ABO

Whether she's writing abou
town in Alaska, Cherise Sin
- Guilty Pleasures Bo

She survived.

Kit survived her abusive husband. Survived imprisonment and beatings from the Patriot Zealots. Now free and healing, she can make a new life for herself and her son...except he has attached himself to a terrifying, scarred, tattooed ex-mercenary.

Women take one look at him and flee.

An ugly childhood and combat left Hawk with scars, a rasping voice, and an aversion to talking. So, why in hell does the four-year-old stick to him like glue?

The kid's pretty mother is smarter. There's fear in her eyes when she looks at Hawk. That hurts. The sweet woman is everything he's ever wanted--loving, affectionate, and patient. But after what she's been through, she sure won't want to be around men—especially the one who killed her husband.

He'd saved her.

Kit agrees with her son. Being near Hawk is the safest place on earth. Beneath the menacing appearance, he's protective...and kind. The better she gets to know him, the more she sees him as a man--a very sexy man. But, considering what had happened to her, she knows--

No man would want her now.

SOAR HIGH

Sons of the Survivalist: 4

CHERISE SINCLAIR

VanScoy Publishing Group

To Kathleen Cole, the Alaska Ice Lady, who fought long and hard. I'm going to miss you so much. Your joy in life was an inspiration to us all. Soar high, my friend.

Soar High
Copyright © 2021 by Cherise Sinclair
ISBN: 978-1-947219-38-0
Published by VanScoy Publishing Group
Cover Art: I'm No Angel Designs
Edited by Red Quill Editing, LLC
Content Editor: Bianca Sommerland

ACKNOWLEDGMENTS

Hugs and so much gratitude goes to my psychology consultants, Ruth Reid and AnnaMaria Boullion. Y'all have the biggest hearts.

I'm so very blessed with my critique partners, Fiona Archer and Monette Michaels. Thank you!

My editors simply rock, what can I say? Content editor: Bianca Sommerland, and copy-editing/proofing from Red Quill Editing with Ekatarina Sayanova, Tracy Damron-Roelle, and Rebecca Cartee.

Many hugs and thanks go to Lisa White, Barb Jack, and Marian Shulman for the amazing beta reading. Y'all have saved me much embarrassment!

My Alaska experts went above and beyond the call of duty with ideas and corrections. Thank you, JJ Foster and Kathleen Cole. Any errors that slipped in are my very own.

Finally, thank you all, my readers, for going on this trip to Alaska with me. *muah!*

PROLOGUE

W*hen everything seems to be against you, remember that an airplane takes off against the wind, not with it.* - Henry Ford.

"Keep up, boy."

The sarge's firm command jerked Hawk's attention from where he trudged along the steep trail behind the other three kids. Kinda like he was in the army. In a lot of soldier movies, the badass sergeant was always yelling at some poor bastard. Mako didn't yell much, but his voice was as big as he was.

Hawk didn't speed up. He didn't want to get up all close with his foster-brothers.

Nah, he shouldn't call them that. The sarge wasn't running a foster home, and he sure wasn't their father. He was just the guy who'd taken—rescued—the four of them from a California foster home and brought them to Alaska.

Because the foster father in LA had been a pervert.

Hawk scowled and fell even farther behind. He could still feel the guy's hands touching him, ripping his shirt. The knee pinning him down to the bed.

1

Sometimes those memories got mixed up with the beatings his real father had dished out. Sometimes he kinda got caught, like in that steel trap the sarge had showed them. Mako'd been pissed off, cuz the trap was all steel teeth that'd dig into some poor animal.

The shit Hawk'd been through had left behind big holes.

Turning, Gabe gave him a worried look. The kid was ten, a year older than Hawk. He was okay, but kinda like one of those weird dogs that rounded up sheep. Gabe got antsy, like, if he couldn't keep track of the other boys, they might get hurt or something.

Hawk looked away. Nobody needed to worry about him; nobody ever had before.

"Caz, where's the closest water?" Mako kept moving up the trail. It wasn't right. He was old, maybe even fifty or something, but he wasn't even breathing hard.

The rest of them were panting like dogs in L.A. during the summer.

"Water. It is..." Caz looked around. He was a year younger than Hawk and Bull—and Hawk liked to call him the baby to piss him off an' make him swear. Not that Hawk usually understood what Cazador said; the baby still dropped into Spanish when he got mad.

Caz's shoulders hunched. "*No sé.*"

Hawk didn't know either.

"Listen," Mako said. "You got two ears; use them. All of you."

They stopped to listen. And yeah, Hawk could hear water running. A creek or something. Keeping one hand on the rock wall, he turned his head to try to pinpoint it. It was somewhere way, way, *way* down the scary-as-shit slope part on the other side of the trail.

Why're we walking up the side of a mountain, anyway?

They all pointed toward the creek.

"Good. Next time, find it before I ask," Mako said. "Which way is home?"

Home.

Hawk scowled. Guess he'd lived in the log cabin like a month now, so okay, maybe it might kinda be almost home. In the loft, he had a bed and even a box for his stuff. Nobody bothered the shit he found—the eagle feathers, the tiny nest, an eggshell littler than a grape.

Suddenly there was a rattle of stones from behind him. A baby elk darted out and dodged past him, heading up the trail past the others.

Jesus, it was cute.

"*Move*," the sarge roared and pointed at something behind Hawk.

What? Glancing over his shoulder, Hawk gasped.

A fucking huge elk charged up the trail—right at him.

He threw himself back—not far enough.

Its giganto-shoulder slammed into him and knocked him toward the drop at the trail's edge. He screamed in terror. "Nooo!"

Grabbing his shirt, the sarge swung him around and tossed him safely against the cliff wall.

Making weird grunting sounds, the elk mama lunged at Gabe like she wanted to stomp on him.

The kid dove away.

"Leave, dumbass!" The sarge threw a big rock at the beast's huge nose.

The elk shook its head, then its ears went back again and—

Huddled against the rock wall, Hawk stared as a giant crack appeared right under the animal's hooves. The trail was falling apart!

"Gabe, get back!" Hawk yelled.

Gabe tried, stumbled, and went down on one knee.

The elk leaped away from the collapsing path and ran after its baby.

Lunging forward, Mako caught Gabe's collar and threw him farther down the trail, even as the ground disappeared right out from under the sarge's boots. In a mass of falling rocks and dirt, Mako went over the edge.

"*Nooo*," Hawk whispered.

"Mako!" Bull shouted. No answer. Bull started to follow, and more of the trail crumbled away.

"*Stop,*" Gabe yelled. "Just wait.

Bull paused.

"Hawk, you got rope, right?" Gabe called.

"Yeah." Hawk dug in his pack and pulled out a bunch of coiled rope. Mako was gonna teach him to use it on the cliffs.

Gabe pointed to a tree off to one side. "Caz, tie it there."

Cazador scrambled to the spot, caught the rope Hawk tossed him, wrapped it around the tree, and made a solid knot. Something else Mako had taught them.

Bull kicked the coil off the side of the slope and held it. He leaned out. "I think he fell all the way down to the stream."

"Let's get him. Bull, you take backup." Gabe grabbed the rope and used it to slow himself down as he went over the edge.

Caz followed.

Hawk slung his pack on, took a step—and tripped as loose rocks rolled out from under his foot. Arm windmilling, he teetered.

Still gripping the rope, Bull grabbed Hawk's shirt and kept him from going over.

Jesus. Hawk latched onto the rope with shaking hands. "Thanks." The word came out in his ugly, rough voice.

"Sure." Bull grinned.

With a steadying breath—and a tight grip on the line—Hawk headed down. It wasn't a cliff like on the other side of the trail but was steep enough he'd have tumbled a dozen times if not for the rope.

Bull followed.

The sarge lay at the bottom of the slope, half in the rushing creek.

"Sarge?" Hawk's hands clenched when he didn't move. Gabe took one arm, Hawk the other, and they dragged him onto the flat bank out of the water.

He didn't move.

Fear was colder than the icy water. "Is he d-dead?"

"Wait." Kneeling, Caz put his head on Mako's chest. "Heart is alive. Breathing. Him arm broked."

Now what? Hawk looked at Gabe. So did Caz.

But Gabe had his arms wrapped around himself and was shaking. They all were. How were they supposed to deal with this? To help the sarge?

"Yo." Bull bumped his shoulder against Gabe's. "What now?"

Gabe blinked, then hauled in a breath and planted his feet like he was getting ready to fight. "O-okay. Um. Guess we're staying here for a while."

"He cold." Caz held Mako's big hand in both of his.

"Right." Gabe motioned to their backpacks. "Dig out your emergency blankets. We'll wrap—"

Deep huffing and growling sounds made them freeze. Hawk knew that sound from the river by the cabin. It was a bear.

Oh fuck. He was shaking so hard his knees started to give out.

The bear was farther down the stream. Looking right at them. It didn't have a hump on the back, so it must be a black bear, not a brown...even though it was kinda brownish.

Mako had said to get real noisy for the black ones.

Hawk swallowed hard and glared at Gabe. "Be noisy."

Gabe nodded and snapped at Bull and Caz. "Start yelling. Scare it off."

Bending, Hawk snatched the giant gun from Mako's holster.

The other boys were screaming and waving their arms.

Damn bear didn't run. Why didn't it *run?*

Hawk gripped the gun and pointed it at the bear. The pistol was really heavy.

"Wait." Gabe leaned over and shoved the safety button thing —and stepped back.

Okay then. Gritting his teeth, Hawk pointed the gun toward the treetops, cuz hitting the bear would piss it off and it'd attack for sure.

He pulled the trigger.

Bam. The gun jumped up in his hands and hit him right in the forehead.

Ow. His face hurt, and his ears were ringing from the noise.

But the bear veered off and disappeared into the trees.

Gone.

The others cheered, then silence fell. Because...now what?

Caz had pulled his blanket out, and they worked to wrap the thin crinkly thing around the sarge.

Mako was so quiet, like he was dead, only he wasn't, was he?

Tears stung Hawk's eyes, and Caz was blinking hard, and Bull kept patting the sarge's chest like he was a dog or something.

Gabe was frowning. "We're gonna need a fire."

"Yeah," Hawk said.

The other two nodded. And looked at Gabe.

Then Mako groaned.

His eyes opened, blue eyes in a tan face that was all scratched and bloody. He started to move, grunted, and scowled at his arm. "What the fuck?"

Bull grinned. "The trail fell apart—and you fell too."

"Smartass boy." A corner of Mako's mouth tilted up. He moved an arm and patted the silver blanket around him. His gaze hit Bull, then Gabe, Caz, and Hawk.

The sarge grinned. "Good job. You men got the makings of a fine team."

Good job. Mako didn't say those words often.

Hawk stood a little straighter. But...

A team?

Yeah, maybe. If the others hadn't been here, he wouldn't have figured out to use a rope to get down the cliff. Would've probably fallen. Couldn't have pulled the sarge out of the creek by himself. Wouldn't know to get Mako warm. Or have remembered the safety.

Without Hawk, there'd be no rope. And the bear might've attacked.

A team might be good.

Because they were stronger together.

CHAPTER ONE

T *wenty-three years later*

The way I see it, every time a man gets up in the morning, he starts his life over. Sure, the bills are there to pay, and the job is there to do, but you don't have to stay in a pattern. You can always start over, saddle a fresh horse, and take another trail. ~ Louis L'Amour

In the tiny garden of the rehab facility, Kirsten Sandersen pulled in a breath of moist, cool air. Springtime in Alaska, and although damaged in body and spirit, she was free. Like the leaves on the plants around her, she was putting out tender, new growth.

Her bag was packed and sitting at the door. The discharge paperwork had been signed, and she'd come to her favorite hideaway to wait for a ride home. Well, not *home*.

I don't have a home.

Or a job.

Or a husband, for that matter. She waited to feel grief for

Obadiah's death. The only thing she felt was regret that she'd been so incredibly stupid. So needy for love that she'd fallen for his lies. His manipulation.

Shame bloomed inside her. Her desire for a strong man had tossed her and Aric right into a nightmare. Eventually, she'd recover, and if she didn't, then she'd deal with it, but her son was only four years old. Would he ever get past the months of fear? Of abuse?

Baby, I'm so sorry.

She brushed the tears from her eyes, feeling like a wimp.

But her counselor had warned her that her emotions would be erratic for a while. *Not a problem.* Soon, she'd be out of this place— and back with her son.

Nothing mattered more than that.

Hearing a man clearing his throat, she jumped to her feet, grabbed her aching ribs, and swore under her breath in a way that would've gotten her caned by the PZs.

Two men wearing button-up shirts, jeans, and sports jackets stood near the door.

She retreated several fast steps.

The fair-skinned one held up both hands in a take-it-easy gesture. "Sorry, Mrs. Traeger."

"It's Ms. Sandersen." Darned if she'd keep Obadiah's name. "I'm sorry, I know we've met, but I don't remember your names."

It seemed as if every person in Alaskan law enforcement had interviewed her.

The shorter man with brown eyes and hair pulled out his badge. "FBI, ma'am. Special Agent Acosta."

"Special Agent Langford." The tall one showed his badge. "We asked the facility to let you know we'd be coming."

Kit let out a pained breath and tried to settle her nerves. *Be brave, Kittycat.* Her father's affectionate name for her always helped. She'd clung to the memory of his voice when she was growing up. Still did. "What with vacation season, the place is understaffed. I'll probably get your message tomorrow."

Langford barked a laugh. "Figures. Sorry, we'd have called you directly if we'd had a number."

"I haven't bought a phone yet." Because she had no money. No income. Her anxiety surged, and she pushed it aside. She'd manage; she always did. "Has something happened? Did you catch Captain Nabera?"

"Not yet, no." Acosta gestured to one of the café tables in the shade. "He holed up somewhere. Maybe in the forests. The rest of the Patriot Zealots have scattered."

Arm pressed against her ribs, Kit carefully took a seat. At least the incision where her spleen had been repaired no longer felt like a burning brand. "Then...?"

"Apparently, your husband was one of Nabera's so-called lieutenants."

They'd probably learned that during their interviews with the other women freed from the Patriot Zealots. Kit nodded. "He was."

"Did Obadiah share any information with you about the Patriot Zealots' future plans—ones they'd been making before they left?"

The night Kit and the other women had been rescued, the PZs had cleared out of the compound and disappeared.

She took a moment to think. "I don't know of anything specific, but Parrish and Nabera were worried. They were losing people and unable to recruit enough to keep the money coming in. They needed ways to get publicity. Um, like confrontations with the law or government officials or attacking a high-profile politician. Nabera said every time a militia group got into a standoff with a liberal, money would flood in."

Acosta's mouth flattened into a grim line. "That's an ugly truth."

"I don't really know anything else. Women weren't..." She

shrugged. Women were less than second-class citizens to the PZ militia. No, they weren't even citizens at all.

"The main reason we're here is"—Agent Acosta shifted in his chair—"while searching the areas around the compound, we found a dump site."

"A what?"

Langford met her gaze. "We were told that Nabera and his lieutenants would dispose of bodies over a cliff."

"They did." She swallowed. "Right after I arrived, Conrad hit a woman too hard, and she died. Obadiah asked Luka what would happen with her body, since there were no swamps here like they use in Texas. Luka said there was a gorge where they just...tossed..."

Her stomach turned over. That's where her body would have been flung if she'd died that night as Obadiah and Nabera had intended. "Is that what you mean?"

Acosta nodded. "We found women's bodies—and some Patriot Zealots who were killed when you and the other women were freed."

The PZs who were killed that night. Like Obadiah? "You found my husband."

"We have a positive identification, yes." Acosta hesitated, obviously not sure whether to offer her condolences or congratulations.

She wasn't sure either.

They hadn't been married that long. Hadn't even known each other very long. She'd been working in a garden center and helped him choose fruit trees that would survive the harsh Texas summers. He was burly and bearded, slow and deliberate. And so polite. He hadn't let her lift the pots, saying a man was given strength for a reason.

Her first husband, Brenden, had died of a drug overdose after trying to quit so many times. She'd been thrilled at Obadiah's interest, at having found such a strong man. Someone who was Brenden's opposite.

But Brenden had been kind, Obadiah controlling and cruel... and now Obadiah was dead.

She couldn't find any regret inside her. If she'd been his only victim, maybe there would be some degree of sorrow, but he'd hurt her son. Only someone evil would hurt a sweet little four-year-old.

And only an idiot would have married a cruel fanatic.

She was that idiot.

She realized the agents were talking. "Sorry, what did you say?"

Sympathy softened Agent Langford's face. "Just making plans for our next stop."

They'd have more people to speak with, wouldn't they? Others had been killed that night.

A memory invaded her thoughts. *Obadiah standing over her, leg raised to kick her. Again. Aiming for her already broken ribs. She stared up at him, knowing she'd die with his next kick. No one would protect her son. But as Obadiah swung his leg, a man was diving across her, tackling Obadiah.*

She shook her head. *Stay in the present.*

As she pulled in a deep breath, the pain in her ribs felt almost comforting. Because she was alive. "Will there be anything you need from me? For Obadiah?"

"No, ma'am." Acosta rose. "The Rescue police chief said he'll make sure you get the death certificate."

The official paperwork wouldn't help anything except her heart. When they moved into the compound, Obadiah had handed over their money to the Patriot Zealots. There was no insurance, no bank accounts.

Langford said, "You're getting out today, I hear?"

When she nodded, Acosta asked, "Are you joining the other women at the shelter here?"

"No, I'm staying with a friend." All she wanted at this point was to leave every thought of the Patriot Zealots behind. Seeing the others would bring it back. "Frankie should be picking me up soon."

"Frankie is picking you up now," came from the doorway. "Hi, agents."

The two men smiled at Frankie—as most men did.

Curvy, with thick dark hair and big brown eyes, the New Yorker just plain liked people—and everyone liked her back.

"I'm glad you're looking better," Acosta said to Kit and laid a card on the table. "Call us if you think of anything we should know or if you have any concerns."

"Thank you. I will."

As the two men strode out of the small garden, Frankie walked over. "I heard the Feds say they found Obadiah's body. Are you okay?" She bent to give Kit an abbreviated, ever-so-gentle hug that comforted without hurting any broken ribs.

There were days Kit felt like a sack of brittle twigs. One that a draft horse had stood on. Twice.

But she was healing.

"I already knew Obadiah was dead." Even before Rescue's Chief of Police had told her. Because she'd seen Hawk's face after. Seen his haunted eyes. Killing Obadiah had wounded his soul.

Lifting her chin, Kit smiled to ease Frankie's worry. "I'm packed and ready for you to break me out of this place." Aric would be waiting. "Is this rescuing stuff turning into a habit?"

"Oh, no, *amica mia*. I'm keeping track and figuring on lots of return favors." Frankie chuckled and motioned toward the door. "Next time, you can save me."

The uncomfortable itch of feeling like she'd gotten charity faded. "Absolutely. I get to be the rescuer next time."

On the way out, the staff of the facility hugged her and wished her a good recovery.

Barely one step outside the facility, Kit's muscles tensed as she quickly checked the area for men. No men, no PZs. Just a parking lot with Frankie's new SUV parked near the door.

Right. It was starting to feel as if her body might heal before her mind did.

Frankie opened the passenger door for her, then stowed the suitcase in the back.

Trying not to groan, Kit eased in. *Ow, ow, ow.* The physical therapist had warned that there was no way to get into a vehicle without twisting the torso at least a little.

Once in the seat, she focused on breathing as the pain in her ribs eased from *I've-been-stabbed* to merely a painful throbbing.

"Poor baby." With a sympathetic look, Frankie buckled Kit's seatbelt for her before driving out of the lot. Once out of Anchorage, they were on the road to Rescue, a small town on the Kenai Peninsula.

Kit felt the uneasy quiver in her stomach grow with each mile. Frankie's man had three brothers, and their houses were together on an isolated bunch of acres. "So why is the place called the Hermitage?"

"Mako—the guy who raised Bull and his bros—was basically a hermit. He did his twenty years in the military, but when he retired, sounds like his PTSD and paranoia caught up with him. He was a total survivalist." Frankie grinned. "The Hermitage will make your gardener heart happy. We have a huge vegetable garden and a greenhouse, and everything's growing like crazy."

Kit smiled. Gardens were the best pain medication. "I can't think of anything nicer. Aric's told me so many stories about the lake and the gardens. And the chickens." And Hawk.

She'd asked Hawk to care for her son—and he was. How could a mother repay the gift of keeping her boy safe? Every few days, he'd brought Aric to Anchorage to see her, and she'd have been lost without those visits.

"Aric loves the Hermitage—although he sure misses you." Frankie glanced over. "You're stewing about something though."

"It's just... It's not my house, and no one knows me, and it feels wrong to simply move in."

"I guess it'd bother me too." Frankie shook her head. "But really, it's fine. Bull's more of a people person than I am; he's the one who suggested that you and Aric stay with us. And hey, your room is downstairs, and our bedroom is upstairs, so you won't be hearing our sexy times."

Startled, Kit laughed and grabbed her side with the stab of pain. "Okay then." After a minute, she laughed again.

"What was the second laugh for?"

"Just feeling grateful for the busted bones."

Frankie's jaw dropped. "What? Why?"

"Being hurt so badly meant I was stuck in the hospital and rehab and pretty much got pushed into counseling. A lot of counseling." Her grin faded. "I never thought my behavior with men wasn't normal, but...I learned a lot about myself in the last three weeks. Like why my choices in men, even before Obadiah, were so lousy."

"Huh. In that case, I'm glad too. Your counseling will continue, by the way." Frankie glanced over. "Caz—the nurse practitioner who runs the health clinic—talked to the rehab discharge planner, and you're booked for physical therapy and counseling at the clinic."

"That can't be right. I told the discharge planner I couldn't afford any outpatient therapies." Kit frowned. "Frankie, I don't have insurance or money. I can't—"

"Um..."

Kit narrowed her eyes. "You look as guilty as you did after you ate *all* my Death by Chocolate ice cream—right before my period and finals, no less. What did you do *this* time?"

"*Che palle*, it wasn't *me*." Frankie heaved a very Italian sigh. "I told you a psychologist friend of the guys talked to Aric, right?"

"Mmmhmm. He said it was okay for Aric to stay with Hawk—and you all." Leaving her son to be cared for by others had been the worst part of being in the hospital. She stiffened. "Did he change his mind? Is there a problem with Hawk or—"

"No, no, relax. I said that wrong." Frankie smacked her forehead twice with the palm of her hand. "Aric's fine. When Doc Grayson tried to see you, you were still unconscious, so he talked with the guys and the hospital staff. He's kind of like a godfather to the brothers, only maybe he's not that much older than they are. I don't think he's more than mid-forties."

Suppressing a snicker, Kit tipped her head back to stare at the roof of the car. Frankie had words; she had *all* the words, far too many words. "Are you planning to get to the point anytime soon?"

"*Cazzo*, I missed you." Frankie snickered. "The point is, Zachary Grayson is rich and wanted to help, and since he couldn't do it in person, he did it with money. He paid your medical expenses, including outpatient therapies for the rest of the summer. After that, you're on your own."

Paid...everything? She'd been figuring on huge bills that would require repayment for the rest of her life. "No way. The hospital bill and rehab and surgery and—"

"Pfft." Frankie waved one hand in the air. "All gone."

Frankie smiled softly. "I think the doc fell for Aric. He knew the guys were worried about you."

Kit stared at her in shock.

"Some rich guys are good people. So, yes, you're booked for PT and counseling, and you *will* be going."

The relief was huge. But still... "I'll pay him back."

"He already said you will not, and he's not one you can argue with." Frankie snorted. "Like Hawk in a way. The shrink wins with words; Hawk wins by walking away."

Kit's lips twitched. When Hawk brought Aric to visit, he'd send her son into the room, give her a nod, then disappear until the time was up. Talkative, he was not—but the deadly-looking, muscular guy sure looked as if he could battle with sharks and win.

He'd saved her. Her and Aric.

But they were talking about money. "I need a job."

"Not for a while." Frankie braked as the rental car in front of them slowed to give a wide berth to a moose cropping grass at the side of the road.

Alaska was just so amazing.

"No yelling about this, either," Frankie muttered, pulled a card out of her pocket, and put it into Kit's lap.

"A bank card?"

"It has two thousand on it—and stop glaring at me. *Cazzo*, it's not charity, it's a loan, okay? You'll be ready to work before the money's gone, and when you're back on your feet financially, you can repay me."

Charity. Only...okay, a loan.

"Hey, we've always traded favors back and forth." Frankie gave her a rueful smile. "Like when I got the flu, and you did my homework, even though you hate math. And you flew to New York to help me when Jaxson dumped me—and then kicked me into gear with some tough love."

Well, yes, she'd done that. "You did the same, oh, birth coach. And you flew to Texas when Brenden died."

Frankie pursed her lips in thought and went for one-upmanship. "You went out in a rainstorm to get me tiramisu after Mama spent an entire evening boasting about Anja and Birgit."

Kit rolled her eyes. Frankie's mother valued only her supermodel daughters, not the child who actually cared about everyone. Although Frankie had said her family now saw her differently, thanks to a Bull-sized intervention.

Okay, my turn. "You took on a part-time waitressing job when you didn't even need one. Just because I was being a wuss." Because, at eighteen, Kit had never worked where there were crowds of people, and she'd almost lost it. She'd been planning to quit before Frankie showed up in the restaurant kitchen and grinned at her.

"Oh, girl, for that one, I owe *you*. I got the job at Bull's road-house because I knew how to wait tables." Frankie's voice turned softer, sweeter, whenever she said her man's name. "I've never been so happy in my whole life."

To have even the tiniest part of helping Frankie look like this made Kit's day.

And maybe she was being foolish. Frankie had made good money back at her New York job. She could afford the loan.

"In that case, thank you." Kit stretched out her clenched fingers. "Seriously. Thank you. I'll pay you back."

Frankie stepped on the brakes, slowing to go around a car parked on the shoulder. Tourists had stopped to take pictures of the snow-topped mountains.

Who wouldn't? This state was impossible to describe to anyone down in the Lower 48. Glacier-fed turquoise rivers, sparkling waterfalls, wide green forests, and craggy mountains covered in snow. The Texans had boasted to her about being the biggest state. Alaska was not only bigger, but also jaw-droppingly spectacular.

"Rescue has lots of jobs, but not till you're moving better," Frankie said.

"There probably aren't horticulture-type jobs, not ones I'll be able to handle." Kit sighed. "I swear, that orthopedic surgeon acted like he'd used safety pins on my forearm bones, and his fancy work would come unfastened if I did anything much."

"What a horrific thought." Frankie gave her a determined glance. "You'll take it easy, or all of us will yell at you."

All of them. Kit bit her lip. There were five houses at the Hermitage. One was empty. One house belonged to Frankie's man, Bull. The giant restaurant owner was probably in his thirties.

One house held Rescue's Chief of Police, Gabe, and his girl-friend, Audrey.

The nurse practitioner, Cazador, and his woman, JJ—a police officer, who worked for Gabe, lived in another.

The fifth was owned by Hawk, the man who'd killed her husband to save her life. Her memory was vague, blurred by pain and physical damage, but that moment was when she'd entrusted Hawk with her son.

Each time he dropped Aric off to visit her in the hospital or rehab, she'd questioned her judgment. Muscular, tattooed, scarred, and silent...the man was simply terrifying.

Yet, when he looked at her, his eyes didn't hold death; they held a haunted kind of pain. And on the rare occasions he actually spoke to her, his deep rasping voice felt like a safety line in a stormy sea.

Maybe she was crazy to have trusted him, but he'd kept her son safe.

Turned out to be a pretty enough day, Hawk Calhoun decided, and damned colorful.

Rescue's Main Street used to be filled with decrepit buildings with faded, peeling paint. Now, it was like someone had handed the store owners a box of crayons and told them to go wild. Thank fuck no one had discovered how to create paisley or plaids. The black and white striped trim against blue paint on the pizza place was gaudy enough.

Holding Aric's hand, he stepped around one of the whiskey barrel planters on the sidewalk and smiled at the red and white blooms. Lillian and Audrey intended to add blue flowers to them for the Fourth of July.

Gardeners were a strange breed.

He and the kid passed four pot-bellied men wearing short-sleeved tropical shirts—in Alaska. No wonder Chevy and Knox kept talking about having Fish and Game declare an open season on tacky tourists.

Seeing Hawk, the garish group parted, giving him lots of room and wary stares. Like he'd whip out a knife and gut them or something.

Wanting to get past them, he lengthened his gait, then felt the tiny hand holding his tighten.

Dumbass. He'd been working to get Aric comfortable enough to walk beside him in town rather than being carried. A glance down showed the kid staring up at him in worry.

Ignoring the tourists on the sidewalk, Hawk went down on his haunches, putting him only a little taller than the four-year-old. "Sorry, kid."

The small body was tensed up, and Aric's grip on his hand hadn't relaxed. Did he think Hawk had been trying to leave him behind?

Probably. Abuse could scramble a brain for a while—especially a kid's developing mind.

Hawk tugged on his ear and manned up. According to Mako, some people found it harder to share something personal than to take a bullet.

The sarge had rarely been wrong.

"I wasn't trying to leave you, Aric." Hawk noted the people walking by. From this height, legs looked like a moving forest. Thank fuck he wasn't this size. "Too many people make me antsy. Piss me off some too. That's why I was walking faster."

Like Hawk, the kid had sandy hair, fair skin, and blue eyes. Only Aric's eyes were big and vulnerable. The boy was so fucking cute, it was impossible to think anyone could hurt him.

Hawk frowned. Had he looked like this as a boy? His father sure hadn't had any trouble hurting *him*.

He shook the thought loose and rose.

Since the kid didn't like to talk, Hawk and his brothers had taught him some of the hand signals used in combat—and invented a few for just Aric. Like the one for *want a ride?*

Hawk bent and held his hands out with palms up.

Aric nodded vigorously.

Okay then. Hawk picked the kid up—so damned light, even after three weeks of feeding him everything he could consume.

Veering past a pungent batch of anglers debating about rods and reels, Hawk sighed. Combat fishing had begun, from battling for positions on the river to arguing about gear, and then, to his brother Bull's disgust, brawling in the roadhouse over who'd caught the biggest fish.

When they passed the grocery, Dante, the owner, saluted them through the display window. Aric gave a shy wave back, and the white-haired Okie grinned.

Across the street, the local handymen, Chevy and Knox, were replacing a cracked window in the hair salon and spa.

"Yo, Aric." Knox held up a hammer in greeting. "Hey, Hawk. We'll be done with this job by tomorrow and free to take on more of your projects."

"Good." Because there were still more buildings to fix. "Call me."

The two men nodded.

Hawk and Aric continued down Main Street. Sometimes it seemed as if there was no end to renovating the buildings he and his brothers had inherited. In the years before his death, Mako bought up a shitload of failing businesses in Rescue to help the people wanting to leave Alaska. Then a ski resort and hotel re-opened nearby, bringing in an influx of tourists. When the sarge died a year and a half ago, he'd left everything to Hawk and his brothers, expecting them to help bring the town back to life.

So, they were choosing good people to lease the businesses—and renovating a lot of the buildings first. For his part of the tasks, Hawk supervised the carpenters, because no way would he deal with the showing and leasing shit. His brothers liked people; he didn't.

He could manage the repair people, electricians, and plumbers, though. And, at the moment, he had the time. With a sigh, he hefted Aric to a better position. With the kid attached to him like this, Hawk wasn't going anywhere anytime soon.

Near the end of downtown, he entered a small building to check on Milo and Orion, his most recent hires.

With a full brown beard and long hair in a bun, Orion was as laid-back as he looked. He was laying down new flooring in the main space.

Clean-shaven with a shaved scalp, Milo was tall and lanky—the opposite of Orion in looks and personality. But he had decent skills and was doing finish work on the built-in cabinetry.

After nodding at their greetings, Hawk set Aric down. "Don't touch the tools, right?"

Aric nodded solemnly. He was so obedient it was worrisome, but there was hope. Three weeks ago, he wouldn't've let Hawk get more than a couple of feet away. Now, as long as Hawk was somewhere in sight, the kid was comfortable.

"Any problems?" Hawk asked the two men.

"Floor in the bathroom has some dry rot," Orion reported. "The boards need replacing."

"Give me numbers. I'll get an order in."

Milo walked over, watching as Aric trotted to a pile of sawdust. "I heard his mother's getting out today."

Nosy bastard. "Yeah."

"I guess she'll be looking for work. Good timing what with it being tourist season."

Orion shook his head. "I doubt she'll be working anytime soon. There was a reason she was in rehab—those PZ bastards busted her up pretty bad."

"Shut it." Hawk checked where the kid was. Thankfully, Aric

was across the room, poking his finger in a hole in the flooring, and probably hadn't heard.

Orion winced. "Sorry, Hawk. I got a big mouth."

Hawk shrugged. Orion was right; the PZs were bastards. And Kit's asshole husband had been trying to kick her to death when Hawk killed him.

"Yeah, you do." Milo shot Orion a cold look and stalked back to the cabinets.

Frowning, Hawk asked Orion, "You two okay?" He'd hired them separately and put them together.

Easy-going Orion shrugged. "Yeah, we're good. He pulls his weight. Just sometimes gets a hair up his ass."

Hawk nodded and took a minute to check over their work, pleased to find it up to his standards.

Across the room, Aric was drawing pictures in the sawdust.

Frowning, Milo was watching him. Seeing Hawk had noticed, he muttered, "Cute boy," and got back to work.

"Let's go, kid." Hawk scooped Aric up.

Smiling happily, Aric grabbed onto Hawk's flannel shirt.

The sawdust covering the little fingers inevitably covered the fabric. When Hawk brushed it off, Aric cringed.

"At ease. Some people give a damn about getting dirty; I don't."

He could almost hear Mako's rumbling voice. *"Never trust a man who's afraid to get his hands dirty."*

The kid hadn't relaxed.

So, taking Aric's hand, Hawk blew on the fingers, sending sawdust over them both.

And got one of the boy's tiny laughs.

CHAPTER TWO

T*he only way to have a friend is to be one.* - Ralph Waldo Emerson

"Here, this room is for you and Aric." Frankie opened the door.

With a hand on her aching ribs, Kit stepped past her friend.

Dark blue curtains matched the blue and green quilt. Bronze-colored lamps and picture frames added warmth. Her eyes prickled at the welcoming atmosphere.

In one corner, rather than a chair, there was a loveseat. What with abdominal surgery and broken ribs, it'd be a while before she could have her boy sitting on her lap. But the loveseat was big enough she could read to Aric with him snuggled up beside her, and there was even a beautiful, comfy throw blanket.

Her bestie was the most thoughtful person in the world.

"The bathroom is here." Frankie opened a door on the left wall, then another beside it. "Closet. I added some warmer clothes."

"Frankie..." Sweet heavens, it was hard to accept charity, even from a friend. Maybe because she'd learned how some people could resent the act of giving. Aunt Norma and her husband, Duane, had raised her after her parents died—and constantly said how she should be grateful for their charity and generosity. Frankie wasn't like them, but the feeling of obligation was heavy, even if it was to her best friend.

Frankie laughed. "I recognize that worried expression. Yes, I did a lot for you, but girl, if I hadn't come here to help you, I wouldn't have Bull. In a way, I feel like I owe you." After rescuing Kit, Frankie stayed in Alaska to be with Bull. She really did have the glow of love about her.

Kit couldn't keep from smiling.

A rumbling laugh came from the doorway. "We both owe you, Kit." Bull walked in slowly, as if he recognized how scary his size was, especially to a woman who'd been imprisoned by the PZs. The man was at least three or four inches over six feet and massive. But his wide smile was friendly, his dark eyes kind—and when he looked at Frankie, it was obvious he adored her.

Looking past Bull into the hallway, Kit frowned. "I thought Aric would be with you. Would—" Would want to see his mother, would be waiting for her...

"Ah, he was." Bull grinned. "He helped make your bed, in fact, but then Hawk got a call. Last week, he flew some campers into the Chugach range and was to pick them up next week, but somebody got hurt. Not badly enough for an air ambulance, but he needed a lift out."

"Aric couldn't stay with you?" Kit frowned. If Bull didn't like little boys, he wasn't good enough for Frankie.

"Aric still won't stay with anyone but Hawk." Bull ran his hand over his shaved scalp. "Whenever we tell him it's all right to stay with one of us or Frankie, he just shakes his head, and we get, 'Mama *said*.'"

"Did I?" Much of what happened after Nabera and Obadiah started beating her was still a blur. The way Hawk had saved her, she remembered that. And his rasping baritone. "...*we'll take her to the hospital. Get her help.*"

The memory of his voice was like a magic wand, a way to banish nightmares.

She remembered his hard blue eyes and how they'd softened when he looked at Aric. How he'd held her son so carefully, so gently. And she'd asked, or maybe *told* Hawk to take care of Aric. Had she done the same with her son? "I'm guessing I told Aric to stay with him? That night?"

"You did."

"I knew Aric was clinging to him, and that was why Hawk was the only one to bring him to visit. But...still?"

"Still. Because Hawk saved you and carried Aric out, Aric feels safe with him." Frankie added, "Doc Grayson, that psychologist friend of the guys, said it might take a while before Aric gets over the need to be with Hawk all the time."

Her poor son. Anger and guilt roused inside. She sat on the edge of the bed, simply wanting to cry.

"Oh, Kit." Frankie sat beside her and put a gentle arm around her shoulders. "He's getting better. He wants Hawk within eyesight but doesn't have to be right next to him anymore. With you here, he'll relax."

"Okay. Right." Kit tried to push the sense of helplessness away and concentrate on what Aric needed. Wanted. "I know he loves flying with Hawk."

"Oh yeah." Bull shook his head. "He'll be pushing for his pilot's license when he hits seventeen."

That... Kit choked. "Let's not go there."

"Way to scare a mommy, *deficiente*." Frankie glared at Bull, then smiled at Kit. "Why don't you take a nap? Hawk and Aric should be back after supper."

When Kit nodded, the two disappeared, their low voices coming from the living area.

Hawk and Aric. The way it was said came out smooth from

repetition. As if the two were a pair, a family. It was a little unsettling to hear.

But she could only be grateful to Hawk for caring for her boy and making the trips to bring him to see her. He rarely spoke, and she'd thought it was merely because he was quiet or didn't like people.

Her stomach sank. Could the man, maybe, resent her for saddling him with a child who clung to him like kudzu?

No matter. It was fine if Hawk disliked her as long as he was kind to Aric. She blew out a breath and started the slow process of lying down without hurting her ribs.

For her part, she'd do everything she could to get on her feet, find a job, and resume caring for Aric.

And even if Hawk felt a bit aggrieved at her for disrupting his life, she'd be forever grateful to him.

In clean clothes after a quick shower, Hawk dropped onto his living room couch. Stretching out his legs, he sighed. Felt good to be home.

He could hear the kid upstairs in the bedroom putting on the clothes someone had left on the bed for him. Everything else of Aric's had been moved to Bull's place.

The kid might take a while, but dressing was something he'd mastered.

Getting clean was another matter, especially on days like today. At the campsite, while Hawk had loaded the client and his gear into the floatplane, Aric had played in the mud.

Hell, more like he'd rolled in it. He'd even had it in his ears. It'd taken two times with shampoo to get Aric's hair back to blond rather than brown. But he'd pass a mom-inspection now.

Speaking of moms...

Hawk rose to get his phone from where he'd dropped it on the kitchen island. Yeah, Bull had texted that Kit was there, and they'd already had supper.

That worked out since the kid was already fed. After landing the floatplane at Lake Hood, Hawk—with Aric—took the client and his stuff to the Anchorage airport for a flight back to the Lower 48. The kid had tried his best to be helpful, so Hawk had treated him to a burger and fries at the Arctic Roadrunner.

Aric trotted down the stairs and swung by his bowl on the shelf to deposit a new rock. He wore the bright blue T-shirt with a dinosaur on it JJ had bought him, jeans, and red sneakers—ones with Velcro rather than shoelaces.

"Good job dressing," Hawk said and was pleased Aric no longer looked surprised at getting approval. "We're going to Bull's. He probably has cookies."

That got an enthusiastic nod.

No words though. Aric still avoided speaking, if possible. Hawk ended up talking more than normal just to counter the kid's silence.

But, in all reality, quiet was good. Since Aric was so obviously fragile, Hawk was damned careful around him.

Hawk wouldn't be triggered into acting like his own father. Like a monster.

They walked out the deck door and down the stairs. Summer solstice was a little over a week away, and the sun was hours from setting. The grass in the courtyard was a vivid green and getting tall. He'd have to mow it tomorrow. Maybe do some weeding in the garden since it was one of Aric's happy places. The chickens would appreciate the greens.

As they crossed to Bull's house, Hawk stopped. "Got news."

The boy froze.

Hell, hadn't meant to scare him. Hawk knelt. "Your mom's at Bull's."

Aric's eyes went wide.

"Go on."

"Mama." The word came out loud enough to be heard, then Aric raced onto Bull's deck and through the door.

A clear cry of happiness came from Kit.

Pretty obvious the kid had no doubt of her love.

Must be nice.

Hawk leaned a hip against the deck railing. They didn't need him in there, and fuck knew, the woman would be more comfortable without him around. Most females found him terrifying—and he'd killed Kit's husband. Yeah, most people wouldn't consider the death of an abusive asshole to be a great loss, but she'd married the guy. Must've loved him at some point, right? He'd seen women return to the men who'd pounded on them.

So, after speaking to her once in the hospital to reassure her that he'd watch her son, he'd kept his distance. He would drop Aric off at the door of her hospital or rehab room and wait down the hall.

Now she was here—and he'd simply avoid her. She'd be comfortable with his brothers who weren't scarred and tatted and who managed to conceal their deadly natures far better than Hawk could.

People liked Gabe—and being a cop probably helped.

Even huge as Bull was, the guy liked people, and they flocked around him.

Caz, with his penchant for knives, did his killing up close and personal and was a unique kind of deadly. Hawk far preferred to shoot from a distance, either in a helicopter or as a sniper. Yet, despite the knives that Caz still carried, the doc could charm just about anyone. He cared about people, and it showed.

Hawk, though, didn't trust anyone except his brothers, and people could tell. Even if he wanted to talk—and he didn't—speaking didn't come easy. Mako had thought Hawk's raspy voice was probably from screaming. Hawk had never told him it'd been fucked up since his father hit him in the throat with a skillet for making too much noise.

It'd been a long time before he managed to talk at all after that.

Hawk shook his head. He had tats and scars. Ugly voice. Bad attitude. Hell, the only women who liked him were the ones who obsessed over violent men and rough sex.

Best he stay far away from the fragile woman who was Aric's mother.

He was halfway to his house when Bull's voice boomed across the courtyard. "Hawk, get your ass back here."

Keep going? Wouldn't work. Bull would just come after him—and talk.

Why did people think they could fix things with talking?

With a grunt of exasperation, he walked back, his gut tightening. At least, Kit had seen him before. Wouldn't be shocked by scars and tats.

He climbed the steps and scowled at his brother. "Aric should be with his mother. Without me."

"Nope." Bull shook his head. "Grayson said Aric might still need you for security, even with her here."

Hawk eyed the door. Aric might need him. Kit didn't, and he sure wasn't into scaring her. "He'll be fine."

Bull laughed and slapped his back. "C'mon, let's go in."

Hawk shot him a glare that should've fried his ass.

If anything, Bull's smirk widened. "If nothing else, the beer's great." The owner of Bull's Moose Brewery would say so, of course.

There was no winning this battle.

With a pissed-off growl, Hawk stepped inside and assessed the room. Good lines of retreat to the windows and doors. Three people in the living area—Frankie, Kit, Aric.

Dark-haired, curvy Frankie, who was Bull's woman, sat at one end of the sectional.

With her splinted right arm in a sling, Kit sat in the middle with the kid standing and leaning against her legs. Still slender, but she'd gained some weight and was no longer hollow-cheeked. An inch or so shorter than Frankie, she might be five-five. The brown hair with sun-lightened streaks was like the coloring of a golden eagle. So fucking pretty.

In the compound the night of the rescue, she'd been bruised, battered, and beaten, but not broken. No, she'd roused enough to help get the other women to leave, had told them, *"Go with Frankie, you idiots."* She'd fought off unconsciousness and ordered Hawk to care for her son. The woman had a solid core of strength.

But she wasn't all steel. When she smiled at her son and her brown eyes turned soft, the warmth was enough to melt an Alaska glacier.

Hawk didn't get a smile.

Then he did. A hesitant one, as if she wasn't sure how he'd react. "Hawk, thank you for taking care of Aric. I didn't realize that you'd be doing...well, everything."

"Everyone helped." And he would be doing nothing now the kid's mother was here. A prickly ache started up under his ribcage.

"We have goodies, everyone." Frankie set a tray of cookies on the coffee table, and Hawk almost laughed when Aric's gaze snagged on the sweets.

The kid didn't speak, dammit. It would be a fine day when the boy felt comfortable enough to ask for something he wanted.

Hawk glanced at Kit to see if she'd noticed her son's desire.

She had. Her busted ribs were obviously painful as she leaned forward, snagged a cookie, and handed it to Aric. Her lips were pressed tight as she leaned back.

Hawk stared at her. Rather than asking for help, she'd hurt herself to give her son a treat. Felt like something he'd do, but it didn't feel right when she behaved the same way.

"Yo, bro. Try this." Bull handed over a bottle of beer.

Hawk checked the label. Bull's Moose Brewery. "Break-up Ale?"

"Yeah, the new one." Bull took a seat beside Frankie. "You'll like the hops."

Hawk stayed standing. He wouldn't be here for longer than it took to satisfy his brother. If the women thought him rude, too fucking bad.

"*Break-up*. You named a beer after something sad?" Kit asked.

"Break-up in Alaska is when the ice on the rivers melts and breaks into chunks." Bull smiled at her. "Around here, it basically means spring."

"Oh. I heard the lieutenants talking about it and didn't understand." Kit shook her head. "Most of us from the Texas compound didn't know anything about Alaska."

"It's a long way from Texas. Why'd the PZs from there come up here?" Bull asked.

Hawk leaned a hip against the couch and sampled the beer. Not bad. Nice and hoppy. Light on the tongue. It was odd that neither Kit nor Aric sounded Texan.

"The Reverend said Alaska had less rules and fewer people to interfere with what he wanted to do." The corners of Kit's mouth twitched up. "He complained a lot about the police chief here. Your brother?"

"That would be Gabe. He enjoyed ruining Parrish's plans." Bull grinned.

Beside Kit, Aric had finished his cookie and was nodding off. Face soft, she brushed a hand over his hair. "I better get him to bed."

Any fool could see she'd never manage to move herself and the kid off the couch without a hell of a lot of pain.

Hawk stepped forward and lifted the boy, draping him over a shoulder with a hand under his ass. In the last three weeks, he'd learned Aric didn't wake up once he was asleep. At least, not if he felt safe.

He glanced at Frankie. "He got a bed?"

"Beside Kit's in the downstairs guest room."

"I'm going to make an early night of it too." Kit struggled to slide forward on the oversized sectional. It was like watching a fawn struggle out of a snowdrift.

Hawk held out his free hand. "Grab on. Go at your own pace." She froze.

Hell, what had he been thinking? She wouldn't accept help from someone who looked like him. Sure wouldn't touch him.

Even as he started to pull his arm back, she took his hand. Her hand was cold and tiny, but as he closed his fingers around hers, he could feel her callused skin. Even three weeks of being laid-up hadn't eradicated the evidence of hard work.

Her wary gaze met his, and then, using him as an anchor, she slid forward on the couch. After rising to her feet, she released his hand. "That helped. Thank you."

Damn. Unexpected pleasure swept through him. She'd let him assist.

Frankie shook her head. "I have trouble extracting myself from this sectional, too, and I don't have broken ribs. We'll find a smaller chair for you to use."

"No, it's fine," Kit protested. "I—"

"There's an extra armchair in Mako's quarters." Hawk turned toward the guest bedroom with Aric and ignored Bull's surprise at his words.

So, yeah, maybe he didn't like change and didn't want strangers touching the sarge's things. Maybe he'd been pissed off when his brothers let Gabe's officer, JJ, stay there. However, Kit needed a chair she could sit in. He was just being practical.

In the guest bedroom, Aric's cot was next to the bigger bed. Same setup as the kid had used in Hawk's bedroom.

Stepping around Hawk, Kit flipped the covers back.

After laying Aric down, Hawk slid the kid's shoes and socks off. "He just had a bath," he muttered.

"Thank you." She tucked the covers around her son. "I can see he's gained weight. Has a suntan. And he isn't terrified all the time." When she looked up at Hawk, tears filled her eyes. "You've taken good care of him."

Hawk backed away. *Crying. Fuck no.* There should be a law or something—no crying around him. "No problem."

Words exhausted, he walked out.

In the living room, Bull and Frankie watched him.

When Bull smiled, Hawk considered planting a fist in his brother's face. "Let's get that fucking chair."

As Kit closed the door of her bedroom, she heard the men talking in the living room. Bull had an incredibly deep voice. Hawk's was almost as deep, but with a gravelly, harsh timbre.

Such different men. Bull was open, friendly, and completely straightforward. He reminded her of a wide, slow-moving river so clear one could see the sparkling stones in the depths.

Hawk was more like a mountain glacier. Slow-moving and unstoppable. Hiding everything submerged within the ice, yet with unexpected sparkling waterfalls.

And so very, very deep.

When he'd seen she couldn't rise without help, he'd offered his hand. And scared her.

Obadiah had considered her fear a prize. Not Hawk. There had been pain in his blue-gray eyes when she cringed. She'd hurt him.

And so, she'd found her courage.

She couldn't blame herself for being frightened of any man, really. But Hawk...talk about intimidating.

He had dark blond hair, cut short, and a trim beard outlined his lean, hard jawline. He moved like...like he was ready for a fight at any moment, and he'd obviously been in a few. The reddish tan of his fair skin contrasted with a long white scar across his forehead and one on his neck. Another scar ran down his cheek into his mustache and was deep enough it pulled his top lip up into a slight sneer.

Rolled-up shirtsleeves had exposed his tattooed forearms. And was it bad that she kind of wanted to look at the tats that were different shades of brown? To see what he'd chosen. There'd been a plane on one forearm and...

Snoopy much, Kit?

She had to laugh because...yes? Maybe she was quieter than her bestie, but people were interesting. However, unlike Frankie, she preferred them in ones or twos rather than a crowd.

And she preferred a fair amount of alone time.

Smiling slightly, she moved around the bedroom, savoring that she had a place for her and Aric. She'd never realized how wonderful privacy could be until the months of living in the PZ women's barracks. During the days, she'd worked in the fields and gardens, cleaned Obadiah's small house, and joined the women in cooking.

In the evenings, after slaking his needs on her body, her husband would send her back to the barracks since Reverend Parrish denounced letting a female get too close. Heaven forbid a man should love his wife or show her any tenderness. She was put on the earth solely to serve his needs and bear his children.

In her head, the counselor's voice whispered, "*Is that what you believe, Kit?*"

"No," Kit whispered back. *No, it's not.*

She'd been a fool.

Or maybe misguided would be more accurate. Her parents had loved her and each other. It was *their* example she needed to follow.

Not the example of her aunt and uncle who'd taken her in after Mom and Dad died. Uncle Duane would've joined the PZs in a heartbeat. They'd been a cold, mean-spirited couple.

Now she knew that while trying to win their love and

approval, she'd opened herself up to their belief that a woman wasn't complete without a man.

She sure didn't believe their idiocy any longer...because she'd learned she was far, far better off without a man.

The sliding groan of his bedroom door snapped Hawk out of sleep. Silently, he put his hand under his pillow and...found nothing.

Shit, right. He'd mounted his pistol in a nightstand gun safe three weeks ago. Because of the kid. Silently, he leaned over, started to touch the fingerprint scanner and—

He narrowed his eyes.

The person in the doorway was short.

Really fucking short.

"Aric." His voice came out harsher than normal, as if he'd spent two days smoking bad tobacco and drinking rotgut.

The kid wasn't scared at the sound. Never had been.

Aric came closer, as silent as Caz was when hunting. The kid didn't speak.

Hawk almost laughed. As a kid, he'd been as uncommunicative —and had annoyed the hell out of his brothers and Mako.

"Your mama okay?"

The gray twilight showed the boy's nod. He didn't look frightened or anxious.

Doc Grayson had warned that any deviation in Aric's life might have him regressing, which was Grayson's fancy-ass-shrink way of saying the boy would get clingy again.

Because, when scared, he ran to Hawk like a baby bird hiding under its parent's wing.

Understandable, but...damn. "Kid, your mom's going to have a shi—uh, will be upset you're not in bed." Hawk scrubbed his hands over his face, trying to wake up. Could hardly send the squirt hiking back by himself. He stood up and made the gesture for *ride*. "Let's go."

Although Aric's mouth flattened—the kid could be right-eously stubborn—he let Hawk haul him up and set him on his hip.

Outside, a brightening of the dusk indicated the first hint of sunrise, which meant it was closing in on 4:30 or so. The dew-moistened grass in the courtyard was cold on his bare feet. As they crossed to Bull's house next door, a light breeze rustled the rushes on the lake shore and reminded Hawk he hadn't put on a damn shirt, either.

The deck door was unlocked. Before Hawk had walked halfway across the living area, his brother slid open the upstairs bedroom door.

Leaning on the railing, Bull looked down.

None of the brothers slept heavy. Not that Hawk had tried to be especially quiet.

Hawk tilted his head at Aric who was half asleep already and shrugged.

Bull let out a snort, shook his head, and disappeared into his room. Because he had a warm, loving woman in his bed.

Envy was a familiar ache in Hawk's chest. He'd never have a wife and kids.

Instead of stewing, he headed down the narrow hallway beneath the second floor. The guest bedroom door was open, and he stopped in the doorway.

Kit was sleeping on her undamaged right side. Her long, streaky-brown hair lay loose over her pillow. Her splinted arm was on another pillow, her other arm stretched out toward Aric's empty cot.

A pang ran through Hawk at the sight, at the knowledge that even in her sleep, she'd wanted to touch her son.

He took a step forward and stopped. Going into a woman's room wouldn't be a smart move.

Hawk silently set the boy down, pointed to Aric's chest, then the bed. He leaned against the doorframe to wait.

Of course, on the way to his cot, the kid bumped into his mother's bed.

Kit sat up in a rush, looked around in obvious fear, and spotted Hawk in the doorway. Her breath drew in audibly.

"Brought your kid back," he grated out before she could scream the house down. "He showed up in my room."

Her hands were clenched on the bed covers, her eyes wide. After a long moment, she pulled in a breath. "Hawk."

Yeah, her brain had booted up. Her gaze dropped to her son who was crawling onto his cot. "Aric, did you go over to Hawk's house?"

The kid nodded.

Honest kid. A guy had to appreciate that.

Hawk half-smiled at the memory of when Mako had taken in Bull, Gabe, and Caz—and him. He'd been a lying little shit back then. But he'd changed. Doc Grayson had talked about the damage a lie could cause in a family. Caz had pointed out that hawks and eagles were the most upfront of the winged species. But, most of all, the sarge had hated dishonesty, and there was nothing Hawk wanted more than to win Mako's regard.

It'd still taken Hawk a year to kick the lying habit.

Aric wouldn't have that problem; his abusive stepfather and the other PZs hadn't turned him into a liar. Maybe because the boy had spent his time hiding and rarely spoke. No need to lie if no one expected an answer.

Over on the cot, Aric pulled his covers up.

Duty done.

As Hawk opened his mouth to say good night, he saw the way Kit's hands were still clenched on her blanket, the tenseness of her shoulders. He could almost hear the fears running through her head. A big half-dressed stranger in her bedroom. A scary one.

Then her pointed chin came up, and she shocked the hell out

of him with a sweet smile. "Thank you for bringing him back. I hope you're able to get to sleep."

Brave woman. The faint twilight through the window high-lighted the ragged scar over her left cheekbone where a fist had ripped the skin.

The light showed more than that. Beneath her loose flannel pajamas, she had high, sweetly rounded breasts.

Not something he should be noticing.

"No problem." Turning his gaze away, Hawk straightened. "Night."

He headed down the hall, across the living room, and out the deck door, attempting to set aside the wish to join her. To touch her, to feel her warmth against him, maybe even have her smile at him again.

Talk about a forlorn hope. After what she'd lived through, the woman would want nothing more to do with the male gender.

And, if she ever did, it'd be a cold day in hell before she would want *him*.

The nice ones never did.

CHAPTER THREE

P *eople who use the phrase "sleep like a baby" must have never had one.*
- Unknown

Captain Grigor Nabera walked out of the small farmhouse in the Matanuska Valley north of Anchorage.

Hiding out like a coward was offensive, but necessary until he knew what needed to be done. When their leader, Reverend Parrish—the Prophet—had been arrested, the members of the militia here and in Texas scattered after a raid on their compound. Although the weak in spirit had abandoned the cause, the faithful went to ground and maintained contact.

When the Prophet called, they would answer, and Nabera would lead them to victory.

"Morning, Captain." Walking up from the barn, Alvin joined him on the small porch. The balding farmer brushed a few strands of hay from his flannel shirt. "Have you heard from Reverend Parrish? How is it going?"

Nabera scowled as he looked out over the fields of beets. "He's been denied bail...because of the women who've accused him of rape and murder."

And other crimes. The list was long.

Nabera glanced at Alvin and added, "Untrue, of course. He'll be cleared, but until then, our course is uncertain."

"Of course." Alvin shifted his weight from one foot to another. Unwilling to give up everything to join the compound, he'd kept his farm and sent money as his way of supporting the cause.

He hadn't been pleased when Nabera showed up three weeks ago.

No matter.

"The missus will have breakfast for us soon." Alvin took a step back. "I need to move the cows to a new pasture."

It was time for a new pasture for Nabera too. He'd had Alvin rent a house in Anchorage. Nabera and his lieutenants would move in there.

If only he could figure out how to help the Prophet. Unfortunately, there wasn't much he could do when Parrish was imprisoned all the way south in Texas, and Nabera was stuck here in Alaska. The state troopers, FBI, and DEA were on the alert, so getting to Dallas was impossible.

Meanwhile, Parrish was waiting for his trial where the women from the Texas compound would testify against him. The blasphemous bitches.

A cold wind swept across the farm, rustling the red and green leaves of the beets, waving the grasses in the pastures. Summer was getting on. Time was passing too quickly.

When running the compound, Nabera would normally make a bloody example of one woman—or child—to frighten the rest into silence.

Nabera growled under his breath. Times weren't normal.

In Texas, the Patriot Zealots had managed to locate and

punish one bitch. After seeing one of their own broken and hospitalized, the rest of the cunts should have shut the fuck up. Instead, they'd let the Feds hide them away in safe houses.

Their testimony would land Parrish behind bars for years.

What could Nabera do from here to change that? Would an example made in Alaska be effective in silencing the harlots in Texas?

Perhaps... If the example was shocking enough.

Despite Aric's late-night visit to Hawk's place, the kid didn't seem any the worse for wear.

How many times this morning had the boy snuck into his cabin to reassure himself that Hawk was still around?

The kid had skills.

Grabbing a Coke, Hawk headed outside and settled into a chair on his deck.

The frequent checks weren't because the boy loved him or anything. It was because Hawk had killed Aric's abusive stepfather, saved his mother, and carried the boy to safety.

Doc Grayson had said, "*Even when she is ready to take him back, she can't give him the same sense of safety that he gets with Hawk. Not right away.*"

From the kid's point of view, Hawk was strong enough to protect him, and his mother wasn't.

Before last night, Hawk had planned to resume a full workload. He and his buddy, Bishop, had served together as helicopter pilots in the 160th Special Operations Aviation Regiment—the Night Stalkers—and had recently pooled their money to buy a helicopter. They had a contract with McNally's Resort to fly tourists to hard-to-reach locations. Bishop usually took the helicopter since Hawk also loved flying his floatplane.

Tourists from the Lower 48 loved floatplanes.

But returning to full time piloting would have to be delayed. It seemed the kid wasn't ready for Hawk to be gone long hours or overnight.

From the chicken pen came the sound of Regan's laughter and chatter. Caz's daughter had drafted Aric to help her gather eggs. With a heart as big as her father's, Regan had taken the boy under her wing.

Since she was out of school for the summer, everyone at the Hermitage had been taking turns babysitting her. Caz said Kit had volunteered for today.

Speaking of which, Hawk spotted the woman walking a circuit around the courtyard perimeter. Her expression was that of an army recruit gutting through morning PT, determined to get stronger, no matter the pain involved. Guess he knew where Aric's stubbornness had come from.

He had to respect her willpower.

Unlike Aric, she looked tired today. Shoulders sagging slightly, dark circles under her eyes. Her arm was in a sling, although he'd seen her take it out when trying to do anything. At least the damage from her husband's fists had healed.

Every time he'd seen her bruised face in the hospital, he wanted to dig the bastard up and kill him again.

The two children appeared, detouring to show Kit the basket of eggs, before crossing the courtyard to the houses.

"The eggs go to Bull's house today. He gets extra cuz you and your mom live there now," Regan told Aric. Followed by the boy and Bull's dog, Gryff, Regan led the way up onto the deck to set the basket on a shelf. She and Aric stopped to pet her giant furball of a cat who'd perched on the railing to supervise.

Hawk shook his head. The Hermitage sure had changed in the last year. The sarge had been one paranoid survivalist-type to begin with. Then, having illegally brought Hawk, Gabe, Bull, and Caz to Alaska from a California foster home, he'd grown even more cautious. When he'd moved to Rescue, the only people permitted on the property were his four sons and Doc Grayson. Later, he'd allowed Dante, an old Vietnam vet friend, to visit and then...Lillian.

Hawk had to admit it'd been a shock to learn that Mako and Lillian had been lovers.

"Way to go, Sarge." Hawk lifted his Coke in a toast.

But the sarge had crossed the river, and shit was changing.

Gabe had started the upheaval. A year ago, Audrey had arrived in Rescue, running from a hitman. The sweet, brainy librarian had surprising courage, and Gabe had fallen hard.

Then, needing help in the police station, Gabe brought in Officer Jayden at the same time Caz had discovered he had a kid. Regan was a hell of a gutsy little girl—and had almost killed herself trying to rescue that stray cat from a fucking blizzard. Good kid.

And JJ was a good woman, as Caz had learned.

Last spring, Bull rescued the brown mutt—a Bernese mountain-shepherd mix—from an asshole who was into dogfighting. Gryff deserved better. So, the Hermitage acquired a damn dog.

Couple of months ago, Frankie came to Alaska to rescue Kit and Aric. Hawk smirked. The New Yorker had a temper, and when she started swearing in Italian, it was the funniest thing he'd ever seen. She and Bull fit perfectly.

Now, Kit and Aric were here. The Hermitage was getting fucking crowded.

Aric trotted off Bull's deck, collected a hug from his mother, and started for Hawk's place, undoubtedly for another covert check.

Hawk raised a hand.

Startled, the kid stood for a second as if to ensure Hawk wasn't planning to do anything unexpected—like leave—then ran to rejoin Regan.

Regan had grabbed a camera case off Caz's deck. "Hey, Aric,

Papá gave me his camera, so we can take pictures of the baby ducks. I can take pictures of you an' your mom too." The girl turned to Kit for permission since they had a rule of no kids near the water without an adult watching.

Kit nodded and angled in that direction.

Good mom.

CHAPTER FOUR

M *ake yourself a sheep and the wolves will eat you.* ~ Ben Franklin

On Sunday evening, Kit followed Frankie across the Hermitage courtyard, and her heartrate increased at the number of people on the patio.

No, no, there weren't so many. Really.

The logic didn't help.

One by one, she named them, trying to convince herself to relax.

Bull was grilling freshly caught salmon.

In a cute chef's hat, ten-year-old Regan was helping him. It was adorable how much she looked like her father, Cazador, who stood nearby.

Prior to her rescue, Caz had set her arm—before Obadiah broke it a second time. The dark-haired, dark-eyed nurse practitioner had been kind, his hands gentle, as he asked her how she'd been hurt. However, with Aric held hostage in the PZ compound, she'd had to lie.

Beside Caz was his girlfriend, JJ. About Kit's height, but far more muscular, the police officer had a strong face, neck-length, curly auburn hair, and bright turquoise eyes. She and Audrey had visited Kit in the hospital to reassure her that they'd help care for Aric.

Rescue's librarian, blonde Audrey, stood at the other end of the picnic table with her fiancé, Gabe. A big man with a rough-hewn, cynical face, the chief of police was JJ's boss.

His eyes narrowed when he saw Kit.

Fear jolted through her, and her feet came to a halt.

Living in Bull's house, she'd gotten used to Bull and his size—as long as he didn't move too fast. Although shorter, Gabe was even scarier.

Audrey slapped Gabe's arm and said something to him. He blinked, and his expression changed. They both moved forward.

Heaven help her, but she wanted to run. *I will not flee.*

Tensing, she held her ground.

Eyes filled with sympathy, Audrey said, "When I first got to Rescue, Gabe looked at me with his *I'm-a-mean-old-cop* expression, and I almost ran too."

Kit's mouth dropped open, and her stomach went tight. "Don't—" But he didn't backhand his girlfriend for hitting him or for the insult.

No, he wouldn't. Normal people didn't act like that.

She pulled in a breath. Although she'd lived only months with the PZs, somehow, they'd warped her world.

After another quick breath, she managed to smile at the police chief. "Forgive me, please. Your...expression...is quite effective."

"All the better to scare the bad guys with." His grin was rueful and charming. "I didn't mean to use it on you. Sorry. I'm glad you're finally here and out of rehab."

At the sincerity in his blue eyes, she relaxed. "Me too." She tried to keep the quaver out of her voice. "Thank you so very much for your part in my rescue."

He blinked, then shook his head. "I'm only sorry we didn't make it in before you got so hurt."

He'd risked his life, yet felt bad the rescue hadn't been faster? Her fear drained away. "Bones heal. You got the children out. Got Aric out. If there is ever anything I can do for any of you, you have it."

"Just work on getting better." He grinned at her. "I'd been wanting to shut those bast—" Audrey's elbow impacted his ribs, and he grunted and amended his words. "Uh, those *PZs* down since I met the first one. I'm grateful Frankie let us help."

She could hear the sincerity in his voice. He really was a nice person, wasn't he? All of them were—and they'd saved her, and even more importantly, her son.

Averting her gaze, she blinked away tears. Where was her son?

There, on the other side of the patio with Hawk.

Tall, broad shouldered, with his sleeves rolled up over muscular forearms to reveal those amazing tattoos, Hawk was helping Aric throw a ball for Gryff to retrieve.

As if he'd felt her gaze, Hawk turned. His eyes sharpened, probably at the tears in her eyes.

At her slightly wavery smile, he gave her a chin-lift.

Aric bounced, waving his hand at her to get her to come over.

"I guess I'd better see what's going on. Excuse me." After smiling at Audrey and Gabe, she joined him. "What's up, honey bear?"

His eyes got wide and uncertain.

Hawk frowned before making an interrogative sound. Did the man have a restricted number of words he was allowed to use in a day?

Still, it was wonderful he could read Aric so accurately.

Reluctantly, she explained what had worried her son. "Obadiah ordered me to only use Aric's name. He said endearments—especially from a woman—would weaken a man."

Hawk's expression hardened.

Yes, she'd been a failure as a parent. She knew that.

He looked down at Aric and growled, "Obadiah was an idiot." His tone made her shiver, yet Aric didn't seem afraid in the least.

She swallowed and owned her failure in a whisper. "So was I."

"You were conned. That's different." His dark blond brows drew together. "No endearments. And Aric whispers."

She nodded. "Only the men were permitted to talk freely. To be loud."

"Yeah, no. He needs to see it's okay to make noise."

"Of course."

Hawk's mouth tightened, and she knew she'd missed something.

Then he asked, "But if his mom's terrified to raise her voice...?"

Aric's mother took a step back, looking like he'd slapped her. Hawk winced.

Hell, he'd fucked up, hadn't he?

How else could he explain that the way she tiptoed around and spoke barely above a whisper would influence the kid? If she acted as if she'd be yelled at for making noise, the boy would never change.

He watched as she recovered. As her gaze dropped to her son.

"You didn't realize," he said slowly.

She shook her head and said softly, "After a while—" Her hands clenched...and then her chin came up, and her voice emerged much louder. "After a while, staying quiet becomes a habit."

Eyes wide, Aric stared at her.

So did Hawk.

She had a beautiful mouth, sweetly curved lips with the bottom one bigger than the top...and it quivered as she smiled at her son. "Aric, Obadiah and those men were wrong to order us to be quiet all the time. Sometimes, whispering is good—like when someone is sleeping, and you don't want to wake them up. But when we're with friends—like now—we can be just as loud as they are."

The way the kid watched his mother as if she was an unexploded landmine made Hawk smother a laugh.

And made him want to pound a few heads together for what the kid had gone through.

But when the slender young woman discovered she had a motherlode of courage inside her? Now that was an honor to watch.

And when she turned and yelled across the patio, "Hey, Bull, I'm starving. When do we eat?" Hawk almost cheered.

Kit blinked and stared up at the ceiling. *Oh look, I'm awake. Again.* For what—the third time tonight? She shouldn't have had that can of caffeinated soda at supper. She knew better. But, oh, it was such a lovely indulgence to enjoy the foods Obadiah had forbidden.

Unfortunately, the caffeine meant her brain kept waking her back up after an hour or two of sleep. Darn it.

Earlier, on the patio, she'd eventually relaxed around the Hermitage residents, although it would be nice if the guys were timid nerds instead of obviously dangerous. But during the meal at the oak picnic table, they'd been thoughtful when speaking to her, using gentle tones and expressions. Much the same as they were with Aric.

Eventually, she might resent being treated as if she was weak, but right now—she wrinkled her nose in annoyance—

right now, she really was a wussy, and their consideration helped.

Because she was also far too inclined to panic. Like when they'd started sitting down. Frankie motioned for Kit to sit beside her near the middle, and Kit had frozen.

Then Hawk looked at her and pointed to the end of the bench. "Sit there."

Also seated in the middle, Audrey frowned. "But we want her near us."

He shook his head and told Kit, "Your instincts want an escape route. For now."

He'd been right. The knot inside her had relaxed when she sat at the end...because she could run away if needed. Or jump out and put Aric behind her.

How had he known? As big and tough as he was, he'd never had fears like hers.

Once settled, she'd had a wonderful time. She'd forgotten how enjoyable it was to eat and talk with pleasant people. Intelligent ones who had busy lives. Ones who could argue about almost anything without getting upset. They didn't believe there was only one way to do things, and no one else should voice an opinion.

The women spoke up as often as the men—and so did Regan.

Although Kit would need to make her own way and couldn't stay here long, the interactions of the Hermitage family were exactly what she and Aric needed to see.

Caring, consideration, and equality.

Aric was already changing. Returning to the young imp he'd been before.

She grinned. He'd played so hard he'd been half asleep when she put him to bed.

Rolling onto her side, she reached out to the narrow cot beside her bed. Just to touch him, to reassure herself he was alive and safe.

The bed was empty.

Her heart gave a horrible thump. Where could he be?

The bathroom? No. The door was open, the room dark.

Arm pressed to her sore ribs, she sat up and pushed to her feet.

Soft footsteps sounded in the hallway. A big man shadowed the doorway and made a snort of exasperation. "See? Your mom's awake." The deep rasping voice was familiar.

"Hawk."

One big arm under Aric's butt, he carried her son in and set him on the cot. Aric stared at him.

"This time, stay here," Hawk said. How could such a stern, harsh voice be so gentle?

Aric shook his head, his lower lip poking out. Her son could be extremely stubborn.

"This time?" Kit asked.

"Second time tonight."

A man had entered her bedroom while she was sleeping. Icy fear slid up her spine.

Hawk rubbed his cheek where a scar parted his beard, then sighed. "Boy, if I bunk in the living room, will you stay put?"

Aric eyed Hawk, then nodded slowly.

"On the sectional?" Kit asked.

"It's big enough." He ruffled Aric's hair. "Go to sleep, kid. I'll be close enough."

As Aric lay down, Kit tucked him in. Even before she kissed his cheek, he was falling asleep.

When she turned, Hawk had already disappeared.

Nice of Bull to keep a couple of heavy throw blankets on the back of the sectional, Hawk thought. He set his boots by the sliding glass door and stretched out. It was a comfortable enough couch for a nap, but he wouldn't sleep that deep or long.

Not on a couch. Not in someone else's house—even his brother's.

Then again, he wasn't getting much sleep what with hauling the kid's ass back over here. But there was no choice. Aric needed to be with his mother.

Such a damn pretty mother. Big, wide eyes and soft mouth. And even soft-looking breasts.

Dammit, don't notice those things, dumbass.

Hawk had expected her to yell—or burst into tears. He'd scared her—and he'd also seen the flash of hurt that her son needed someone else.

But she'd sucked it up, and as he left, she'd been tucking her boy in. Kissing him on the cheek.

Lucky kid. What would it feel like to be the recipient of all that love?

CHAPTER FIVE

H*ope for the best, but prepare for the worst.* - Unknown

Midweek, in her Toyota 4Runner, JJ glanced over at her passenger and winced at the way Kit was holding her side. It wouldn't do the woman any good to arrive at her physical therapy appointment already in pain.

JJ slowed the vehicle a bit more. "Sorry. I know how much bouncing can hurt."

"That sounds like the voice of experience. I bet police work gets pretty rough."

"Sometimes." JJ hadn't spent much time with Kit, but she was finding the woman was just as sweet as Frankie had said. "Back in Nevada, I got on the wrong side of a bullet during a drug gang's takedown."

At Kit's wide eyes, JJ laughed. "No, no big holes. I had on body armor. But just the impact cracked a rib."

"Sheesh, what a job."

When they went over the next dip, Kit bent forward, making

a pained sound. "Why does this section have so many ruts? The rest is in decent shape."

"You can thank Mako for that."

"Why?"

JJ shook her head. "You know this was Mako's place at first, with the guys just visiting, right?"

"Actually, no."

"Okay, let's see. The sarge was retired career military, and he raised the guys out in the middle of nowhere, but when they grew up and left, he got..." JJ had slowed the car to a crawl. "During his service, he'd been deployed to Vietnam and some uglier areas, and suffered from PTSD and paranoia. Caz said he had a sense of impending doom—as though the world was going to go up in flames at any moment. He wanted to be prepared."

"Frankie said he was a survivalist."

"Big time." JJ thought of the arsenal that would put most police station armories to shame. The tunnels under the houses. "He went way past the basic prepper stuff, like the solar panels and generators and stocking up on food."

Kit gave her a smile. "I love the way the Hermitage is set up, actually. It makes my permaculture heart happy."

"Agreed. The houses even shrug off earthquakes," JJ said with a laugh. "But, back to the road. The sarge designed it so that, from Swan Avenue, it seems to dead-end. If someone *does* make it around the U-curve, this section is so rutted, it appears impassible. I must admit his strategy is effective. No tourists try to visit this side of the lake."

As JJ stopped the car before turning onto Swan, Kit turned slightly to look behind them. "I see. You can't even tell that the road turns and continues."

"Right?" JJ pulled out onto the nice, smoothly graveled main road and was relieved to see Kit relax. "Sorry about the ride."

"It's certainly not your fault. I'm surprised the guys haven't graded the road though. Since Mako isn't here any longer."

"They seem to have inherited some of his wariness." JJ shook her head. "God knows they all saw combat, and maybe having a secure fortress for a home lets them sleep better at night.

And if a rutted road was what it took for Caz to feel at peace, she'd hack a few holes in it herself.

Although Kit might not feel the same.

At the soft sound of understanding, JJ glanced over.

"When I woke up in the hospital, I felt like I had the worst of lives, had made the stupidest choices, suffered more than most people. So self-centered." Kit snorted. "But most of us run into bad stuff—and then have to figure out how to compensate for it. If the men who served our country need a rutted road, then that's what we'll make sure they have."

JJ blinked in surprise, then pleasure. Here was a woman with a wagonload of compassion. No wonder she and Frankie were best friends.

Kit gave her a firm nod. "Next time, I'll bring a pillow to brace against my midsection when we go over the bumps."

A couple of hours later, Kit trudged out of her physical therapy appointment, wanting nothing more than to crawl onto a couch somewhere and take a nap.

Thank goodness her PT and counseling appointments were on the same day, and she wouldn't have to suffer going down that road more often.

She was lucky that Soldotna's agencies sent various therapists to Rescue's medical clinic several times a week. Driving to Soldotna twice a week would not only have hurt, but also made her feel even more of a burden on Frankie and the others. Although JJ had been wonderful this morning, insisting that it was no problem to bring Kit in with her. The officer was a really nice person.

Kit looked around and sighed at the total lack of comfy sofas in the big municipal building lobby.

With a muffled groan, she settled into a wooden chair on the health clinic side. She could divert herself by watching the people coming and going from the clinic, the police station on the other side, and the town offices upstairs. The place was busy.

All the visitors stopped at the semi-circular receptionist desk staffed by a middle-aged, solidly built blonde. The nameplate on the desk read "Regina Schroeder."

Two men in rubber boots, stained shirts, and jeans were telling the woman how one got injured. "Yeah, the damn bear wanted my damn fish, and excuse me, but *I* caught that salmon. I figured if I yelled loud enough, it'd leave."

The receptionist snorted. "And how did that work out for you?"

"The bear charged him." His friend grinned at the unhappy salmon owner. "You should've seen the way you dove into those bushes—with an Olympic medal-worthy dive."

"Well, duh. Did you see the size of that animal?"

Kit shook her head. The poor fisherman had rips in his clothes and bloody scratches here and there.

The friend shook his head. "Trouble is, I think he sprained his wrist."

"*Trouble* is the goddamn bear got my salmon," the man said morosely.

Ms. Schroeder didn't laugh out loud, but her lips were twitching. Receptioning in this place must be a crazy job.

Sitting back, Kit listened as Ms. Schroeder sent people upstairs to the town's record office, the library, called JJ to report a fistfight at the post office, and juggled medical appointments. Incoming clinic patients got paperwork to be filled out for the medical aides.

Kit sighed, wishing she'd taken something for pain before

coming in. At least there was an hour to relax before the counseling appointment.

Physical therapy was tough work. Since Kit was up and moving around, the focus had changed to her arm that was full of metal plates and pins and stuff. Talk about painful. The therapist, a very competent, kind, older woman, had just laughed when Kit accused her of practicing BDSM.

Grimacing, she shifted her throbbing arm to a better position in the sling.

It was all good, though. True, her muscles were weak and her fingers still fumbly, but her arm was improving.

Realizing she was going to get back to normal was so very heartening.

"Are you doing well there, Ms. Sandersen?" The receptionist sat down next to Kit. "Can I get you anything?"

Kit chuckled. "Was I looking pitiful?"

The answer on the woman's face was easy to read.

"Really, I'm fine. I have a counseling appointment in another hour—and my arm aches from PT, so I thought I'd just sit here rather than wandering around town."

"That makes sense." The woman tilted her head. "I'm Regina, and you're Frankie's friend? When I saw her last night at the diner, she asked me to watch out for you."

That was totally Frankie. "Yes, and it's Kit. I've enjoyed watching you. You're like a New York City traffic cop, sending patients, residents, police officers, and health staff to the right places at the right times."

Regina chuckled. "There are days it's more like trying to steer a batch of grizzlies."

Kit laughed. "Yet you're enjoying it."

"You betcha. It sure beats sitting at home. Or it used to. My daughter and her husband moved back here from the Lower 48 last winter." Regina's eyes were all alight. "They presented me with my first grandchild last month. My days have gotten lively."

"Congratulations on the new baby."

"Thank you." Regina beamed. "If I might ask, what do you do for a living when you're not laid up?"

Kit smiled. Regina reminded her of the Hermitage guys. Right to the point, but with no malice. Just interest. "Before I married and got pressured into the Patriot Zealots"—a nod showed Regina understood—"I worked in a garden nursery and did landscape design with an emphasis on natural systems."

"Interesting. Did you like it?"

"Yes. I miss it so much. It's the best of all worlds, really. Helping the earth to be more beautiful and productive. And helping people too. I like people"—Kit half-grinned—"um, in small numbers."

"I hear you." Regina laughed. "Put me at a party where I have to make small talk in a group, and hell, I'd rather go bare-ass ice swimming. But this"—she waved at her reception desk—"it's like you said. Helping people. Keeping things working right."

The phone at Regina's desk rang. She gave Kit's knee a quick pat, then bustled across the room to answer.

Kit returned to people watching.

A person went into the police station, two more into the health clinic. Not a busy day. After studying the receptionist desk, the off-white walls and hardwood floors, she was bored silly. Next time, she'd bring a book and a thermos of coffee.

She eyed the glass-fronted doors to the street. Wasn't there a coffee shop around here?

No, girl. Coffee isn't in the budget. No. She was being extremely careful with the money Frankie had loaned her. It had to go a long way.

To her right, a man said, "Kit" in a smooth, dark voice.

She jumped and squeaked when she twisted too fast.

"*Dios.*" Caz held up his hands and took a step back. "Sorry, *chica*. I forget to make noise when I walk."

"It's fine." She'd been watching the front door, not thinking about someone coming out of the clinic. Blindsiding her.

From now on, she'd know better.

He went down on his haunches, relieving her anxiety of being at a disadvantage before it had a chance to register. "I'm taking a break and getting us both some coffee. Do you want your coffee here or would you like to join me across the street?"

She almost smiled. Caz's Spanish-accented voice was the auditory equivalent of melted chocolate. So different from Hawk's.

Her brows drew together at the way he'd phrased his question. She *would* be getting coffee. Joining him was optional. He must have realized she'd refuse if he'd asked her if she wanted coffee. "Were you born tactful and sneaky, or did you learn that in school?"

He laughed. "I will answer your question across the street." Standing, he stepped back so she could rise.

As they walked across the room toward the door, Regina tossed Caz a satisfied salute.

"She called you, didn't she?"

He didn't pretend to misunderstand. "*Sí.* She knows I enjoy company with my break."

Charm like his should be considered lethal. Yet there was something even more satisfying about Hawk's completely blunt, whittled-to-the-minimum kinds of answers.

The bell over the coffee shop door clanged lightly as they entered. With a sweet, old-fashioned décor, the room had wooden pews rubbed to softness forming booths along the front window and right side. A few people sat at tables and chairs in the center.

Behind the glass-fronted pastry display to the left, a lean brunette waved a latex-gloved hand. "Doc, your usual? And we have apple empanadas. Want one?"

"Yes to both, please. A drink and pastry for Kit, here, too." When she started to shake her head, he simply smiled. "After being tortured by our physical terrorist, you deserve caffeine and something sweet."

His charm was a thin mulch hiding a very stubborn personality. She wasn't going to win.

He leaned an arm on the counter. "Sarah, this is Kit, who is staying with us out at the Hermitage. She's Aric's mother. Kit, this is Sarah. She and her husband own the shop."

"Aric's mama?" Sarah clapped her hands. "He must be happy you're on your feet again. He's simply adorable."

Anyone who liked Aric had to be a wonderful person. Kit beamed. "He really is, thank you." After a quick study of the handwritten menu on the chalkboard, she picked a plain coffee and indulged in an old-fashioned apple fritter. Because Caz was right; she deserved it.

But somehow her list of people she owed kept getting longer. How ever would she pay everyone back?

Drinks and food in hand, they sat down at a table at the back.

Caz studied her for a moment. "Can you share what has you worried?"

Darn it. With Obadiah, she'd grown skilled at hiding her emotions. Free of him, it'd felt painfully good to drop that mask. But now...

A denial was on her lips, but no. She didn't want to be a person who wasn't honest in words or expressions. Even if it required being brave enough to drop her defenses.

After a moment, she realized Caz had leaned back, simply sipping his coffee and waiting.

"It's like this," she said. "I can't work just yet, and Obadiah gave all our money—including my savings—to the PZs. You folks are putting me up, and although Frankie loaned me some money, I'm going to need it for food, future rent, and getting a car. So, although I needed this coffee more than life itself"—she smiled at him—"it's eating at me that I can't pay my own way. Or pay anyone back for quite a while to come."

He took a bite of his hand pie and considered her words. "*Comprendo.* I'm not as prickly at receiving help as Gabe and Hawk are, but none of us enjoy feeling dependent on others."

That he understood was incredibly comforting.

Relaxing, she nibbled on her fritter. The pastry had a lovely fried crunch. There were pieces of apples in the sweet glaze. So yummy.

And it would be her last treat for a very long time, she figured. Her mouth tightened. How soon before she was healed enough to get a job?

"Hey, Hawk, what would you like?" Sarah called from the counter. "Black coffee and...?"

Kit startled and winced at the jab of rib pain before turning to look.

Hawk stood near the door, his intent blue-gray eyes meeting hers. His thick hair was all the shades of caramel, his beard trimmed close to his jawline. He wore a plain black T-shirt and jeans—no pretenses there—yet the well-worn fabrics, which clung to his muscular chest and thick biceps, gave hints of washboard abs and molded over hard thighs.

He frowned at her before turning to Sarah. "Yeah, coffee and..." He half-turned, revealing Aric behind him. "Kid, pick a—"

"Mama!" With a delighted cry, Aric darted across the room and dodged a customer. At the last minute, he remembered her ribs and skidded to a stop.

She leaned forward to hug him. "Honey bear," she whispered into his soft hair, inhaling the unique scent of little boy.

He nestled close, and his adorably crooked smile appeared. "We checking the happy-men."

"The...what?" Happy men? "What happened to the sad men?"

"No, no, *mijo*, they're *handymen*," Caz corrected Aric. "People who fix buildings."

"Handymen," Aric said agreeably and whispered to her, "They have hammers 'n' saws 'n' everyt'ing."

"Kid." Hawk took a coffee from Sarah. "Choose something."

Aric ran back to the counter. With his usual thoroughness, he studied the display of pastries, moving ever so slowly.

Kit tensed, then realized she'd let her fears mess with her perceptions.

Even though Hawk totally looked as if he snapped necks for a living and would garrote someone who delayed him, he was sipping his coffee and waiting for her son's decision with apparent infinite patience.

Her heart melted a bit.

Napkin-wrapped donut acquired, Aric carried it carefully over to the table while Hawk brought a glass of milk, coffee, and his own apple fritter.

He nodded to Caz and her. Seeing her pastry, his lips quirked. But he didn't speak.

She smiled at him. The PZ men were constantly giving the women orders or lecturing. They'd inflict their opinions on everyone. Hawk's silence was so refreshing.

It was also tempting to nudge him a bit to get him to talk.

Bad Kit. He might not be nearly as patient with her as he was with Aric.

Only, somehow, despite his deadly appearance, he didn't frighten her nearly as much as other men did. If anything, she felt safer when he was nearby.

Usually. There had been a few times when he'd move unexpectedly, and her body would take over, swamping her with panic.

"You upsetting her?" Hawk asked Caz as he sat down.

What? Kit blinked at the irritation in Hawk's voice.

"No, no, not me, 'mano. Life is." Caz gave her a smile. "She doesn't enjoy being forced to accept help."

"Why's today different?"

Hawk's question was easy to interpret. After all, she'd been accepting help ever since she'd been beaten into the ground.

His sharp gaze dropped to her coffee and pastry. "Ah. Sucks to be broke." He'd figured it out in two seconds.

Caz nodded. "Her husband gave his money—and hers—to the PZs."

"The pissers." Aric gave a tiny *heheheh* laugh.

"The what?" She tried to smother her own laugh, but how she'd missed his infectious high giggles.

"Regan renamed the PZers to pissers." Hawk's teeth flashed white in a quick grin—and his face went from rather terrifying to compellingly masculine.

She blinked, realizing she'd forgotten to breathe. Until Aric giggled again. *Pissers.* "Oh, heavens. As a mother, I should disapprove, but..." She could only laugh.

Hawk met her gaze, sharing her amusement at her son. Then he frowned. "Parrish has the PZ money?"

"He's probably using it to pay his lawyers." Caz looked as if he'd bitten into something nasty. "What if Nabera has access to the accounts?"

"Wouldn't be good." Hawk pushed the glass of milk closer to Aric.

Have access. Kit's mouth dropped open. "I forgot to tell the Feds about the cash."

Hawk raised an eyebrow. "Cash?"

"Obadiah oversaw the militia's money. And they were always talking about war or being attacked by the Feds, so they kept a stockpile of cash in a secret spot." She tried to smile. "It reminded me of pirates and their treasure stash."

Obadiah hadn't found her comparison funny.

"So Nabera does have money." Caz made an annoyed sound.

"Maybe?" Kit frowned. "He wouldn't have had time to get it before the PZs fled the compound."

Hawk snorted. "It's buried or something?"

"The money's in a cave in the forest. It takes a while to get there."

"Nabera might not have retrieved it then," Caz said. "The alphabet agencies only left yesterday. Before that, it was like an ant hive, and the road was blocked off."

"Really?" Nabera wouldn't risk getting caught by the Feds, but he might go after it now. If she moved fast... She sighed. She could barely move, let alone fast. She slumped back in the chair.

Hawk studied her. "You know where the cave is?"

"I'm surprised the *cabrón* who was your husband would share that with you," Caz said.

She hesitated, then decided she wouldn't go through her life distrusting people. These men had risked their lives to help her. "Obadiah needed an extra person to help carry."

She'd been his beast of burden.

"The asshole," Hawk muttered under his breath.

His comment kind of made her day.

Money would come in so useful right now. For her and... She bit her lip. "If I retrieved the hoard, could I share it with the other women rather than turning it over? They're in the same fix I am."

"Hmm." Caz tapped his fingers on the table. "Perhaps. You were a member of the PZs; it's your money too. Legally, as a victim, it should be yours."

Hawk took a sip of his coffee. "Possession is nine-tenths of the law."

It took her a second to realize they were agreeing with her.

"However," Caz added, "we will not share this information with the chief of police."

Hawk half-laughed, then his gaze ran over her in open assessment. "Sounds like it's a hike."

There was no way she'd be able to get there. Or be able to tell them how. Her shoulders sagged. "I think we walked for miles."

His eyes narrowed. "Did it have a clearing nearby?"

Jesus. Three hours later, the simple helicopter trip had expanded from three people to five. Hawk had planned to take Kit along after her counseling appointment as well as Aric, who was still attached to his side.

He'd figured the chance of running into the PZ bastards was slim. How would they even know the Feds had left?

To be safe, though, Caz said he'd come along.

Of course, Caz told Bull, who invited himself on the trip. Hawk snorted. The nosy big bastard just wanted to see the site.

In the helicopter, Kit was in front next to Hawk. Bull and Caz were in back. So was Aric who was buckled in with the kid restraint system and wearing child-sized headphones. The boy pouted at losing his shotgun position, but to give directions, Kit needed to see out the front.

Hawk got everyone arranged for an equitable weight distribution. At least one thing had gone right—since there was fog in the lowlands, the helicopter hadn't been booked for any tourist flights.

Accompanied by Aric's muted squeal of joy, the helicopter lifted off from McNally's Resort landing pad.

I agree, kid. With an unspoken whoop, Hawk took the helicopter straight down the mountain toward the compound. Fuck, he loved this machine. The Airbus H125, aka the Squirrel, was a hell of a workhorse.

In the headphones, he heard a sharply drawn breath, and he glanced to his right. Was Kit panicking?

Then he grinned. Like her son's, her wide smile was a tiny bit crooked...and just as filled with joy.

The woman liked flying.

Relaxing, he settled in to enjoy the flight—because being in the air was happiness, no matter how often he flew.

A few minutes later, he could see that the private road leading to the PZ compound was still blocked to traffic. The fence gate was closed.

But the law enforcement vehicles were gone.

Keeping the helicopter at a low height, Hawk flew over the compound and hovered by the back fence.

"I don't see a trail." Bull's voice came through the headphones.

"That way." Kit motioned toward the east. "The path is almost invisible when near the compound. Obadiah didn't want it to be used. Once in the forest, there's an animal trail to follow."

Hawk made a couple of passes.

"There." Kit leaned forward and pointed. "It's that thin line. Do you see it? The cliff near that stream is where we're going."

Hawk glanced around, checking his surroundings, height, speed.

"I can see that'd be quite a walk," Bull said.

As they got closer, Kit motioned to the right. "The caves are there, beside the waterfall, and"—she made an unhappy sound—"the open area is smaller than I realized."

Hawk shrugged. No wind. No fog. Easy enough. He'd dropped into tighter spots.

Piece of cake, although he noticed Kit held her breath as he centered and lowered the helicopter into the clearing. After landing on the stream bank, he shut down the engine.

Before removing his headphones, he told Kit, "Wait for me to help you out."

"Sir, yes, sir." The bubbly laughter in her voice didn't sound like her.

Ah, right. "First helicopter ride?"

"Oh, yes." Her huge brown eyes were luminous with delight. "It was awesome. And you do this all the time?"

"I take my floatplane more often than the helicopter, but yeah. This is my job."

He unlocked his gun safe, donned his holstered Glock, then jumped out and surveyed the area.

To the east, was the cliff. Scattered trees, boulders, and thick brush ran along the base. Water splashed noisily from the top into a curving stream. Mud-loving Aric was going to be happy. Dense forest covered the other three sides.

As Bull and Caz got out, Hawk walked around the Squirrel to open Kit's door.

She'd only needed a small boost to climb into the helicopter, but he knew from the times he'd been injured getting out was a whole different story.

She stalled in the door, trying to figure out what to do.

"Want help?" He held out his hands and waited until she nodded.

With her busted ribs and abdominal surgery, he couldn't grab her around the waist. *Okay then.* Putting an arm around her lower back, another under her sweetly curved ass, he pulled her against him and lifted her out, then bent his knees until her feet touched the ground.

She was a slender little female, and he couldn't deny that he enjoyed feeling her against him. But he released her quickly, moved back, and waited to get yelled at.

Her color was pink, her eyes flashing. Within a second, her anger disappeared, and she said ruefully, "Thank you. I couldn't figure out how to get down without giving my ribs a good jolting."

He nodded. "Been there, done that."

Caz gave her an assessing look, then chuckled. "Nice job of transferring the patient, *'mano.*"

"Where to, Kit?" Having already strapped on his revolver, Bull had Aric on his shoulders. The kid was giggling because he usually grabbed Hawk's hair to hold onto, and it wasn't possible with Bull's shaved head.

She pointed at a patch of brush in front of the steep bluff. "There."

Darkness behind the bushes turned out to be the cave.

After handing Aric over to Hawk, Bull waded through the underbrush, pulled out a flashlight, and ducked inside. A minute later, he called, "All clear."

Kit went in.

Seeing there wasn't room for anyone else in there, Hawk set Aric down beside some rivulets that had forked off the stream. "You okay here, kid?"

"Uh-huh." Aric crouched and picked up a shiny rock.

Hawk grinned. A big bowl in his living room was already filled to overflowing with Aric's finds.

Apparently not willing to shout over the waterfall noise, Caz signaled that he'd patrol the area from the helicopter and southward.

Hawk nodded and took up guard to the north. Even if there weren't any PZs in the neighborhood, the bears and cougars would consider a four-year-old to be a fine snack.

"Well, damn." Bull's booming voice could barely be heard over the splashing of the water. "That's a hell of a lot of cash." A couple of minutes later, he emerged from the cave with plastic-wrapped, shoeboxes.

Kit followed, looking shell-shocked.

"Kit?" Hawk took a step toward her. "You okay?"

"There's money. So much money."

Hawk glanced at Aric, but the boy was happily splashing in the streamlet and hadn't noticed his mother was upset.

"Money's a good thing," Hawk said cautiously.

"Um. Yes." She shook her head, and her brain apparently turned back on.

He almost grinned. When young, he'd enthusiastically pumped a car's gas pedal, then had to wait until the flooded engine could recover and start. Like the vehicle, the little gardener had been swamped with too much of a good thing.

Her face brightened, and then her laughter bubbled out. "This is *wonderful*. I can't wait to divide up the money with the other women. We'll have a chance to start over."

"Okay then." He studied her. Apparently, she hadn't even considered keeping it for herself.

As if unable to believe the good fortune was real, she followed Bull to the helicopter to watch him stow the boxes away.

Hawk made a quick check of his half of the area...and saw two birds burst upward from the forest canopy to the west. A few more birds went up. Closer to the clearing.

The trail was in that direction.

"*Hsst*." His snake-like warning carried over the sound of the water, and his brothers turned toward him.

Catching a glimpse of movement and a glint of metal from down the trail, Hawk made the hand signal to his eyes and pointed. *Enemy in sight.*

"*Dios*," Caz said under his breath. Closest to Aric, he snatched the boy up and disappeared into the forest to the south.

"Kit, we have company coming," Bull said in a low voice and motioned to a boulder north of the cave. "Hide behind there."

Instead, seeing her son carried away, she started to run that direction.

Hell. Hawk grabbed her wrist and pulled her to the boulder. He kept his voice quiet and cold. "Get *down*. Stay put."

Panting, she stared up into his face, then regained control and crouched behind the boulder.

Good enough. Getting Bull's attention, Hawk motioned to her.

Bull nodded. He'd protect the civilian.

And Hawk would do what he did best. Taking the area of less cover, he ran to the northeast along the base of the cliff.

Bull moved toward a stand of trees. It was far enough away from Kit's hiding place return fire wouldn't come near her but close enough to intervene if she needed protection.

A boulder-strewn cliff ledge about ten feet up was Hawk's goal. Scraping the shit out of his arms, he scrambled up onto it.

Yeah, from here, he'd be damned difficult to spot.

He settled into the prone position with arms outstretched and a Glock 19 in his hand. He was slightly on his side, resting on his right lat, elbow in the dirt, cheek on his biceps. Good stability. Nice elevation. No wind.

Just in time.

Three bearded men carrying AR-15s jogged out of the forest, spotted the helicopter, and came to a full stop.

"What the fuck!" With angry shouts, the three brought their AR-15s up.

Hawk held his fire. Because good guys didn't shoot first. *Dammit to hell.*

Something banged and rattled on the stones near the cave. Bull had tossed a rock to keep the bastards' attention focused there.

The militia bastards simply opened fire. No talk. No warning. *Fuck.*

Bullets peppered the cave and terrain around it. Anyone inside would've been torn to ribbons.

Hawk gritted his teeth. *Mustn't kill the assholes.* Gabe'd get pissed. He'd go for shooting arms rather than head shots.

Acquiring a target, he breathed out, fired, acquired the next, fired. The two men dropped their rifles with shouts of pain.

With the deep boom of Bull's Redhawk revolver, the third asshole went down. Yeah, the fist-sized hole from a .44 Magnum would do that.

One of Hawk's targets proved stubborn and pulled an automatic with his other hand. The fucking asshat aimed for the helicopter.

Not. Happening. Hawk's next shot destroyed the guy's arm. Still pissed-off, Hawk considered shooting again and taking him right out of the gene pool.

But their courage broke. Two PZs fled back down the trail, carrying the third between them. If they were smart, they'd stop to bind up their wounds before they bled out.

Not his problem.

Knowing Hawk would remain on guard, Bull ran over to the

trail opening. "Sounds like they're still running," he called to Hawk, then shouted loud enough for Caz to hear, "Clear, bro."

Hawk holstered his Glock, slid off the ledge, and jogged to Kit's boulder.

Brown eyes filled with fear, she still crouched where he had left her, watching his every move. Shaking, dead white, but maintaining position. He'd known soldiers who would've run.

He waited, letting his presence register, letting her get control. Wanting so fucking much to sweep her up and hold her. Let her know he'd protect her with everything inside him.

That would be a dumbass thing to do. "The bastards are gone." Slowly, he bent and offered a hand.

Kit was shaking so hard it was hurting her ribs—and her knees felt like the joints had turned to pudding.

Hawk said something, and it took a few seconds for the words to make sense. Gone. The PZs were gone.

But she knew that, didn't she? Unable to tolerate not seeing if someone was coming at her, she'd peeked around the edge of the boulder. Had seen the PZs spraying bullets. Could see Hawk lying flat and calmly shooting as if he was out for a lazy afternoon at a target range.

Under his fire, the militia men had staggered back, rifles dropping.

She'd watched them run.

They'd *run*.

"Need a hand?" The dark rasp cut across the memories.

She blinked. Swallowed. And reached up.

His big hand engulfed hers, the warmth wrapping around her icy fingers. He didn't move. "Say when."

She braced her ribs with her other arm. "Now."

Carefully, slowly, he pulled her to her feet and gripped her waistband to steady her. "Okay?"

She looked up and met his calm, patient gaze. He'd tucked that violence away; only his concern for her remained. Unable to hold back, needing contact, she leaned against him. Still holding her hand, he didn't even sway. He was all rock-hard muscles, broad shoulders, wide chest.

Her anchor. She could stay like this forever.

Instead, she pulled in a slow breath, stepped back, and managed to smile. "Thank you, Hawk."

"Fuck," he said under his breath, looking away.

He looked oddly disconcerted.

Well, that made two of them. She moved toward the forest. "Aric?"

"Caz'll have him back in—"

And there was her boy, following the doc out of the forest. Aric saw her and charged forward, little legs pumping, and when he hit her legs like a rocket, she didn't even care. He was all right.

She shed a few tears as she bent to hug him. "I love you, baby. Love you so much."

Off to one side, the men were talking in low voices.

"Kit, time to get out of here." Bull wiped blood off his face and caught her staring.

"Ricochet," he said nonchalantly. "A few bullets hit my tree and sprayed me with bark."

Dear heavens, the bullets could have hit *him*.

Don't have hysterics. "You're not going after them, are you?"

Bull shook his head. "No, we can't leave you two here alone."

Relief ran through her even as she puzzled it out. It would take one person to guard her and Aric—especially Aric—and another to shoot. And one person going after three didn't sound wise, let alone how he'd get three wounded men out of the forest.

"Okay." Her arms were refusing to let go of her boy. Reluctantly, she released him and straightened, and only then realized Hawk had his hand on her lower back. He'd been standing behind her the whole time, bracing her to keep her from being toppled over by Aric.

He took a step back, raising his hands as if he thought she might hit him.

A laugh broke from her. "Thanks. I'd probably have landed on my butt if you hadn't been there."

The sunlines beside his eyes crinkled. Then he nodded at Aric. "Good job hiding."

Aric took a step closer to Hawk and confided, "There were *cabrones* here. Did you see 'em?"

Wasn't that Spanish for bastard or something? Kit shot Caz a frown, and he winced.

"Yeah." Hawk nodded gravely. "*Cabrones.* We chased 'em off."

"With guns," Aric agreed, then took Kit's hand. "'S'okay, Mama. They're gone now."

It seemed Hawk and her son had both decided she needed to be protected. Fine, she'd give them that, but darned if she wasn't going to learn to do something more productive than cower behind a rock. Even if the thought of action was terrifying.

Until then, she was surrounded by tough guys. Even her little blond one. She smiled at them. "I guess we can get moving, hmm?"

CHAPTER SIX

B oy, *everything you can put your hand on can be turned into a weapon. Use your fucking imagination.* - First Sergeant Michael "Mako" Tyne

Hearing the thump-thump-thump of a helicopter landing outside the Hermitage, Gabe walked out his garage side door to see what was up. Hawk didn't usually bring the helicopter home; it stayed at McNally's Resort.

Bull and Caz jumped out. Gabe saw Aric and Kit still seated as Hawk strolled around.

Did they need help? Moving forward, Gabe noted his brothers' tenseness. Looked almost like post-combat jitters, except they weren't in the sandbox. "What happened? Is there a problem?"

"Yeah, you might say." Bull had a grim smile on his face. "I need a soda—and I'll tell you."

Yeah, something had gone down. However...Bull had the look he got when he was planning a snow job.

"I could use a drink too." Caz said.

Bracketed by his brothers, Gabe was escorted back into his

cabin. Undoubtedly to keep him from seeing what was still in the helicopter.

"You smuggling in a woman?" he asked as he handed out drinks from the fridge.

"Nope." Bull sat at the dining room table, turning the can in his big hands. "It's like this... We heard the Feds had left the PZ compound, and Kit wanted to pick up something she'd left there."

Gabe slammed the fridge door shut hard enough to rattle the shit inside. Had they really endangered civilians? "You went out to the compound?"

"Not...exactly."

No longer interested in sitting, Gabe stood at one end of the table and tried to set aside his anger long enough to figure out what he *wasn't* being told. The compound was easy enough to reach in a vehicle. "Why the helicopter?"

"The location was too far for her to walk to in the shape she's in," Caz answered. "Hawk volunteered to take her."

That was...interesting. The hawk avoided women, at least ones who weren't occupying his bed. "You said there was a problem."

So they told him. A cave in a remote location. Getting Kit's stuff, whatever it was. Three PZs came into the clearing and—

A noise caught his attention. On the deck, Kit was setting Aric up with a coloring book and crayons. As the boy lay down to color, Hawk and Kit came inside.

"Let me get this straight," Gabe said slowly. "You took Kit and the boy onto PZ land—"

"We weren't on PZ land," Hawk pointed out. "It wasn't in the compound."

"Even if it was in the national forest, you were in an area they consider theirs." Gabe crossed his arms over his chest...and saw Kit's shoulders hunch.

Hell. He couldn't yell at his brothers, not within her hearing.

Growling under his breath, he went to the fridge and grabbed a couple more Cokes. He set Kit's in front of her very gently and smacked Hawk's can down hard enough the bastard would get sprayed when he opened it.

Laughter lit in Hawk's eyes. "Thanks, bro."

"You're wel—" Gabe's eyes narrowed.

The sleeves of Hawk's flannel shirt were streaked with blood.

Caz and Kit appeared intact, but Bull had a gash in his cheek. The air around them held the acrid sulfuric stink of gunpowder.

Seriously? Gabe rubbed the back of his neck, feeling the onset of a headache. "Are the three PZs alive?"

Bull grinned.

Gabe sighed. Back when they were kids, and Bull burst out laughing after being chased by a fucking moose, Gabe should have known he was crazy. Should've backed away then.

Too late now. He kept his voice level with an effort. "What happened to the PZs?"

"They ran," Hawk said. "All three. No bodies to worry about."

"Mmmhmm. And how many holes did they have in those bodies?"

Caz snorted a laugh.

Kit's eyes were wide, and he wasn't sure if it was a reaction to what had obviously been a firefight or if she expected him to whip out handcuffs and haul them away.

The thought was fucking tempting.

"Holes, hmm..." Bull counted on his fingers. "Eh, only four holes between the three of them."

"Only four." Gabe kept his voice level.

"They sprayed the area down, Gabe. No talk, no warning. Just hosed the place," Bull said.

"No bodies," Caz pointed out again. "Hawk didn't go for the kill."

Because Hawk could easily have slaughtered them all.

"Hey, I shot one," Bull protested with a wink at Kit.

When it came down to it, all three of his brothers were deadly.

Gabe sighed again. "Thank you for not littering the borough with corpses."

"And for doing it outside of the town's boundaries?" Bull downed half the Coke in one long gulp.

"Yeah, that too." Gabe grimaced. Time to make some calls, starting with the Feds and the state troopers. They needed to know the PZs still had an active interest in the area and that three of them might be seeking medical attention.

Doubtful that they'd show up at a hospital. No gunshot victims had been reported after the fight at the compound last month, indicating the PZs found someone to treat them off the record.

So...what did Kit get at the cave? His brothers didn't want him to know, which probably meant they didn't want the Chief of Police to know.

How far should he push?

They'd called it her stuff, but *was* it hers? "Kit, did you personally put that *stuff* in the cave?"

"Yes, I did." Her chin came up, reminding him of Audrey. Yeah, he rather liked this woman.

He glanced at Caz, the most law-abiding...somewhat...of his brothers.

Caz shook his head slightly. *Don't ask.*

So they thought she was justified in taking whatever—he'd guess it was money—but the actual ownership was probably questionable.

"All right. You went to reclaim your property on unowned land, got fired upon by three men who were probably PZs, defended yourselves without killing anyone; they fled the area, and you left. Do I have that right?"

"You got it," Bull agreed.

"Okay then." Gabe smiled at Kit. "First, I don't want to frighten you, but you need to remember the Patriot Zealots are obviously still in the area. Be careful when you leave the Hermitage."

He hated how her face paled. But she nodded.

"Second, can I get you to join Aric so I can yell at my brothers without upsetting you?"

"Oh. Of course." She rose slowly and started away.

Then she turned around. Her hands were clenched, and her muscles tensed as if preparing for a blow. "Chief, the guys were only there because I needed help. You should yell at me, not them."

Despite what she'd been through, she was ready to endure his anger to protect his brothers. No wonder Frankie adored this woman.

Bull and Caz grinned. Even Hawk was smiling.

"Kit, if I yell at you, I'm the one who'll end up full of holes," he explained patiently. And Mako would reach out from the grave to smack him upside the head. "But shouting at them will help my headache feel better, and I know you wouldn't want me to be hurting."

He saw her start to automatically agree before she caught on. She frowned at him. "I thought it was just these three, but all four of you are crazy."

Shaking her head, she headed out to her son.

Gabe grinned.

Then he slapped his palms on the table, leaned forward, and channeled the sarge. "What the *fuck* were you thinking to take a civilian and a child into a fucking fire zone!"

———

By the time Gabe started shouting, Kit and Aric were most of the way to Bull's house.

Good grief, but the chief sounded just like those movies where some drill sergeant laid into a recruit who'd dropped his gun or something.

Safely on the deck, Kit sighed and watched her son. He was talking to Gryff and showing off the shiny rocks he'd picked up by the stream.

The dog wagged his tail for each new stone.

She could only smile. Her son hadn't been traumatized by the battle...because Caz had carried him way back in the forest. The doc said the noise from the waterfall had drowned out most of the shooting. Guns didn't upset Aric. In the compound, the men had always been shooting their weapons.

Really, her son was doing far better than she was.

But had Gabe's yelling bothered him?

As they went inside, Kit said, "I know Gabe loves his brothers, but he probably shouldn't shout at them."

"Hawk says Gabe is *bossy,* an' he yells when they don't listen to him." Aric giggled. "An' he said Gabe can be a butthead."

Kit blinked. "Oh. Well, then." Guess that took care of that, although she and Hawk might have to discuss appropriate language one of these days.

"Here, why don't you eat some peas while I check on something." She pulled out the sugar snap peas she'd picked yesterday. Opening the pods would keep someone's little fingers occupied.

While Aric had his snack, Kit went into their bedroom and opened the closet where Hawk had stowed the boxes of money. The first shoebox was filled with packets of $100-dollar bills. The other shoeboxes were full of $20 bills.

She just sat there for a while, staring at the money. Daydreaming a little.

"Kit." Hawk's rasping voice came down the hallway and set up a tingle deep inside her.

She walked out.

Hawk stood in the living area in clean clothes, hair still wet from a shower. "The helicopter goes back to McNally's. Want to come?"

"Yes!" Aric bounced up and down beside Hawk. "Mama, can—"

"Yes. Yes, we'll go." The answer popped out before she even thought about it. She shouldn't.

But oh, the feeling of being up in the air made her feel as if her spirits lifted too. The sheer beauty of the world so far below made her problems shrink to nothing.

Besides, she needed...activity. A way to avoid thinking about what had happened, about being shot at by three men.

Yes, Hawk was a man. He scared her now and then.

Yet she loved how he cared for her son, how his blunt speech was balanced by his gentleness. There were times the sadness in his gaze made her want to hug him as if he was Aric's age. She'd seen the quiet pleasure in his face when he simply sat and watched the lake, and she'd wanted to sit beside him.

And his laugh—those rare laughs lit her heart.

Without further talk, he packed them back into his helicopter and took off.

After a glance at her face, he flew a few circuits around the Hermitage and then the town, naming landmarks in an extravagance of two- or three-word sentences.

Then he flew them up the mountain and did the same with McNally's Resort.

The resort had a huge hotel surrounded by numerous other buildings. A tram led upward to a small day lodge perched near the head of the chair lifts.

"What a beautiful place," Kit said, peering out the window.

"It died a decade ago. Pretty much killed Rescue. Reopened last year. The town's coming back to life too."

She grinned. He'd used more words today than she'd ever heard before. Maybe gun battles were good for him.

After setting the helicopter down, he opened the back door,

undid her son's seat restraints, and let him clamber out on his own.

Then Hawk helped Kit out.

She could feel her cheeks warm at feeling his hands on her body, at being so close. He hadn't taken advantage of her at all, but there was a very male look in his eyes when he released her and stepped back.

Aric took her hand and asked Hawk, "Can we get burgers?"

She watched the man's hard face turn gentle. He glanced at Kit. "My treat."

When her son gave her a puppy-dog-look, she couldn't refuse, no matter how much it hurt her pride. "All right, sure."

Hawk led them around the side of the massive hotel building, giving her a chance to admire the landscaping, before they entered the restaurant.

One breath brought her the aromas of grilling burgers and french fries, and her stomach growled.

"I guess I'm hungrier than I thought." She put her hand over her embarrassing belly.

"Me too," Aric stated.

Back in the kitchen, someone shouted.

Aric jumped and moved closer to Hawk, latching onto his jean's pocket. Hawk didn't seem to mind, just set a hand on her son's shoulder.

"Have you two been here before?" she asked Hawk.

He nodded. "My partner and I haul McNally's guests around. Aric's my co-pilot."

When her son's chest puffed out, she had to smother a laugh.

"They got fries 'n' everything," Aric told her, pulling her and Hawk forward.

A glint of amusement appeared in Hawk's eyes. "We'll eat outside."

"A wise choice." Kit smothered a grin. Dealing with even a

quiet Aric had probably pushed Hawk's patience to the limits at times.

After ordering and collecting their food, they went out onto a wide patio overlooking the grounds. Mountains encircled the resort, and the air held a crisp tang from the still snowy peaks. Ski season was over, and the people on the patio ranged from tourists with children to couples in shorts and hiking boots, to fishermen in flannel shirts and rubber boots.

She started to take a center table, but Hawk pointed to one near the wall of the building.

After setting Aric up with food and squirting ketchup onto the plate for french fries, Kit took a bite of her own cheeseburger and moaned happily. "I missed burgers."

Hawk grinned. "Welcome back to this century."

"As it happens, I prefer the twenty-first century." She glanced at her son. He wasn't paying any attention to them, perfectly happy with drawing ketchup circles with a french fry. "In spite of their preference for the good old days, the PZs seem perfectly happy using modern weaponry."

"Yep." Hawk frowned. "You need to stay on guard."

She stiffened. That was essentially what Gabe had said. She'd relaxed too much, hadn't she? "It bothers me that I didn't see them coming today. And I didn't know what to do when they did."

His nod indicated she'd messed up. She'd kind of been hoping for a pat and a *don't worry your pretty little head about it*. Only that would have annoyed her too. "What should I have done differently?"

"Good for you." A corner of his mouth lifted, then he deepened his voice. "Mako would say, '*You fucked up, boy. Now tell us how you'll avoid stepping on your dick next time*'."

She laughed. *Those poor boys.* "Okay, tell me."

"Close your eyes."

She stiffened. Not a chance.

"Ah, right. Don't look—and tell me who's on the patio."

"I..." She bit her lip, trying to think. "A couple of men to my right. A family, I think to the left. And...I don't know. Who should I have seen?"

She looked up at him.

He motioned to the two men. "Middle-aged males. Jogging gear, no weapons."

A motion toward the family. "Young couple. Two toddlers. No weapons." He held her eyes without looking around. "Patio door —three unarmed older women. Railing—two hikers in their twenties, unarmed. Right railing—four fishermen in their thirties. One has a handgun, three carry knives."

Her mouth dropped open. "I didn't even think of looking at people like that." What if there'd been PZs in the crowd? She'd been watching her son, enjoying the flowers, anticipating the food. Not watching for trouble.

"Situational awareness. Be aware. Sit or stand where you can keep an eye on things."

That was why he'd chosen a table where he could view everything around him. His back was to the wall. *Oh.*

Mouth tight, she angled her chair outward so she was still beside Aric but could see the entire patio.

He nodded approval. "Check the people—and hazards— around you."

"Go on."

"Where's your line of retreat?"

"Like finding the exit in a movie theater?"

His lips twitched. "If the armed fisherman starts shooting, do we defend or retreat?"

Dear heavens, did he do this with everything? Her jaw clenched. "Tell me."

He rapped on the table. "Too thin to stop bullets, so we attack or run."

She eyed the door into the restaurant.

"No, too many windows." He pointed to the railing. "Jump it and hide."

He didn't even look around. He'd already done his own assessment. She realized whenever he looked at her or Aric, his gaze also swept the area.

"What else?"

"Watch for anomalies. At a resort, people should be relaxed. Are they uneasy or too interested in you?"

She looked around again. No one was paying any particular attention to them. Everyone appeared relaxed. "Anything else?"

"What if you can't run?"

The thought made her stomach clench. "I don't know."

"Kit, find a weapon."

"Here?" Weapons? "Like the chairs?"

"Good." He tapped the table knife and fork. "For stabbing."

Turning, he picked up a fist-sized decorative stone from the planter box. "Throw it. Or hit someone in the head with it." He swung it and stopped like he'd smacked someone's forehead.

What a horrible image. "Um, right."

He unscrewed the lid of the pepper shaker and smiled at her. "Chemical warfare if thrown in the eyes and mouth."

The planter box again. He touched the dirt. "Throw it in their eyes."

"Huh, I get it. We're surrounded by weapons, aren't we?"

His slight nod said, *now, she was catching on.*

When two men sat down at a nearby table, she observed them. Dressed in suits. No observable weapons. Not uneasy. Not paying her or Hawk any attention.

Frowning, she pulled in a breath. "At the cave...what should I have done?"

"You did okay. Stayed put."

"What about before that?"

He gave her a considering stare. "Next time, trust us."

Ouch. She'd delayed them by not obeying Bull's order immediately. "I'm sorry."

"A team is stronger than a person alone. But it takes trust."

"Oh." That might be difficult. "You and your brothers are a team."

"Yeah. Now." He rubbed his neck. "At first, I didn't trust them to have my back—or for Gabe to give orders."

"And how old were you when you learned?"

His eyes filled with laughter. "Around eleven."

They'd been a team for a long, long time. Why did that feel awfully sweet? Smiling, she leaned back to study the area, the people, the possible weapons. What she might do if anything happened.

Hawk let her think, while he used a french fry and ketchup to draw a stick figure on his almost empty plate, then pushed it over so Aric could add arms and hair.

After a couple of minutes, Kit sat back. Assessment was complete. Now she could enjoy the view. "I love places that use color coordination. Did you notice how they planted purple petunias to match the colors on the welcome sign?"

Hawk followed her gaze. "You studied horticulture?"

Frankie must have told him. "Mmmhmm. After I got my degree, I worked in a garden nursery, doing landscaping consultations. Trying to teach Texans to work with nature instead of against it. The idea of natural landscaping is catching on."

"Yeah?" He motioned to the grounds they could see. "What would you change?"

"Hmm." She studied the grounds now, although, in her head, she'd totally criticized everything on their walk here.

She pointed downslope. "The trees they planted there require massive amounts of care—and some of Alaska's native plants would work just as nicely. I love your red-twig dogwoods and mountain ash. Over there to the right, a patch of crab apples would be gorgeous in the spring and the apples would draw in animals for the tourists."

He started smiling as she continued her imaginary changes to the grounds.

"Okay, I know I get carried away." She laughed and wasn't able to resist adding, "You said the resort wants to stay open all four seasons and summer tourists tend to bring their children. So really, they need a small playground so munchkins can work off their energy. When traveling, it's nice to be able to finish a meal while the kids play within eyesight."

She nodded at her son. Aric had smeared ketchup all over the plate and partly down his front.

Hawk's snort was slightly exasperated and mostly amused.

Smiling, Kit poured some water from her bottle onto a napkin and wiped down her boy. "There you go, nice and clean."

When he gave her a worried look, she laughed, kissed the tip of his nose, then poked him in the tummy. "And all full, too."

He giggled—and wasn't that amazing?

Hawk ruffled Aric's hair. "Time to get back."

As they rose, Kit realized the two men seated nearby had been listening—and were watching her. Probably not PZs, though. The pissers weren't the kind to wear suits.

One of them nodded at Hawk. "Calhoun."

Hawk gave him a chin lift and hoisted Aric back up onto his shoulders. "Hang on, kid."

With a huge grin, Aric gripped Hawk's thick hair and gave a bounce.

Envy rose inside Kit. From Aric's expression, he'd discovered being with Hawk was the safest place in the world.

She knew just how he felt.

CHAPTER SEVEN

If you think you are too small to make a difference, try sleeping with a mosquito. - Dalai Lama

Late Saturday afternoon, Kit had a chance to see what Hawk had meant about teamwork.

When Bull announced that he and his brothers planned to celebrate the solstice today with combat games, Kit had politely mentioned that solstice was two days ago. And what were combat games anyway?

Bull had simply laughed.

Shaking her head, Frankie told him she was a civilian and staying home to taste-test a new recipe. Kit had planned to help her until Hawk showed up to get Aric.

Her *son*. Playing war games.

Like she'd let him do that without her to supervise. *Uh-uh.*

Hawk had loaded her and Audrey, the noncombatants, into his pickup. Everyone else piled into the truck bed for the short drive down the dirt road to the forested area.

"This is crazy," Kit muttered. She and Audrey were sitting in camp chairs in the pickup and holding umbrellas because—of course—it was pouring rain.

Aric would be fine. He was bundled in a dark sweatshirt, heavy jeans, with a camo stocking cap on his head.

After the four brothers, JJ, Regan, and Aric had loaded mini-water balloons into belt pouches, they'd jogged into the forest.

"It *is* crazy," Audrey agreed.

Kit glanced at the blonde. "You could have played. I wouldn't mind."

"I join them for games I enjoy. Sneaking around in a muddy forest in the rain? I decline." Audrey snorted. "I'm a librarian, not a soldier."

Kit grinned and leaned forward, trying to see what was going on. What with the rain and the murk of the forest, she could only catch mere glimpses of the combatants.

As far as she could tell, the adults were going easy on the children—but not much. Her boy was holding his own, and Regan was excellent.

Except the girl had been caught by Bull, and he'd sat her down beside a tree and was tying her wrists. "I can't believe he—" Kit squinted. "Is that toilet paper?"

"Isn't it funny?" Audrey laughed. "Gabe said it's Aric's turn to save someone. The last couple of times, Regan rescued *him*, but now he knows what to do."

"Oh, won't he just feel amazing if he gets her free." What a lovely way to build up her boy's confidence.

Kit watched Hawk send Aric creeping forward. Sneaking around a forest kind of looked like fun. "I'd like to try. Maybe. When I can actually move."

Audrey gave her a sympathetic smile. "You'll have a chance. They love games like this. The snowball wars last winter were great—and I got surprisingly good at tactics."

Tactics? "Is a war different from a snowball fight?"

"Mmm, less of a free-for-all. They'll set up a flag for a target, and the defenders will try to keep the invaders from capturing the flag." Audrey laughed. "At least we can see them today. In the winter, the sun goes down so early, we play in the dark. It's a little eerie.

"I bet. Oh, look, there's Aric."

Her son crawled forward so carefully the underbrush barely moved with his passage. He reached Regan, then pulled a knife.

"Tell me that isn't a real knife." They wouldn't; surely, they—

"It's so soft a rubber that it bends if you look at it hard," Audrey said. "I think the guys bought some last Halloween."

Aric sawed at Regan's "ropes" with his fake knife, and the already wet toilet paper dropped off her wrists. Dropping the knife, Aric covered his mouth with his hands—so obviously trying not to giggle that Kit started to laugh.

A second later, both children disappeared back into the underbrush.

"That was so cute."

"It was. But it's not always like this." Audrey frowned. "The games can get kind of intense. Maybe scary. Aric's pretty little."

"That's what I was afraid of. My son is very good at sneaking around and hiding"—Kit's mouth twisted bitterly—"because it was the only way to keep from being hurt. But Gabe and Hawk said it might help Aric if he realized those skills can be used for fun. Even for *offensive action* as Hawk called it."

Audrey tilted her head in consideration. "They might have a point. And throwing water balloons isn't exactly frightening."

"That's what I hoped, but I wanted to be here…just in case." Gabe had thought she shouldn't come, what with her ribs and all.

But Hawk had agreed with her. When he'd said, "*She's a good mom*," she had to blink back tears.

Farther down in the forest, Aric emerged, then crouched behind a shrub, almost vibrating with excitement.

Regan knelt behind the next bush over, cleverly hidden from

Bull and Gabe, the defenders of the flag. Turning, the girl grinned at Aric.

He grinned back, obviously still having fun.

After creeping up behind Aric, Hawk knelt and made a gesture, like breaking a stick. Then he pointed at JJ who was sneaking away to the right.

Aric nodded and started forward again.

"I think he's going to be fine," Kit said, almost whispering. "Look at him crawl."

"He's so little, he's almost invisible," Audrey murmured.

Standing behind a tree, Hawk exchanged grins with Caz as they watched Aric squirm his way toward where Bull and Gabe guarded the red flag.

"I saw Aric yesterday with Sirius on his lap—I swear the cat is almost bigger than he is. Aric was petting him and singing a lullaby," Audrey said. "And Sirius was eating it up. Despite what he's been through, your boy has a gentle heart."

Guilt swept through Kit. It was her fault he'd been through so much. "You know, when I married Obadiah, he kept pushing Aric away, and I was furious with him. Then he moved us to the compound—and I was so relieved that Aric was in the children's barracks and escaped most of his abuse."

"Asshole men," Audrey said under her breath.

"Listen to you." Kit laughed. "You've been around the Hermitage guys too long."

"Mako's sons are foul-mouthed creatures," Audrey agreed, then leaned forward, trying to see. "You know, if Aric didn't have his hair covered, he'd be a lot easier to spot."

"My little blond. I love his hair." Kit smiled. "He got my face, but his coloring is his father's."

"Your first husband?" Audrey flushed. "Sorry. Frankie mentioned Obadiah was your second husband."

Everyone was curious; of course, they were. And it wasn't like her past needed to be a secret. Kit didn't mind sharing. "When I got pregnant with Aric, I wasn't married. I was just having fun. As it happens, condom effectiveness isn't one hundred percent."

Audrey snickered. "I did research for a women's group presentation—so I know the stats. Ninety-eight percent only if you're perfect. Effectively, it's more like eighty-five percent."

"Exactly. Now, I'd have told Aric's father about him, but he was in New York for only a few days, and I never even learned his last name." Kit blew out a breath. "I regret that, because I can't tell Aric anything about his birth father."

"You could do a DNA test to locate familial connections. When he gets older, he might get cranky about the whole no father around thing, but he'll manage." Audrey wrinkled her nose. "My mother went for artificial insemination, and I don't know anything about my sperm donor. Well, aside from Mother saying he was brilliant."

Kit's mouth dropped open. "Um. Did you get...cranky?"

"As a teenager, I expressed my negative views about it. Or I tried. She was unconcerned about my opinions, so that was a failure." The sadness in Audrey's expression was fleeting. Her lips tipped up. "So was Frankie around when Aric was little?"

"We were roommates, and she was my birthing coach." Kit rolled her eyes. "You should have heard her swearing when she thought the obstetrician should have been more helpful. Thankfully, no one understood the names she was calling him."

"I can imagine." Audrey pulled out her phone and displayed an Italian/English translator. "I've looked a lot of those swear-words up. The ones they'll list."

"Clever." Kit checked her son. He was sneaking through the trees, moving very slowly. So patiently. "When Aric was almost three, I married a sweet man, and we moved to Texas. But Brenden died. And before I really got over him, there was Obadiah."

Two husbands in two years. She was certainly doing things wrong.

No, don't think that way. Brenden had tried his hardest to stay clean; he just hadn't been strong enough.

Obadiah was simply a lying abuser.

"I know this might sound bad"—Audrey pulled in a breath—"but I'm really glad that jerk Obadiah is dead, and you're free of him."

Kit blinked back tears. It was exactly what she needed to hear. "Thank you."

As they turned to watch the game, Kit saw that Caz and Hawk had moved far apart, approaching the target flag from different sides.

Bull and Gabe spotted the two men, but the children were also creeping forward. Down low where there was more cover.

"I saw you planting seeds into trays. More veggies for the garden?" Audrey asked.

"No, they're flowers. I'm going to make autumnal hanging baskets to thank the people in town who saved us from the PZs. I think they'll flower right around the beginning of August." Kit shook her head.

"You know you don't have to thank anyone." Audrey smiled. "But they'll love it if you do."

As the wind carried a spray of rain under the umbrella, Kit frowned and leaned forward. "Where'd the children go?"

Audrey pointed. "There's Regan."

The girl was crouching behind a bush. Farther away, something crashed.

"Was that JJ over there?" Audrey asked.

"I lost track of her." Kit noticed Gabe and Bull turned toward the noise too.

Regan sprinted forward and threw her water balloon at Gabe.

The police chief dove to the ground, only half escaping her excellent pitch.

Bull threw at the same time Regan tossed a balloon at him—and both hit.

A high scream of victory ran through the forest. "Got it, got it!" Having grabbed the flag, Aric waved it over his head, yelling and bouncing.

Everyone cheered. Gabe set Aric on his shoulders, Bull did the same with Regan, and moved close enough the children could exchange fist-bumps with each other and their other teammates.

And they headed out to the road where Kit and Audrey waited.

"Did you see me, Audrey?" Regan was yelling. "JJ was the first di—diversion, and I was the second, and I got Uncle Gabe and Uncle Bull anyway."

"You showed awesome skills," Audrey agreed.

Laughing, Gabe lifted Aric from his shoulders and set him in the pickup bed. "Aric and Regan are an amazing team."

"I did it, Mama," Aric boasted.

He sounded so much like he used to that her words could barely escape the thickness in her throat. "You did. You were amazing." She held out her good hand to get a fist-bump from him, lost her battle to restrain herself, and pulled him in for a hug.

His giggle was high and infectious, and when she let him go, his face was flushed and his crooked smile simply huge. "We was all good. Cuz Hawk 'n' Caz moved fast so they'd getted looked at 'n' JJ made a big noise 'n' Regan was a-tillery."

"Artillery," Hawk corrected.

"That's me," Regan agreed and gave Hawk a big hug.

When his blue-gray eyes turned soft, and his hard face turned gentle, Kit's heart went to mush. The man might present himself as a hardass, but he loved that little girl—and Aric.

"Crew." Bull's laugh was deep and hearty. "Frankie said, if Aric and Regan's team won, they'd get cupcakes."

More cheers echoed off the trees.

Even as Kit's mouth watered, she was appalled. Frankie's sugar-loaded, sprinkle-covered frosted cupcakes?

They'd never get the children to calm down tonight.

"While we eat, we'll debrief—what we did wrong, what we did right, and what we can do better next time." Gabe punched Bull's shoulder. "Neither of us expected a four-year-old to sneak past us."

"True that." Bull eyed Hawk. "You've been working with him, haven't you, bro?"

"Some." Hawk pulled Aric's cap off and ruffled his hair. "Caz is up next."

"He has skills." Caz nodded. "I'll take him when Regan and I go out."

Regan grinned. "Papá is the best."

Kit eyed the combatants and saw they agreed. Sneaking was Caz's skill—and he'd work with Aric. They were playing to their strengths. Building on them. Working together to achieve the goal.

She could hear Hawk's voice when he'd talked to her after the firefight at the cave. "*A team is stronger than a person alone.*"

What would it be like to be part of a family who felt that way?

It was something she'd never know. And all too soon, she'd be moving away from the Hermitage.

But maybe if she and Aric stayed in Rescue, they'd still be friends. Aric could have their support in growing his skills. She'd have Frankie—and maybe Audrey and JJ too.

She just needed to find a job.

I can do that.

CHAPTER EIGHT

There will come a time when you believe everything is finished. Yet that will be the beginning. - Louis L'Amour

On Monday afternoon, Hawk was in his armchair reading while listening to the murmur of the kids. Seated on the floor, Aric and Regan were clicking pieces together to create a marble run. Each new twist, chute, tube, or spinner involved a discussion.

Perched on a chair, Sirius supervised. Regan's oversized fluffy cat was probably just waiting for the marbles to start rolling.

At a tap on the door, he looked up to see Kit on the deck. She'd been in town for her PT and counseling appointments.

Without rising, he waved her in and pointed at the kids. "Building isn't done."

Aric scrambled to his feet and ran over to hug her—a sight that never failed to make Hawk smile...and feel a bit of envy.

"Can I finish, Mama?"

"We're almost at the end," Regan called. "We want to see a marble go through."

"I..." She glanced at Hawk.

He pointed her to the couch. Now he'd have to talk with her. It wasn't as if he was unwilling, too much the reverse. She was easy to talk with. And far too fucking appealing.

Clicking a spinner piece into place, Aric let out a squeal of victory. Regan clapped her hands for him, and Kit let out a low laugh.

Jesus. Hawk frowned, realizing he had three people in his house, none of whom was a brother. The isolation of the Hermitage was coming to an end.

So was his, it seemed.

He tried to find anger or irritation, but what the hell, all he felt right now was an odd sense of contentment.

Hard to object to a pretty woman in his home.

Kit's face was tender as she watched her son.

A while back, Regan had taken a picture of Kit and Aric. Aric had given him a copy, and Hawk had tucked it into his wallet. Because somehow, the girl had captured the soft look of love.

Hawk could vaguely remember his own mother having the same expression...before his father had taken notice of him, and his childhood had gone straight to hell. He and Aric had a lot in common.

He watched the boy for a minute. The kid was recovering.

Hawk had helped with that—and the knowledge was immensely satisfying. Far more than anything he'd felt in the military or the mercenaries.

Being back here with his brothers made him...happy. Having children around? Hell, it was amazing.

That was why he was ignoring the job offers from various merc units, security firms, and even old combat buddies. This was his life now, and he was damned glad of it.

A soft sound of pain drew his attention.

Brace off, Kit was wiggling her fingers

"New exercises?" he asked.

"Yes. I wanted to run through them once to make sure I remember what the therapist said to do."

"You're moving better."

"I am." She beamed. "As soon as I get a little more flexibility and strength, I can look for a job. Well, a job that isn't too physical."

As he watched, she finished the exercise and started to massage her hand, stroking upward. What with only being able to use the one hand, her efforts were ineffectual.

"You're not getting anywhere." With a huff, he sat beside her and took over the massage. He tried to apply enough pressure to be therapeutic, but not so much he hurt her. Fuck knew, he had strong hands.

After a minute, the silence registered.

She was staring at him, immobile with terror.

Hell. She'd been in his helicopter. Had lunch with him. Hugged him. He hadn't thought she was afraid of him any longer.

He stopped. Considered moving away. But no. "I won't hit you," he said quietly, returning his attention to the massage. "Or hit on you."

Her swallow was audible.

"Sorry," she whispered. A second later, she said in a stronger voice, "I'm sorry. I know that. I just..."

Had a fucking panic attack. Because he was an idiot.

"Want me to stop?"

Her jaw muscles went tight as she fought against her body's fear. "No. Keep going...please."

He nodded.

Her fingers were cold. Trembling slightly.

Panic attacks—he'd had his fair share. And he'd just moved right in on her, was treating her the way he would one of his brothers. "Sorry. I shouldn't have—" And why the fuck had he? He shook his head and glanced at her. "Guess you feel like family."

Her expression brightened. He wasn't the only one who valued family, it seemed.

"I'm sorry too. I think I'm doing better and still...this happens."

"Instincts aren't in the thinking part of the brain. Makes 'em hard to control." It'd taken therapy for him to accept that shit.

He concentrated on what he was doing. Her hand was warming up. Relaxing.

"So I'm finding." The wry humor in her light voice made him look up. Although she was still pale, her lips curled up. A dimple appeared.

Her smiles were coming more often.

As he worked, her hand gradually turned a pretty pink with decreased swelling.

"Done." He let go, rose, and settled back into his big chair.

Her hand felt better, less like her fingers were fat little sausages, although the massage had made the muscles ache in a different way.

Leaning back, she considered taking Aric home now even if it did mess up his game. But no, if she surrendered to her nerves every time she had a panic attack, she'd turn into a hermit. Or so her counselor had warned.

Fine. Pretending to be comfortable, she glanced around Hawk's house. And realized she'd never really looked at his place.

Although the structure of the Hermitage houses was identical, each of the brothers had very individual décor.

Bull's place was warm browns and creams with a massive plushy suede sectional.

A bit starker, Gabe's house had whiter walls, and the sectional was a chocolate brown. Rather than a woodstove, he had a fireplace.

Caz had gone for luxuriant with dark reds and oriental carpets.

All three were comfortable. Almost cozy.

Hawk's place was rougher and more rustic. As with the others, the living area was open to the two-story roof. His had dark wood beams like Gabe's. Only here, the wood appeared as if it'd been cut with a chainsaw and left unfinished.

The big dining table was battered and old, yet still sturdy. The flooring was what she would call filled with character, holding an aged patina. Very distinctive. "Are your floors made from reclaimed wood?"

"Yeah." The scarred corner of his mouth tilted up. "Good eye. The sarge re-used anything he could; I do the same."

Interesting. She stroked her hand over the coffee table that was a glossy long slab of wood and raised her brows in inquiry.

"A friend cut down a backyard maple."

And Hawk had turned it into something lovely. "I love when a house has some history." Kit tried to spot more. The wood stove sat in a recessed area of stonework with a heavy wood mantel. "The mantle?"

His grin flashed. "Mining camp."

"That is so cool. You like the history but aren't fanatic about it. Your furniture is really comfortable." The two overstuffed chairs were upholstered in a soft brown leather and bracketed a dark blue couch large enough to suit Hawk's big frame, but not as massive as Bull's sectional.

Hawk glanced around. "Not as comfortable as Bull's place."

She rolled her eyes. "Please. At the PZ compound, I lived in a barracks with an assigned bunk bed and no possessions. This is wonderful."

"I had help." He half-smiled. "I had the two chairs and a woodstove. Audrey and JJ decided I needed more."

"You said no?" When he nodded, Kit bit her lip against a smirk. She could guess who won.

He snorted. "At Christmas, I ended up with a couch, rugs, pillows, and the blanket."

She considered how stark the room must have looked before, and a bubble of laughter escaped. "Who decided your décor would be brown and blues?"

"That'd be Lillian." The amusement in his gaze took her breath away.

When his lips tilted up or when the sunlines at the corners of his eyes deepened with his smile, he was as gorgeous as his brothers. Or maybe more so because the change was so marked.

She averted her gaze and swallowed, searching for something else to say. "I, um, ran out of things to read at Bull's." Although Audrey had offered to bring her books. "I don't suppose you have anything?"

He pointed at the shelves adjacent to the woodstove surround. "Help yourself."

Perfect. She edged forward on the couch and—

"Here." Once again, Hawk stood in front of her, hand out.

She hesitated, realized she wasn't scared, and took a grip.

His hand was warm, callused, strong.

Once she was up, she registered again just how big he was. Not Bull's height, but their powerful musculature was very similar.

After an assessing look, as if checking that she was steady on her feet, he stepped away and returned to his chair.

Before she checked out the books, she noticed a bowl on one shelf. It was filled with sparkly rocks of assorted sizes, shapes, and colors. Her lips twitched, and she glanced over her shoulder. "Aric's?"

Hawk nodded.

Uh-huh. Mr. Tough and Deadly had given her son a special bowl and a place to keep his rocks. She suppressed a little sigh.

The books on the shelves were a glimpse into his mind. Louis L'Amour, Zane Grey, Larry McMurtry. Even Tony Hillerman. A gurgle of laughter escaped her. "Why do I get the impression you wish we were back in the days of the cowboys?"

"Westerns are fun to read; not so much to live." His grin flashed. "No planes."

Yes, she'd watched him piloting his helicopter with utter concentration and, even more, a deep joy.

He walked over, and as he reached past her, she breathed in the scent of warm male skin and the lingering fragrance of his soap—like the ocean with a hint of citrus. *Mmm.*

His finger slid over the books, then he pulled out a Louis L'Amour and handed it to her.

"*The Cherokee Trail*"? She flipped it over. The blurb talked about a woman managing a rundown stagecoach station.

"About a woman," Hawk said. "She had guts—reminds me of you."

With a nod, he headed into the kitchen, leaving her standing there, utterly flabbergasted.

Utterly delighted.

CHAPTER NINE

To know even one life has breathed easier because you have lived, this is to have succeeded. - Ralph Waldo Emerson

"That's wonderful. I'll be there, thank you." In Mako's house, Kit set the landline phone down on the end table with a sigh of relief and a bit of anxiety.

Done. Now she could relax. With that in mind, she picked up her book—the third loaner from Hawk in the last three days.

Louis L'Amour—and his Sacketts—had become her favorite occupation for downtime. Maybe because the heroes reminded her of Hawk. The Sacketts were rugged men, their speech blunt, their social graces awkward. More than anything, they were honorable and honest—and treated women with respect. It was wonderful to be reminded that not all men were like the...the pissers.

Back out on the deck, she smiled at the children sitting in the grass and painting the rocks they'd gathered and washed.

Because the garden paths needed some decoration—or so she'd declared.

"Look, Mama." Aric held up his latest creation. "A rainbow."

"Perfect choice, honey bear. I love rainbows."

Fingers now multi-colored, he beamed at her and started on the next one.

"Look, Kit." Regan held up her own in beautiful swirls of green and turquoise.

"That's beautiful, Regan. I know just the place for it in the garden."

Regan grinned, then told Aric, "Here, want some of my yellow for that rock?"

The girl was a sweetheart, infinitely patient.

Aric was turning back into the active little monkey he'd been before. Happy and free. Could anything be more wonderful?

Across the courtyard, Frankie came out of her cabin, spotted Kit, and disappeared back inside. When she came out again, she had a tote bag in her hand as she headed for Kit. "Did you call the shelter? What's going to happen?"

"I did, and the staff will have everyone together in a private room so I can talk to them at two o'clock tomorrow."

Frankie dropped into a chair, setting her feet up on the railing. "Perfect." She placed the tote in Kit's lap. "Here is the money Bull switched over to hundreds for you."

All the twenties had been too bulky. Packets of $100-dollar bills would be much easier to hand out and conceal. "Awesome. Tell him thank you."

"I will." Frankie tapped her lips. "So, we'll drop you off at the shelter, then go to Bull's restaurant and let Hawk, Aric, and me enjoy munchies while my poor man gets stuck with the management stuff. Afterward, we'll pick you back up."

"Wait." Kit snickered. "You get the munchies, and Bull is stuck in a boring meeting?"

"Of course." Frankie put her nose in the air. "I manage the Rescue roadhouse. His restaurants in Homer and Anchorage—and the brewery—are his problem."

"Oh. Right. I knew that," Kit said agreeably, knowing that sneaky Bull would eventually talk Frankie into managing more than just one restaurant.

"Are you okay, *amica mia?*" Frankie reached over and squeezed Kit's hand. "Will it be hard on you to see them again?"

"Mmm, some? It helps that Aric will stay with Hawk." Kit smiled at her son, so happily playing with Regan. "I don't think it'd be good for him to go to the shelter. He saw too many of the women and children getting hurt."

"So did you," Frankie said softly. "How close did you get to the other women?"

"We weren't really friends, exactly. The men didn't allow us to talk with each other."

At Frankie's appalled stare, Kit grimaced and deepened her voice, " *'Gossip is the devil's work'*. Unfortunately, some of the women who were true-believers would tattle on any rule breakers."

Kit had been caned twice before she'd accepted that friendship wouldn't be part of her life.

"Tomorrow will undoubtedly bring back ugly memories." Kit rubbed her cheek, feeling the slightly raised line of the scar. "I want to put the PZ stuff behind me, but I need to hand out the money from the cave."

"Bull or I would go instead, you know."

Kit smiled. "You really are the bestest friend."

"Then—"

"No. Bull probably wouldn't even be allowed in. And the women might refuse to see a stranger, even you."

This was also a rather questionable appropriation of funds. She wouldn't risk getting Frankie or Bull in trouble for it.

And no staff would be in the room when she handed each woman her stack of bills. If any PZ or official found out about the money, Parrish might claim it, or the police would impound it. The women sure wouldn't see any.

They were in the same boat as Kit. Savings gone. Belongings sold by their husbands. Like Kit, they needed a way to start over.

Kit would be the one going in. She just...didn't really want to go.

No choice.

She'd have to suck it up and deal with her fears.

Hey, what was one more terror in the midst of so many, right?

CHAPTER TEN

*A*lways *remember to pillage BEFORE you burn. -* Unknown

Midmorning on Thursday, Nabera heard a car door outside, then Alvin's voice calling a greeting to someone.

Luka had arrived at the farm. It was about time the lieutenant showed up to explain what had come up.

Cell phones were useful, but the government was on the hunt. The libtards were sure the authorities didn't eavesdrop, but Nabera knew better. The Feds spied on everyone.

His mouth twisted in bitter memory of the phone call he'd gotten last week. His men had been cautious with their wording, but the meaning was clear. The three men sent to retrieve the Patriot's emergency cash had been ambushed by an overwhelming force of at least ten heavily armed men. The money was gone, and his men had been shot. Even worse, they'd had to draw from their limited funds. The doctor had to be bribed not to notify law enforcement of firearm injuries.

Fuck, fuck, fuck.

Nabera tugged on his black beard, frustration growing. What else could go wrong?

Word had reached him from Texas. The Prophet was still in jail, awaiting trial, and spending money on lawyers and bribes.

Nabera had really needed the money from the cave.

Then again, at least he was comfortable. The Prophet was locked up with no comforts. No women.

Both of them had enjoyed the rewards of being at the top with all the women available for their use. Nabera had been given the right to punish the unholy and disobedient. Sex was most enjoyable when accompanied by screams, sobs, and pleading.

Sometimes even death.

"Captain. How are you, sir?" Luka entered the kitchen.

"Good." Nabera looked him over.

His lieutenant had let his black buzz-cut hair grow. It was now trimmed in a modern style. Clean shaven, as usual, he wore jeans and a T-shirt with a rock band logo.

"You look like an Anchorage college student." Nabera's nod of approval made the man stand straighter. "What was so urgent you needed to see me today?"

After discovering their children and traitorous females were at a bleeding-heart women's shelter, Nabera had assigned Luka to charm one of the facility's volunteers. The dark-haired man had a way with women, and he'd been feeding the female a steady diet of sex and drugs.

"It's about the women's shelter. There's a limit to how long anyone can stay in the facility, and the time is up for our bitches."

"Is it now…" Nabera stroked his beard. He wanted to make examples of them, to show the Texas sluts what would happen if they testified. Once out of the shelter, he could get to them quite easily. "Good."

"Maybe not. Only a few are staying in Alaska and moving to reduced income housing while they find jobs. The rest are leaving the state to move in with relatives, wherever they are. Most are flying out tomorrow."

"Shit." Nabera scowled. "Then we need to act today." He reached for his cell phone.

"Yes, sir." Luka frowned. "One other thing."

"Yeah, speak up."

"Obadiah's woman—she's supposed to show up this afternoon at two. Probably to say goodbye to the rest of them."

"Kirsten." The hot rage hit Nabera so quickly that it felt as if he'd dropped into a lake of lava. "That traitorous bitch."

Luka's expression held the same anger. "The cunt destroyed our lives. Got Obadiah killed."

Somehow, the slut had sent word to a friend about the Zealots. The bitch friend arranged for her lover and others to break into the compound. Not only had Kirsten escaped, so had the children and most of the women. The traitorous cunts had spilled their guts to the Feds.

It was Kirsten's fault that Parrish was in prison. Nabera had sworn he would see her dead even if it took his entire fucking life.

Now he had his chance.

And even better... "If she's there to see the others, they'll be gathered in one place. Is there a way to get in?"

"It's a women's shelter so they have good security. Cameras, alarms. But"—Luka smirked—"if I tell Arella I'm going out of town and offer some ecstasy and a quickie, she'll let me in the side door. The staff turned off the alarm on that door so they can go outside and smoke."

This was his smartest lieutenant. "Go on."

"I'll knock Arella out and take care of the desk receptionist. Once I shut down the security system, our men can just waltz in the front."

"I like it," Nabera said. "Set it up, and I'll call in the men."

"Maybe we can get the children back."

"Perhaps." Children would be a pain in the ass. But some of

his men wanted their offspring. "We will for certain make an example of the women."

A spectacle of the horrifying, gory deaths of the Alaska PZ women would ensure the Texas women would be too cowed to testify.

Nabera smiled. "Our Prophet will be pleased."

And there would be all the screaming a man's vindictive heart could desire.

Holding the oversized tote that Frankie lent her, Kit shut her emotions down tight as she waited in a side room for the shelter worker to finish talking to her aide.

Instead, she gazed out a window at a tiny children's playground. It would be nicely safe. Before entering the shelter, she'd seen the corner lot was completely enclosed by an eight-foot privacy fence.

"Ready to go?" The staff worker joined her.

Kit motioned to the playground. "I see you used privet hedges to make a dedicated space for the children?"

The volunteer said, "We have plenty of small private spaces with the hedges to divide them up. Like here, the only way into a space is through a house door."

"Other spaces outside?" Kit tilted her head. The little children's area was adorable. What else might they have?

"You bet. We have a couple of secluded garden meditation rooms, a small veggie garden and greenhouse, and a big lawn area for kickball and games."

"That's awesome." When using the tiny garden in the rehab facility, she'd always wished it had been more private. "Your residents are lucky to have you."

"Thank you." The worker smiled. "Let me show you the room where your friends are gathered.

"Right." As memories of the PZs filled her, Kit shivered, wishing she could have stayed with Hawk, Aric, Bull, and Frankie. They'd dropped her off and gone to have lunch at Bull's restaurant here in Anchorage. They'd be back later to pick Kit up.

Kit followed the woman to the back of the huge two-story house. The hallway held the strong scent of a cleanser—and the lingering stink of vomit. Not a surprising smell.

How often had she puked as she'd tried to process everything that'd happened to her?

"Everyone is in here." The volunteer waved Kit into a spacious room filled with armchairs and couches. Children played quietly in one corner.

The center of the room was filled with women. Standing in groups of three and four, they stared at her. No one was familiar.

No, wait.

Slowly, she recognized features.

Miriam's big nose.

Serena's brown eyes. But she was wearing makeup, and the eye shadow and mascara made her eyes huge.

Mary's gray hair. Rather than to her waist, it was now in an attractive short bob.

Everyone looked different. Of course they did. There were no ankle-length dark skirts or long-sleeved blouses. No long hair pulled into buns. Instead, they wore colorful T-shirts and jeans. Some had on makeup. Hair was in a range of styles and new colors.

Kit gave a half-laugh. "You've...changed.

They burst out laughing—another surprise. Women rarely laughed in the PZ compound, especially loudly enough to be heard.

Everyone gathered around to hug her. Whispers and murmurs filled the air. "We were so worried." "You were hurt so badly." "I can never thank you enough."

Eventually, Mary clapped her hands together. "Sit, y'all. Let the girl breathe."

Smiling, they backed away, merging into one big blur through Kit's tear-filled eyes. She blinked hard. "Look at you all."

They were no longer gaunt. No one had bruises or cuts or black eyes. No one limped as they took seats on the couches, chairs, and the rug.

In the corner, the teens watching the younger children waved at Kit.

She waved back, and her heart felt...happy. After being reluctant to see the women again, now she was glad she had come.

A chair had been left empty for her, and she sat, putting the tote at her feet.

"Okay, I just need to put this out here." Miriam leaned forward, hands clasped together. "Kit, thank you. On that night, you were only half-conscious, and still, you cared enough to order us to get off our butts. To escape with your rescuers. I was frigging scared, but you got me moving. Thank you."

A chorus of agreement filled the air.

Kit felt a knot inside her ease. She'd felt incredibly guilty that people had risked their lives to rescue her. But if they hadn't, these women would still be imprisoned and abused in the PZ compound.

"You look better than I thought you would." Mary had always been the unofficial leader of the women. "Did you just get out of the hospital?"

"It's been about two weeks. I'm staying with my friend, Frankie. She arranged our rescue."

"But what about therapy?" Serena said hesitantly, "We get counseling here, one-on-one and group sessions and all that. It's... I..." She glanced at the others and caught their encouraging smiles. "We needed it. You might too."

"Oh, I did. I do." Kit half-laughed. "Even before I was

released, they were wheeling me to counseling sessions. And now I see a counselor at the local health clinic."

"Not group?" someone asked.

Kit shook her head. One-on-one was good. Group, well, she wasn't so keen. She'd managed to avoid it so far.

"I'm glad you're seeing a counselor," Miriam said. "The group therapy, though. It helps in a different way."

Daisy nodded. "The sessions are hard, but somehow, it helps hearing others went through abuse too. Learning how they handle problems, and what worked and didn't work and—"

"And not feeling like I'm the only idiot or coward in the world," Ellie added. "Try it, Kit."

The rest nodded.

Ugh. Groups really weren't her thing. But everyone was looking at her, willing her to agree. "I'll give it a try," she said reluctantly.

Once. She'd go once.

"Anyway, on a brighter note," she said. "I came today since I heard everyone is leaving for different places."

Kit relaxed back into the soft chair as they chimed in. Sharing their plans. Telling of legal affairs—divorces and custody and restraining orders. Some planned to stay with family. Others were getting help in finding jobs or obtaining schooling. Daycare and low-income housing had been arranged.

No one was returning to Texas, even if they had family there. The PZs were savage with anyone who escaped.

"It's going to be rough," tiny, slender Ellie whispered, "Starting from scratch. It makes me so mad that I listened to Bryson. That I gave up everything for him."

Kit pulled in a breath. She wouldn't have a better lead-in than this. And really, she needed to get things moving. Her friends and Aric would be here soon to pick her up.

Rising, she glanced around, checking that it was only the women and their children in the room. No shelter workers.

From their months of oppression, the others recognized what she was doing. They fell silent.

Letting the children's play drown out her lowered voice, Kit opened her tote. "If you didn't know, Obadiah handled the PZ bookkeeping—and their when-the-shit-hits-the-fan funds."

"Like disaster funds?" Daisy asked.

"Remember how they kept months of stored food in the locked building in case of war or disasters?"

Mary snorted. "It was one of the few things I actually thought made sense."

A few others nodded.

Layla's lip turned up in a snarl. "I would've approved except their so-called storage meant me and my daughter didn't get enough to eat."

That got a general murmur of agreement.

"It'd make sense that the bastards would keep money for disasters too. Heaven knows they had enough funds coming in through the website." Miriam's man had handled the website and donations. "It's a shame we'll never see any of that money."

Layla rolled her eyes. "The good reverend has probably spent it on lawyer fees by now. Or Captain Nabera will have used it to buy more weapons. He's still running around somewhere, remember?"

Every woman visibly shrank at the thought.

Kit did too. The Prophet was bad enough—a fanatic who felt that only he knew the truth, and everyone was there to serve him. Nabera was not only devoted to Parrish but was also...warped. He loved hurting women. Would boast about killing "the bitches." He was terrifying.

She swallowed, trying to shake off the nauseating memories of the night he'd "cleansed" her—of the stink of his breath, the revulsion of his touch.

A shriek of glee broke into Kit's memories, and she straightened.

In the corner, a little girl did a happy dance of victory at winning the children's game. The child had overcome the habit of silence.

Kit's hopes lifted. If the girl could do it, so could Aric.

"You wanted to tell us something?" Mary prompted.

"Oh, right." Kit turned back to the woman. "The Zealots had their big bank account, but like with the food storage, they also stockpiled cash. In a cave."

Eyes widened.

Miriam whispered, "I don't suppose…"

"Yes. I retrieved the money from the cave." Kit hauled in a breath. "I divided it up evenly between those of us here. Anyone who didn't leave with us will have PZ support, so the money I have here is just for us. We shouldn't tell anyone about it."

"Or someone will take it." Mary nodded her understanding. "Kit makes sense—and she took a risk in fetchin' the money. So, no talking about where this money came from, agreed?"

To Kit's relief, everyone nodded. PZ women knew how to keep secrets.

One-by-one, she handed over the flat packets of money, quietly so the children wouldn't notice.

The money disappeared into the women's clothing.

"Those were hundred-dollar bills," Ellie whispered, her eyes still wide. "How much?"

"We each got a little over ten thousand." Kit sat back in her chair, her tote bag now empty. "It's enough for a start."

Serena's eyes filled. "You could have kept it. Instead, you shared."

"Of course. We women have to stick together, right?" Because they had, even if silently.

Kit smiled at Serena. "When Obadiah broke my finger, you stacked the firewood in my arms so I wouldn't have to pick it up." Being damaged or ill wasn't considered a reason to excuse a woman from working.

"When I burned the bread," Serena nudged Mary, "you took the blame."

"After Bryson left me so bruised I could barely move"—Ellie turned to Layla—"you abandoned your own chores to take on my job doing the laundry."

There were smiles and misty eyes as they shared and remembered.

"We women stick together," Kit repeated softly.

"Yes. That's right." Mary's lips trembled, but she nodded firmly.

Mary had been married for thirty years. Her husband hadn't given her a choice in joining the PZs and had refused to let her leave.

"Hey, we totally forgot. The staff put out drinks and snacks for us." Layla rose. "Over on the table—"

A crash came from outside the room. Then a man's shout, "Bitch, where are our women?"

Kit jumped to her feet at the sound of the voice from her worst nightmares. Her mouth went dry.

"That's Captain Nabera." Layla was whimpering.

Doors slammed. Near the front of the building, women were screaming.

Nabera shouted, "Door-to-door search."

There was the hard sound of boots on wooden floors.

"They're here. Dear God, they're here," Serena moaned.

Children scrambled from the corner, fleeing to their mothers.

Run, run, run. Heart hammering, Kit turned in a circle, frantically looking for an exit.

She didn't know how to escape the room.

Situational awareness. Why hadn't she paid attention as Hawk had said?

A child shrieked, and Kit almost panicked, thinking it was Aric. *No.* Her son was safe with Hawk.

There were other children here. Her fear was pushed aside by determination. *Help the children.*

She spun and snapped out, "Miriam, block the door."

Dashing across the room to another door, she yanked it open, hoping it would lead to somewhere that could be barricaded better.

It was a closet only big enough for one person. Worthless.

At the door to the hallway, Miriam braced a chair under the handle. Others pushed more furniture against the door and the chair.

A man's voice came from the hallway. "There's someone in there. Sounds like kids."

Mothers immediately silenced their children, as he rattled the handle and tried to open the door. "It's braced shut," he hollered. "Fucking cunts."

A bullet came through the door—and someone let out a shriek.

Other men were talking.

"Yeah, got women in here."

"Might have some fun before we leave, huh?"

"Get that door open." The voice was Captain Nabera's. "Get a hatchet."

Shaking started deep inside Kit's body as if her very bones vibrated with fear.

Think, Kit, think. "If someone has a phone, call 911." Living in the compound, the women had lost the almost instinctive response of calling the emergency number.

One woman whipped out a phone.

When the men break in, we'll be trapped here. Kit headed for the door to outside.

"Yes," Mary agreed. "We need to get out of this room." She started shoving women and children that direction.

Kit shoved the door open and went out with the wave of people.

Outside, she could almost hear Hawk's voice. *Where is your line of retreat?*

She moved away from the building to look around. The outside area was a small meditation spot. A thick privet hedge with no openings divided it from the other sides of the yard. The far wall was the six-feet tall privacy fence that enclosed the grounds.

They'd never get the children over that fence before getting caught.

Kit scowled. Screaming wouldn't help. The area was residential. No one would come running to help.

Loud thumps showed the men were battering down the door into the room.

"Block this door too," Mary ordered. She'd pulled a folding chair out with her.

Men's voices came from the other sides of the privet hedge, sounding frustrated. The thick bushes blocked them for the moment.

The women would soon be *flanked,* as Hawk's westerns would say.

Those western heroes—the Sacketts—often escaped pursuit by fleeing up a mountain. "Where's a darn mountain when I..."

Her voice trailed off as she spotted a ladder leaning against the side of the house. Stacks of shingles and tools were scattered on the roof.

With yells of success, the men made it into the room and started rattling the handle of the outside door.

Fear swamping her in a cold deluge, Kit ran toward the ladder.

No. Not without the others.

She shoved her panic down and grabbed the nearest woman. "Up the ladder, Serena. Now."

Serena climbed the ladder onto the roof, followed by Daisy. The older children followed, scrambling up like monkeys. Women carried their babies and younger children, getting help from the unencumbered.

Finally, Mary went up.

Kit had her hands on the first rung when men kicked out the glass and came out the windows into the meditation garden.

She went up the ladder like her feet were on fire and swung onto the roof. "Pull the ladder up!"

The women were herding the children to the steep valley between two roofs—one over the original house and another over a garage add-on. The V would provide a hiding place rather than making them easy targets.

Two of the strongest women started lifting the ladder, hand over hand.

The men let out a yell and grabbed it.

Noooo. Snatching up loose shingles, Kit flung them down at the PZs.

Yelling in pain and outrage, the men batted at the barrage.

The ladder was free.

"Pull," Mary shouted, and the women hauled the ladder up and out of reach.

The crack of a gunshot sounded, and something stung Kit's outer arm. Following the others, she dove for the V to get out of sight.

"Well, well, if it isn't Obadiah's treacherous bitch up there."

At the sound of Captain Nabera's cruel voice, Kit felt her courage shrivel into a tight ball of fear. Her mouth was too dry to swallow.

She edged out enough to look at him. *I'm out of reach. He can't touch me.*

The knowledge didn't help.

His gaze met hers, and his mouth curved in a vicious smile. "Come down, cunt, and I'll let you live. Otherwise, all they'll find of you will be tiny pieces."

As if to make sure she understood, he snapped at another man, "Set the explosives, inside and out."

They'd blow up the house? Her mouth went dry.

"You're one of us, and Obadiah's gone." Nabera softened his voice. "Lower the ladder, Kirsten. Come down to me, and you'll live."

The twisted lust in his gaze turned her stomach until she thought she'd heave. She'd seen his expression while Obadiah was kicking and punching her. In his hands, she wouldn't live; she'd die screaming.

Never. She'd never let him get his hands on her again. Death would be better.

He read her unspoken answer, and his face darkened with fury.

In a huddled cluster, the women hadn't moved, and she heard the same resolve in their whispers. *I'd rather die.*

"Fucking bitches, get down here." Frustrated, the PZs started shooting.

Bullets peppered the steep sides of the V. As the sharp fragments of shingles and wood tore into their skin, the women flattened down even further into the security of the lowest part between the two roofs. Children whimpered and sobbed.

Kit's face and arms stung and bled where shards had hit.

In a pause during the gunfire, there came the sound of a car in the street. The vehicle stopped.

A PZ yelled, "Incoming, Captain."

"Finish planting the explosives. We'll hold them off," Nabera shouted.

A car door slammed. Another.

"What the *fuck*." Bull's booming bass came clearly.

Her friends. *Yes!*

The relief flooding Kit drained away even faster. Aric was in the car. *No, no, no*. Her hands clenched. *Get Aric away. Please.*

Bull snapped, "Get the fuck out of here, Frankie."

"*Leave*, Yorkie." Hawk's dark bitter order brought fresh fears. He wouldn't leave—he could get hurt. Killed.

The car engine roared, and then tires squealed. As the sound of the vehicle receded, Kit sagged in relief.

She might die here; they all might die here. But her baby would live. And Frankie would be alive to care for him.

CHAPTER ELEVEN

*A*nything *worth shooting is worth shooting twice. Ammunition is cheap; life is expensive.* - Rules of a Gunfight

Hawk took the paddle holster with a Glock 19 and an extra magazine his brother handed over. Bull had grabbed weapons from his SUV "armory" before Frankie sped away.

At least the yorkie was safe. Now to extract Kit from the clusterfuck of undoubtedly PZs. Hawk shoved the holster onto his belt and tucked the magazine away. Bull had already donned his in-town firearm—an M1911.

Sporadic shooting came from somewhere near the rear of the house. A man shouted something about explosives.

Explosives. Talk about complicating the hell out of a clean assault. *Dammit, Kit, stay safe.*

Needing info, Hawk swung up onto the privacy fence, using his arms to hold him high enough to see, hoping he didn't get his head shot off.

Fuck. Thick hedges divided the outside area into small, contained spaces. There was no way through the damn bushes.

He could barely see the heads of men in the back left corner. Why were their weapons pointed upward?

Oh, fuck. Hawk dropped down to the ground. "The women are on the roof."

Bull's eyes narrowed. "I go inside; you go around."

"Roger that." Hawk jogged to the corner to scan down the fence line. He could... Yeah, a tree at the far corner had branches overhanging the fence. *Perfect.*

Bull disappeared into the house.

Time to move.

Hawk sprinted down the outside of the privacy fence, jumped, caught a branch, and swung himself up.

A PZ was already in the tree, pistol in hand, trying to get a good angle to shoot at the women. He saw Hawk and fired.

Missed.

Dropping onto his belly over the branch, Hawk swung his legs around, nailed the asshole's shoulder, and knocked him into the trunk. Hawk followed up with a fist to the PZ's jaw and sent him nighty-night.

One down.

After far-too-fucking-gently dropping the man onto the ground, Hawk drew his Glock. The whole area held the sulphuric stink of gunpowder, and men dotted the contained space inside the fence.

Target-rich environment for sure.

He snapped a bullet at the farthest one out, then another. Two down.

Bull's big Colt .45 cracked loudly.

In the distance, police sirens wailed.

"Call for pickup." Nabera yelled. "Head out."

As the chickenshits jumped the fence, Hawk swung down on the branch and kicked the nearest in the head with a solid *thunk*. The man dropped, out cold.

The rest sprinted away and piled into two vans that had drawn up to the curb.

As the vans peeled away, Hawk holstered his Glock and scowled. The vans' rear license plates were covered with mud and unreadable. They'd be on the Spenard Thruway and gone before the cops made it here.

Not his concern. He needed to check on Bull—and get the women to safety. Fuck knew if the bastards had finished planting the explosives.

On the roof, the women were moving the ladder. On the other side of the house, Bull's voice boomed, directing them to put it out in front.

Good enough. He'd join them there. After tying up the two unconscious PZs, he dragged them closer to the fence and away from the house, then glanced around. The two he'd shot were dead.

Back over the fence, he jogged to the front of the house.

At the foot of the repositioned ladder, Bull was helping the women off and directing them to the house across the street. The shelter's staff and other residents were already clustered there.

The sirens were closer now. The PZs wouldn't risk returning.

Where was Kit? His gut clenched when he didn't see her.

No, there she was, still on the roof, waiting for the others to go down. Face dead white, eyes wide. He scanned her quickly. Scratches, mostly. Right sleeve was bloody.

She was upright and moving, though. His gut unclenched.

She saw him. After looking him up and down, just as he had her, relief filled her expression. The last to leave, she came down the ladder after an older woman.

Just as she set foot on the ground, a loud explosion shook the building.

Scooping her up, Hawk sprinted after Bull, who'd grabbed the older woman

On the other side of the street, Hawk set Kit on her feet, keeping a hand under her arm, just in case. "You good?"

"Yes." She leaned against him for a moment. "Thank you. Again."

"Can't think of anyone I'd rather rescue." The words were out before he could recall them.

She blinked, then color swept across her face.

And she smiled at him.

Another boom sounded.

"Seems the bastards got their explosives planted." Bull set the older lady down. "You okay, ma'am?"

"No. But thank you." Tears streaked the woman's face. She hurried over to join the others.

Unhappiness filled Bull's expression. "I must have hurt her when I—"

"You didn't hurt her, Bull," Kit said softly. "Mary's husband is the explosives expert in the PZs. It's hard to realize your husband of thirty years is willing to kill you rather than let you go."

Hawk froze. *The fucking son of a bitch.*

He saw the same fury in Bull's expression. And the sadness in Kit's face. She'd only been married to her bastard of a husband for a few months, but yeah, she must know what Mary was feeling.

Fuck if he knew what to say. Instead, he ran a hand down her back and then set himself to checking out the damage to her arm.

———

Kit wasn't sure how much time had passed. Rather than traumatize the women with a trip to the station, the police had interviewed them at the neighbor's house where they had the support of the shelter staff and each other. It wasn't as if there was any mystery to what happened. During the questions, Arella, a shelter volunteer, had burst into tears and confessed she'd let a "boyfriend" inside.

A nice female officer had spoken with Kit, then handed her to the paramedics to get her arm bandaged.

Waiting for the police to finish talking with Hawk and Bull, Kit spotted Bull's SUV moving past a cop at the barricaded road.

Hope rose inside her.

The SUV stopped behind the police cars. Frankie jumped out and opened the back door where Aric was in his booster seat.

As Kit ran forward, she could hear him screaming, "Mama!"

The second he was out of the car, Kit dropped to her knees and hugged him. "Baby."

His arms were around her neck, half strangling her. "Mamaaaaa." He was crying uncontrollably.

A sob choked her as she pressed her cheek to his hair. All she wanted was to break down and cry with him.

But he was safe. That was what mattered.

She looked up at her best friend in the world. "Thank you."

Frankie's eyes were wet, too, but she gave a nonchalant smile. "All part of a godmother's duties. Although he's really mad at me since I took him away from you and Hawk."

"Thank God," Kit muttered.

"I wanted to stay and help, but *cazzo*, when Hawk gives an order, he's even scarier than Bull." Frankie huffed a little, then grinned. "I can't believe Bull carries extra weapons in the SUV. I mean, I could see maybe a rifle or something, but he has, like, an armory."

"Well, yeah." Bull walked up and tucked an arm behind Frankie to pull her close for a thorough kiss. "Gotta have enough to share with my brothers. You never know when some assholes are going to attack a women's shelter, after all."

"He'll have to re-stock." A gravelly laugh came from behind Kit. "The cops kept our weapons."

"Hawk!" When Aric squealed, Hawk picked him up, set him on his hip, then held a hand down for Kit.

She took his hand. How often over the past few days had he'd casually held out his hand to help her to her feet or out of the helicopter? Always just offering and letting her decide.

Now, she didn't even think before taking his hand.

Once she was standing, he tugged her close enough so Aric could cling to her hand.

Kit glanced at the smoking, half-destroyed shelter. Her baby didn't need to see that. "When can we leave?"

"Now," Hawk said.

"The police know where to find us." Bull chuckled. "We mentioned our bro is Rescue's Chief of Police and lives next door."

Kit gasped. "You were suspects? I can't believe—"

"We killed people. Naturally, they'll look at us closely," Bull said.

They'd killed...for her. *Again.* Kit stared up at Hawk. "I'm sorry. I'm so sorry."

He touched her cheek. "Did you invite the assholes to come here?"

"No, of course not."

"Don't shoulder guilt that isn't yours to carry."

"I..." He was right.

His hard blue gaze softened.

"Kit," Bull said. "Did you accomplish your goal?"

In other words, did she distribute the money? "I did." Her gaze was on the shelter. Firefighters were there, putting out the fire started by the explosives. "I guess it's good no one had a chance to put the packets in their rooms."

Frankie glanced around. "Were any of the women or children hurt?"

"Some splinters, a few scraped hands and legs. Nothing serious." Kit looked at Hawk. "Did any of the shelter people get injured?"

He nodded.

Bull elaborated. "The volunteer who let them in has a gash on her head. The lady at the front tried to fight and got knocked out. She's got a concussion. Two others were caught in the edge of the explosion. Nothing life-threatening."

"Let's go," Hawk gave Aric a small bounce. "The kid needs cookies."

Rather than laughing, Aric laid his head on Hawk's shoulder—without releasing his grip on Kit's hand.

Her boy had been traumatized. Again.

Anger stewed inside her, even as she nodded agreement. Then she sighed.

Aric would heal, especially since he had his own personal protector right there to hold onto. Because of Hawk and Frankie and the others, her son was with her, not held hostage in the PZ compound. They were free.

Kit squeezed Aric's hand and smiled at Hawk. "Yes, we totally need cookies."

After soaping down several times in the shower—because damned if any kind of combat left him feeling as if he was covered in blood—Hawk paced around his house, trying to relax.

A text from Bull dinged on his phone. *-We're all eating at Mako's. Come on over. -*

He scowled at the display and tried to decide if he wanted to join the others.

Eating might be smart, and being around his brothers after a fight would settle the uneasy feeling in his lizard brain. He could relax because it wasn't only him watching for danger.

But being around others? Despite showering, it still felt as if anyone seeing him would spot the darkness in his soul.

He was a killer. The son of an abuser. A fucked-up mess by any standard.

Jesus, get over yourself, dumbass. Pulling in a breath, he ran through the talk with his counselor after the rescue at the PZ. His counselor was a combat vet and had seen some shit. The doc had given Hawk two questions to ask himself to work through the aftermath.

One: Why did I kill today?

The answer was plain enough. To keep helpless women and children from being murdered.

Two: Could I have done anything else?

Not without risking the lives of the innocent.

Okay then.

Another text came from Bull. *- Can you stop by my house and bring Kit and Aric? -*

Ah, Kit still didn't have a phone. Once she started getting out on her own, she would need one.

He texted back. *- K -*

Over at Bull's house, he called out, letting her know she had company. "Kit."

"Back here." She poked her head out of her room in the back hallway, then leaned on the door frame.

He joined her and saw why she hadn't left. At the kid-sized dresser, Aric was wearing only briefs as he pulled a red T-shirt and dark blue overalls out of the drawer. Dressing was a serious matter at four years old.

"Why'd he pick only shit color combinations for me?" Hawk muttered. Like pairing purple plaid shorts with a garish orange-paisley shirt. The combo'd made Hawk's eyes bleed.

A corner of her mouth tipped up in a smirk. "Because I only put a few shirts and bottoms in the drawers—all of which work no matter what gets mixed with what. I hide the other clothes and change them out now and then."

Hawk lifted an eyebrow. "You're sneakier than you look."

"I have mad mommy skills." Her luminous brown eyes lit with laughter and struck him speechless with their beauty.

She frowned. "Were you looking for Bull?"

"No. Fetching you. There's food at Mako's."

"Oh. Huh." Her frown deepened. "I guess sitting and stewing about things isn't a good idea."

They were a lot alike, weren't they?

Clothes on, Aric fastened the Velcro straps on his sneakers and ran over to Hawk. "I'm hungry."

To hear Aric demanding food like a normal kid made Hawk's day. "Me too."

"Me three. Let's go." Kit turned and winced.

"You're hurt." He put a hand on her shoulder, felt her tense before relaxing.

"Not really. My ribs are sore from climbing a ladder. And throwing things..."

"Throwing things?" Aric asked.

Hawk winced. Perhaps not a good example for a child. Still, it wouldn't hurt to know his mother wasn't defenseless. "She threw stuff at the bad guys to keep them from hurting anyone. Pretty damn brave."

Aric's eyes went wide. He'd seen the PZs hurt his mother and figured she was defenseless. Powerless. The kid was too young to realize *he* was the reason she hadn't fought back.

They walked together over to Mako's place and were greeted by everyone there.

The meal was a good one. Craving Mexican food, Caz had gone for a fix-your-own meal. There were platters of warm tortillas, crispy taco shells, a spicy beef-and-bean mix, cheese, lettuce, sour cream, and guacamole. The health-nuts, who sure didn't include Hawk, made themselves taco salads. The kids went for tacos.

After having some nachos, Hawk had a couple of burritos and one of Bull's beers.

To his surprise, he felt all right, despite the crowd. Audrey, Frankie, and JJ were good people. And he liked having the children close where he knew they were safe. Same with Kit.

Yeah, he felt better. Although the night wouldn't be a good one. It never was after he killed someone.

While eating, everyone offered a summary of their day, good and bad. Caz told about the mother who'd brought him a home-made strawberry pie for treating her daughter last week. He caught hell from Bull and Gabe for sharing it with his medical staff rather than bringing it home.

JJ got laughs from telling about the traffic jam—in their two-block town—caused by a moose and baby.

For a historical author, Audrey had researched what people used before toilet paper. Corn husks and mullein leaves were common. Rolling her eyes, she mentioned the commonest mistakes—like using poison ivy.

Jesus.

Discussion about the shelter battle had been postponed to after clean-up was done.

Now the dishwasher was running, and everyone relocated to the living room. A couple more armchairs were added for places to sit other than the massive sectional.

When Kit settled into one chair, JJ grinned and dumped a pile of pillows and blankets at her feet—an instant lure for Aric and Regan.

After giving JJ an approving nod, Hawk sat on the sectional closest to Kit and the kids. If talk about the PZs upset Aric, he'd be close.

Joining the children in the pillow pile, Gryff lay down with his muzzle on Aric's leg, and Sirius, Regan's big cat, curled up in her arms.

Even before Kit started talking about her part of the fight, the children were falling asleep.

They looked so fucking peaceful. The uncomfortable pressure in Hawk's chest eased up, then disappeared. Even as the group discussed the fight and explosions, the pressure didn't return.

"That's it," Bull said finally, concluding with the police interviews. "Might be they'll give you a call, Gabe, since we dropped your name."

"That fancy *Chief of Police* title is good for something, I guess." Gabe grinned, then turned to Kit. "Now you've had some time to think about the action, what would you do differently? What did you do right—or wrong?"

Kit stared. "Wh-what?"

JJ snorted. "Welcome to your first debriefing. It's one of the downsides of being around Mako's sons."

"Like you did with the children after their game?" Kit turned to Hawk as if he had the answers.

Felt...different. Good. He nodded and added, "Looking back is how you get better."

"Everybody screws up sooner or later. But making the same mistake twice—that can be avoided," Gabe said quietly.

He'd been their leader even before they left the foster home. Although Hawk still wanted to kick his ass at times.

Not so much recently. The bitterness of what had happened when they were mercs was pretty much gone.

"Mistakes." Kit chewed on her lower lip as she thought. "I'm not sure what—"

"When you heard the PZs arrive, did you know how to get out?" Caz asked softly.

"Oh. Oh, I get what you mean." She gave Hawk an unhappy look. "I wasn't doing what you taught me—not until I got out of the room. Inside, I didn't know what the windows looked out on or what one of the doors went to, like a closet or an exit."

"It was a closet, I take it?" JJ asked in a dry voice.

"Uh-huh." Kit pulled in a breath. "I messed up."

"It's how you learn. Watch how Hawk automatically checks out a room." Gabe motioned to Aric. "Your son too. They're probably better than any of us."

Kit's brows drew together, and she turned to Hawk again. "Why you and Aric?"

Even if it felt like he was ripping scabs off old wounds, she deserved an answer. "Beatings. You mark out the quickest way to escape. It's instinctive."

"I don't have that instinct."

He wanted to take her hand, to comfort her. Instead, he gave her honesty. "You weren't allowed to escape. Kids...it's their first defense."

"Aric is good at it," she whispered. "He needed to be." Pain and guilt showed in her eyes as she looked at Aric. She hadn't been able to defend him.

Then her gaze lifted to Hawk's, and he could see she'd realized what he had in common with her son. As children, they'd been forced to escape from adults.

Rather than pity, her expression showed only respect. "Then I'll keep learning from you...and Aric."

Damned if he could find the right words to say. He just nodded.

"Good enough," Gabe said in approval. "How about getting you a pistol?"

"No, but thank you." She smiled at the three women in the room before telling Gabe, "They offered to teach me, but...quite honestly, I don't think I could shoot someone. Hit them, yes. Shoot, no."

Gabe glanced at Hawk, who nodded. He'd already gotten that read on her, but it was impressive she knew her limits.

"In that case." Gabe turned to Frankie and JJ. "When she can move better, work with her on self-defense. Escaping if grabbed. Running."

"Sweet." Frankie grinned at her friend. "I've been trying to get you to learn since forever. Now you're stuck."

JJ laughed. "I have some evil moves that work for women our size. It'll be fun."

"Oh, boy." Kit chewed on her lip, then nodded. "Okay. I don't like being helpless—I'd appreciate your instruction."

She wasn't a fighter, Hawk knew. Didn't have a predatory bone in her body, but she had an internal strength he respected. She'd push herself to gain the skills needed to protect herself and her son.

Not that she'd need to use those skills. Not while he was around.

Bull gave her a nod. "At the shelter, once you got outside, you pulled it together. You figured out that being on the roof would put you out of reach. You got the women up there and kept the PZs from following. Good job."

The pink that crept into her cheeks made her face glow.

Hawk's eyes narrowed. She wasn't used to hearing she'd done good, was she? He knew how that felt. As a kid, he'd fucking cried the first time the sarge had said, "Good job."

He'd have to remember to tell her when she did well. It was easier with Aric. Not so much with a woman.

But she needed that reassurance, so he'd get his ass on that job too.

CHAPTER TWELVE

I f you could kick the person in the pants responsible for most of your trouble, you wouldn't sit for a month. ~ Theodore Roosevelt

The night had been as fucked-up as Hawk expected.

He woke in a cold sweat with the day's battle playing in his head. Shooting in slow motion and seeing the nauseating damage each slug had done. Each replay had been slightly different, and in the last one, he'd been too slow. The PZ in the tree had shot him, and he'd been unable to move as Bull got gunned down. Then the house exploded beneath the women.

Their screaming had kicked him out of the nightmare, thank fuck.

He wiped off the sweat with a washcloth, letting the cold bite ground him, and then slugged down a glass of water to rinse the bitter taste from his mouth.

Once outside, he checked the courtyard. The night was gray and cold. Reassuringly silent. Barefooted, he patrolled the perimeter to reassure himself there were no intruders.

His behavior was a lot like Mako's sometimes.

He half-grinned. There were worse role models than the honorable first sergeant.

As his gut settled, Hawk pulled on a flannel shirt and socks, fetched his violin, and settled out on his deck.

As he tuned the strings, streamers of fog drifted across the lake like lingering ghosts from his dreams. Beneath the fog was the black, still water.

The lake was his talisman. Infinitely changeable. Birthing life; cruelly taking life. Always beautiful.

Often enough at night, he played to the Lady of the Lake, offering her the sad haunting melodies from his heart. And she would gift him with a few hours of peace.

As she did now.

When his fingers grew too chilled to play, he went back to bed for a few more hours and rose at his usual time.

Dressed in sweats and a T-shirt and ready to run, he was tying his shoes when Aric slipped in the door.

"Hey, kid."

Still looking sleepy, Aric leaned against his knee, pressing close. Yeah, Hawk wasn't the only one disturbed by yesterday.

"Hungry?"

A nod of the blond head.

Hawk stroked a hand over silky hair that was softer than puppy fur. "All right." A banana and milk would tide the boy over until breakfast. "Your mom still asleep?"

Another nod.

Figured. She'd had a fucking shitty time yesterday.

Hadn't they all. He needed to run it off.

As the kid ate, Hawk walked onto the deck to check the lights in the other three houses. It was Saturday, so Bull and Frankie were probably sleeping in. Same with Caz and JJ. Gabe had planned to go into the station early—and there was a light in his house. Audrey might be up.

In case Kit woke up, Hawk wrote out a note and taped it to his sliding glass door. *"Aric's at Audrey's."*

Finished, he told Aric, "Let's go see Audrey."

Never unwilling to visit—as long as Hawk went along—Aric slid off his booster chair. Onto bare feet. Hell.

Hawk made the "want to ride" gesture, and Aric nodded. After setting the kid on his shoulders, Hawk jogged to Gabe's house, the first in the line, then tapped on the sliding glass door.

In the kitchen, Audrey waved for him to come in.

"Good morning, you two. What's up?" She looked confused for a minute then laughed. "Let me guess. You're dying to go running and want me to watch Aric?"

"Yeah. If it's okay?"

"I like company." She smiled at Aric and probably noticed the way the kid's hands tightened in Hawk's hair.

Maybe a run wasn't a good idea. Or he could put the kid on his back and—

Audrey tilted her head. "How about we climb up to the...the..."

"Sniper's nest?" Hawk guessed.

"Yes, that, and we'll be able to watch you as you run. Okay, Aric?"

The grip on Hawk's hair relaxed. "'Kay."

Setting Aric down, Hawk pointed to the hallway. "Mind if I leave through there?"

"Go ahead." She took Aric's hand and led him toward the stairs. "You're going to like this. You can see everything."

After Hawk went out the garage's side door, he took a minute to stretch out. He wasn't a young pup any longer to be able to bust out running. Injuries and age had taught him the benefits of warming up.

He started off at a slow jog down the dirt and gravel road toward Swan Avenue.

After passing the strip he used for his plane in the off seasons when he couldn't land on the snow or the water, he stopped and turned to look back at Gabe's house.

No way to spot motion up in the tiny attic space. That'd been part of the design. The logs and shingles concealed sliding hatches at various locations and heights. Each house had a sniper's nest that provided an excellent field of fire.

Mako had insisted.

Assuming Audrey and Aric were watching, Hawk held up his hand in a wave, then resumed his run, picking up the pace as he went.

The air was brisk with the damp scent of the lake and green growth. A pile of fur at the side of the road showed a moose calf had ended up being dinner for something—probably a hungry brown bear.

The young of any species was vulnerable.

His speed increased as anger...and determination...roused within him. The Hermitage had two young ones. Nothing—and no one—would harm them.

Or the women either. Especially not Kit.

But she was an adult, and despite what she'd been through, she wouldn't stay hidden here where it was safe. She'd asked Caz and Gabe what jobs were available in town, ones that wouldn't require a lot of lifting.

And each day, Aric was less dependent on having his mother or Hawk around. The boy might even join Regan at the summer school program.

It was good that the two were moving on with their lives.

It was good that Kit would soon be recovered enough to move to her own place.

Wasn't it?

———

Heavens, but she'd slept hard.

Still yawning, Kit went in search of her boy. He wasn't in Bull's house.

Next choice would be over at Hawk's. She heard Aric's high giggles even as she climbed the deck steps.

When she knocked on the sliding glass door, Aric ran to let her in—and gave her a happy, little boy hug.

A sticky one. He smelled of maple syrup, and the house held an enticing, almost pastry-like aroma.

Hawk was seated at one of the long kitchen islands eating pancakes. That was what she'd smelled.

Disappointment swept through her that she hadn't gotten up in time to have some. She kissed the top of Aric's head. "Morning, honey bear. Morning, Hawk."

Holding onto her legs, Aric leaned back so he could see her face. "Mama, I went up high. With Audrey. So high. We watched Hawk."

Wasn't it wonderful to hear his chatter? "Did you now?" She didn't remember any climbable trees in the courtyard. Audrey wouldn't take Aric anywhere unsafe, would she? "Where was this?"

"Up."

Oh, that was helpful. Kit frowned at Hawk.

"Attic room. I was jogging."

Kit smiled at Aric. "That sounds amazing."

Except for the fact that she was creating work for everyone else. She'd just have to make sure she got up earlier. "I'm sorry I slept so late. It won't happen again."

Hawk snorted. "You're allowed."

"Sometimes I ride Hawk," Aric said proudly. "In a kid-pack."

"You run with Aric on your back?" she said slowly. "He's not exactly light..."

"Lighter than combat gear."

She had to shake her head at someone whose comparisons measured a child's weight against battle stuff.

"So…" Hawk took a sip of his coffee, gave her a considering look, then turned to point at the garage door at the end of the hall. "Bad guys are busting in from there. What do you do?"

"*What?*" Just the question sent ice up her spine. Then the momentary chilling fear turned into annoyance. "Seriously? I haven't even had *coffee* yet."

He snorted and turned toward the garage door to call, "Guys, no shooting till the target gets coffee."

When he raised an eyebrow at her, she wanted to yell at him. That he wasn't being fair, that—

Life wasn't fair.

Well…darn it, anyway.

She crossed the room to join him at the island, and okay, maybe she glared at him. A little.

His lips twitched with his amusement.

With a loud sigh, she put an arm around Aric, hugging him to her so she'd remember what was important. "I'd grab Aric and run out the deck door to whoever is home to warn them."

"Good try." He pointed at the coffee as an obvious reward.

She poured herself some and wrinkled her nose at the pitch-black color.

"Sugar." He pointed to canisters on the counter, then the fridge. "Milk."

After doctoring the sludge to a better color, she heaved a pleased sigh and started imbibing sweet caffeine. "Why did you call my solution a good try? Instead of perfect."

"There're gaps between the houses."

She frowned. A gap meant someone on the road could see her and Aric. And take a shot. "Oh. Right." That really wasn't good. "Okay."

"If you're here alone?"

Her hands clenched at the terrifying thought. Having people around was one of her safety blankets. To be here alone and have men come in. What if *Nabera*…

"Kit." Hawk's deep voice yanked her out of her head. He didn't reach for her—just offered his hand.

She gripped his hand with both of hers. His fingers were strong. Callused. Warm.

Her mind cleared enough she could think, and she still didn't know what to do.

He glanced at Aric. "Hiding places?"

Aric pointed to the upstairs.

Hawk nodded. "Good doors; good locks."

She found a breath. "So run and hide and call the cops."

"And us." He motioned toward the lake. "After dark, you can hide in the reeds."

"Unner the deck." Aric made the hand signal for "go prone".

Hawk's lips quirked.

Kit started to smile. Apparently, Aric had hidden under the deck a time or two. "Would it be best to leave the courtyard entirely?"

"Too exposed. Mako was a paranoid bast—" Hawk glanced at Aric and substituted, "man."

Sitting on the stool next to him, she considered. The small dirt road ran past the semi-circle of houses before ending. On the other side of the road was Hawk's landing strip. The forested area where they'd played games with the children was back where the road curved near the lake, much closer to Swan Avenue. There were no trees near the outside of the Hermitage. "I never thought about any of this."

He nodded. "Knowing escape routes might let you...settle."

"Settle?"

"After combat, soldiers stay on high alert. Preparation helps." His tone was serious. Deadly. "Evaluate shit everywhere. Like the grocery—where are the exits? Hiding places."

Her eyes started to tear. "I don't want to live like that."

"Woman, you already do." The blunt statement was like a slap in the face.

Denying the truth was like whining that life wasn't fair. It did her no good. Captain Nabera was still out there, would kill her if he saw her. And Nabera wasn't the only predator in the world.

Even if there was no one actively wanting to hurt her, after what she'd lived through, her subconscious probably didn't believe anywhere was safe. The best she could do would be to convince it that she could handle whatever happened. "Okay. I get it."

His gaze stayed steady on her as he waited for the rest.

"And you're right. I'll work on it. And let you tell me the stuff I missed seeing."

He gave a low humph of acknowledgement and agreement, then pointed at the oven. "Your pancakes."

Her day went from sour to sweet. "I get pancakes?" She couldn't keep from beaming at him.

And his head tilted slightly, his expression changing to one that was very masculine. "Do I get a hug too?"

Her mouth dropped open in surprise. At herself. Because she wasn't immediately revolted; instead, the thought was intriguing —like another way to step out of the desert of non-touching she'd been in.

Before she lost her courage, she stepped between his knees, leaned forward, and hugged him around the shoulders. The very broad shoulders.

A tingle of interest sizzled up her spine.

He smelled different today. A green kind of clean—cypress and lavender. Maybe the tang of sage. She breathed in, wanting to rub her face against him. Against Hawk.

Her hand curled around his neck, under his hair, and she couldn't resist running her fingers up through the strands. So thick and soft.

He closed his hands on her hips and pulled her closer.

Hard hands moving her.

At the feeling of being drawn forward, she felt the room turn icy cold, too cold for even air to exist. Her heart raced as she gasped, unable to breathe.

Wrenching away, she staggered back, hands up in a futile defense for when he...

He didn't move.

He would. Soon enough he would. Nausea twisted her insides, and she choked, black spots in front of her eyes.

"Mama!" The cry pulled her head up.

Hawk had an arm around Aric. "Wait, kid. Grabbing her isn't smart."

Because she might not realize it was her son touching her. The knowledge was bitter. And forced her to get control.

Seeing her expression, Hawk let Aric go. "Slow, kid."

Aric ran over, stopped before slamming into her...and hugged her leg.

Bending, she put her arms around his shoulders. He was shaking almost as hard as she was.

It took a minute, two, an eternity before her breathing returned to normal. *Okay, okay.* She had this. She was fine.

When she straightened, Hawk wasn't in the room any longer.

Over at the wooden smoker, Hawk checked the state of the salmon strips there. Because he needed something for his hands to do.

Jesus, he'd sent her right into a fucking panic attack. What the fuck had he been thinking? That she was *interested* in him?

Not hardly. She tolerated him because of Aric, because her kid needed him. She might even like him in a friendly way. Not because she saw him as a man.

Pretty fucking familiar, wasn't it?

He rubbed at the ache in his chest. He hadn't intended to

scare her, but hell, it seemed that she saw him as being as terrifying as her rapists.

Most women did.

The knowledge was bitter. Because he...liked her. Liked everything about her, from the haunted brown eyes to the thin, callused hands. The way she adored her kid and the unhappiness she showed when she had to accept charity.

He liked her spirit, her courage...and yeah, he was a guy, so he'd noticed the sweet breasts, the curve of her hips. He wanted her in his bed, under him and over him. If she wanted to sit on his face, he'd be all for it.

Instead, he'd scared her into nearly puking.

Now, every time she looked at him, she'd want to run—be looking for those escape routes she'd just learned.

Way to go, asshole.

A minute later, he heard Aric's high little voice. Over at his house, they were leaving. Obviously, Kit wasn't sticking around to eat pancakes.

He pulled in a slow breath, unhappiness settling like an unbalanced load in his gut. The Hermitage was home, his sanctuary, but Kit *needed* to be here. She didn't have anywhere else to go while she finished recovering.

She wouldn't accomplish much healing with him here, scaring her.

Aric was pretty much back to normal. If he had his mom, he'd be fine. Hawk wasn't his security blanket any longer.

No point in hanging around, was there? He let out an unhappy sigh. Time to go shut up the house and get his ass out of here.

That evening, Kit was still waiting for Hawk to return.

A while after her panic attack, before she'd mustered the courage to find him, she'd heard a motor in the courtyard. She'd run outside to see his plane taking off from the lake. Water streamed off the floats and glittered in the sunlight.

Now, supper over, the Hermitage people—except Hawk—were in the gazebo, having drinks.

And singing.

She really did love the musical evenings. Regan, who was learning violin, and Audrey, who was new to the guitar, joined in on the easy tunes. JJ occasionally played her flute.

Between Caz's knees, Aric "helped" him drum.

Oddly enough, her son didn't seem concerned about Hawk's absence, which was such a relief. If he'd started crying for Hawk, she might have joined in.

Boy, she'd really messed up.

Hawk had been trying to help her. Giving her advice, being blunt and teasing as a friend would.

Then she'd gone and hugged him and touched him. Like, in a sexy way. Because she was...interested...in him.

Talk about stupid. No guy wanted another man's dirty leftovers.

And she was definitely used goods. She swallowed, feeling as if she'd rolled around in the chicken yard and everyone could smell the filth covering her skin.

Hawk probably could too.

To complete her humiliation, she'd had an ugly meltdown right in front of him. How absolutely pitiful. If he hadn't already realized she was damaged, she'd sure made it clear.

No wonder he'd walked out of the house.

As they were finishing up another song, multiple phones chimed with incoming text messages. Gabe, Bull, and Caz checked their cells.

When Bull scowled, Frankie asked, "What?"

"Seems Hawk's taken an undercover job down in South America for a friend who needed a pilot and extra guard."

Guilt swept over Kit, darkening her world like the blackest of nights.

It was her fault.

He'd left his family—his home—to escape her.

"If he's undercover, he won't get in touch until after it's over," Caz said.

Gabe's brows drew together in annoyance. "It doesn't say when he'll be back." After making a growling sound, he shook his head and texted something back.

"What did you say?" Audrey asked, leaning against his shoulder. "Nothing too angry...?"

"No, Goldilocks." Gabe sighed. "Although I might pound on him a while when he gets back."

Bull chuckled. "Good luck with that."

With a rueful smile, Gabe flipped him off, then turned his attention back to Audrey. "I just sent him what Mako used to say whenever Hawk took off from the old cabin."

"Of course." Smiling slightly, Caz looked up to where the mountains met the sky and said softly, "Soar high, *'mano.*"

CHAPTER THIRTEEN

E *ach time women gather in circles with each other the world heals a little more.* - Unknown

Almost a week later, Kit was getting ready for her group session at the counseling center. She still wasn't comfortable with it, but the anxiety was decreasing. Sitting on the bed, she pulled on a pair of jeans and a loose top—one that would survive tears.

She walked down the hallway and out onto the deck. JJ had volunteered to watch Aric along with Regan, and her son was already over at Caz's house. Or not. She spotted JJ and Regan on the patio, but Aric was...

Aric was near the dock, although not past the yellow line Gabe had spray-painted on the grass. The no-children-past-this-line boundary.

Holding a maroon-colored blob—a stuffed animal or something—her son stood, staring at the dock. As he had, several times a day, since Hawk had left.

Like her, he was probably seeing the bare place where the floatplane should be.

Shoulders slumping, Aric shoved the maroon object into the hoodie's kangaroo pocket and trudged up to the house and onto the deck.

"Hawk didn't come home, Mama." The tears in his eyes simply broke her heart into pieces.

Damn Hawk anyway. How could he do this to her baby?

Dropping into a deck chair, she pulled Aric close, hearing the almost silent sobs.

Tears filled her own eyes. "Hawk will be back, honey. I know he will."

But maybe not soon, and little boys of four years didn't understand time. Days flashed past for her. For Aric, the hours were so very long.

Damn you, Hawk.

She wanted to hit him for every single tear her son cried. But how much of this was her fault? He wouldn't have left his home and his brothers if she hadn't been so very stupid. How could she blame him for escaping from an awkward situation?

If only he'd call so she could explain.

Yeah right. Hawk—have an uncomfortable conversation on a phone? That would happen about never. And Gabe had mentioned if Hawk was undercover, he wouldn't call home.

"Hey, Aric," Regan yelled from next door. "C'mon. We're gonna look for tadpoles."

Kit lifted her head and saw JJ watching with an understanding expression. Yes, she'd undoubtedly been in the same position— unable to help a heart-wounded child.

Moving her boy back a step, Kit wiped his damp cheeks with a tissue she'd stuck in her pocket in anticipation of a stormy group session. "Here you go, honey. Blow your nose. Then give me a hug since I have a meeting to go to tonight."

He did and then trotted off the deck, heading for Regan.

Sirius streaked across the grass, then slowed and followed at a dignified distance, puffy tail held high.

Aric crouched to pet the giant cat, and his little chuckling laugh carried up to Kit.

Okay. Okay then. He'd be all right. For now.

Come home, Hawk. I'll stay away. Just...come home.

An hour later, in the town of Soldotna, Kit sat in a circle of women.

The room in the counseling center was soothing enough. The pale green walls, warm lighting, and thriving philodendrons created a calm atmosphere. Chairs upholstered in blues and greens sat a comfortable arm's width apart in a circle.

And yet...

Group counseling sure wasn't for cowards.

Across the circle from Kit, Fernanda cried while telling how she'd hidden in her house for a month after being raped. Unable to leave, unable to sleep, spiraling down and down. "And then my sister, she pounded on the door and used her key and came inside."

"Oh, thank god," someone whispered, and Kit felt the same.

"She..." Fernanda smiled a little. "Big sister. Bossed me into the shower, into eating, and when I couldn't sleep, she crawled into bed with me. And eventually, I could tell her what happened."

"Talking about it is hard, isn't it," Diana muttered and got a chorus of soft agreements.

"She was with me when I left the first time. Got me into a counselor." Fernanda shook her head. "And I am back to work again."

Kit joined in the gentle applause.

Every woman in the group was a survivor of sexual assault. Their attackers had been spouses, dates, and strangers. With some women, the abuse had occurred years in the past. A few, like Kit, were only weeks or months away from the assault.

Kit hadn't felt as isolated as the others here, probably because the women in the PZ compound had been abused. To avoid being beaten, most of them submitted to their husbands and to the "cleansings" by Parrish and Nabera. And each time, she'd felt used. Like a thing. But at least she'd had the other women there. They'd offer each other silent support—a surreptitious pat on the shoulder, an extra ladle of soup, a quiet smile and sympathetic look. They all understood.

Shaking the thoughts away, Kit returned her attention to the circle of women.

Diana was talking about her husband. Last night, when he'd hugged her in her sleep, she'd panicked and run to the bathroom to vomit. He'd held her hair back and given her a washcloth to wipe her face.

Blinking away tears, Diana smiled at the group. "There really are nice men in the world. Now I just have to convince my body of that." Huddling into herself, she whispered, "I just don't know if I can."

Remembering how Hawk's silent gestures of support helped, Kit leaned over and offered her hand. "Need to hold on?"

Diana shook her head no, then choked on a laugh. "God, yes." She gripped Kit's hand hard.

Kit knew the relief of feeling anchored to someone else.

And deep inside, she could feel her own healing. She wasn't broken completely if she could still help someone else.

CHAPTER FOURTEEN

When I hear somebody sigh, "Life is hard," I am always tempted to ask, "Compared to what?" - Sydney J. Harris

How long had Hawk been stuck in this damn billionaire's mansion in Brazil? He tried to count off the days. Almost two weeks? Seemed like fucking forever.

Last week, the Hermitage would've celebrated the Fourth of July. Not with fireworks since sunset was around 11:30, and the sky just didn't want to darken. But there would've been grilled salmon and various dishes from the garden's produce. Vegetables grew like crazy when the sun barely set. JJ probably made a cake decorated for the holiday, so Aric would've been on a sugar high. Hawk could almost hear his giggles.

No matter how crazy the kid got, Kit would still look at her boy with those soft eyes.

Jesus, he missed them. All of them. Especially Kit and Aric.

How the fuck had that happened?

Growling under his breath, he picked up his eReader and paged to where he'd lost the thread of the story.

A few minutes later, Zander deVries walked into the two-bedroom suite they shared. The hard ass ex-merc was laughing.

"What's so funny?" Hawk growled.

"The cook thinks we're brothers."

"Yeah?" Hawk eyed his friend. They were the same general build—thickly muscled and 6'2". They both had short, dark blond hair. Hawk had a trim beard. Both were fair skinned with deep tans and light eyes, though deVries' were grayish-green rather than blue. "Maybe."

Although deVries had grown his hair out to look less like a bodyguard, an observant pro might ID him from the way he moved and the cold, evaluating gaze.

Another way they were similar, Hawk admitted.

"You know, if you want to be my brother"—deVries grinned—"you'll need a whip."

"Fuck no. Get me a beer instead."

"Bro, sadists have more fun." Laughing, deVries retrieved beers from the small fridge.

"Hard pass." That was another result of a crappy childhood and abusive father—the thought of hurting someone for fun was nauseating.

To each his own, and, at least, deVries didn't play his BDSM games without full consent. "I've got enough brothers, thanks."

"You got good brothers." At Hawk's look of surprise, deVries added, "Met them at Mako's funeral. I was there, guarding Zachary Grayson."

"Right. Bull mentioned the doc had a bodyguard." Hawk hadn't even heard about Mako's death until after he returned from a merc assignment. "The sarge probably enjoyed having a gunfight at his wake."

"It did get lively." After handing over a beer, deVries dropped onto the fancy-ass sofa.

Hawk nodded his thanks for the drink. "How's the client?"

"He'll be up and around soon. Until then, we're stuck here

with nada to do. Dammit, who ever heard of getting pneumonia in the summer?"

"Sucks to be him." Hawk had gotten so fucking bored, he'd gone shopping yesterday and then remembered how much he hated that shit. But he'd found a hoodie the kid would like. If he ever got home to give it to him.

He'd wanted to buy something for Kit, too, but that would've been the ultimate in stupidity.

Hawk drank down some beer to clear the ache in his throat. "Gotta say, this might be a crap job, but the jet and helicopter are sweet."

Especially the jet. It was why deVries had wanted Hawk, since he was rated to fly small jets. In Alaska, Hawk traded helicopter flying time with a pilot who owned a small private jet so they'd each get enough hours to keep current.

"At least you get toys. Fuck, but I miss my woman."

"Never figured you for permanent." The sadist was more of a fuck 'em and leave 'em sort. Or had been. "How long?"

"Closing in on three years." Smiling, deVries said, "I started to fall when she told me I probably couldn't find my ass with a flashlight and a search warrant."

Hawk stared. The woman had balls, big brass ones.

"I knew I was in trouble when I found her defending a kid from a gang," deVries chuckled, "and her crap-shit apartment had rodents, and she'd named the mouse François."

Courage, big heart, sense of humor, naturally deVries had fallen hard. Fuck, and now Hawk was missing Kit, and she sure wasn't his. She'd probably not even noticed he was gone.

Aric would've. But Hawk had talked to him, prepped him. With luck, he wasn't taking it too hard.

"But not having Lindsey here means that out-of-country assignments suck ass," deVries said.

Hawk blinked. "Why'd you take it? You're senior enough to pick and choose."

"The client's brother is a friend of Simon's," deVries grumbled. "Simon asked me to do it as a favor."

Simon owned Demakis International Security, which had a sterling rep in the industry. He was not only deVries' boss, the two were friends. It was tough to refuse a buddy's request...as Hawk knew.

Leaning back, deVries thumped his feet onto the coffee table. "He didn't realize how long this would take. The briefing implied the bastards would act right away."

Last month, Sanchez escaped an attempted assassination and discovered an old enemy had contracted a hit on him. Since the timing indicated someone on his staff was taking bribes, Sanchez hired Simon's company to expose the traitor. He'd pay a bonus if the next attempt on his life resulted in enough gore to deter future assassins.

Hawk had a cynical feeling the enemy wouldn't last long after this.

The problem was that the hitmen hadn't made their move yet. "Now what?"

"As soon as Sanchez is up and around, we'll go easy until he's back in his routine. Then we'll scatter bait for the informant. Leave the perfect opening to score a kill." With a shake of his head, deVries added, "It'll just take longer."

Hawk grunted, tempted to say he was out.

"Sorry about this, Hawk. But I'm damn glad you were free. There's not many I'd trust to have my back for a bait and switch."

Hawk sighed. He and deVries had worked as mercenaries in different outfits. Been in fights together. He couldn't leave a friend in the lurch.

Not even to get back to Aric and Kit.

Dammit, Kit. He should have stuck around and talked to her. But he was shit at talking. And face it, she'd panicked because of what he'd done. Who he was.

Eyes narrowed, deVries gave him a questioning look. "You good?"

"Yeah." Hawk took a sip of beer. "Bait and switch?"

"Exactly. We bait the hook with what looks like an easy kill. Then the switch."

"They get us instead." *Surprise.*

With two tired children in the backseat, Kit was filling up her car at the Rescue gas station. It'd certainly been a full day. First, she'd bought a car. Happiness bubbled up inside her, and she gave the steering wheel a pat. The Jeep had more than a few dents, but it meant independence. And it was red too.

To celebrate her new ride, she'd taken the kids to the town park. While they explored the small playground, she'd stretched out her sore muscles. Frankie and JJ had no mercy when it came to teaching their forms of self-defense.

Thigh muscles could really hurt.

As the pump dinged, she put up the nozzle and replaced the cap on her Jeep's gas tank. "All done, kids. It's time to head home."

"Hey, there's Papá." Regan pointed toward the other pump.

Kit turned to see Caz talking to the owner. Seeing her, the doc excused himself and strolled over.

He ran his gaze over her car and nodded. "Very nice choice." Bending to look in the open back window, he smiled. "Regan, Aric. You two look as if you had a good day."

"We were at the playground, Papá. It's got a climbing thing now."

Kit grinned. The mini-climbing wall let Regan get up to the tallest slide.

"Ah, that does sound fun, *mija*. And Aric, did you climb too?"

Aric waved his hands. "I roded a dinosaur."

Caz's brows drew together. "Do we have dinosaurs in Alaska?"

Snickering, Regan informed him, "No, Papá."

"There were a batch of animals on springs that bounced," Kit said. "One was a T-rex."

"A tyrannosaurus. That was very brave, Aric." Caz turned. "Kit. If you aren't on a schedule, Regina, our municipal receptionist, left word she wanted to speak with you."

"About what?"

"I'm certain Regina will tell you." The doc smiled, waved at the children, and went back to talk with Zappa.

Huh. What in the world could Regina want?

Probably a medical paperwork problem. Kit slid into the driver's seat. She could swing by now and deal with the problem.

Once downtown, she parked and walked into the building with Regan and Aric. "You two stay with me."

Inside, she stopped short. Two men stood at the receptionist desk. Rough-looking, with gray hair and beards, they looked like PZs.

Aric squeaked and moved behind Kit. When she picked him up, he buried his head against her neck.

Before Kit could grab her, Regan ran forward. "Hey, Tucker. Hey, Guzman."

"*Regan.*" Kit hurried forward, put a hand on the child's shoulder, and angled to move slightly in front.

Just in case.

Regan gave her a confused look.

"Kit." The receptionist's gaze met Kit's, sympathy showing. "They might look like they kick puppies, but you'll never find nicer guys. They were in the group that busted you and the others out of the PZ compound."

Kit felt like an idiot. This was Alaska, for heaven's sake. There were rough-looking men everywhere—and she needed to get past the way she reacted.

The shorter man eyed them. "Who're your buddies, Regan?"

"She's Kit." Regan patted Aric's leg. "He's Aric. Those pissers were mean to him, so he's kinda scared of guys. But he's okay—he's not a stupidhead or anything."

As Regan talked, Regina was saying on her phone, "Hey, Audrey, want a couple of kids?"

"Not a stupidhead. That's good to know." The man with a bulbous nose gave the girl a solemn nod.

Mouth almost hidden by his full beard, the other man nodded at Kit. "Miss, I'm Tucker. This is Guzman."

Balancing Aric on her hip, she held her hand out. "Tucker, Guzman. I can never express how grateful I am for the rescue. Thank you so much."

"Oh, hey, now." Tucker flushed and shifted his weight.

And she realized in surprise...he was shy.

"Nah, no thanks needed." Guzman took her hand and gave it a gentle squeeze. "It was a kick in the pants to get to help out."

Regan bounced on her toes. "Can we go fishing again soon?"

"If your pops says yes." Tucker bobbed his head. "Audrey said she wants to go too."

"See, now, Tucker?" The other man shook his head. "We'll have to give that Gabe a lecture. He's getting' busy with po-lice work and forgettin' to cast a line now and then."

They obviously knew Gabe, Audrey, and Caz, if Regan went fishing with them. Kit relaxed.

"Tucker, what good timing." Audrey crossed the lobby to the receptionist desk. In tan jeans and a button-up pink shirt, she looked casual, but professional. "The movie you requested came in today."

Guzman's smile appeared within his thick beard, and Tucker's grin was even wider.

"Be worth running the generator for a couple of hours," Tucker said to Guzman. After nodding to Kit and Regina, the two men headed toward the stairs to the library on the second floor.

Audrey smiled at Regan and Aric. "Kit and Regina are going to talk about boring stuff, but I have coloring books and picture books."

Regan edged closer to Audrey and whispered, "Can we get a Coke on the way up?"

Kit smothered a laugh. Regan's father had firm opinions about what children should eat, and sodas weren't on the list. No one at the Hermitage was strict about following Caz's rules—and Regan knew it.

"Yes, but only if a Coke means I get quiet children in my library." Audrey glanced at Kit. "Bribes are an accepted practice in child-sitting."

"Absolutely." When Aric squirmed to get down, Kit laughed. "Are you sure you want two children on your hands?"

"I'll love it. The library closes in half an hour, so go run errands, and I'll drive them home. I still have one of Aric's seats in my car."

Over the past weeks, the people at the Hermitage had acquired extra car seats and passed them around as needed.

"If you're sure, then thank you." As her son and Regan followed Audrey like quiet little mice, Kit shook her head. "I'll have to remember the power of a bribe."

Regina grinned. "A mother needs many tools in her parenting toolbox."

"Look how big he's getting. I swear, just yesterday, he was just a tiny baby." Kit made a cradle of her arms. "And now? I'm going to need bigger tools."

"For sure. Wait until he's a teenager. I needed a whole new toolbox then." Regina shook her head solemnly, then smiled. "Do you have a minute to talk?"

Worry swept through Kit. Did she owe money for the medical visits? Maybe her benefactor, Doc Grayson, had changed his mind? "Caz said you needed to see me. Is there a problem?"

"Oh, no, girl. I heard you're job-hunting."

Possible employment? Kit straightened to look more job-worthy.

Unfortunately, after playing with the children, she had grass stains on her jeans and dirt streaks on her T-shirt. "Yes. Do you know someone who's hiring?"

"I am." Regina patted her desk. "Right here."

"But..."

"As it happens, I have a beautiful new granddaughter." Regina picked up a photo off the desk to show a two-month-old little girl with wispy hair, a button nose, and a rosebud mouth.

"Ooooh, she's precious."

"She really is." Regina smiled fondly at the photo. "Lauretta doesn't want to lose her job at McNally's and asked me to babysit three days a week. Later, they'll use the day care onsite at the resort, but—"

"But not when her baby is this young." Kit felt hope rising inside. "You want me to be receptionist for the three days you're babysitting until you return to being full-time?"

"That's it in a nutshell." Regina nodded. "Monday, Wednesday, and Friday. The job will be part-time and temporary, but it'll bring in some money while you're still healing up."

Hope rose inside Kit. Rescue's pre-school and summer school were open on those days, and just yesterday, Aric had attended with Regan and done fine. He'd come home filled with enthusiasm about his new friends and the caregiver named Erica. "I think that would work great."

"Part-time will be all right?"

Kit sighed. "Much as I'd love full-time, less is probably better right now. My strength is improving, but not quite there yet."

"Excellent." Regina slapped her hand on the desk. "C'mon around. Let's get started on the paperwork."

"Yes, let's." As hope for the future set up a bubbly sensation inside, Kit sat beside the older woman.

With a job, there would be money coming in. She wouldn't have to move to a bigger town. Could stay where her friends were.

And maybe Hawk would come back someday.

CHAPTER FIFTEEN

There's nothing better than a best friend—unless that best friend has chocolate. - Unknown

Just over a week later, Kit stepped into Bull's Moose Roadhouse and stopped to let her eyes adjust to the dimmer light inside. Halfway through July, the sun was still high and bright at seven in the evening.

The bar always felt warm and welcoming with its golden log walls decorated with antlers, antiques, and pictures from years past. What with it being Friday during tourist season, the tables were mostly filled.

"Hey, Kit."

She smiled at the greetings from Tucker and Guzman, who were seated near the door. "Hi, guys."

Obviously hearing, Felix turned and waved. The slender, flamboyant server was one of the friendliest people she'd ever met. Working in a restaurant and bar was totally his jam.

"Hey, kittycat." He headed across the room. "How's the homework going? Want a squeeze?"

After the Fourth of July, she and Frankie had been here, drinking piña coladas to celebrate summer, and Felix had joined them.

Being out of drinking practice, Kit had gotten chatty and confessed she was having trouble being touched because of the PZs. She told them she'd assigned herself the homework of giving and accepting hugs.

"My hugs are getting so much better." She held her arms out and wiggled her fingers. "C'mere."

Laughing, he let her give him a hug, waited a second, then hugged her back.

When he let go, they were both grinning.

"I give you an E for Excellence." Felix pointed to a table in the corner where JJ, Frankie, and Audrey were sitting. "Your crew of troublemakers is over there."

"Thanks, Felix." She patted his arm. "Really. Thanks."

"Girl, I'm here for you anytime you want a hug. But for anything sexier, you'll have to find a different stud-muffin." He batted his eyeliner-rimmed eyes.

She laughed. And her mind immediately supplied a picture of Hawk's rugged masculinity, how his solidly packed muscles flexed beneath his T-shirt, and the disconcerting way his steel-blue eyes could turn so gentle when he looked at Aric...or her. Now there was a stud muffin—and it was pitiful she should be thinking that.

With a wave, Felix headed back to his customers, and Kit went the other direction.

"Hey, people." She greeted the women at the table. "Sorry I'm late."

"No problem." Frankie pushed a chair out for her. "I was hoping there wasn't an emergency or anything."

"No emergencies. Caz had a backlog of patients, and I didn't want the last one sitting in the lobby alone, so I stayed until she got in to see him."

"That's what Regina does, and Caz really appreciates it." JJ smiled her approval.

Audrey poured a glass from the pitcher of sangria and handed it over. "How is Aric doing with the summer school?"

"Really well. He's handling it far better than I thought he would." And hadn't that been such an amazing relief? "Hawk leaving without warning was hard on him. He still keeps running down to the dock to see if he's returned."

Every time her son cried after visiting the dock, she wanted to yell at Hawk...and then she'd remember she was the one who'd driven the man away.

"I get it. I check the dock for his plane too." Frankie shook her head. "Who would've thought that someone so quiet and—face it—grumpy, would make such a hole by leaving?"

As the other two nodded, Kit's guilt increased, and she hastily changed the subject. "I'm so glad Aric has Regan at the school with him. He says she watches out for him. You should be proud of her, JJ."

"She's an incredible kid," JJ agreed.

Audrey smiled "And just as protective as her daddy—and her mama."

JJ flushed. "I never thought I'd love being a mother so much, and I'm so grateful mine was such a good example."

"It helps. From the little I remember, my parents were amazing." At the questioning looks, Kit added, "They died when I was ten, and I went to live with my aunt and her husband."

Frankie made a face. "From what you've said about your aunt and uncle, they sound an awful lot like PZs."

Which was why Kit had moved out of their place before even graduating high school.

Audrey wrinkled her nose. "Ew. I can't imagine being raised by Patriot Zealot types."

"They weren't pleasant." Kit ran her finger around the condensation on her glass. "I told my therapist I must be really stupid to marry a guy like my uncle. She said it wasn't stupidity, but that, when stressed, it's easy to be drawn to someone who feels familiar, like someone from the past, especially if that someone had a major effect on you."

"Even a harmful effect?" Audrey questioned.

"She said it didn't matter. The familiarity was what sucked a person in."

JJ blinked. "You know, that might explain some couples who don't seem to belong together at all."

"That's why I was so receptive to Obadiah," Kit said. "My first husband had died, and I felt lost and alone, and here was a take-charge guy who had all the answers. It seemed like we fit."

"You totally didn't fit," Frankie growled under her breath. "But familiarity—that makes sense."

"Ooooh, speaking of strong men... Kit, might I interest you in some book boyfriends?" Audrey dug in her bag and handed over two library books. "I checked out a couple of westerns for you since Frankie said you'd been reading Hawk's."

Wow, how awesome was this? "He got me addicted to westerns but, Audrey, I don't have a library card."

Smirking, Audrey tapped the card sticking out a book. "You do now."

Kit took the card and saw KIRSTEN SANDERSEN in official lettering.

Seeing her birth surname rather than Obadiah's, she felt something snap home, as if she'd reclaimed another tiny piece of herself. "Thank you. Really, thank you."

"Hey, I love adding people to my library rolls. Next, I'm going to get you to join one of our book clubs." Audrey frowned. "Only we don't have a discussion group for westerns. Would you like romance, maybe?"

Kit snorted. "I haven't read one since I met Obadiah. He didn't approve of romance novels."

"Too much competition. He was probably afraid you'd realize

he was lacking." Frankie poured herself more sangria and refilled the others' glasses. "Bull loves when I read a hot romance, because I usually jump him afterward."

Jumping a man. Having sex. Kit pulled in a breath. Over the past couple of months, the notion had gone from nauseating to interesting. Almost tempting, even.

Frankie was watching her, probably remembering, of the two of them, Kit had been the one more interested in sex.

Someday, it would be true again. It *would.*

"By the way, I bought presents when I was shopping with Bull in Anchorage," Frankie announced.

Audrey tilted her head. "What's the occasion?"

"Because I wanted to?" Frankie tried to look embarrassed and totally failed. "Ms. Librarian, you know how you're a sucker for office supply stores? That's me when it comes to bed-and-bath shops."

"So true. If you're with her, avoid those shops like the plague." Kit rolled her eyes. "She'll sniff every candle, fondle all the linens, test the lotions."

"Naturally. And—ta-da—even the Hermitage can have luxuries." Frankie plopped three gift bags on the table. "These have lotion, foam bath, and body wash. Audrey, yours is the one with a hint of lemon. JJ, orange and cedar. Kit, you get the lavender-vanilla combination."

As JJ and Audrey oohed and ahhed, Kit opened the top of her lotion and sniffed. Lavender was good for relieving stress and enhancing relaxation. Mingling with the clean, crisp scent was the lovely fragrance of vanilla.

"Thank you. But that was sneaky, Yorkie," Kit said, using Hawk's nickname for the New Yorker. By giving gifts to the three of them, Frankie'd ensured that Kit couldn't protest getting charity.

"Devious, that's me," Frankie said smugly, not at all fazed. Not much upset her—and when it did, everyone knew. She'd yell, swear, and cry with equal ease.

Wouldn't it be nice to be so uninhibited? Or to be as comfortable in her skin as Frankie was?

Kit had liked her own body...before. Now, after the PZs, it sometimes felt as if her body was a hotel room where no one lived. As if her mind wasn't linked to it at all.

The counselor had told her she should try getting in touch with her physical parts. Like, *hey, breasts, how are you feeling today?*

Kit had laughed at the time. Today, though... She picked up the gift bag. Maybe it was time to get back in touch.

CHAPTER SIXTEEN

Q : *What's the difference between God and a Night Stalker?*
A: God doesn't think he's a Night Stalker.

Hawk squinted against the blinding sunlight, then donned his sunglasses as he strode across the long expanse of tarmac. In the cloudless sky, a plane buzzed like an annoying bee as it circled, then came in for a sweet touchdown.

Pleasure swept through him. If he couldn't be in Alaska, at least he was around planes. Speaking of which...

Yeah, there was Sanchez's jet. The small executive airport had excellent service, and the plane had been moved out of the hangar for them.

He headed that way, the light breeze ruffling his uniform shirt. August in Brazil was pretty—although damned if he wouldn't far prefer to be home.

Over the past two weeks, he and deVries had tried to uncover the informant in Sanchez's staff. Every few days, a different suspect would be fed advance notice of their boss' plans. Each time, deVries and Hawk prepared a trap. So far, no results.

Today, Sanchez had done the song and dance for his administrative assistant, saying the CEO of his Rio de Janeiro company called, and he needed to be there right away. He grumbled that two of his three bodyguards were out with a stomach flu, leaving him short on guards.

Hawk hoped the trap would be snapped today. He'd met the pompous asshole of an administrative assistant. It'd be a pleasure if the culprit was him.

And it was time the damned assignment ended.

Hawk winced as guilt swept over him. He'd bailed out in the middle of tourist season, leaving his brothers to supervise the repairs and remodeling of the various properties that the sarge had left them.

He'd abandoned the mission that the sarge had given them:

Death has been part of your lives. Time to create something instead. Bring this town back to life. That's an order.

After Mako's death, Hawk had been slow to join his brothers in Rescue, and now, he'd walked out on them. The sarge would kick his ass if he were still alive.

And what about Aric? Was the kid okay? Hawk had done what he could before leaving, but he hadn't intended to be gone this long. Remorse cut like a knife. The boy didn't need more trauma.

With a sigh, Hawk curled his fingers around the dark granite rock in his pocket, the treasure Aric had solemnly given him earlier in the summer.

Maybe he was a fucking idiot, moping over a rock as well as the picture of Kit and Aric in his wallet. But, dammit, he was too far away from them.

If he survived this mission, he'd head home without delay. He'd stuff his feelings for Kit into a box and latch it down good. He'd be fucking polite. Proper.

If getting too close made her uncomfortable, he'd stay at a distance and keep her safe from there.

That would work. It had to. Being away from her—and Aric—

made him feel like he had a hole blown in his chest. He even missed his damn brothers.

All of them.

Yeah, well, focus, Calhoun. A bullet in the brain would fuck up those plans.

With shoulders rounded and taking care not to dislodge the pot-belly padding beneath his flight jacket, Hawk did a slow prep on the exterior of the small jet.

If he ever grew a gut like this, the sarge would reach out from the afterlife and shoot him dead. And slouching made his back ache.

Yeah, it was past time to get this shit done with.

As he went up the steps into the plane, he saw his partner mosey across the tarmac. In a gray-haired wig, glasses, and uniform, deVries was dressed so he'd be taken for the usual flight attendant.

Inside, Hawk secured one side of the cockpit curtain, thus forcing anyone to enter only on the pilot's side. He stationed himself on the co-pilot side.

Quiet footsteps in the cabin indicated deVries was onboard.

Waiting silently, Hawk ran a finger over the creamy leather of the co-pilot's seat and glanced around the fancy cockpit. The passenger cabin was even more luxurious.

What did it say about him that he preferred his sturdy float-plane and his helicopter?

Of course, he'd also loved the Black Hawks he'd flown as a Night Stalker. Who wouldn't get off on having missiles, rockets, and cannons to play with, let alone the ability to fly nap-of-the-earth?

Yet this job brought it home that he didn't miss the action. He'd rather live quietly at the Hermitage and have his battles be against the forces of nature rather than men.

Dammit, he wanted to go home. To get a hug from Aric and

enjoy Regan's snark. To play his violin to the lake. To hang out with his brothers.

To see Kit, even if it meant from a distance.

Pitiful, man. You're homesick.

Lovesick.

From the other side of the curtain came the sound of the passenger door opening. Whoever had entered was trying to be stealthy—and there were several people.

Perfect. As they'd hoped, the killers were here, planning to take over the plane from the pilot and cabin attendant, then ambush Sanchez and his lone bodyguard.

Silently, Hawk drew his firearm and went motionless. His heart rate picked up; his muscles tensed.

Playing the part of cabin crew, deVries would be in the aft part of the cabin.

Unfortunately, the law said the intruders must be given a chance to make their murderous intentions known.

A muted *whap* and thud came from the cabin. That was a silenced firearm—and the sound of a bullet hitting something hard.

Seems like *those* intentions were crystal clear, Hawk figured.

There was the soft whish of clothing brushing against the narrow passage to the cockpit. The curtain beside him rippled as someone pushed it aside to enter.

A big man holding a silenced pistol stepped through. Seeing the pilot chair empty, the killer started to turn, and his finger tightened on the trigger.

Hawk fired. One clean shot of a hollow-point .22 to the brain. Lightweight pistol, but he hadn't wanted any chance of a stray bullet taking out a civilian.

The guy dropped like a rock, and someone shouted.

A knife slashed through the curtain and ripped across Hawk's left forearm.

Fuck. As pain burned across his nerves, Hawk yanked the

curtain back—and shot. The bearded bastard went down. He wouldn't be doing any more slice and dice.

Hawk stepped over the body. He'd only heard the one gunshot from aft. Had de Vries—

His friend came down the center aisle. "How many?"

"Two." Hawk grabbed some paper towels from the server station and put pressure on the slash down his forearm. "You?"

"One." The stink of blood and bowels hung in the air, and de Vries sniffed, then shook his head at the bodies behind Hawk. "I'm glad we're not liable for damage or cleanup. You left a mess."

Hawk snorted. "At least I didn't get blood on the instrument panel." As if he'd ever let that happen.

"Pilots and their priorities. Then again, Sanchez may give us a bonus for the gore." Huffing a laugh, de Vries pulled out his phone. "I'll let Sanchez know we're done here."

When de Vries finished the call, Hawk led the way out onto the asphalt to escape the stench. "Any trouble from Sanchez?"

"We're good. The weasel is ID'd, and that was what Sanchez wanted us for. His regular bodyguards can handle everything else."

Hawk nodded.

"I'm past ready to get home to Lindsey. You know, I used to think men who moped for their wives were pussies."

Hawk grunted. Kit wasn't even his wife, and he fucking missed her.

"You too?" With a smirk, de Vries pointed. "Yeah, I recognize that look. You got a woman back home."

"Not for me."

"Why's that?"

"When did you get so nosy?" When his friend didn't answer, Hawk caved in. "She was married to an asshole in a fanatic militia group, the Patriot Zealots. When we busted her out, her husband was trying to kick her to death. She won't be interested in men—especially an ex-merc."

Frowning, deVries didn't disagree. "Patriot Zealots. They in Texas too?"

"Yeah. Their so-called Prophet was arrested there."

"Thought I recognized the name. Lindsey's Texan. Her family told us about the scandal when they investigated the compound there. The families of the kidnapped women were pissed off and creating a ruckus."

As they crossed the tarmac, deVries glanced at Hawk. "Seems like you're surrendering without giving the woman a vote. You can't win a battle if you don't step onto the field."

Before Hawk could answer, deVries shook his head. "Let's get you stitched up and get headed home."

The Hermitage was a quiet place when Kit walked out onto Bull's deck. Behind her, at the kitchen island, Frankie was talking on the phone with her mother in New York.

Earlier, Bull, Caz, Aric, and Regan had left with a batch of groceries for an off-the-grid woman who was home after a heart attack. Although, someday, she'd have to live with her daughter down in Iowa. For now, the woman was stubbornly staying in her cabin. The guys planned to do some chores while the children helped put the groceries away.

JJ was at the police station, Audrey at the library, and Gabe was probably still asleep. He'd worked late last night when some drunken tourists rampaged through downtown after the bar closed.

Taking a seat on the deck, Kit gave the railing planters a satisfied smile. A while back, she'd switched out the faded spring pansies for bright red geraniums.

Next door, blooming petunias filled the hip-high planters she'd helped Audrey buy for Gabe's deck. The flowers matched his gray-blue shutters.

At the other end of the semi-circle, Mako's entire deck was awash with the autumn pansies she'd been growing to give away. Over the past month, she'd painted the inexpensive pots and macraméd the hangers. Everything was ready now.

The tiny pot at one end was Aric's. Her son had carefully transplanted the purple pansy with his own two hands.

He made her so proud.

And flowers made her so happy—especially the old classics like geraniums, daisies, and petunias.

No matter where a person was, there was always room for flowers. Her gaze ran over the courtyard in assessment. Really, the patio around the grill called out for some flowerbeds or planters to liven up the space.

And down by the dock. Wouldn't it be...

No, bad Kit.

This isn't my home. Not forever. She needed to remember that, no matter how much she loved this peaceful courtyard facing the ever-changing lake. Let alone the view that went upward from lake to the sprawling town to the towering mountains.

In the chicken house, a hen made a *buk-buk-buk-buk* sound, announcing she'd laid an egg. On the lake, occasional quacks came from the ducks bobbing around the dock with their offspring paddling furiously to keep up.

Wasn't it strangely wonderful how the toughest men she'd ever met had created such a sanctuary?

But, really, she was so happy to still be here.

On Monday, after receiving her second weekly paycheck, she'd started phoning around for possible places to live, and Frankie had heard her.

Minutes later, Gabe showed up, sat her down on Bull's deck, and firmly said, since she was ready to be on her own, she'd be staying in Mako's place. Because he couldn't protect her adequately if she lived in town. Because Nabera was still on the loose.

If it'd just been her, maybe she'd have said no, but she wouldn't risk Aric for pride. She'd agreed—and when Gabe had yelled out, "She said yes," cheers had filled the courtyard. Everyone had been in on the plan and waiting for her answer.

They'd swarmed out of the houses and carried her stuff over to Mako's and then celebrated with a meal downstairs. She'd come close to bursting into tears several times that night.

The only one who hadn't been there was Hawk.

He'd been gone since the end of June, and tomorrow was the first of August. Aric no longer checked the dock several times a day but was still missing him.

Kit didn't miss him at all.

And, whoa, look at the lie I just tried to tell myself.

Every single day, she felt his absence, which didn't make sense. It wasn't as if he talked much. Still, he had a way of filling space just by being present.

Whenever Aric did something adorable, Kit would look to see if Hawk had noticed and to share a smile.

And she kept expecting to feel him next to her. She hadn't realized how often he stood beside her until his warmth was gone.

"So, girl, what's got you looking so unhappy?" Frankie handed her an iced tea and took the adjacent chair.

Kit felt her color rise. "Nothing."

"Oh, please." Frankie pointed an accusing finger. "From the way you're blushing, I'd guess a man."

Frankie knew her too well, yet she didn't. "I wish."

At her friend's raised eyebrow, Kit sighed. "I'm better, and I think, eventually, I'll be ready to deal with men. Maybe even have sex again, someday."

After all, she could now get herself off again.

While thinking of Hawk, dammit.

"But?"

"But who's going to want someone like me? Someone who's been...used."

"What kind of bullshit is that? No one will feel that way." Frankie's gaze darkened with anger.

Tears pricked at the backs of Kit's eyes. "They will. He did."

Frankie went still. "Who?"

"Hawk." Kit swallowed hard. "Oh, damn, Frankie, I...I made a pass at him, hugged him, and then—then I had a stupid panic attack, and when I got over it, he was gone. I disgusted him so bad, he left his own home and hasn't come back."

The thickness in Kit's throat grew. "I'm dirty. Used goods." She pulled in another breath. "I drove away the man who'd saved me. Because I'm filthy."

Tears ran down her face.

Taking the iced tea out of her hand, Frankie hugged her—and let her cry.

Confusion mingling with anger, Gabe stayed where he was.

Earlier, roused by Bull's pickup, he'd come onto his deck, discovered he was still exhausted—damn drunken tourists—and had stretched out in a sunny patch beside Regan's cat.

An Alaskan enjoys the sun wherever he finds it.

He'd fallen back asleep and woke when the women started talking. He'd have let them know he was there if it wouldn't have embarrassed the hell out of Kit.

So he heard a lot more than he wanted to. Or expected.

When Kit finished crying, the women headed over to Mako's place.

Sitting up, Gabe rubbed his hands over his face. "For fuck's sake."

Guess that explained the hawk's unexpected flight. However, to hear that he'd rejected Kit for what she'd been through?

Gabe shook his head. That didn't ring true. His brother would never think that way.

But, if she'd made a pass at the taciturn bastard and made him uncomfortable? Would his brother walk away without a word?

Yeah, he would.

Gabe ran a hand down Sirius' sun-warmed fur, hearing the cat's rumbling purr in response. Wouldn't be the first time. Like when Hawk had transferred out of Gabe's merc unit to another with no explanations. No nothing. He'd just left.

But hell, couldn't the dumbass have thought about what his reaction would do to a woman with Kit's traumatic background?

Dammit, Hawk.

CHAPTER SEVENTEEN

I *f your advance is going well, you are walking into an ambush.* – Murphy's Laws of Combat Operations

Hawk stepped onto the dock at the Hermitage and pulled in a long breath of pleasure. Despite the worry about seeing Kit, he couldn't deny the rising sense of contentment.

I'm home.

The flight from Anchorage had reminded him of everything he loved about Alaska. Sunlight sparkling on Cook Inlet. The stunningly jagged mountains. Swathes of vivid pink fireweed in full bloom. Brown bears wading into the rivers for their summer salmon treats.

There was nowhere quite like Alaska.

As he secured his floatplane to the ramp, ducks with half-sized offspring rode the wake from the Cessna's passage

He'd missed out on watching the babies grow. Missed most of an Alaska summer.

Missed seeing Kit healing and hearing Aric's giggling.

With a couple of loud *woofs*, a streak of brown and black barreled down the dock.

"Hey, Gryff." Hawk braced his feet to keep from getting knocked off the dock. Bending to pet the enthusiastic dog, he kept his stitched-up forearm out of harm's way.

At least one of the residents of the Hermitage was happy to have him back. The rest—there'd be some backlash coming.

Hawk walked off the dock onto the grass with Gryff bouncing beside him. Around the courtyard, the family had obviously just finished a Sunday evening supper. He saw Gabe and Audrey, and Bull and Frankie coming out of their houses. The others were still on the patio, probably on clean-up duty.

Good, he'd hoped to arrive after the meal—because salmon wouldn't have been the only thing getting grilled.

"'*Mano*, we've missed you." Caz strode down the slope to greet him with a handshake and half-hug. He studied Hawk with a professional gaze. "How much damage this time?"

"I'm good, Doc." Good thing he'd worn a long-sleeved shirt rather than a tee.

Joining Caz, JJ said in her warm, husky voice, "Welcome back, Hawk."

"You home for good or just passing through?" Bull asked in a loud voice, stepping off his deck.

Yeah, he'd pissed off the bull. Hawk tried not to wince. "For good. It was just a favor for a friend."

"I'm so happy you're back." Audrey pushed forward to give him a quick hug. "We were worried about you."

Blondie was a fucking sweetheart. Gabe better appreciate her.

She was followed by Frankie who also hugged him before stepping back. "You have some explaining to do, I hope you know."

"Dream on, Yorkie."

The quirk of her full lips defeated the glare she tried to give him.

"Uncle Hawk, where've you been?" Regan wrapped her arms around his waist.

His heart twisted with a painful twang. "I'm back now."

Hell, he hadn't thought about how she might take his absence. After losing her mother, her sense of security was probably shaky.

And there was the other kid he loved, dammit.

Partway to the houses, Aric stood next to Kit, both silently watching. Tears pooled in the boy's big eyes.

Fuck. Fuck me. He'd done what he could to keep Aric from worrying. It obviously hadn't been enough.

Hawk went down on one knee. "Hey."

With a heartbreaking wail, Aric ran forward, and Hawk wrapped his arms around the small body.

Crying, Aric held on for all he was worth—and burrowed right into Hawk's aching heart.

Hawk cleared his tight throat. "I told you I'd be back."

"You didn't come. Didn't, didn't, didn't come."

"Took longer than I'd planned." Remorse sliced another gash in Hawk's chest. Time worked differently for a kid. To adults, a month was a drop in the bucket. To a kid, it was a huge part of their life. *Hell.* "I should've called. I'm sorry."

So incredibly sorry. The pain of disappointing the boy, of hurting him, was like a knife to the gut.

Aric's head came up. Surprise at the apology showed in the tear-filled blue eyes.

Hawk's smile failed miserably. Instead, he used his fingers to wipe the wetness from the kid's cheeks. "I'm home now."

"You stay home," Aric said firmly.

"Yeah. No more long trips." He'd just have to suck it up and deal with the discomfort of being around a woman he wanted for more than a friend.

Wouldn't be the first time now, would it?

"I gotta unpack." He stood. "See you in the morning, right?"

He got another hug before Aric ran back to his mama, who was holding a stack of dirty dishes. "He's going to *stay*."

Seems someone had found himself a healthy yell. *Good for you, kid.*

Hawk met Kit's gaze. Her expression was composed and cool...and her lower lip trembled. She gave him a nod, then bent to her son.

Yeah, she was establishing boundaries right from the start. He'd keep his distance.

As they walked away, his chest hurt like he'd come home with a gunshot wound. With a sigh, he rubbed his neck. Time to hide in his cave and get his shit together.

Naturally, that was when Gabe moved forward and told the others, "Give us a minute."

After a second, Caz returned to cleaning up the patio while the rest headed back to their houses.

Considering the shit expression on Gabe's face, Hawk planted his feet solidly on the ground.

"Leaving without warning." The cop looked Hawk up and down. "Guess I expect that kind of dick move from you."

Hawk's jaw clenched. When his brother got on his high horse, the need to plant a fist in his face grew almost intolerable.

"Not sending word if you were alive," Gabe growled. "Same."

Hawk crossed his arms over his chest and set to endure.

"What you did to Kit—that was fucked-up."

Hawk winced. "Yeah, okay. I thought... I misread the situation and yeah, I fucked up."

"No shit. She liked you and thought—"

"Bullshit." Hawk dropped his arms, his hands fisting. "She's terrified of me. Women don't 'like' me."

"Bullshit yourself." Gabe's brows drew together. "You've had a shitload of women."

"Tag-chasers and the ones who get off on being scared. No one wants more than a fast fuck."

"Don't give me that *poor pitiful me* crap." Gabe shoved him back a step. "You've had girlfriends. Like back in Nicaragua with Jami—no, *Jazeera*, that was her name, right?"

Jazeera. The memory of the dark-eyed beauty was a bucketful of bitter dumped on his head. He'd dated her for a month while the merc team recovered from a job and set up for the next. One night, he drank too much—they both had—and told her he was falling for her. She'd laughed at him. "*No, no, big man. You're a god in bed, but not for serious. I just wanted a way to get in with your magnificent brother. Mmm. That Gabe, him I could marry.*"

And Gabe couldn't even remember her name.

"Yeah, *bro*. Jazeera." Hawk's soul was turning to ice. "She wanted to marry my *magnificent* brother. I was just a stepping-stone to get close to you."

No woman wanted Hawk for more. They wanted Gabe. Caz. Bull. All his life, he'd fought the envy. He loved his brothers. Would die for them. But...that shit with Jazeera? That'd gutted him.

Gabe stared for a second, then blew it off, the fucking asshole. "That doesn't excuse the crap you pulled with Kit. I can't believe you—"

Hawk's control snapped. His right hook impacted Gabe's self-righteous chin, getting the bastard out of Hawk's space real nice.

Gabe rubbed his jaw and growled, "Like that, is it?" He waded in, swinging fast and furious.

And then it was down to it.

Growling, grunting, and punching. Taking painful blows, landing harder ones. Lunging forward, retreating. Hawk had more muscles and hit harder. Gabe's talent for tactics evened the playing field.

"*Noooo.*"

At the high-pitched scream, Hawk backpedaled to check for a new attack.

Aric ran between them and shoved at Gabe. "You *hurt* him. You're bad."

"I... No, Aric, we're just having fun. We fight like this all"— Gabe's expression turned to dismay—"Hell, bro, you're bleeding."

Hawk glanced down. The left sleeve of his pale blue and gray shirt was now dark red. Blocking Gabe's punches must have ripped open the stitches. "Yep."

Hawk went down on his haunches. "Kid, c'mere."

Aric's face was dead white.

Shit. Can I mess this up any more? "Aric, I had a...cut, and when we were play-fighting, it pulled the...scab...off."

Behind Aric, Gabe shook his head.

Bullshitting wasn't exactly in Hawk's skill set. He ruffled Aric's hair. "I better put a new Band-Aid on it, huh?"

The kid nodded.

Thank fuck.

Gabe went down on one knee to get to Aric's height. "Bull, Caz, Hawk, and me—we've been fighting like this since we were only a few years older than you. When Frankie gets upset, she yells, right? When we get upset, we throw punches, only we never fight too hard. Not so anyone gets hurt bad. If I'd known Hawk had a...an ouchy"—Gabe glared at Hawk for a second—"I wouldn't have let him fight."

Hawk snorted. "Like you could stop me, cop."

At the retort, Aric blinked, and a tentative smile appeared.

"Get your ass to bed before your mama yells at us." After a quick hug with his good arm, Hawk pointed at the kid's chest, then at Bull's house.

The boy ran off—toward Mako's house.

Gabe sighed and rose.

"They're staying in the sarge's place?" Hawk accepted Gabe's hand up.

"Yeah. She wanted to get a place in town, and I wouldn't let her." Gabe shook his head. "I know you don't like people in Mako's house, but, hell, Hawk, Nabera is still out there."

The thought of the PZs getting their hands on Kit was intolerable. "You did right."

"Huh." Gabe turned and yelled, "Hey, Doc."

At the grill, wire brush in hand, Caz turned. His eyes narrowed, then he tossed the brush onto the table and jogged over.

"*Mano*, what did you do?" He pointed toward his house. "Let's go."

Hawk shot Gabe a disgusted look. "I can sew myself back up."

Gabe smirked. "Now you won't have to." Annoyingly, the bastard followed them onto the deck.

"Sleeve up. Sit." Caz disappeared into his house.

Hawk obeyed. No one argued when Caz was in medic mode.

Inside the house, JJ's voice was audible. "Sounds like the boys are done with their games, Regan."

Hawk almost laughed at her irritated tone. Gabe hadn't lied to Aric—fights were common between the brothers. After the first few times, the women had accepted it—although JJ had waded in a couple of times to smack them if they got rougher than she approved of.

JJ was saying, "While Caz fixes Hawk's arm, can you take his suitcase to his house?"

"Sure." Regan trotted out, slowing to frown at Hawk's bloody arm. Fetching his suitcase from the dock, she pulled it across the courtyard and onto his deck. He winced; it probably weighed more than she did.

She ran back and past him and Gabe.

When he tossed her a two-fingered salute for thanks, she grinned before disappearing into the house.

Good kid. Tough kid.

With a bag of medical shit, Caz sat down on Hawk's left side.

Setting a hip on the railing, Gabe eyed the long slash on Hawk's forearm. "Knife?"

"Yeah." Hawk stayed immobile as Caz injected a local.

Hell, guess he owed his brothers a bit more information. "Remember deVries?"

Gabe nodded. "The merc who joined a security company? He was at the sarge's funeral."

"Yeah, him. He was sent to worm out an informant for a client. The pilot he'd hired had an appendectomy."

"You wanted to be gone for a while," Gabe said thoughtfully, "or you'd have only subbed long enough for deVries to hire someone else."

Hawk shrugged.

"Numb?" Caz tapped near the sliced-up flesh.

After Hawk nodded, the doc efficiently cleaned, stitched, and bandaged the wound.

"Done. Be more careful, *sí?*"

Hawk nodded. "Thanks."

"Mind if we sit here for a bit?" Gabe asked Caz.

"Stay and talk." After setting his bag inside, Caz headed back to the patio.

Hawk glared at Gabe. "What now?"

"Couple of things. The woman. Jazeera. She used you? To meet me?" Gabe's jaw was tight.

Hawk nodded. Her plan hadn't worked, had it? "You hardly remember her." And Hawk had been fucking gone on her. Then again, it wasn't as if he had much experience having a girlfriend.

With thumb and index finger, Gabe rubbed his eyes, then met Hawk's gaze. "I only remember I was glad you found someone who made you happy."

Hard to stay angry when he said shit like that. "I got taken in."

"It's why you quit the unit, isn't it?"

Hawk looked away.

"Fucking-A." Gabe pushed off the railing to pace the deck. "Dammit, I'm sorry. I didn't know. I'd never—we don't—"

The code they'd established as teens meant they didn't poach a brother's girl. Jazeera wouldn't have gotten anywhere with Gabe, even if he'd noticed her.

"Not your problem. Not your fault." His brothers couldn't help being good looking and able to talk to women.

And Hawk had thought he was past that bitterness...right up until Gabe gave him shit about Kit.

Gabe still looked worried. "But—"

"No, bro. I overreacted." Hawk held out his hand in the sarge's way of indicating: *fight over, move on.*

Gabe studied him for a minute, nodded, and they shook hands.

Hawk started to stand.

"One more thing."

Jesus *fuck.*

Gabe rubbed his chin, examined the blood on his fingers. "You got me a good one, asshole," he said mildly. "About Kit..."

Hawk considered punching him again. A lot harder.

"I think there's a"—Gabe grimaced—"Audrey'd call it a miscommunication." He paused as if trying to be diplomatic.

Not one of Gabe's skills. Hawk's either. "Spit it out, for fuck's sake."

"She thinks you left because she made a pass at you, and you were disgusted. That you see her as dirty. As used goods."

The words hung in the air, not making any sense. Hawk tried to pick them apart, phrase by phrase. *Made a pass at him?* He'd thought that at first, and that's why he pulled her closer, only she'd...

Abandoning that memory, he went on to the next phrase. Kit thought Hawk had been *disgusted?* What could he possibly be disgusted about?

Next phrase. See her as dirty. As... "*Used goods.* What the hell?"

"Ahhh." Gabe glanced at Hawk's fists and held up a staying hand. "Law enforcement—we get training on dealing with sexual assault. In our screwed-up society, a woman who's been raped often blames herself. Feels dirty. Used."

Dirty. Used. Because some fucking bastard attacked her? She thought *Hawk* saw her that way?

He rose. "We done?"

"Yeah." Gabe palpated his ribs, and a corner of his mouth tilted up. "You hit harder than you used to. I'm going to curse you when I get out of bed in the morning."

"Same." Hawk headed down the stairs, hesitated, turned. "Thanks. For the intel."

Without it, he'd never know about this...miscommunication. Bullshit word. This was a total goatfuck.

Realizing he was still bloody, he headed to his own house.

Shower first, then he and Kit would have a *chat*. And there'd be no fucking *miscommunication*.

In the bathroom in Mako's upstairs apartment, Kit sat beside Aric as he splashed and played in the tub.

Determinedly, she pushed Hawk out of her thoughts to focus on the here and now.

It wasn't easy, especially since, when she'd been in the kitchen doing dishes, her son had disappeared to check on Hawk again. Aric had returned just as she'd realized he wasn't in the living room where she'd left him.

He knew he wasn't supposed to leave the house without her. But she couldn't scold him very hard; not today when his hero had returned.

In fact, her boy was in a wonderful mood. The yellow duck entered the water with a decided splash.

Aric crowed. "Run away, whale. Swim."

The bright blue whale squirted water, thankfully not too high, as it tried to escape the oversized duck.

Who would have thought rubber ducks had a feral side? That orange beak might give any animal second thoughts.

When the whale escaped, Kit cheered along with Aric. Then tugged his hair. "Time for bed, my man."

Aric eyed her, so she put on her "serious face". With a gargantuan sigh, he unplugged the drain and giggled as the water swirled around his toes.

He dried off—with some help—and she picked him up and swung him out of the tub.

Wasn't that the best feeling?

She still instinctively guarded her ribs and abdominal incision, and her arm ached if she used it too much, but she was pretty much back to normal. Even working as a receptionist no longer wore her out. She was making money and standing on her feet again.

Mostly.

As she followed her naked child into the area the guys had sectioned off as "Aric's bedroom," she sighed. Living here rent-free wasn't exactly being independent.

She'd also hoped to be gone before Hawk returned.

As if following her thoughts, Aric started talking about him, the words muffled as he pulled his pj top over his head. "Hawk said sorry."

The big bad mercenary had apologized to a little boy? "Sorry about what?"

As Aric's head popped out, he struggled to get his arm in one sleeve. "Cuz he didn't come back when he was s'posed to, and he shoulda called."

"He told you he should have called."

"Uh-huh." Aric gave a firm nod. "He shoulda."

Wait a minute. Where had this "supposed to" notion come from?

She studied her child. "Did Hawk tell you he was going to leave? Before he left?"

"Uh-huh. He gave me his ber... His ber... His hat." Squatting beside his small bed, Aric opened the wooden box she'd given him for his treasures. He pulled out a maroon beret.

Huh. She'd occasionally seen Aric carrying it, and she'd thought it was a particularly limp stuffed toy. Regan had given him a few of her old ones.

It looked like military headgear. "That was Hawk's?"

"It's from when he be'd a soldier." Aric's eyes were shining with awe. "A pilot."

Kit took the beret. The emblem on the front had the words "Night Stalkers" with a winged centaur holding a sword. "He gave you this?"

"To hold on till he comed back." Aric's lip quivered. "But he didn't come."

She'd hated Hawk for leaving her son without a word. How *could* he?

Yet, she hated herself for being the cause.

But he hadn't just walked away. He'd told Aric he was leaving and offered a token to show he'd be back. "Why didn't you tell me?"

"He said it was a secret." Aric patted the beret. "Our secret."

She really felt like stomping her foot and having her own version of a tantrum. But the secret wasn't one a mother had to know, so Hawk hadn't overstepped the mom-rules.

"Well." Her emotions felt like someone had whisked them into a froth. "I'm glad he made it back safe."

"He got an ouchy." Aric scowled. "He and Gabe fighted, and Hawk got hurt. There was blood."

"He was hurt?" She'd thought Aric had just run back there for another hug.

It took a while, but he told her the story of the fight. Except for *why* the brothers had been brawling.

She'd probably never figure it out. Male reasoning didn't follow logical patterns.

"All right, honey bear, pick out your bedtime story."

———

An hour later, Hawk walked into Mako's place and was oddly reassured the place didn't look different from in the past aside from small changes.

A children's book lay on the sectional, a box of crayons and coloring book on the dining room table. Two small socks had been abandoned near the door.

A juice box on the kitchen counter sat next to an open storage container of cookies. Someone had gotten a bedtime snack.

Wanting his sons to hang out here when at the Hermitage, Mako had furnished his house accordingly. The apartment upstairs had been his private quarters—and he'd decreed the downstairs to be public space.

Since anything in the kitchen was considered communal, Hawk helped himself. Damn, he did love peanut butter cookies.

The pocket door to the apartment upstairs was closed, but he could hear Kit singing a lullaby.

A funny feeling brewed in his gut—like nostalgia for something he'd never had. No one had ever sung to him at night.

After pouring himself a glass of lemonade, he took a seat at the island and waited. The kitchen was spotless, except for the cookies and juice box, which meant Kit would undoubtedly come to tidy up.

Before he could indulge in a third cookie, she walked downstairs and was halfway across the room before noticing him.

There, she froze, obviously unsure of what to say.

Jesus, the two of them were too much alike.

He gestured to her—*keep coming*.

Silently, she approached.

He studied her, pleased with how healthy she looked. Back to a good weight. Skin tanned with a light sunburn on her arms. Shoulder-length, brown hair now glossy with golden streaks.

She moved like nothing hurt any longer. The splint was gone, and she had new muscles in her arms. The slice on her cheek had healed to a pale pink line.

He nodded. "You look better."

"You don't."

A laugh escaped. He'd lost weight, the nightmares of how close he'd come to being gutted meant he was losing sleep, and he'd picked up another knife scar. "Yeah."

She waited a minute, gave up on him talking, and busied herself disposing of the juice box and putting the cookies away.

"I stole a couple. Good cookies."

Her lips curved slightly. "I leave them down here so anyone can help themselves. I'm glad you liked them."

Her voice was the way he remembered. Not husky like JJs, but with a pure, perfect clarity that delighted the musician in him. Her soprano when singing was just as beautiful.

"Kit." He stopped, unsure of what to say next.

She looked up at him, her lustrous brown eyes the color of the mocha coffee Frankie liked to drink. Then she folded her hands over her waist in a way that reminded him of a nun.

In the forest, he could sneak up on deer, on bear. Damned if he could figure out how to sneak up on a conversational subject. So he just put it out there. "I don't think you're dirty. Or used goods."

Eyes widening, she took a step back.

Great, he was screwing this up already. "As a kid, I got beat up. A lot."

Her eyes softened. "Hawk."

"I'm not dirty because of it. Rape is a way of beating someone up—a shitty way, but still. You're not dirty because of it."

Shock had filled her face.

Unable to figure out what else to do, he crossed his arms over his chest. "Yeah, that's what I wanted to say."

She swallowed. "But you left."

"I touched you, and you panicked." After turning his forearms over to show the sleeves of tats, he ran a finger down the scar on his cheek, the one that lifted his lip like he was growling. "I get it. I scare people—and this is a place where you should feel safe."

"You thought I was afraid of you? You left so I'd feel safer?" Her expression changed in the way that the light brightens at dawn when the sun first clears the mountaintops. "You don't scare me, Hawk. You saved me."

He shook his head. "You don't know what—"

"I've seen you with Aric. With Regan and Gryff. Under the scars and tats, you're a really nice person."

Nice? He stared at her.

She pulled in a breath and lifted her chin. "I have a kind of PTSD. Some things—especially with men—swamp me with bad memories, and I'm still trying to figure out what can set me off. The counselor calls them triggers."

PTSD—shit, he wouldn't have put that together with rape and beatings, but it made sense. Fuck knew he'd had problems from his father pounding on him. Like when the sarge'd raise his hand to point at something, and Hawk would duck. "I had that. As a kid. Then after combat. Nightmares. Flashbacks."

"A flashback is pretty much what I had that day." She bit her lip for a second. "I've been practicing hugs to get past it."

"Practicing?"

Her cheeks turned an appealing pink. "In case I had a chance for a do-over." Her gaze dropped. "Although, I didn't think that would happen."

Think *what* would happen? That she'd get a chance to hug him?

Far be it from him to deny this woman anything she wanted. He stepped forward...and pulled up, stalling out.

Way to be a dumbass all over again. "Do-overs are good," he said as gently as he could manage with his shit voice.

When she looked up at him, he opened his arms wide—and held very still.

The next move needed to be hers.

Her breathing stopped. Then she stepped forward and put her arms around him, resting her cheek against his shoulder.

He stayed perfectly still even as he savored the feeling of her body against his and her slender arms around him. Her scent drifted up, a heady mix of lavender and vanilla.

"Both of us are supposed to hug," she said in a small grumpy voice. She gripped his wrists and put them behind her back before resuming her hug.

All right then. Carefully, he hugged her, and with a sigh, she relaxed.

Snuggled.

"Fuck, I missed you." His voice sounded like someone had grated his vocal cords.

Her breathing hitched. "Me too." With a low sob, she started to shake, and then she cried.

Appalled, shaken, he held her, even as contentment welled up inside—because she trusted him with her feelings.

The entire time, her hold on him didn't relax an iota.

CHAPTER EIGHTEEN

When things get out of control and everyone around you is screaming and losing their minds, look for the quiet one and stick to him. He's fixing to cut fence and sort some bastards out. - Unknown

Fog drifted through the forest like ghosts of time past.

Leaning against a tree the next morning, Caz studied his brother with the skill of a medic—and the experience of his own soul-deep wounds.

Last night, he'd visited Hawk to check the stitches, both of them knowing he was really there in case his brother needed to talk.

He hadn't but was in good spirits. Having seen Hawk emerge from Mako's house, Caz had an idea of why...and heartily approved.

This morning, though, his brother seemed enveloped in a murky cloud of pain and memories. Not surprising. Often after a period of happiness, darkness would surge back in, overwhelming the lowered defenses. Thankfully, there were ways to recall the light—love, belonging, satisfying work.

Mako had often retreated into the wilderness to restore his balance. His sons did the same.

Today, Hawk would get some time in the forest as well as receive the best soul bandage in the world—the enthusiasm and laughter of children.

Smiling, Caz caught his brother's attention and signaled him to move north and away from the dirt road.

Hawk gave him a two-fingered salute and obeyed.

There was no summer school today since some of the care providers had a teachers' meeting for the upcoming school year. It was Caz's turn on kid-watch duties, and he'd drafted his brother for a game.

Hawk hadn't argued. None of them would turn down a chance to teach the next generation the sarge's skill-building exercises.

The children's goal was to sneak up and grab Hawk, who would dial down his wariness to about eighty percent.

Although the kids were familiar with the woods closest to the Hermitage, the dense fog changed everything. The thick mist could be more disorienting than darkness.

Caz followed the children at a slight distance, listening for fabric brushing against bushes, vegetation rustling, a bird taking off, and insects and small animals going silent.

He could see Hawk's footprints. Short and light, the children created less sign than Hawk, but there was grass springing back on two paths. The children had separated, probably hoping to flank him. Caz smiled his approval.

Back when Aric moved in, Caz had expected his daughter to display only-child territorialism. But the boy had been so damaged and frightened that Regan's big heart was engaged. Rather than pushing him away, she'd decided he'd be her little brother.

No youngster could have a fiercer protector than Caz's little girl.

Caz shook his head, wondering how he'd been so lucky.

. . .

Heart pounding in excitement, Regan glanced to her left where Aric was supposed to be. The fog sure made everything weird, and he was so little he just disappeared.

Big and tall, Hawk was easier to spot, although he was pretty good at moving quietly in the forest. Not as good as Papá, but no one was as good as him.

I will be someday. I will.

But he was proud of her, and that was just...just dope.

He loved her and so did JJ. Regan sighed a little cuz she'd really like to call JJ Mamá. Anyway, she had uncles and Frankie and Audrey. Having family was *everything*.

Aric had only his mama, although Kit *was* pretty Gucci. Kind of quiet, but she knew everything about the garden. And when she read stories to them, she'd cuddle Regan just like she did Aric.

It'd be major if Kit and Aric stayed at the Hermitage, and then Regan could have a little brother.

Papá and the uncles made a team. She and Aric could be their own team and protect each other like Papá and his brothers.

Realizing the tiny noises from Hawk walking had stopped, Regan froze for a second.

Nothing.

Silently, she moved forward, checking each place her foot would land and avoiding branches that might rustle.

When the fog swirled, she spotted Aric's light hair to her left.

And in front, there was Hawk.

Foot raised, she stilled.

What was he doing? Leaning against a tree, he was staring at...

Bunnies!

Uncle Gabe said the rabbits here were called snowshoe hares, and they turned brown in the summer.

Another one hopped out, and Regan almost squealed. Three little gray-brown bunnies. So cute!

After a minute, she blinked. *Oh, oops. Bad Regan.* Uncle Gabe would be frowning and ordering, *"Focus."*

She totally hadn't.

And Aric? He'd probably lose it worse than her and run toward the bunnies.

No, he was crouched and waiting. He sure acted older than a preschooler. Papá said it was because the pissers had been mean to him. She wanted to kick them all.

Focus, stupidhead. Hawk wasn't moving. *This is our chance.*

Aric turned his head to look at her.

She was team leader, so she pointed to him and made a curving motion. *Go around Hawk.* Aric was even quieter than she was, so he'd be better at sneaking around Hawk

Then she pointed to him again and pretended to snap a stick in half. He knew that signal cuz Papá showed them how to make little noises for diversions—even if Aric couldn't say the word.

He signaled *okay* and headed off.

Taking her time, she crept closer to Hawk.

A stick cracked across the clearing.

Hawk looked that way.

Regan dashed across the small space, slapped his leg, and dove to the ground. *Win!*

Sitting up, she blinked as she heard a really rare sound.

Uncle Hawk was laughing.

Monday evening, as Kit got out of her car in Soldotna, she realized she'd been thinking about Hawk most of the day.

Last night, she'd cried all over the guy. He'd simply held her without talking, making a soothing, growly sound.

After she'd stopped bawling like a baby, she'd rested her head on him and listened to his heart beating, felt how his chest rose and fell. His iron-hard arms were gentle, but...unyielding. He hadn't released her; her crying hadn't upset him.

Being near him was like being enclosed in a bubble of peace. She hadn't felt so sheltered since...

She frowned. There'd been no safety with her aunt or, really, any of the guys she'd been with. Maybe not since her parents died.

In the counseling center, Kit entered the group session room and breathed in the air lightly scented with jasmine.

Taking a seat, Kit exchanged greetings with the others. When the clock hit seven, the counselor started the session, talking about sex after surviving sexual assault.

Kit shifted uncomfortably. Wasn't this just a timely subject?

After the lecture, the discussion started.

A couple of women volunteered that they had no interest in sex whatsoever.

Fernanda never wanted to be with a man again but might have found a girlfriend.

Diana, who was married, had resumed sexual relations, but Signy was having plenty of problems. Her husband had grown impatient at how long she was taking to get back to what he considered normal.

Getting back to normal would really be nice, wouldn't it? Thinking of Hawk, Kit bit her lip.

The counselor, darn her, noticed. "Kit, where are you at in the journey?"

"I'm..." She felt warmth searing her cheeks. "First, I feel weirdly guilty because I haven't lost interest in sex."

"At all?" Fernanda asked, obviously shocked.

"Uh, right after, for a couple of months, even the thought was sickening. But now, things seem alive again, and..."

"And?" Diana prompted.

"I've always liked sex—a lot. The physical parts of it and getting off. I'd like to have a sex life back, only"—she pulled in a breath—"I feel kind of like a slut or something."

The response from the others was so reassuring.

Even better, Fernanda with the new girlfriend felt the same and had the same disconcerting guilt—as if she shouldn't want sex any longer, but she did.

Which was stupid when it came right down to it. Did Kit want Obadiah and the other creeps to steal something she'd always enjoyed?

No, she wasn't about to let them win that game in her head.

"Do you have someone in mind?" Diana asked. "To have sex with?"

"Um, yes?" Oh, God, how could she talk about Hawk?

How could she not?

She almost laughed. Thank goodness the group sessions were in Soldotna rather than Rescue. "He...he's the one I asked to care for my son."

They'd all shared their stories at this point, so Signy clarified, "The one who saved you and killed your husband?"

"You have the hots for your rescuer," another said. "That could be like some hero syndrome or something?"

"Maybe." The counselor frowned slightly. "Tell us about him, Kit. The good and the bad."

Hmm. "He doesn't talk much. Part of it is that his throat was damaged when he was a kid; partly, I think he just doesn't like to talk." She smiled a little. "And he swears a ton and sounds grumpy all the time. He has tattoos up both arms. And scars—a lot of those. He was a mercenary after being in the army."

"Did you know you'd asked a mercenary to watch over your boy?" Fernanda sounded horrified.

"Not at the time. I was pretty shocked when I found out." Kit half-laughed. "And even more when I watched him with his brother's dog. He was telling the dog that he didn't like dogs and the stupid thing should leave him alone. And I thought I really *had* screwed up to trust him with my son."

The women looked appalled.

"But even while he was grumbling, he was petting Gryff into a puddle of happy dog." Kit smiled at the chorus of *awwww*s.

Her smile faded. "Then the jerk took off without telling anyone and was gone for over a month, and I was so mad at him because Aric kept looking for him."

"Yeah, that's a jerk," Diana muttered.

"Only then I found out that he'd talked to my boy before leaving. Even left his military beret so Aric would know he'd be back."

"Something tangible to hold onto." The counselor nodded approval.

Kit exhaled and fessed up. "The reason he took off was because, when I tried to hug him, I had a panic attack, and he figured I was scared of him. Big bad mercenary, right? He didn't want me feeling threatened by his being around. Especially since he likes me."

Signy raised her hand. "I changed my mind. He sounds maybe good enough for you."

"You seem to see him pretty clearly," the counselor said. "And now, you're wondering how to move forward."

"Or even if I should." Kit sighed. "I'm such a mess."

"There aren't many—if any—people who aren't a mess at one time or another. Or lots of times. You've gone through a hellish thing. Try to remember that the people around you could have had their own distressing incidents or phases." The counselor shook her head. "Here at the center, we see people for crappy childhoods, homelessness, car accidents, cancer, amputations, combat, disastrous relationships. Even losing a loved one or child."

Kit blinked. So many things could derail a person over the course of a lifetime. Yes, she'd just had a bad season and had felt much like a drought-ridden, dying plant. But she could almost feel the new green growth in her spirit.

Who would have thought budding out was such hard work?

The counselor looked around the circle. "You all have work to do to get your lives back together. That doesn't mean you're bad or permanently damaged. You're amazing women. Look at you—still moving ahead despite having run into a messy patch."

Her words sank in. Kit could hear the sincerity.

"Okay, back to the interesting stuff," Fernanda said with a grin. "Kit, you've been practicing hugs and touch and stuff. Did it work?"

"It did." Kit bounced a little. "I told him I'd practiced hugging, and he opened his arms, and I hugged him, and then I had to pull his arms around me, and it was wonderful. And"—she rolled her eyes—"and then I cried all over him."

"Oh, no." Diana's brows pulled together "Was he upset?"

"He just held me, and it was great."

The counselor nodded. "There's potential here. From those of you who've gone past hugging, what obstacles did you run into and how did you work around them?"

The ones further on the journey chimed in with their stories and their triggers and workarounds.

The one warning they gave, though, was that—whether Kit's guy talked or not—communication was essential.

And didn't that just suck? Talking about sex was a lot more difficult than just stripping and jumping in bed.

Sex with Hawk.

An unsettling mix of anticipation and nausea swept through Kit as she remembered their first aborted hug and the disaster that had followed.

Huh. Maybe talking wouldn't be a bad idea.

CHAPTER NINETEEN

*W*orrying is like paying a debt you don't owe. - Mark Twain

Tuesday morning, in his dining room, Bull studied his brother. It had always annoyed Hawk when his attempts to hide his emotions behind irritability and a wall of reserve didn't work. But the dark circles under Hawk's eyes were a dead giveaway of stress.

And when he'd flown away without any warning? They'd known something had pulled the hawk's tail feathers.

But he'd come back to them.

"You might've lost sleep while you were away, but you don't look like you lost weight." Bull put a plate of scrambled eggs and hash browns in front of Hawk, then dished more for himself and Frankie.

Dancing a little to the Huey Lewis on the sound system, Frankie set a plate of bacon on the table and added a platter of toast. Gryff took up position nearby.

"Rich client." The corner of Hawk's mouth tipped up. "With a chef."

They settled at the table, and Bull had the gratification of watching his brother chow down with open pleasure.

After a few minutes, Hawk sat back with a contented sigh. "You're a better cook than the fancy chef, bro."

"Hey," Frankie said indignantly. "I made the eggs."

"You, too, Yorkie. Takes talent to make even the basics taste amazing."

"Ooooh, that was a very good compliment," Frankie said. "I guess I'll have to bake something sweet to welcome you home."

Hawk's eyes lit.

Bull grinned. His woman had never been fazed by Hawk's appearance. "It's good you're back. We kept your crew of carpenters busy but haven't had time to check their work."

From what he'd seen, the men seemed solid, but still... Hawk was as exacting about construction as Bull was about cooking.

"I'll get on it tomorrow." Hawk pushed his plate away, empty except for a piece of bacon that he tossed to Gryff.

The dog caught it mid-air and gave a thump of his tail.

"What's planned today?" Frankie asked, saving Bull from trying to disguise the same question. Hawk might answer her; he'd probably shut Bull down.

"Kit wanted help to deliver her flowers."

Bull glanced toward Mako's deck, which overflowed with blooming plants. Tomorrow, it would be empty. "That's a shame; I've been enjoying the view."

"I'm glad you'll be with her," Frankie said to Hawk. "She's going to get all emotional—and she hates that."

Bull expected his taciturn brother to think of ways to bail. Instead, Hawk's eyes narrowed, and then he nodded. "Got it."

Hell, had he missed something going on between Kit and Hawk? Bull eyed Frankie. But she wouldn't share Kit's confidences.

"Is Nabera still in the wind?" Hawk asked.

"Unfortunately. The *stronzo*." Frankie scowled.

"The PZs dropped out of sight again after that mess at the shelter," Bull said. "Haven't been seen since."

Hawk frowned. "Nabera wants revenge on Kit. He won't give up."

"I know. We're trying to keep an eye on her," Bull said. "It was easier before she bought a car and started driving herself."

"Shit," Hawk muttered. When his mouth went tight, Bull knew they'd have one more person keeping an eye out for Kit.

"How's Aric?" Hawk rested an arm on the table, the white gauze of a dressing a reminder of how deadly the ex-merc could be.

"So-so." Frankie tipped her hand back and forth. "He's talking and playing like a normal four-year-old. We're working on helping him with his emotions."

Bull smiled at her. His woman was incredible with children. Someday, he hoped to talk her into a Frankie mini-me. Or two or three.

Frowning, Hawk made a *give-me-more* gesture.

"If he's lonely, hurt, sad, or frustrated, it comes out as anger, and he throws things." Bull shook his head. "Doesn't yell much, doesn't hit. I bet Obadiah threw shit a lot." And kids learned from what they saw.

"What are we doing about it?" A muscle in Hawk's cheek twitched. Bull realized Hawk's whole body had gone tense.

Aric's behavior probably brought some memories back, Bull figured. Because Hawk had been that kid once. Only Hawk *had* hit—and hit hard. Because of him, his brothers knew some of the steps to take.

"Right after you left, he started with counseling. He and Kit have sessions together." Frankie idly stirred the leftover eggs on her plate. "It helps that he's never doubted her love, and they weren't in that PZ camp too long."

Bull added, "We're supposed to help him identify his

emotions. Shit like getting him to talk about what he's feeling and what caused it. Deep breathing."

Hawk was listening intently. "Sounds familiar."

"Like Doc Grayson's assignments for you—and us?" Bull smiled, remembering the early days at Mako's off-the-grid cabin. They'd experienced bad foster care homes and street living. At least, Bull, Gabe, and Caz had started with decent parents. Hawk's father had liked beating the crap out of his kid, and from what they'd overheard when Hawk talked to Grayson, his mother had eventually joined her husband in being abusive.

"You know how..." Bull's voice trailed off at the lack of expression in Hawk's face.

No surprise, really. Bull had tried, hell, each of the brothers had tried to talk with Hawk about his past. And the reticent bastard had shut them down. Just like he was doing now.

Dammit.

Hawk rose. "Thanks for breakfast." And headed out the door without another word.

Frankie looked over at Bull. "That didn't go well."

Over at Mako's cabin, Kit tied her sneakers and looked for Aric.

He was in the bathroom, getting the grass out of his hair. He'd been playing with Sirius outside. "Are you ready, honey bear?"

"Uh-huh." On his step stool, he admired himself in the mirror and put his comb down.

She stilled. Had her baby grown again?

He *had*. Now getting lots of food, sleeping well, and running around like a normal child, he'd had a growth spurt,

Her eyes started to burn, and she gave them a quick swipe. "Very nice job getting ready. That's a great hoodie." The black hooded shirt had a picture of a hawk soaring through a gray sky.

"Hawk got it for me in South 'Merica." Aric patted his chest. "Cuz he was thinking of me."

"Of course he was." Kit lifted him off the step stool and kissed his soft hair. "I'm sure he missed you a lot."

"Uh-huh."

She adored Hawk for the certainty in her son's voice. "Let's get going. Hawk's finished loading the pickup with our presents."

Hawk was awfully quiet on the trip to town—more so than normal. But when he looked at her or at Aric, she could swear his hard face softened.

Maybe he'd just had a rough night?

Once in town, Hawk parked in front of Dante's store. While he released Aric from the child seat in the back of the supercab, Kit slid out and paused.

Situational awareness. A car in the other lane held two gray-haired women. No one sat in the parked cars. A young couple stood hand-in-hand in front of the coffee shop. A man was walking into the municipal building. Two men came out of the sports store.

On previous trips, she'd searched out the safest escape routes. Nothing had changed there.

Finished, she gave herself a mental pat on the back. *Good Kit.*

She joined Hawk as he lowered the tailgate. The entire bed was filled with her plants.

Aric clapped his hands at the pretty sight.

The pansy seeds she'd sown at summer solstice had been transplanted a couple of times into bigger pots. Now, in full, glorious bloom, some were dark blue and white, some purple and violet, the rest a vivid yellow. With inexpensive pots, paint, and macramé cord, she'd created attractive hanging baskets.

Her timing was excellent, since petunias, the usual plant for hanging baskets, were getting scraggly. Her cold-loving pansies would keep flowering for a long time during the fall.

"Which one for Dante, Aric?" she asked.

"This." Her son liked the bicolor blue-and-white flowers.

"All right." Nerves jittering, she picked it up.

Hawk held the grocery store door open, and Aric trotted in with her.

Behind the counter, Dante held up a hand in greeting. "Kit, Aric, y'all are looking good. That's a beautiful pot. Pansies?"

"Um, yes." She pulled in a breath, and her carefully rehearsed speech disappeared. "I-ah-I grew these for you"—her voice cracked—"t-to try to say thank you for helping get me and Aric out of the PZ compound."

For saving us.

Blinking back tears, she handed him the basket over the counter. This was a lot harder than she'd thought it would be.

Hawk's rough voice broke in. "She's been growing them out at the Hermitage. Fixed up the pots. Did the macramé herself."

"Hey, now, that's a purely fine thank you." Dante smiled at her, then Aric. "And you're very welcome. Both of you."

Aric piped in, "We can pick Ms. Lillian a pretty one to match yours. Cuz we are thanking her too."

The white-haired Okie's expression turned soft. "Happens that blue is her favorite color."

Aric's chest puffed out.

"She'll be tickled to have a hanging plant on each side of our door. She loves fancy flowers."

Consulting her list, Kit and her crew continued handing out flowers to the people who'd helped during the rescue.

To her delight, Hawk spotted Chevy and Knox at the post office, fixing a gutter. During the rescue, Kit had been unconscious, but Chevy was the one who'd carried her down the long trail away from the PZ compound. Knox had been there too.

Knox was a tall lanky guy with a bushy red beard. Chevy was short and stocky. She'd gotten to know them when Principal Jones hired her to landscape the new school grounds. The guys had been spending their off hours there building a playground.

Presented with the bright yellow pansies, the two handymen looked flabbergasted, then Chevy grinned. "The missus will love these. I'll be a hero when I get home."

"Yeah? A hero?" Knox studied his plant thoughtfully.

Hawk chuckled. "You still seeing Erica at the summer school?"

Color rose in the handyman's face until it was the same color as his beard. "Mebbe."

Hawk glanced at Kit. "S'okay if he uses flowers to get the girl?"

Aww, the deadly mercenary wants to help Knox with his love life. How sweet is this? Kit smiled at Knox. "The pansies are a thank you for risking your life for me and Aric and should be used however you wish, especially to treat your women. Dante's pot is going to Lillian so she can have one on each side of her door."

"Erica really likes flowers." Knox's smile grew.

The man was totally a sweetheart. "Your lady is lucky to have you, Knox."

He grinned. "Yellow's her favorite color."

"P-perfect, then." Kit forced her lips to turn upward. She didn't want to ruin the moment for him. Bending down, she took Aric's hand. "Come along, my young warrior."

After a minute, Hawk caught up and walked beside her. When they reached the pickup, he stepped in front of her. "What upset you?"

"It's nothing."

His voice turned growly. "Kit."

She pulled in a breath through her nose. "They were sweet, both of them."

"Okay." Hawk's light brown brows drew into a frown.

"It's just... Obadiah gave me flowers only once. On our first date." She could still see that bouquet of red tulips. She'd been so thrilled. Now? She knew she'd never grow tulips again. "He never bothered to learn my favorite color and sure never looked like Knox—happy to be giving me something."

"Ah." Hawk lifted his hand, giving her time to pull back if she wanted, then ran his fingers down her cheek and over her quivering lower lip. "Obadiah was an asshole."

"Obadiah's an asshole," piped Aric, nodding.

Hawk burst out laughing.

Kit stared.

His laughter—it never failed to fill her with joy. When Aric started giggling, her own laughter erupted like a fountain.

Obadiah *had* been an asshole.

And she was well shed of him.

But, oh, dear heavens, the word *asshole* would now be a permanent part of Aric's vocabulary.

When Hawk exchanged fist bumps with her boy, she narrowed her eyes. "You, sir, are going to be the one to explain to his preschool teacher about his vocabulary."

A corner of his mouth tilted up. "Now that's just fucking mean."

———

An hour later, Hawk parked the pickup in front of the Bull's Moose Roadhouse. This was the last stop, he decided, no matter what Kit said.

Every thank you she'd spoken had been from the heart—and she was worn the hell out. The kid needed a nap, and so did Hawk.

After the breakfast with Bull and Frankie, Hawk'd been tense, feeling like he'd fuck everything up for the kid. But Aric hadn't suddenly changed into a spoiled brat—he was the same loveable kid he'd always been. Nothing there to set Hawk off into acting like an asshole.

It'd be all right.

He turned to Kit. "After this, we head home." He waited for an argument.

She tipped her head back against the seat. "I should argue, oh, bossy one, but I'm too tired. Agreed."

Hell. "Sorry." When she looked confused, he clarified, "About ordering you around."

"I know I can disagree, and you won't get upset. That's what matters to me." She leaned over the center console, kissed his cheek—like the touch of a butterfly—and slid out of the pickup.

Leaving him trying to re-assemble his heart.

As she and Aric disappeared into the restaurant, he frowned. About half a dozen of the restaurant staff had helped in the rescue. Since most walked to work, they wouldn't have cars to stash their plants in, and there wasn't room for the flowers inside the restaurant.

He studied the thick posts that supported the overhanging roof of the one-story building. There was heavy-duty rope in his cargo box.

After attaching his rope between two posts, he hung the pots there. The line of flowering plants looked good. Colorful and shit.

Felix popped out of the restaurant, followed by Kit and Aric.

"Holy handbaskets, girl." Felix stared at the flowers. "Those are incredible. And I get one?"

"Absolutely." Kit beamed at Hawk. "What a great idea. Now they can just pick them up on the way home."

"Yeah." Movement caught his attention.

Milo and Orion, two of his carpenter hires, were walking down the sidewalk on Sweetgale toward the roadhouse. Must be their lunch break.

"Hawk." Kit patted his chest to get his attention. "Aric and I are going back inside, but we'll be done in just a few minutes."

She had a hand on him, so it was probably all right to touch back. He ran his fingers through her hair, stroking it back from her face. "I'll be here."

"I know," she whispered.

Her wide brown eyes were more beautiful than any he'd ever seen. Was it because they were always so warm?

She looked down at her son. "Let's go thank Raymond now."

As they headed inside, Hawk watched, then scowled at Felix's wide grin.

"Oops, my bad." The server took a step back. "Would you happen to have carpenter tape in your pickup?"

Hawk gave an affirmative grunt and fetched it.

As he was handing the roll over, Milo and Orion strolled up to the roadhouse.

"Hawk." Milo gave him a chin-lift.

"Hey, boss," Orion said, then grinned at Felix. "Yo, cutie. What's going on?"

"My man, look at these." Felix gestured to the hanging pots. "Remember I told you how we helped save people from some cray-cray fanatics? The woman we really went for—Frankie's bestie—was Kit. Being into gardening, she's giving flowers to all of us who helped bust her out."

Milo stared at Felix, then sneered. "*You* helped?"

Scowling, Orion turned, and one big hand clenched into a fist.

Hell. Hawk stepped between them. Bull got irritable about brawling in the parking lot.

"Not every fight requires fists." Unfazed, Felix smirked at Milo. "I helped with the diversion. We staged a car crash at the front gate to draw off the guards and made enough noise that the others"—he nodded to Hawk—"could get the women and children out."

"Staged a crash?" Orion looked delighted. "You didn't mention that."

"Zappa donated two rust-bucket clunkers." Felix rolled his eyes. "Our piece-of-shit spewed smoke like a forest fire. Anyway, Erica's crew raced ours, and we smashed the cars together at the gate and put on a drunken screaming fight."

"Played right into your thespian talents. Way to go, love." Orion set his hand on Felix's shoulder. "That took guts."

From the looks of Felix's glowing happiness, someone was smitten.

"We weren't in that much danger since the guards totally fell for it." Felix tried to look nonchalant. "The pissers are... Let's just say they're about as bright as Alaska in December."

When the sun barely rose. Hawk grinned.

Orion considered the flowers. "It seems Kit has a green thumb and a good heart."

"They're flowers," Milo snapped. "Big fucking deal."

Hawk stiffened. If the asshole said that to Kit, Hawk would—

"Dude, a verbal thank you is easy. Trying to give something back is far more rare." Orion tugged on his three-inch brown beard and gave a firm nod. "I'm impressed."

"Me too." Felix pulled a pen from his pocket. After writing, "Property of Felix," on the carpenter tape, he attached the strip to a pot of blue-and-white pansies.

Orion barked a laugh. "Ensuring you get the right colors?"

"Duh. The yellow would clash with my décor." Felix leaned against Orion and batted his eyes. "As you know."

Milo's mouth twisted as if he'd stepped in dog shit. After a glance at Hawk, he told Orion, "I got something to do. I'll grab food from Dante's."

As he walked away, Orion snorted. "Not like I wanted to eat with him anyway. Gotta say, boss, he's got some skills, but every time he opens his mouth, I want to punch him."

Felix snickered. "Since Orion's a pacifist, that's saying something."

It was hard-held truth that some people improved after a few punches; Milo might be one of them.

No. Bad boss.

Hawk sighed. "I'll try to find you someone else to work with." And at the end of the month, he'd hand Milo his walking papers.

The door of the restaurant opened. Bull came out with Frankie and stared at the hanging pots. "Give me a minute." He walked down to the parking lot entrance and stood there, studying the roadhouse.

When he returned, he was scowling.

"You're upset?" Frankie put her hands on her hips. "How in the world can you be unhappy with *flowers?*"

"It's not that. Those yellow blooms brighten the place up and would catch people's eyes from the road." Bull ran his fingers down his goatee. "I have a feeling telling the staff to leave their plants here might cause a mutiny."

"Don't you touch my flowers, boss. Uh-*uh*. Mine's already marked." Felix pointed to his tagged plant before hurrying into the building.

Frankie laughed. "I bet he's warning everyone to claim their plants before you confiscate them."

"Figures."

Bull did have a point, Hawk decided. The bright blooms were more effective than any *welcome* sign. He pointed to the horizontal log between the posts. "I could put hooks in that beam."

Arms crossed over his chest, Bull considered and nodded. "Do it. I'll bribe Kit to macramé the right length of hangers for pots."

"No bribe needed." Kit startled Bull, who obviously hadn't seen her come out. "I owe you and Frankie far more than I can ever repay."

The sincerity in her soft voice was heartwarming...because this was who she was. The woman held up her end. Paid her dues.

The sarge would've liked her.

CHAPTER TWENTY

*W*hen it is dark enough, you can see the stars. - Ralph Waldo Emerson

Kit hadn't been to bed long when something roused her from sleep.

Was that music? It was soft. Haunting. Like a violin. As she sat up in bed, it stopped, and she heard the faint sound of men's voices before it started again.

Someone was playing a violin.

All of Mako's sons played an instrument. Hawk was the one who played the violin.

Pulling on the long, fluffy robe Frankie had given her in the hospital, Kit tiptoed down the stairs, across the living area, and out onto Mako's deck.

To listen.

Oh, such a lie. Partly to listen. Partly because simply looking at Hawk made her pulse quicken.

A bit before midnight, the only light came from the thin crescent moon overhead. But she could see him just fine.

He was standing, facing the lake, not even wearing a shirt. Probably barefooted too. The temperatures had dropped into the 40s, but Alaskans seemed to think if there wasn't snow, it wasn't cold.

She leaned against the railing. The music was slow and mournful in the way only a violin could achieve, singing of losses and a sadness so deep it made her chest hurt. Tears filled her eyes and spilled over.

Silhouetted against the pale sliver of a moon, an owl flapped over the lake with the soft *whup-whup-whup* of wide wings.

When the music halted, she straightened to go inside.

Catching the movement, he turned his head. Looked at her.

Rising, he walked inside.

Her throat tightened painfully. She shouldn't have intruded on his solitude. On his music.

Her head bowed. She'd been thoughtless. Unkind.

Then she heard footsteps. With a flannel shirt on, but unbuttoned, and wearing shoes, Hawk came down his deck steps and strode across the courtyard.

Toward her.

Her wish to flee faded as he grew closer. The moon glow lightened his hair and short beard to blond, shadowed his eyes, and streaked the scars on his forehead, his neck, and the side of his face.

His expression was unreadable as he climbed the steps onto Mako's deck.

She straightened. If he was angry, well, she deserved it.

"I didn't mean to intrude." She laced her fingers together. "The music was so beautiful, but I'm sorry for—"

"Intrude?" He frowned, then shook his head. "If I cared who listened, I'd fiddle in the forest." His gaze swung across the semicircle of houses filled with people.

A long exhalation of relief escaped her.

His eyes narrowed. "Worried, huh?" He cupped her chin and

gently brushed the tears away with his thumbs. "You should complain I woke you up."

Her gaze went past him to the dark, quiet lake. "That would be like complaining about moonlight on the water."

He studied her for a moment. "Is Aric asleep?"

"Um-hmm." His unbuttoned flannel shirt gave her glimpses of a very muscular chest.

"Kit." His palm under her chin lifted her head. Her gaze met his. Was that laughter in his eyes? "You're cold. Let's go inside."

"Right." Disappointment rose as he opened the door for her. She turned to bid him goodnight and realized he'd followed her in.

Realized he'd said, "*let's go inside*," not "*you* go inside."

Her heart started a heavy, suggestive beat. "Um, can I get you something to drink?"

"No." He opened his arms. "Hug?"

She couldn't think of anything she'd like better. Stepping forward, she put her arms around him and pressed her cheek against his chest—his *bare* chest.

Shock froze her for a moment, then she inhaled. His skin smelled clean, but of the woods rather than citrus or sage.

His hands settled on her waist, waiting...until she rubbed her face against him. Just the right amount of short, curly chest hair covered his warm skin and hard pectoral muscles.

He looked and smelled nothing like Parrish or Nabera. She tried to push the thought of them away. "Can you talk to me?"

His laugh was wry. "Not much for talking."

Against the warmth of his skin, her lips curved up, because whenever he spoke, his deep gravelly voice somehow firmed the ground up beneath her feet, giving her a stable place to stand. As the shadows of the past dissipated like fog in the morning sun, she tightened her arms around him. "The sound of your voice is all I need."

. . .

What the fuck? His voice? She was hugging him harder, so Hawk slid his arms around her waist. She was so damn breakable. "No one likes what I sound like."

His parents sure hadn't, maybe because the broken sound was their fault.

The women he'd bedded would complain. *"You have a horrible voice." "Don't say anything." "I can't stand it when you speak." "Just shut up and don't talk."*

"I like when you talk." Her exhalation made a warm patch on his chest. "I heard you that night in the compound. When you told Aric you'd take me to the hospital. Would get me help."

Huh. He'd always wondered how much she remembered. She'd been so fucking close to dying.

"To me, you sound like hope," she whispered. "Like safety."

Happiness unfurled inside him, but he knew no way to show her. He stroked a hand down her hair. Soft, silky.

He'd be content to simply hold her all night.

Pulling back slightly, she tilted her head up. "Can we..." Her tongue swept across her plump lower lip. There was desire in her eyes.

"Kiss?"

The dim lighting in the room didn't conceal the way her cheeks darkened. Or her nod.

Setting one hand on the side of her face, he bent and brushed his mouth against hers. Her lips were so soft. Willing but tentative.

He was damned good at rough sex. The women he'd fucked—that was what they wanted.

She was the first to want him to be kind. Gentle.

With his lips, he coaxed, lured...

Giving a tiny sigh, she went up on tiptoes for more.

He gave her more.

How in the world had they ended up on Mako's couch? Still fully clothed, Kit shook her head and almost laughed. Somehow, she was straddling Hawk's hips as he reclined against the armrest. A large erection pressed against her buttocks.

Even better, it didn't upset her to know he was aroused. Instead, the feeling was wonderful.

He *wanted* her.

Smiling, she pushed his shirt open and ran her hands over his hard muscles, enjoying the sensuous tickling of his chest hair. She traced the hollows above his collarbones, then the deeper one at the base of his throat.

As she leaned forward, he tangled his fingers in her loose hair and gave a small tug to pull her down for a kiss.

Everything inside her tightened, froze, and her mind blanked. Fear swept through her. Her arms went stiff, bracing against his chest to keep him from—

"Whoa, eaglet. Breathe." His open hands ran up and down her arms.

It took long moments for his voice to penetrate the fog of fear, to realize he wasn't gripping her. Not at all.

She pulled in a breath, concentrating on what she smelled. The lingering aroma of cookies, Hawk's clean masculine scent, the faint lavender and vanilla from the lotion she'd used earlier.

Under her palms was warm skin.

Outside, an owl hooted. A response came from farther away.

She was at the Hermitage, not in the compound. This was Hawk. "Sorry."

"Nothing to be sorry about. Things'll set you off." Very slowly, he ran his hand through her hair again—carefully not pulling. "We'll avoid them. Or work through them."

He wasn't upset. Relief swept through her. "What did you call me—eaglet?"

"Your hair's like a golden eagle's."

Her eyes narrowed. "But eaglet. Isn't that like a baby?"

"Young." His lips twitched. "Short flights. Crash and burn landings."

She started to laugh. "Like now."

"Nah, you just clipped a wing." He stroked his knuckles over her cheek. "Keep flying."

After more kisses and under his slow, patient hands, she managed to get her robe off. Then the shirt of her pajamas.

And then she had another "crash and burn". Somehow, that sounded so much less fraught than calling it a panic attack.

But look at me.

She was half-stripped. Even if she was shaking and panting. His voice anchored her in safety, brought her back.

And they went back to kissing.

"You're going to go crazy with this forward and backward, and—"

"Woman, I got you sitting on me, kissing me. I'm more than good."

His gruff no-shit response made her glow inside. Because she felt the same way.

Oh, sure, her body wanted more, throbbed for some action down below, but this was simply amazing.

So was he.

None of the PZs let a woman be on top. "I kind of like sitting on you." She bent to kiss him. His lips were firm, yet velvety soft, and his beard was soft too.

"Good." Under her lips, his mouth curved up. "One day, you'll sit on my face."

On his *what*? A shocked gasp escaped her, and then she was laughing. And kissing him. And laughing some more because his rough words had sent heat through her whole body.

Not tonight. But...

Swallowing hard, she sat up, took his hands, and set them on her breasts, and pressed him to her.

At the feel of his warm palms, she sucked in a breath, and every nerve under his hands came to life.

Slowly, gently, he touched her, massaging lightly, kneading. His fingertips teased her nipples to hard aching peaks, then circled. Fondled.

It felt as if her insides were the epicenter of an earthquake, and she whimpered.

He stilled, studying her for a long minute. "We'll go no further than this tonight."

She managed a nod, unsure if she was relieved or disappointed. Both, really.

"No further." A glint of heat appeared in his eyes. "So I'll enjoy the hell out of this much."

His thumb slowly circled one nipple, sending a stream of molten heat to her pelvis.

Over the next hour, he played with her, simply and obviously enjoying himself. Over and over, she'd get so very aroused, and then her desire would fade as ugly memories surged up.

And he'd smile and change his technique and drive her up again. Gently, sweetly, and so very patiently.

Finally, he brushed the hair away from her face. "Time to stop. You need sleep."

As if she'd sleep now, with her breasts swollen and her clit throbbing. At her snort of exasperation, his grin flashed.

He lifted her off of him and rose, then held her pajama shirt for her to put on. As he fastened button after button, his knuckles brushed the insides of her breasts.

She tried to suppress a moan and only half succeeded. The sound of his very male chuckle made her toes curl.

He pressed a quick kiss to the top of her head. "Come and lock the door."

When he was on the deck, he turned and held her chin, bending to kiss her slowly. Tenderly. Pushing her back inside, he closed the door. She could see him through the small window, waiting, arms crossed, for her to engage the lock.

When she did, he nodded. His footsteps sounded firm and solid as he strode off the deck.

Hers didn't. She was so full of happy bubbles, her feet might not have even touched the stairs. She simply floated up.

CHAPTER TWENTY-ONE

*O*ur most basic instinct is not for survival but for family. - Paul
Pearsall

The results were in, and even hours later, Audrey wanted to dance
and shout...and then maybe hide for a while. Talk about erratic
emotions.

Settle down, Audrey. She was good at appearing calm—she'd
certainly had more than adequate practice as a child.

Tipping her head back, she enjoyed the feel of the sun on her
face. After two days of rain, she was ready for warm and dry.

"We're here," Gabe called from in front of her. On the still-
damp trail behind her, the others responded with cheers.
Everyone at the Hermitage had decided the Sunday activity
would be berry picking. But she hadn't expected quite such a
climb.

Emerging from the foothill's thinning forest, she saw a wide
sunny slope. Brushing her hair out of her face, she pulled in a
breath. Even though the sun was hot on her shoulders, the air
held a decided chill.

"Here?" With Aric beside her, Kit frowned. "Where are the berry bushes?"

Audrey grinned, remembering how she'd asked that same question last year.

"Look down." Walking forward with his arm around Frankie, Bull waved at the ground. "Our wild blueberries don't even make it to knee-high."

"Stop." Hawk's voice snapped out, and everyone halted. "Got a bear. Make noise."

A *bear*. Mouth dry, Audrey started to back toward the trail.

"Hold up, Goldy." Gabe put an arm around her, pulled her close, and began whistling loudly.

In a loud voice, Bull was telling Frankie what berries to avoid picking.

Pulling one of his numerous knives, Caz tapped the blade against a rocky outcropping in an annoying rhythm.

A rustle came from a small hollow, then a brown bear lumbered away across the meadow.

"Humans. So irritatingly noisy," Gabe said, obviously amused.

Audrey's heart was going a mile a minute. "You didn't even draw your gun."

His biggest pistol was holstered on his belt with a can of bear spray on the other side. His brothers and JJ also carried bear spray. Next time, she would too.

Gabe tugged her hair. "No need. He wasn't interested in a fight. There are plenty of berries."

He was right. The low bushes were loaded with blueberries. "In that case, I better start picking."

JJ grinned at her. "Pick with me. I want to hear what I missed at the book club."

"Sure." Audrey tried to remember the highlights of the SFF group. Knox had brought up the best points as they discussed whether Earth should assume aliens were friendly or not. He'd come so far since last year when he'd torn pages out of a book because he couldn't read. She was so proud of him.

"Aric, catch." Off to the right, Regan was picking berries—and tossing some at Aric. Little troublemaker.

Grinning, Audrey popped a blueberry in her mouth. *Yum.* The fruit was smaller than store bought, but the flavor was fantastic. What a lovely way to spend a day with family.

I have family. The thought still overwhelmed her at times.

As they worked, one of the guys would start singing or humming. Sometimes it seemed as if melodies ran like a river beneath their skin.

Now, with a smile for Aric and Regan, Bull started to sing, "Do-Re-Mi".

Laughing, Gabe harmonized, and everyone joined in, including Kit in her beautiful clear voice. Audrey loved that she finally had another soprano to sing with.

As the children figured out the words, they piped up.

Hawk stayed silent, but from the contented expression on his face, he enjoyed the music just as much.

As the song ended, JJ shook her head. "We need more children."

"*Princesa*, what do you mean?" Caz asked.

"It felt like I'd fallen through a space-time continuum and landed in an overly-testosteroned, Alaskan version of *The Sound of Music*. But we don't have enough children to do it justice."

Making a tsking sound with his tongue, Caz shook his head sadly. "I need to budget your science fiction reading."

With a threatening sound, JJ bounced a blueberry off his shoulder.

Audrey grinned. JJ giving up SFF would happen about…never.

"What's *The Sound of Music*?" Regan asked.

"A romantic musical." Hawk chuckled and pointed at Bull. "The sarge would've tossed him in the river for singing it."

Bull laughed and agreed.

It was amazing to see Hawk laughing more. As Audrey smiled, she noticed he and Kit were working so close together their shoulders rubbed.

Now, wasn't that interesting?

Gabe grinned. "You should watch the movie with JJ and your father, Regan. Especially your father."

A knife landed between Gabe's knees, far too close to his boy parts.

"Behave, Cazador." Audrey scowled. "You're setting a poor example for your child." And that was something she'd been thinking of a lot in the last week.

Caz blinked, noticed JJ was nodding, and sighed. "Sorry."

Gabe's lips quirked up. "Excellent reprimand, Goldilocks."

"It was," Bull called. "She's got that pissed-off-mommy tone down pat."

Oh no.

She *had* sounded just like Kit and JJ when they scolded the children. Which meant she really, really needed to talk with Gabe.

Pushing to her feet, she poured her berries into JJ's bag and grabbed Gabe's hand. "Come and walk with me."

He gave her an odd look, then strolled with her toward a small cluster of trees.

Behind her, Hawk said, "*Walk with me*—pure Doc Grayson."

Bull laughed. "Words to strike fear into any soul. '*Let's take a walk, Bull*'."

What? Oh, right. Doc Grayson was the psychologist who'd visited the boys. No wonder Gabe had looked at her funny.

"Uh, Gabe. I'm not planning to psychoanalyze you."

"There's a relief."

Audrey choked on a laugh.

In the shady grove, the temperature dropped several degrees

to pleasantly cool, and the air held the tangy sweet scent of evergreens.

"We're out of sight. Very nice." Smiling, Gabe put his arms around her and drew her close. Hand cupping her ass, he tangled his fingers in her hair to pull her head back so he could kiss her, long and deep. Then nuzzling her cheek, he whispered, "Was this the reason you led me back here?"

Oh boy. Whenever he pulled her against his rock-hard body, or face it, any time he touched her, her heart sped up, and her brain went foggy with lust.

"Yes." Her voice came out husky, breathless. "No, wait. No. I mean, I need to talk to you. *Talk*."

He straightened to gaze down at her, and the amusement in his blue eyes disappeared. "What's wrong, sweetheart?"

Great, now she had him worried. "I'd planned to talk with you this morning, but—"

"But I got caught up with booking some asshole burglars."

A couple of entitled college students had been breaking into rooms at the B&B to get drinking money. *Idiots.*

"I'm sorry." Kissing the top of her head, Gabe rubbed her back. "It's not easy for the family of a law enforcement officer. The hours are rough on—"

"No, it's not that. You were born to protect others—your brothers, your fellow soldiers, your town. Your family."

His arms tightened around her, and she could feel his relief at her acceptance.

"I...um..." She cleared her throat delicately. "I just wanted you to know your family will be increasing by one."

Oh, that came out awkward. She flushed, trying to think of words to say it better, then realized he'd gone completely still.

"What?" His voice was hoarse.

"We're having a baby." She rubbed her forehead against his shoulder. "You're going to be a daddy."

He took a step back, and her anxiety shot sky-high. What if he—

Wonder filled his expression, then joy. "A baby."

His gaze ran over her. Pulling her back into his arms, he kissed her, telling her without words exactly how he felt.

JJ watched Gabe and Audrey emerge from the small grove of trees. *Hmm.* Suppressing a laugh, she nudged Caz. "If I was doing drug tests, he'd be my first choice. He looks like he's walking on air."

Caz glanced that way. And she had to wonder how a devastatingly gorgeous man managed to get even hotter just with a smile.

Wait... She narrowed her eyes. "Why do you look so smug?"

"She finally told him."

"Told him what?"

"We're going to have a baby," Gabe yelled out for everyone to hear.

"Oh. Oh, wow." She joined the cheering and laughed as berry picking was abandoned for hugs and congratulations.

Standing beside Regan, Aric frowned at Gabe. "Where's the baby? Did you leave it at home like Gryff?"

Gabe coughed and glanced at Audrey, then Kit. "This falls into female territory."

Kit laughed and knelt next to her son. "Audrey will be growing the baby in her tummy for lots of months. Her stomach is going to get big."

"Ooooh." He considered Audrey's stomach before asking his mother, "Can I get a baby in my tummy? I can grow it good too."

Kit shook her head. "Sorry, honey bear. Nobody makes babies until they're a lot older."

He scowled. "Kids don't get to do anything."

JJ felt like clapping—because his objection was loud and

perfectly normal. "Children get to help pick berries, and the ones who can cook will put them in blueberry muffins."

"I can cook." Short legs pumping, Aric ran back over, so cute she just had to pick him up and hug him.

After she settled the children side-by-side at a new patch of berries, Caz took her hand. "Did you want to get married, *princesa*? And have babies?"

"What?" Was he joking?

"Tell me, please." His melting dark brown eyes were serious. Concerned.

Her heart turned into a puddle in her chest. God, she loved him. "Ah, married, yes. One of these days. So Regan can feel as if she has two people to count on."

He put a rock-hard arm around her, firmly pulling her closer. "Is that the only reason, *mamita*?"

Pushy doctor. "Maybe because I love you. A little."

His grin flashed, white in the brown face. "As it happens, I love you much more than a little."

Honestly, he took her breath away. "Do you want more children?"

He moved his shoulders in a nonchalant shrug. "If you aren't in a hurry, I'd rather you and Regan get to feel more settled. Then we can make some babies if you want. Or adopt. Or not. I'm happy with a big or small family as long as you and Regan are in it."

Her eyes prickled with tears. If she let him continue, he'd reduce her to a sappy mess. Putting her arms around his neck, she kissed him.

"Same here," she whispered and kissed him again.

"Aric, look," Regan said in a low voice. "They're always doing that stuff."

"So does Mama." Aric whispered back. "With Hawk."

"Ooooh, does your mama like him?"

Caz tilted his head to hear the answer, and *snoopy JJ*, she was doing the same thing.

"Uh-huh. I like him too."

Right. At four, he wouldn't understand the sexier versions of *like*.

"Hawk and Kit?" JJ murmured to Caz. "I didn't see *that* one coming. What should we do?"

"Get some popcorn and enjoy the show?" He laughed when she tried to kick him.

CHAPTER TWENTY-TWO

M*y kid is turning out just like me. Well played, karma.* **Well-played**. ~ Unknown

Kids were damned crazy.

Hawk sat at the kitchen island in Mako's cabin as rain pattered out on the deck. The rising wind created white-topped wavelets across the lake.

The kids had summer school on Mondays, Wednesdays, and Fridays. But today was Thursday, and they were home. Since tourists didn't want to fly in the storm, he'd volunteered to watch the kids.

Which went to prove that he really was crazy as a hoot owl.

Thankfully, he remembered a game he and his brothers had played when snowbound in the sarge's tiny cabin. *Good times.*

After hijacking blankets and rugs from the rest of the Hermitage, he'd moved furniture around, then strung rope in long stretches through the downstairs of Mako's house.

With strategically draped blankets over the rope, tables, and chairs, he and the kids built a vast tunnel city. Inside the tunnels, throw rugs and pillows covered the bare hardwood.

With Gryff and Sirius following, Regan and Aric had disappeared into the maze.

Later, when the kids took a break to fetch eggs from the chicken pen, Hawk hid "treasure" in various places in the tunnels.

Assigning each kid half of the system, he set them to hunting.

Seated at the kitchen island, he drank his coffee and enjoyed their excitement. Had the sarge felt this odd sense of contentment when Gabe, Bull, Caz, and Hawk had been immersed in their games?

A high squeal broke the silence. Exiting one opening, Aric stood up to wave his first find—a dinosaur.

"What'd you get?" Popping out of a tunnel in her area, Regan ran to see.

A few minutes later, back inside, she yelled her happiness at finding the *Mulan* coloring book JJ had suggested.

Funny how noisy squeals and giggles could transform to a feeling of peace deep in his soul. Taking another sip of coffee, he let himself savor the pleasures of the previous week.

Simply being home. Evenings with the family. Making music together in a way that felt as if the songs were creating bonds between them in the same way the tunnels here connected to each other.

Several times, he'd joined Aric and Kit for supper and spent the evening. They'd played preschool board games or hide and seek, watched kid movies, and read books.

After the boy was in bed, Hawk would stay downstairs with Kit—for talking, for kissing, for touching.

Last night, he'd gotten her off with his fingers, then held her when she cried. She'd insisted it was happy crying.

He shook his head. Shedding tears for happiness wasn't in his toolbox. Maybe it was a female thing.

Fuck, he liked being with her. She had a quiet spirit. She'd talk when she had something relevant to say but didn't need to fill silence with empty chatter.

And he didn't have to come up with a bunch of shit to say, either. She was comfortable when his side of a conversation contained a hell of a lot fewer words.

Even the standard this-isn't-a-serious-relationship conversation had been reduced to almost nothing. Kit had looked at him and shook her head. *"I know this won't go anywhere, but I'm really glad you're here now."*

Her acceptance of a lack of a future together had hurt, down inside, but was a relief too. *Short-term.* He could handle that.

Just as he could handle the slow pace as they learned about each other. Kit liked to snuggle, but he didn't touch her without giving notice. She'd realized he didn't like being grabbed, either. Yeah, they were moving carefully.

Because the three of them were, in their own way, more than a bit fucked up.

That afternoon, as the kids put their lunch dishes in the dishwasher, Hawk glanced at the schedule created by the parental authorities—Caz, JJ, and Kit—and saw no changes had been made since he'd gone to South America.

This was still supposed to be quiet time. Sounded good. The morning had been damned energetic and noisy.

"Regan, pick a book and sack out somewhere."

"'Kay." She pulled a book from the shelves and curled up in a blanket pile by the windows. "I want to watch the rain too."

"Good choice, kid." He ruffled her hair, heard her snort in the way of all children ever, and saw the tiny happy smile on her face.

She really was a good kid; Caz had gotten lucky.

He headed back to figure out a good spot for Aric. Upstairs in his corner, maybe? No, he'd want to be down with Hawk and Regan.

Hawk dropped pillows, a blanket, and a picture book at one of the tunnel exits. "Here, Aric."

Standing by the toybox, the boy held up a T-Rex and scowled at Hawk. "I want Regan to play with me."

"After quiet time, you can ask her."

Turning red, Aric stomped his foot. "No. Now."

Fucking-A, look who'd turned into a regular kid. Hawk barely kept from laughing. "Sorry, boy. We got a schedule, and it's quiet time."

"No!" That little foot kicked over the box, and then Aric started throwing toys everywhere.

Hawk's gut clenched, then he relaxed. Regan wasn't in range. Mako's place was designed for roughhousing. There was no damage the kid could do.

Breathing out slowly as he watched the tantrum, Hawk found his center to ensure he wouldn't lose his temper.

But ignoring the behavior wouldn't do the boy any favors. Hawk knew the harm that could happen from unrestrained anger.

Well, since the kid lived in the sarge's house, seemed only right that he'd receive the discipline the sarge used to dispense.

Gripping the kid's collar, Hawk, gently, but firmly guided him outside and across the deck. Rather than being frightened, Aric struggled, still spitting mad.

It was still raining. Off the deck, the splatter of cold drops brought the boy's fighting to a halt.

"Tough to be you, kid." Hawk let go and retreated a couple of steps back under the deck roof.

Water streamed over Aric's face, flattening his blond hair.

"When I got angry and started throwing things"—usually his fists—"the sarge made me run laps till I cooled down. You can do that now."

"Huh?" Wide blue eyes stared up at Hawk.

"Run to the smokehouse and back. Then ask me—politely—if you're done."

Aric didn't move, and fuck, it felt as if he was kicking a puppy. *Dammit, Mako.* It'd be easier to kill a few insurgents than deal with this.

Man up, Calhoun. Hawk forced his voice to stay level. "Get started, boy, before you get cold."

The kid turned and trudged toward the smokehouse. Slowly.

"Hey."

Aric turned.

Holding his arm up, Hawk pumped his fist up and down in the army hand signal for *go faster.*

Aric took two stubbornly slow steps, then his nerve broke, and he started to run. He reached the smokehouse and sprinted back. At the foot of the steps, he caught his breath and looked up at Hawk. Water soaked his hair; his clothes were sopping.

Hawk kept the sympathy off his face. "What's your gut feel like? Still angry that it's quiet time?"

Aric scowled.

Yeah, not there yet. "Go again." Hawk motioned to the smokehouse.

It was a long way for a four-year-old, and by the time Aric got back, he was flagging.

Hawk winced. Kit might murder him for this. Then again, she wasn't a pushover when it came to her son's behavior.

Hawk looked at Aric, and this time, his question obtained a shake of Aric's head rather than a scowl.

Aric stayed quiet even as Hawk helped him into dry clothes and brought him back downstairs. It was fucking tempting to just drop the matter and simply hug the boy.

Finish the lesson.

Hawk tossed a stuffed owl onto the pillow pile at the tunnel opening where he'd left the book. Sitting down, he pulled Aric into his lap.

Aric went stiff, then snuggled against him.

The relief was enormous. "You got angry about quiet time, yeah?"

Head down, Aric nodded, his fingers picking at his shirtsleeve.

"We all get angry when we don't get our way." Hawk ran his hand down the damp hair. "But throwing things is a bad choice. I guess you saw Obadiah throw shit?"

After a second, Aric nodded, not looking at Hawk.

"You don't want to be like him."

Aric shook his head, chin firming up.

"When I was little, I pretended my anger was a smoke monster that I had to blow away." Doc Grayson came up with the weirdest shit. But it'd worked.

The big blue gaze turned up to Hawk. "Smoke monster?"

"Yeah. If my gut got pissed-off"—Hawk patted Aric's stomach—"it'd make a smoke monster." He'd get so furious, he'd go berserk.

"It's hard to think with a smoke monster in your face." When Hawk waved his hand in the air, Aric's eyes widened as if he could see the imaginary smoke.

"Blow real hard. Make it go away."

Aric puffed. Over and over.

"That's it." Hawk nodded. "When the monster's gone, it's easier to figure out what to do."

Aric's brows drew together as he considered.

Smart kid. Could make a guy proud.

"We'll work on it," Hawk murmured. Unable to resist, he gave Aric a squeeze. "Good job running. You're damned fast."

The kid's eyes brightened.

At the tug in the center of Hawk's chest, he cleared his throat. "Bunk down or read the book."

After crawling in and curling up in the pillow nest, Aric gave the stuffed toy a dubious look.

"Owls sleep during the day. He's your nap buddy."

As if that made perfect sense, Aric wrapped his arms around the owl and was asleep within a minute.

Picking up his own book, Hawk settled down on the sectional...and was too shook up to read. How did parents survive this shit for eighteen years?

And how fucking pitiful was it that he'd give anything to be one of those parents? To raise that boy over there.

Sadness swept through Hawk. He'd never be a father; he knew better.

CHAPTER TWENTY-THREE

When trouble comes, it's your family that supports you. - Guy Lafleur

On Saturday, Hawk walked out to his deck to enjoy the sun. Maybe he'd take the canoe out on the lake. Kit and Aric might enjoy that.

He caught sight of Gryff making his rounds of the courtyard, sniffing near the electric fence. Probably some predator had been lured too close by the scent of the chickens and gotten zapped.

Next door, Caz stepped outside. "Nice day, 'mano."

Hawk nodded, pleased that this brother, at least, wouldn't interrogate him about being with Kit and Aric in the evenings. Without a doubt, his brothers *had* noticed.

Hawk sighed. There'd be shit coming his way soon enough. There was no way they'd approve of him getting serious about Kit —because no one in the fucking world would want Hawk to be a father. They knew, if nothing else, his parents had gone to prison and he'd had a shitty childhood. They might well have figured out that his father had been an abusive asshole.

Sooner or later, he'd have to explain that he knew better than to get involved—and Kit wasn't serious about him, anyway.

"Where's your girl?" Hawk asked.

"Which one?" Caz grinned. "JJ is working. Gabe and Audrey took Regan and Aric off for a fishing lesson, since Tucker and Guzman acquired kid-sized poles."

The two backcountry men were rapidly turning into doting honorary uncles.

When Hawk's phone dinged, he checked the text message and sighed. So much for his day off. He tapped in a reply.

"Work?" Caz asked.

"The campers I dropped off last week. A bear got their supplies."

"Good thing they took a satellite phone and are high enough to get a signal. Do they want you to fly them in some food?"

"Yeah." Hawk pulled up the aviation weather unit. Fog in the forecast, dammit. "I need to hurry. Did Kit go fishing too?"

"No, she doesn't have a license yet. Why?"

Hawk bit back his first response—*none of your business*—and went for honest. "She likes flying."

Caz opened his mouth. Closed it. "Ah. Then you two have a good day. If Aric gets back before you, one of us will look after him."

"Thanks." Hawk didn't care if his brothers knew he was interested in Kit. Growing up in a tiny cabin meant they'd gotten used to the lack of privacy. However, he did care if they gave Kit any grief.

Caz had manners. Gabe and Bull—they might tease Kit.

They'd learn better. Hawk examined his scarred-up knuckles. Wouldn't be the first time he'd punched a brother for poking his nose in where it didn't belong.

Kit held her breath as Hawk made a pass over a high mountain clearing to check the wind.

Below them, several tents were set in a circle. A man sitting beside a big camp stove waved a ladle in a welcome.

Centering the helicopter, Hawk landed them as gently as a falling feather.

She pulled off her headphones. "You are an incredible pilot."

"When you love something, it's easy." His grin flashed for a second. "You garden like I fly."

The compliment set up a happy glow inside her, especially since it was true. She really did have a green thumb. And he'd noticed.

Smiling, she jumped out, delighted that nothing hurt any longer. Her ribs and healing incision were fine. Although her arm ached occasionally and wasn't as strong as her left, it was improving.

Life was good.

She drew in a long, slow breath of crisp, cold air scented with evergreen.

"Woohoo! The supplies!" Five men burst out of the forest and converged on the helicopter. As the guys greeted Hawk, he started handing out boxes.

Kit took a step forward to help with the carrying. But...all those men. Her heart started to thud within her ribcage. As her palms turned clammy, she rubbed them on her jeans.

How about a nice stroll, staying in sight? She glanced back at the helicopter and realized Hawk was watching her.

He tilted his head in an obvious query. *Are you all right?*

She nodded and managed a smile.

For the next few minutes, she strolled around, staying in sight, yet at a distance from any of the men. Now and then, she'd stop to simply enjoy the beauty of the mountain scene. Aside from the men talking, the world was incredibly quiet.

After unloading was complete, the man who was cooking

wandered over to exchange handshakes with Hawk before returning to the camp stove.

On Kit's next circuit, she saw the guys showing Hawk the mess the bear had made. They'd hung their food packs from a tree limb, but bears could apparently climb when given the right incentive. Who knew?

So Hawk was instructing them on how to keep their food safe. She had to smile at the way he was standing, his back to the helicopter. Probably so no bear could sneak up on him.

Or... When his gaze met hers, she realized he'd positioned himself so he wouldn't lose sight of her in her rambles around the clearing.

It took her a second to blink away the burn from her eyes, and then she smiled at him. *Thank you.*

His eyes crinkled, and he continued talking to the men.

On her next lap, the cook called, "Ma'am." When she walked over, he gave her a quiet smile and handed her a big mug of coffee. "Hawk said you use creamer and a couple teaspoons of sugar."

"That's perfect, thank you." Hawk remembered how she liked her coffee. The knowledge made her feel funny inside.

"It's good to see him with a nice woman."

Oh, boy, she might need to process that statement for a while. "You know him? Are you from Rescue?"

"That town of his? Nah, we were both deployed in Afghanistan." His mouth flattened, then he shook his head, much as she did when reminding herself to stay in the present. "The Night Stalkers—they're hell of incredible. You know about them, ma'am?"

"It's Kit. And no, I don't." That was the name on the beret Hawk had let Aric hold to prove he'd return. Just the name was ominous. "Who are they?"

"They're Special Ops pilots, and their helicopters are seriously hi-tech. They flew us in, provided close air support when we needed it. Did recon sometimes. Always in the thick of it."

Her skin went cold. "That sounds awfully dangerous."

"Hell, yeah. The bastards saved my ass more than once. Hawk was one of the best." The man smiled. "It's nice to see him here, making himself a good life."

The grim note in his voice told her he was still working on that good life.

The past wasn't easy to escape, was it, but they all coped as best they could. Hawk played his violin. She grew flowers. This man was here fishing.

"I think he'd say the same about you," she said quietly, then grinned. "Well, he would if you could get him to use that many words."

Ruston's guffaw joined with Kit's clear laughter and caught Hawk's attention. She didn't laugh nearly enough.

Turning, he saw the burly Marine Raider grinning down at her.

"Don't often hear Ruston laugh like that," Foreman muttered. "Your woman's got a way about her."

Hawk nodded—*she did*—and then continued his instructions.

Once they'd learned how to keep their food safe, he checked the sky. "Time to go. There's fog coming in."

It'd not only suck to fly into a mountain, but he wasn't about to risk Kit's life. Ever.

He joined Ruston and Kit at the camp stove.

"I like her," the retired Marine announced. "You should keep her."

Kit sputtered, but her eyes danced.

"I like her too." Hawk held his arm out and was pleased when she leaned against him so he could pull her close. He was enjoying the silent dance of consent between them. "We need to be off."

"Okay." Kit handed the Marine her mug. "There's supposed to be fog in a while."

"Damned stuff." Ruston shook Hawk's hand. "Fly safe. We'll

need a ride out of this place in another week or so."

Hawk lifted his chin in acknowledgment.

As he tucked Kit into the cockpit, he saw the men working on stringing up the food storage wire between two trees. He'd also left them some bear-proof containers to use on the ground.

After strapping in, Kit donned her headphones.

He tossed a salute at Ruston and Foreman, then lifted into the sky and started the flight toward home.

Unfortunately, before they were halfway down the mountains, billowing white fog had started to conceal the passes.

Damn. He shouldn't have brought Kit.

"That doesn't look good," she said quietly.

"Nope. We need to set down for the night."

"But—Aric."

"He'll be safe. Best if we get you home to him in one piece."

Her eyes widened, but although her hands tightened in her lap, she stayed calm.

Hell of a woman. A touch could send her into a panic attack, but a possible helicopter crash? She had it under control.

"We land, spend the night. The sun and wind will lift the fog in the morning." He handed her the satellite phone. "Let Gabe know."

"Right. Okay."

As she talked with Gabe, he circled, keeping high enough the phone would work.

"He says he'll let Frankie know." Kit turned off the device. "And that she'll like playing godmother."

Frankie adored Aric. "Yeah." Hawk dropped them into the next valley, searching for a spot to land.

Near a stream, the fog was patchy enough to see the ground— and there was a small flat clearing just calling his name.

He took them down.

Why did her phone always ring any time she left it upstairs?

Grumbling, Frankie ran up to the master bedroom. There it was. She'd left it on the dresser when she changed. Gabe's name showed on the display.

"Hey, Gabe. What's up?"

"The fog is going to keep Hawk and Kit from making it back tonight. They'll spend the night in the mountains."

Cavalo. Her knees went weak, and she dropped onto the bed. "Are they all right?"

"They're fine." Gabe's easy-going laugh was reassuring. "Hawk's flown into enemy fire, at night, into shitty terrain. A little fog isn't a worry."

"But what if he doesn't make it down?"

"He stayed high enough for the sat phone to work to give me a call and has probably already landed. He had a spot picked out." As if he could feel her heart speeding up, he added, "Relax. Hawk's careful, especially when he has passengers."

The reassurance was what she needed. And really, he'd probably be even more careful with having Kit along. Frankie had seen how his hard face softened when he talked with her bestie. And when she'd asked Kit about him, her friend turned red and flustered...and her face softened too.

Frankie'd decided she'd be hands-off, although, okay, she was totally cheering them on. "What about camping? I mean, it's going to be cold and everything."

"He carries everything he'll need for both of them."

Of course he did. The man had been raised by a survivalist, right? "If they call again, you can let them know Aric's safe with me."

"Thanks, Frankie."

Shaking her head, she returned to the others in her living room.

On the sectional, Audrey and Lillian were discussing the newly purchased portable school buildings.

At the dining room table, JJ sat between the two children, drawing pictures for Aric. He loved when he could get someone to freehand designs for him.

"What color should our bird be?" JJ asked.

He held up a crayon.

She just raised her eyebrows. "What's color is that?"

Grinning, he shouted out, "Pink!"

"You're right." She took the crayon. "It will stand out nicely in this snow." Grinning, JJ started working on a...a penguin?

In pink? The poor bird would hide in shame. Smothering a laugh, Frankie winked at Regan, who was giggling.

Now...how in the world was she going to tell Aric about his mom?

"Oh, there's a worried expression," JJ said. "Was it a bad call, Frankie? Is there a problem at the roadhouse?"

Audrey looked over the back of the couch. "You law enforcement types are such pessimists. That's exactly what Gabe would ask."

"Not the roadhouse." Trying to be discreet, Frankie waved toward the wall of windows that faced the courtyard. "See how pretty the lake is?"

JJ gave her a puzzled look. "I can't even see the lake for the fog."

"Exactly. Gabe heard from someone who's spending the night elsewhere. Because of that white stuff."

Catching on, Lillian, Audrey, and JJ glanced at Aric. Since their rescue, the boy hadn't spent a night without either Kit or Hawk to put him to bed.

Frankie bent and kissed his silky-soft hair. He smelled like a child who'd had a wonderful day. Of grass and mud. Chocolate smeared his chin from when he'd helped her make chocolate chip cookies.

He tipped his head back to look up at her with his endearing crooked smile.

Cazzo, she loved him. She pulled in a breath. How to give him the news?

Maybe start with family? She went down on one knee beside him. "Hey, Aric, did your mama tell you I was there when you were born?"

"You were?"

"Uh-huh. I was in the hospital with her and got to hold you." She made a baby-holding curve in one arm and patted it. "You were only this big. That was the day she asked me to be your godmother."

On the other side of JJ, Regan stopped coloring. "What's a godmother?"

"A godmother is kind of like having a second mother." Frankie patted Aric's knee. "That's why, when your mama said the pissers wouldn't let you leave, I came to help."

"Papá said you flew all the way from New York." Regan looked at Aric. "It's a really, really long way, and he said Kit was lucky to have Frankie for a friend." Her voice dropped. "That's the kind of friend I'm gonna be."

"Oh, baby." JJ made a choking sound and put an arm around Regan. "You already are."

Frankie thought so too.

"Godmuvver," Aric said slowly, as if trying on the word for size.

Frankie leaned against him. "Mmmhmm. So whenever your mama can't be with you, you have a second mama to watch over you."

She'd wait until after supper to tell him that tonight was going to be one of those times.

Little forehead wrinkled, Aric started coloring again...because he was a young man who liked to consider things carefully. The damn PZers had obviously taught him what happened to children who acted before thinking.

Frankie's heart ached. "Want me to draw the next penguin?"

Aric studied her with solemn eyes, then handed her a purple crayon.

"Ooooh, purple." She held it up.

"Uh-huh. Cuz purple's your fav'rite." The most adorable child in the world gave her a sweet smile. "Godmuvver."

In the mountain range, Kit stretched her feet toward the fire. "I'm glad we have a fire—and that you're so careful with it."

The campfire Hawk had made was downstream of a tiny waterfall in an area of patchy grass. After digging a fire pit, he'd lined the edge with river stones.

He was seated on a low canvas camp chair—another treasure from his helicopter. "If it hadn't been a wet summer, we'd be using the camp stove now."

"I guess that means the fire won't burn all night to keep the bears away?"

"No fire." He pointed to an open area across the creek and uphill. "We'll sleep away from the creek and the smell of food."

She sipped her hot chocolate, savoring the hazelnut taste from the Frangelico Liqueur he'd added. Rather than a horrendous survival experience, this felt more like a mini-vacation.

"Want another?" he asked.

"No, I'm good." She grinned to herself and caught his raised eyebrows. "Frankie teases me about being a lightweight since more than two drinks makes me sick. And she can outdrink a lot of guys."

"Yep. Seen that." His smile faded. "I'm sorry I can't get you home to Aric."

"Fog is hardly your fault, and I think you know how much I love flying." She sighed. "Aric's getting better. Even his counselor is pleased with his progress."

"Counselors." Making an irritated noise, Hawk ran his finger over the tattoos on his arm as if tracing memories.

She laughed. "The visits leave me frazzled for a while afterward, but I'm really grateful to have help for me and Aric. And the group sessions are..." She couldn't find the right word.

"Helpful?"

"In a different way, yes." She tipped her head back. The fog was so thick she couldn't even see the dark sky. "It helps to hear others talking about the same problems I have and that the way I react is, kind of, just part of dealing with the aftermath."

"What about one-on-one?"

"I'm done for now. She said to return if anything came up." Kit poked a stick in the fire. Seeing how much she enjoyed feeding the fire, Hawk had assigned her the job, then crushed her hopes by refusing to let her build a six-foot blaze. Darn it. "Have you ever seen a therapist? I mean, soldiers do, right?"

"We should. I didn't till this year." A corner of his mouth tilted up. "Got the same guy the sarge saw."

"That'd be strange. Does it bother you?"

Hawk shook his head. "Mako got better. Was even seeing a woman."

"Someone in town?"

"Lillian."

"Whoa. You mean seeing, like the *in bed* kind of seeing?"

Hawk's raspy voice held amusement. "Yep."

"Huh." From what she'd heard, the sarge had been a hard-ass military lifer, tough as nails, and paranoid as all get out. How'd he win the elegant British actress? Then again, Lillian obviously liked rugged men, since she lived with Dante, also a veteran. "From the stories, your sarge must have been scary when you were a child."

"Yeah, some." Hawk took a sip of his drink. "We were lucky he found us."

She snorted. "Found you? That sounds like he tripped over you on a walk or something."

"Pretty much."

Seriously? He wasn't going to explain? She gave him a *"use-your-words"* look.

Making a grumbling sound, he continued, "We were in foster care. In California. The guy in charge had a thing for boys."

Kit's eyes widened. "Like a pedophile?"

At the memory, Hawk felt his jaw clench, his gut twist. "He grabbed me." *Pinned face down on the bed. Screaming, fighting, biting, doing everything he could to keep his pants from being ripped off.* "I fought back."

He'd been losing.

Kit made a horrified sound.

"Gabe, Bull, and Caz jumped in." *Gabe first. Bursting through the door and charging Phillip—who knocked him to the floor. Hawk scrambling up, diving at the man. Hearing the screaming, Bull and Caz ran in—and attacked.*

The boys weren't his friends or anything—Hawk hadn't had friends—and they were street-smart enough to know no one could win against a foster parent. Yet they'd come to his rescue.

The wonder of that moment had never left him.

And despite the mess, there'd been high points. "Caz nailed the pervert with a baseball bat to the crotch."

Kit burst out laughing. "Good for him."

Yeah, he knew he liked her. She might not like violence, but she didn't hide her head in the sand.

Even better, she hadn't dissolved into a bunch of uncomfortable sympathy over his story either. Which meant he could continue.

"Mako was visiting next door. Heard the yelling"—shrieking was more like it—"and walked in." Like Hawk's brothers, the sarge had that protective gene. "He brought us here."

"To Alaska from California?" Kit blinked. "A single father

from another state? That must have taken months to get the paperwork done. Did the social workers at least move you to a safer— You're laughing. Why are you laughing?"

"He stuffed us in his car, and we left."

"That's kidnapping!"

Hawk shook his head. "He asked us first."

"Oh, my heavens, that's so wrong." She stared at him. "What about here? Suddenly a guy has four children. Didn't anyone question that?"

"We lived in an off-the-grid cabin deep in the forest. Alaskans don't ask questions."

Her outraged expression was adorable. "How old were you?"

"Nine." And really fucked up in the head. But she didn't need to know that, did she? She'd already figured out he'd had a shit childhood.

And, fuck him, but he needed to remember he wasn't the right man for her. Not for serious. They were friends. She hadn't asked for more. He couldn't allow himself to want more, even if he did, damn him for a fool.

He liked being her friend. Best he keep his ambitions confined to that.

"If you were in foster care, were your parents—"

Not going there.

"What about yours?" he interrupted. "Are they alive?"

"No." She swirled her hot chocolate in the mug. "They died in a car crash. I was ten when I went to live with my mom's sister and her husband."

Hawk studied the way her body had closed in on itself. The animation had left her face. "Assholes?"

"Not...exactly." Her lips twisted in a wry smile. "Some. Counseling showed me how thoroughly they messed up my thinking."

"Yeah?"

When she didn't speak, he gave her the same raised-brows,

head-tilt shit she used on him when he wasn't spitting out the words.

She laughed, and there was the resilient woman he knew. The one willing to tackle problems head on.

"They were exceedingly conservative, Bible-thumper types, colder than your Alaska winters, and more judgmental than Judge Judy." She set her mug on the ground with an angry thump. "Uncle Duane said my parents deserved to die since they'd never gotten married. And that a woman isn't complete without a husband."

"Yeah, assholes." Hawk studied her. She'd said her thinking was messed up. "How'd that affect you?"

Hands clasped tightly together, she averted her gaze. "I went kind of crazy when I left, rebelling by having lots of one-night-stands."

"Youngsters." He went with a noncommittal response. "Most of us like sex."

"Me too," she agreed, "but counseling showed me that my subconscious wanted me to find someone like Uncle Duane—because a woman isn't complete without a husband. Then I had Aric without a husband."

Fuck, no wonder. "You were easy pickings for Obadiah."

"I really was." She sighed. "It's funny though. I can remember my parents enough to know they weren't like that."

Seems like they'd been about the same age when their brain programming got rewired. After all, that was what adults did—imprint kids with expected behavior.

Going from abuse into Mako's gruff version of love, Hawk had absorbed his strong moral code. Kit had gone from loving parents to real bastards. Had she tried to adhere to their code to win affection from them?

Probably.

Yeah, he and his brothers had been damn lucky.

Thank you, Sarge.

At the dinner table in Mako's house, Regan did what Uncle Hawk called "chowing down." Cuz it all tasted awesome.

Frankie'd planned to make some fancy French stuff, but instead, she and Audrey cooked fried chicken, mashed potatoes, and gravy.

Audrey called it comfort food.

Totally. Sirius had thought so, too, when Regan sneaked him little bits of the chicken. He'd kept putting his paw on her foot when she stopped.

After they cleaned up, Regan curled up beside Papá on the humongo couch, feeling all full and happy. His leg was hard but made a great pillow.

JJ tucked a snuggly blanket around Regan, then sat on Papá's other side.

Dante and Lillian had come over for supper and stayed to talk. They were sitting in the chairs and holding hands like the teens did. Very chill.

Uncle Bull was supposed to be bartending at the roadhouse, but he'd come home.

Everybody was here except for Uncle Hawk and Kit.

Was that why people were acting kinda weird?

Even with comfort food and her favorite fuzzy blankie, she had a wiggly feeling inside. Like there was something wrong. Only nobody was shouting or anything.

Close to Regan's feet, Aric was sitting beside Frankie with Bull on Frankie's other side.

"*Cazzo. Mannaggia a me,*" Frankie muttered.

Regan frowned. What did that one mean? She'd learned some cool swears from Frankie—and Papá too.

Like when she'd been helping Dante in his grocery store and dropped an egg, and it splattered, and she yelled, "*A la verga.*"

A Latino tourist guy got major frowny-faced. "*Chiquita*, you should not *say* such words." And she said *sorry*, even though Dante was laughing. Really, *a la verga* was better than saying *fuck,* wasn't it? She'd already taught it to Niko and Delaney.

She'd have to look up *cazzo* on the internet...if she could figure out how to spell it. Italian was weird.

Sitting beside Frankie, Bull took her hand. "Man up, sweetheart."

She made a face at him—Frankie had the best faces—then pulled Aric into her lap and hugged him. "Aric. Remember I'm your godmother?"

He nodded and started getting all stiff.

Uh-huh, Regan knew it. Something wasn't right.

When she sat up, Papá put his arm around her. "Shhh, *mija*."

Frankie was telling Aric, "You know your mama and Hawk took food to some campers. Up in the mountains."

Aric nodded again.

"Right. See how it's foggy outside?" Frankie waved at the windows. "Helicopters aren't supposed to fly in the fog, so Hawk landed beside a pretty little stream so they can camp there tonight."

When Aric didn't move, Frankie talked faster. "The fog will blow away tonight, so they'll be home tomorrow morning. They're fine, Aric; they just can't fly in a fog. So they can't be here tonight."

Oh, no.

Aric's eyes got wet, and he didn't yell like Regan would. But he was shaking worse than Niko's dog did when there was thunder.

Frankie hugged Aric again. "I'm here, *tesoro mio*. You'll stay with me and Bull up in our room tonight...because you're our family."

Regan scowled. Aric was still crying so Frankie's stuff wasn't working. But what she said was smart, cuz when Papá couldn't be home and Regan got scared, having JJ hold her was really nice.

Having family was like comfort food.

Pulling away from Papá, Regan crawled next to Aric and bumped him with her shoulder. "Hey. You know you kinda-sorta belong to Hawk, right?"

Aric looked at her, and his mouth got all scrunchy, like he wanted to say, *mine*. He nodded big.

Regan got it, cuz that's how she felt about JJ. *Mine*. "Yeah, so since Hawk is my uncle, and you belong to him, then that makes you my...my..." There was a word.

"I believe you want to say cousin, *mija*." Papá was smiling like he was proud of her.

That made her heart go gooey.

She turned to Aric. "There, see? We're cousins. Like brother and sister, but with different moms and dads."

Aric wasn't looking as scared, and when she took his hand, his cold fingers squeezed hers. He said *cousins* only no sound came out.

"Spot on." In one of the chairs, Lillian clapped her hands like she was all happy. "Since you're Hawk's boy, and you're cousins with Regan, and she's my grandchild, I do believe that makes you my grandson. You'll have to call me Grammy like Regan does, and I will get to lavish you with treats."

Oh, Lillian was tricksy. Regan had shown Aric the super-cool backpack Lillian had bought her for school. She leaned forward and whispered, "Grammy gives the best presents. Papá says she's spoiling me, an' now she can spoil you too."

Uncle Bull's laugh was really big. "Guess that makes me your Uncle Bull, yeah?"

On the other side of the sectional, there came another laugh. "Uncle Gabe. That's me, Aric." Regan turned to see Audrey kiss Uncle Gabe's cheek. And the cop grinned. "I like the way the family's getting bigger."

Aric was still holding Regan's hand, and she smirked.

She was going to get to keep him.

CHAPTER TWENTY-FOUR

D*amn the torpedoes, full speed ahead.* - Admiral David G. Farragut

As Hawk stowed the pots and dishes in the helicopter, Kit rubbed her hands up and down her arms.

What was Aric thinking? Was he crying? Afraid?

Just a bit ago, she tried to call on the satellite phone, but Hawk said the mountains around them would probably block the signal. He was right. Darn it.

There was nothing she could do. She was stuck here. So far from home. Behind the fog, the glow of the sun was descending behind the mountains. Night was coming.

Anxiety skittered across her skin like tiny pinpricks.

Hawk had been wonderful, but what if he stopped being so nice? Men changed—they did, and she was alone with him. No one was around for miles and miles.

Slowly, she backed toward the forest as her heart set up a horrible thumping inside her ribs.

As if he'd heard her move, he glanced over his shoulder. "Kit." One word in a quiet baritone.

She stopped. Shook her head. Pulled in a breath. *Get a grip, girl.* "Sorry. What?"

"Got a tent for you. Or you can sleep in the helicopter."

"My own tent?"

He nodded, watching her carefully. His movements were slow.

What should she choose? The helicopter had a door, yet there wasn't any flat space. The seats sure weren't comfortable.

Hawk would be able to get inside it anyway.

No, don't think that way. She tried to unclench her fingers. "A tent would be great. I can help put it up."

Since the bendy, light poles threaded through long tubes on the outside of the domes, the two tents went up so easily it was ridiculous. Hawk tossed a sleeping bag and inflatable pad into each.

"You're awfully prepared," she said.

"I keep extras for my brothers." He half smiled. "Never know when we might get stuck somewhere."

Like right now, huh?

The tents weren't that small, but— "I can see how you wouldn't want to share with Bull."

He snorted, then pointed to her tent. "Set up your shit."

Leaving the door unzipped, she crawled in, inflated the pad, and laid out her sleeping bag.

Over by the stream, Hawk doused the fire before disappearing into the trees. When he returned, he handed her a small tote bag.

She peeked in to find an unopened travel toothbrush and paste, a bottle of water, several towelettes, and a flashlight. The surge of happiness made her laugh. It really was all about the little things in life. "This is awesome. Thank you."

"Right. Come." The half-hidden laughter in his voice was a warning.

He led her to where a strand of yellow flagging marked their dishwashing location. "This area is for cleaning up. Watch." He showed her how to open a bear-proof container. "Leave your tote bag in the container. Garbage goes in this sack."

Bear precautions, right. "Got it."

Hawk patted a pile of clothing. "Wear these. Your clothes'll go in the helicopter for the night.

"Sure, but...why?"

"Best not to sleep in clothes that were around food." He pointed to an area farther away with red flagging. "That's the latrine."

Easy enough to find. "All right."

"Clean up. I'll hear if you yell."

In other words, he'd be close enough to help, but far enough for privacy. "For a deadly mercenary, you're awfully thoughtful."

In the dim twilight, his teeth flashed in a grin. "Mako had rules about women."

How sexist—and how reassuring.

When he walked away, she hurriedly brushed her teeth, then stripped down and did a thorough job of washing up. The towelettes' peppermint fragrance sure beat smelling like wood smoke and sweat.

The spare clothes were obviously his. The drawstring on the sweatpants kept them up, but she had to roll the legs up. The soft t-shirt and sweatshirt were huge and still smelled faintly of laundry soap.

After she returned to the tents, Hawk took her dirty clothes to the helicopter.

Standing in front of her tent, Kit wrapped her arms around herself as she looked around. The twilight was fading into black, and the shadowy trees around the clearing were closing in. Anything could be hiding in the darkness.

A shiver ran through her.

Her tent sat right next to Hawk's and still seemed awfully far away.

"Problem?"

She jumped. Hawk stood in front of her. He'd approached so silently. Did bears walk that quietly? Or cougars? Or...

"Can I sleep with you?" she blurted out.

He chuckled. "I'm less scary than bears?"

Looking down, she shook her head. How cowardly could she get? "Nevermi—"

"Hey. Kidding." He touched her cheek, featherlight. "Bet you didn't camp out as a kid."

"No, I'm pretty much a city girl."

"Mako had us in the woods from the day we arrived." He leaned down, lowered his voice. "We were scared spitless."

Her embarrassment lifted, even as she protested, "You were little boys."

"Hardened street kids. New is scary, till you know the dangers and what to do."

"Oh." He was right. "Thanks."

"And yeah, you can sleep here. There's room." He ducked into his tent to move his bag and pad to one side.

In a tent with him. All alone.

Yet the thought wasn't frightening any longer. Well, not much.

She deflated her pad, then set everything back up beside his sleeping bag in his tent. Unzipping her sleeping bag partway, she scooted into it. Even through her clothing, the chill made her squeak.

Already in his own bag, he chuckled, and the sound relaxed her even more. There was no superiority or meanness in his amusement.

And he was letting her stay in his tent.

The need to show gratitude grew uncomfortable, and she raised up on an elbow and leaned over to kiss him. Her mouth had just brushed his when he gripped her shoulder with one hand.

"Not a good idea." His low voice filled the tent.

"But—" How could she thank him?

He ran a finger down her cheek. "You need sleep, and so do I."

Her shoulders hunched with shame. With humiliation. He didn't want her. Didn't want—

"If you jump me in the middle of the night, okay. Only I don't have condoms." His rumbled laugh stroked over her skin and eased the ugly feelings inside.

"Oh." He was giving her a chance to settle. To think before she acted.

And he'd spoken of condoms. It felt as if her face was bright red. This talking about stuff was hard, wasn't it? "Um. I have an implant, actually, so I can't get...um, pregnant."

She had it before marrying Obadiah, and avoiding an argument about not having a child right away, she'd never told him. Her wariness about discussing important matters should have been a red flag telling her not to get involved with him. Later, she learned he'd searched her medicine cabinet to make sure she wasn't taking birth control pills. The jerk.

"I was tested for everything at the hospital." At least the PZs hadn't given her any STDs.

Lying on his side, looking at her, Hawk was immobile. After a second, he said in a gravelly voice, "I get checked; all good. No one since the last test."

Oh. Were they really going to do this? She held her breath.

He shook his head. "It's a small tent. Let's see how you do."

As if she were Aric's age, he pulled her sleeping bag up over her shoulders, tucked her in, and brushed her hair out of her face.

Without a word, he settled back into his own bag.

She closed her eyes, feeling the fabric warm around her.

As her muscles relaxed, she realized she wasn't aching with unfulfilled arousal. Because she hadn't wanted sex for her own pleasure, but because she felt as if she needed to thank him.

Old patterns of behavior could sneak right up on a girl, couldn't they? She let out a sigh. "You're right. Thank you, Hawk."

"Never thought I'd be up for sainthood." He huffed a laugh.

The man had no idea. Because he really was a saint.

And, huh, wasn't it funny that now...*now*, she wanted him. That laugh, his scent, the way he'd tucked her in, his powerful hands so very gentle. Arousal simmered low in her belly.

No sex right now, but oh, she might see what happened when the moon rose.

A faint sound woke Hawk. Kit was sliding out of her sleeping bag. A latrine run, maybe? He waited, unmoving, eyes closed. Rather than unzipping the tent, she moved closer.

Her lips brushed his cheek. Tiny kisses covered his cheek, his jaw, then his mouth. Nibbles on his lips. A kiss—a serious fucking kiss that demanded participation—had his dick springing from a semi-chubby to a cat-couldn't-scratch-it erection.

The light from the full moon lit the tent with a soft glow. Out of her sleeping bag, Kit knelt beside him with her hands on his shoulders.

Threading his fingers into her hair, he kept her still long enough to thoroughly plunder her mouth and—

What the fuck was he thinking? This was Kit.

He released her immediately.

She gave a husky laugh. "It's okay. I thought you might react that way." She kissed him again.

Mmm, he could do this all fucking night.

Although, yeah, one hand had already slid under her oversized T-shirt bunched up around her waist. Her skin was so damned smooth. Her breast fit in his hand just right—high and soft. The velvety nipple jutted into a hard peak under his fingers.

He'd learned how she liked to be touched. She wasn't into pain, but firmness—definitely. When he found the right notes in the song of sex, he'd feel the tiny wiggle of her hips, hear how her breathing would pause.

She didn't want to lead in bed, but she'd panic if he took over completely. That was fine. They'd find a good harmony.

He kissed and teased, feeding the flames, and grinned when she unzipped his sleeping bag, then pulled his shirt up and over his head.

Sliding a hand downward, he discovered her sweatpants were gone. He stroked over the warm curve of her hip. "Jesus, I like your ass."

She gave a huff of a laugh and nipped his earlobe before removing her t-shirt. Her next kiss had the interesting side effect of rubbing her breasts over his chest and putting her ass up in the air.

Massaging one sweet butt cheek with his right hand, he ran his left down her belly to between her legs.

Very nicely wet. His cock gave an interested jerk.

He slid a slickened finger up and over her clit, very lightly, like the first soft notes of a song. Getting the audience's attention, giving them a hint of what was to come.

She was in charge of the kissing part—and he cooperated fully, even as he slowly woke her down below. No hurry. Good music took time to build.

With every sense, he absorbed the clues she sent. The way her breathing stuttered as he stroked the perfect spot at the edge of the hood and clit. How her kisses grew deeper, hotter, and her fingers clenched his shoulders.

He squeezed the soft roundness of her ass, enjoyed the rub of her breasts over his chest.

There was nowhere in the world he'd rather be.

He was driving her *mad*. She didn't want to come, not without him inside her, but when she tried to move away, his hand held her bottom in place...and his finger never stopped rubbing her clit.

Low in her pelvis, she felt the pressure building with every slow stroke of his finger.

His right hand massaged her ass, even as his left hand moved to slide a finger inside her.

She moaned and shivered at the penetration. Then froze as memories of other hands slid into her head.

"Kit, look at me." The rumbled low command was in the voice that surrounded her in safety.

Her panic receded, and she pushed up far enough to look down at him.

In the moonlit tent, his gaze met hers. Held hers, even as his finger stroked in and out, so very slowly, rousing every nerve down there to a searing need.

Feeling his hand on her ass, holding her, she felt the slice of panic again, and he stilled. Waited. His gaze never wavered, because he'd pause if she was scared. He had before, each and every time she'd grown afraid—and then would re-start everything.

She didn't want to pause again. Heat vied with fear—and heat won out.

The sunlines beside his eyes crinkled. Ever so gently, his right hand caressed her bottom, moved down to tease the crease between the cheek and the back of her thigh. With his left hand, he slowly drew a finger over her clit, making it throb and burn, before thrusting inside her again, stronger this time. He set up a pattern, first rubbing her clit, then sliding inside. In and out, over and over, as everything inside her tightened, tightened...

His finger on her clit swept over, paused, and wiggled there, right on top, just enough to—

"Oh God!" Pleasure exploded through her in vast sweeps of sensation, roaring through her veins until she surely must glow brighter than the moon.

A minute...or many...later, she realized she was draped over him like a blanket. His right hand was still on her bottom, the left stroked slowly up and down her back.

"You're mean." She pouted. "I wanted to come with you inside me."

"Then get off again." His laugh was a raspy growl, so very sexy. "It's a female perk."

Oh. She'd managed two orgasms in the past. Before Obadiah. Rarely, but *hmm.* Anyway, even if she didn't come again, she wanted him to get off.

As if he'd heard her thoughts, he made a noise. "We go on only if you're into it. If not, I won't break."

The man didn't expect enough out of life. Not for sex, not for himself.

As tenderness washed over her, she kissed him, tracing the scar on his upper lip with her tongue.

When she lifted her head, his expression was unreadable. Like he'd pulled a plastic mask over his face.

"Hawk, what?"

"You don't seem the type to hanker after a scarred-up merc. A *sneering* one."

"I don't think about you being a mercenary. Not when we're like this." She ran her hands over his chest and could feel the scars there too. Dear heavens, what he must have lived through.

But he'd lived.

However, the scars were not only on his skin, but in his soul as well. So she used the same words she might have for Aric. "It makes my heart sad to know you've been hurt."

Shock filled his eyes.

She touched the scar at the corner of his mouth. "Just so you know, this only makes you look like you're sneering when you're not smiling. With even a tiny smile, it disappears."

He stared at her as if he didn't know what to say.

That made two of them.

Her lips curved. "I guess I'll just have to get you smiling more, hmm?" To get a good start on that, she dragged his sweatpants down his ridged belly and off completely.

His cock bobbed up, and she had a momentary qualm. Could she do this?

"Sugar, we can stop. Or hands—"

"Aren't we a pair, worrying over each other." And wasn't that what love was about?

Wait—no. She didn't have that thought. *That* word didn't belong in her vocabulary any longer, not when applied to an adult male.

She shook the thought out of her head and ran her hands up his legs, feeling the thickened skin of a scar that ran from calf to thigh. Her fingers paused in awe, in respect. He'd had a hard life— and somehow had still preserved the gentleness in his heart.

Yes, she could do this.

Bending, she kissed his flat abs, then wrapped her hand around his erection. He was a bit longer than what she was familiar with and definitely thicker. His cock totally matched his build. Velvety smooth skin lay taut over the iron shaft beneath, and bulging veins ran upward to a thick helmet with a spongier texture.

Smiling, she used both hands, up and down, teasing him as he'd teased her—and then she swung a leg over him and moved on top.

Jesus, the woman was going to kill him.

Hawk froze as Kit straddled him, one knee on either side of his hips. Her wet, hot pussy flattened his dick before she raised up and curled her fingers around him. She positioned his shaft right there at her entrance.

"Kit." His voice sounded as if he'd eaten rocks for supper.

A shiver ran through her, even as she tightened her hand around him. "If I need you to, you'll stop. I know you will."

Her trust in his honor flattened him. "Always."

"Um, and if *you* need to stop, it's fine too."

Damn. The discovery that she didn't need him to be invincible was startling.

Freeing.

Pulling in a breath, he studied her face. "How about a kiss first?"

Her laugh was a bit high, then she abandoned his dick to lean forward and kiss him again. Her pussy pressed him down, warming him with future promises. Her mouth was soft, and as he roamed his hands over her hips, her ass, and the sides of her breasts, her breathing sped back up.

There was that wiggle again. One of these days, he'd bury his face in that pussy and really make her squirm.

By the time he finished kissing her, she was several degrees warmer in his arms.

Sitting up, she lifted her ass and, once again, gripped his dick.

An inch went in, two inches. She came to a full stop, sucking air as if she'd run a mile.

"Slow as you want," he reminded her. "Or we can quit."

He had too many of his own memories of his father's beatings. Of being helpless. Whatever she needed, he'd do. He rested his hands on her thighs and waited.

He'd wait forever if that was what the music called for.

"It's weird, Hawk. I want you so bad I ache, and then I get scared, and then I want you." Her lips pressed together, and she lowered herself—no, she fucking *dropped* right onto his cock.

They both gasped.

Jesus fuck, she was hot and wet and tight, and his dick had just hit heaven. Her cunt made small ripples, adjusting to his size— and bathing him in velvety heat.

"Ooooh, yes," she whispered and started to lean down.

Which swung her beautifully plump breasts right into his

waiting hands. As he fondled her and rolled her nipples gently, her pussy tightened on him like a fist.

When he didn't move, her impatient squirming made him grin —and wait for her to do something about it.

She didn't. "Hawk... Can you...can I be on the bottom? Only I'm not sure I can."

"We'll try it." Slowly, carefully, he rolled them over and braced himself above her, still deep inside. "You with me? Look at me."

Her gaze lifted, her eyes wide and vulnerable, and he held perfectly still, despite the way his cock was demanding action.

"Breathe, sugar. Nothing happens until you say."

Staring into his eyes, she pulled in a breath. The next one was deeper.

He nuzzled her cheek, remembering the techniques he used when he hit the wall. "What do you smell?"

"You," she whispered, then giggled. "We both smell like peppermint and wood smoke."

"What do you hear?"

Her eyes unfocused for a second. "The little waterfall. Wind in the trees. No bears."

"No bears," he agreed. "What's under your hands?"

"Your shoulders." Her palms slid down his arms, over his biceps, back up to his shoulders. "I like your muscles."

When she beamed up at him, he chuckled. The release of intense fear could take a brain off-line, almost like being drunk.

"Wiggle your toes." When she did, he touched her cheek. "Now wiggle something else."

She giggled and did, making his dick one very happy body part.

Damn, but he needed to move.

Feeling her slender body beneath him, seeing her gorgeous eyes, feeling her heat surrounding his shaft left him in awe. Her need for him was honest, her trust humbling, and, once again, he tightened his grip on his control.

Resting his weight on one elbow, he played with one sweet breast. The way she sucked air in at his touch was simply fucking great.

"Ready for me to move?" He tugged on her tightly bunched nipple.

"Move," she whispered.

He balanced carefully, keeping his weight off her, staying low enough he could feel the heat of her body, could brush his chest against her breasts.

Slowly, he pulled out, then slid in, inch by inch, until he was fully seated. "Fuck, you feel good," he growled and bent down to nuzzle her temple.

Out, in. He picked up speed in the most gradual of increments. Oh yeah, it was all good.

And different. Maybe because he was so intently present and focused on her every breath. When her eyes started to close, and her breathing quickened, he knew. When her cunt tightened around him, he grinned and increased his force slightly, then lifted enough he could slide a hand between them.

His hand was almost too big, but when his fingers found her slick little clit, she gasped. Her ass rose, pinning his hand, but he managed to get in a few strokes before her cunt fisted around his cock.

He could feel her body shake as the waves of her climax crashed over her.

His dick took over then—and he kept it within bounds, thrusting fast, but not hard, feeling her tighten and loosen around him. The heat in his balls grew to searing before boiling up and through his cock. He went rigid as the sensations grew unbearable before shooting out in hard spasms of pleasure.

He started to relax, caught himself, and rolled onto his back so she was on top.

And look, he had himself a limp, satisfied, warm blanket of woman.

Smiling, he tugged her sleeping bag over them both, then kissed the top of her head, not finding any words to go with the gesture.

There was a deep satisfaction in knowing she understood anyway.

Using filtered water, Hawk had made her *coffee*.

Yes, he was pretty much perfect. On a camp chair beside the small crackling woodfire, Kit tipped her head back and watched sunlight spill over the mountain peaks into their small valley. So beautiful.

With a contented sigh, she scooped up another bite from her bowl. The rolled oats were sweet with honey and dried fruit with tons of walnuts and almonds. Instead of eating it dry, she'd followed Hawk's lead, pouring some of her thoroughly-creamed coffee into the bowl. It was just plain yummy. "Who made the granola?"

"We take turns." He eyed his bowl. "This batch was Gabe's. Mine's better."

Granola one-upmanship. She didn't quite manage to muffle a snicker.

He heard. Of course he did. "Behave or you'll walk home."

This time, her laugh came out loud and clear—and earned her a half-smile. Sweet heavens, he was sexy as anything in faded jeans and an unbuttoned flannel shirt. The rising sun lightened his eyes to a stunning blue.

They'd already taken down the tents and packed the sleeping stuff away in the helicopter. As soon as the fog cleared a little more, they'd be on their way home.

She wanted to hold her son so badly it was painful.

Yet she wouldn't have missed this wilderness adventure for the world. She'd had the chance to share the world Hawk came from.

The one he loved. As he moved through the forest, made a camp, cooked over a fire, he was as relaxed as he was in his living room.

And last night...

Just wow. At the start, she'd simply hoped she could manage to have sex with a man—with Hawk. Instead, the night had been amazing. She'd come so hard she could swear the tingles still ran over her nerve endings.

But what they'd shared had been more than mere sex. It was as if she'd asked for a flower, and he'd given her an entire garden. She'd never felt so safe and cared for and...cherished. Yes, that was the word.

Not loved, Kit. Don't go there.

Dear God, was she really so foolish? She was.

I love him.

And who wouldn't?

Not just because of the wonderful sex—or how he'd somehow calmed her panic attacks. It was because he was...kind. Thoughtful. Honest. Didn't anyone realize how rare those traits were?

Tipping her head back, she watched the fog on the mountainsides silently wafting upward.

She no longer believed she needed a man to make her feel complete. At long last, she'd wiped out Uncle Duane's misogynistic programming. She was complete, in and of herself.

She and Aric could manage fine on their own. The receptionist pay was good, and her next job would be even better. Besides, she still had most of her share of the PZ money.

So how she felt about Hawk wasn't because she couldn't manage without him. It was truly love, somewhat like her love for Aric and Frankie. Loving them made her happy.

He made her happy—and oh, so much more. Every time she saw him, it felt as if her heart had become the sun, radiating through her. When she heard his voice unexpectedly, every nerve in her body danced with joy. The way he held Aric turned her insides to mush. And the way he held her?

Mmm, bad Kit. Now she wanted to see if they could warm the sleeping bags again.

Another patch of fog lifted upward, revealing the deep green of the evergreen forest.

Wouldn't Obadiah hate that she'd realized she was better off without him. That she'd moved on after he'd tried so hard to break her. He'd seen strong women as a threat. Probably Nabera and Parrish did too. But they were out of her life, and she'd never have to think of them again. And she *wouldn't.* The bastards.

"Hey."

She jumped at the rough sound.

Hawk had crouched beside her. He touched her cheek with the tips of his fingers. "You're growling. Problem?"

Oh, oops? "Just thinking of the past."

And wishing for a future that would let her have him. The chances for that were slim. He'd obviously never settled on one woman before. And what man would want a girlfriend who not only came with another man's child but a ton of issues?

But that didn't matter. She was going to simply take each day at a time and enjoy their time together.

Putting her hand over his, she pressed his palm to her face. "Time to leave?"

"Fog's cleared enough." His thumb stroked her chin gently.

"Then we better get moving." She had a son to get home to.

CHAPTER TWENTY-FIVE

You miss 100% of the shots you don't take. - Wayne Gretzky

Hawk had spent the day flying a batch of tourists up to a mountain lake, then dropping off supplies for some isolated cabins.

Back home, as he'd gotten his supper, he noticed the bacon in the meat drawer. Not unusual. In his mind, bacon was a staple. But it reminded him that Aric had asked what a BLT was. That seemed like a serious lack in the kid's education.

So, after eating, he'd headed into the greenhouse to pick tomatoes. He breathed in the air, filled with the scents of tomato plants, peppers, and moist, rich soil. Although there were more tomato plants in the garden, they always had some heirloom varieties in here that would mature early and would often produce for a while after the first freeze.

He'd picked a few perfectly ripe ones when the door swung open.

Kit squeaked in surprise. "Sorry, I didn't know anyone was in here." She was clad in jeans and a *"Weed 'em & Reap"* T-shirt that

Audrey had bought her. No makeup, long hair pulled back into a tail...and she looked fantastic.

It'd been three days since their unexpected overnight in the mountain. When they returned the next morning, Aric had been frantic and spent the day hanging on to one of them. He'd even shown up in Hawk's bedroom that night. When Hawk carried him up to Kit's bedroom, it'd been fucking difficult to leave. "Aric okay?"

"He's back to normal and sleeping like a rock."

Hawk nodded.

Kneeling by the salad greens she'd planted in July, she started thinning the beets. "Sorry, little guys, but your friends need more room."

Was she apologizing to the plants? *Tenderhearted woman.* "It's good you're here." When she looked up, he motioned to the fall and winter plantings. "Seems no one remembered until too late last year."

He hadn't been around last summer, and he regretted it. He'd hung onto his resentment at Gabe far too fucking long.

Kit set a batch of tiny beet leaves in her basket. "Greenhouses are great, but what do you do when the sun pretty much doesn't bother to rise in midwinter?"

"Use grow lights in our houses. If it's too cold, the greenhouse isn't worth the energy to heat." Solar energy only went so far when there was too little daylight.

Mako's house also had grow lights, but would she still be here then?

The thought of her leaving was like getting gutted.

Shocked at the pain, Hawk stared down at her. Jesus fuck, had he fucking *fallen* for her?

Unable to get past the idea, he watched her picking peppers.

After she added a couple of tomatoes and lifted her basket, he took it from her. "I got it."

"Um, okay." Her brow furrowed as she looked at him.

He carried her produce and his back to Mako's cabin. After setting it on the kitchen island, he hesitated as she put away the greens. Dammit, he didn't know what to say or do. He wanted to be with her...and continuing down this path was a fucking terrible idea.

"Hawk." She shoved the fridge door closed and handed him a beer. "Why don't you drink this and tell me what's wrong."

That wasn't going to happen.

Something else could, though. "Where's Aric?"

"JJ and Regan are making sugar cookies and invited him to help decorate them."

Hawk stared. "Christ, even a bath won't get that shit off."

"Mmmhmm. He'll have colorful hands until the food coloring fades." Kit chuckled, totally unworried about her son's appearance. Because she was the kind of mother who simply wanted her boy to be happy.

Hawk set his beer down unopened. When he put his hands around her waist, he expected her to tense.

She didn't. Because she trusted him.

He wouldn't betray that trust. Not ever.

Setting her palms on his chest, she tilted her head. "What are you up to, mister?"

Her dark eyes were the color of mahogany polished to a lustrous shine. "You have beautiful eyes."

Those eyes narrowed.

So suspicious. She should be.

He smiled slightly. "Frosting cookies usually takes a while."

It took her a moment, then her gaze lifted to her quarters upstairs.

Yep, she got it.

Dear sweet heavens, Hawk had *skills*.

When they'd gotten into her bedroom, he'd stripped her and

somehow, she'd ended up on her back on the bed. With an evil smile, he said their time was limited so she'd need to get off quickly, and he pushed a pillow under her ass. Still clothed, he'd knelt on the bed between her legs and kissed his way down her body.

Only...he kept going. Past her breasts. Past her stomach. He edged back on the bed so he could reach her thighs. His lips were warm, his beard somehow both scratchy and soft and so distracting.

"Hawk, no," she whispered. He'd wanted to do this in the tent, and she hadn't let him. Obadiah—heck, all the PZs—never went down on their women, saying women were smelly and foul and nauseating.

"Kit, yes," Hawk murmured. His big hands ran up and down her thighs, then his thumbs stroked the tender skin next to her groin. "I doubt your fuckwit husband was into this, which means it shouldn't trigger you. Right?"

His thumbs edged inward, over the outside of her labia. Teasing her.

Her hips wiggled—and he grinned.

"I-I guess."

"I love this." His dark blue gaze met hers. "But if you hate it, I'll stop."

Darn it, it was impossible to argue with an argument like that. Especially since, if it was possible, her clit would be doing a happy dance. She used to love oral sex.

Damn Obadiah anyway. "Okay. But...but, if *you* don't like it, then—"

His only response was an exasperated snort. And then he was there, his mouth on her. His tongue slid in circles around her clit, so very warm and velvety and perfect. Her hips tried to rise for more, to get him to lick her there—

And he pressed her down, even as his thumbs opened her more fully.

"Mmm. You smell like vanilla." He licked again, moving his left hand to the top of her mound, the fingers holding her open as his right hand dropped.

His finger slid inside even as his tongue grazed over the very top of her clit.

The exquisite sensations were almost too much. "Oh. *Oh*."

"Nice." His finger began a slow in and out, as he licked the sides of her increasingly engorged nub, then closed his lips around it.

He sucked and licked, thrusting and teasing, and her world narrowed to just the slow slide of penetration, to the demanding sensation of his tongue. The pressure inside her tightened inexorably. He sucked even stronger and rubbed his tongue over the top.

"Oh, oh, oooooh." Pleasure rolled over her, tossing her like waves on an ocean, And his tongue and finger continued drawing out more glorious spasms.

When she heard him laugh, she realized her hands were in his hair, holding him to her.

"Sorry." She released him immediately.

He was still laughing as he moved off the bed and onto his feet. "If I go bald because I get you off, it's a total win."

Opening his jeans, he pushed them down to let his cock spring out.

"Come here, woman." He pulled her down to the edge of the bed. Gently, but firmly, he lifted her legs, resting them on each side of his chest. Her butt was still elevated on a pillow, and most of her weight was on her shoulders. "Okay?"

Somehow her trigger had melted into a pool of happy goo. "Okay."

The bed was high, and her pussy was just at the right height. He entered her slowly, giving her a moment to adjust to the startling sensation of being filled, being stretched almost to discomfort.

As he moved closer, her legs slid upward until her calves were on each side of his head, and her vagina pulsed around his thickness.

Leaning forward slightly, he sank in—and oh, having her ankles on his shoulders, let him penetrate even deeper.

His hands were free, she realized, as he leaned forward and fondled her breasts with one hand. His other hand curled around her right thigh, anchoring her as his thrusts grew stronger, faster.

He'd pound, then slow and move side-to-side, then up and down.

And her arousal wakened and grew. How did he do that to her? His fingers tugged on her nipple, squeezed, the sharply exquisite pain jolting all the way down. Her pussy clenched around him.

He laughed.

"More." The words escaped, and she slapped her hands over her mouth.

But his gaze grew as hot as the blue flame in the center of the fire, and his smile was wicked as he trailed his fingers down her belly. The heel of his hand rested at the top of her mound and pressed down each time his shaft withdrew. His hand pulled upward when he drove in—and that tugged right on her clit too—even as his thick cock filled her completely.

Dear sweet heavens. Her toes curled.

His pace picked up, and the rhythmic sensation on her clit, the hammering inside, drove her up and up, until the heat grew into a brilliant torment.

And sent her right over.

Her legs pressed down on his shoulders, as her hips bucked. "Oh, *Haaawk*." The release tore through her in a storm of sensation, whipping waves of pleasure across her body until even her hair seemed to shimmer.

"Nice." His hand tightened on her thigh, holding her as he

hammered into her. She was still coming even as he reached his peak, and she could feel the jerking of his shaft inside her.

His jaw was tight, his muscles tensed—and his eyes held hers in a long, wonderful moment.

Eventually, he moved, running his hands up and down her thighs before lowering her legs. After pulling up and zipping his jeans, he moved her up on the mattress and stretched out on top of her.

His weight pressed her into the mattress, and she stiffened, then breathed in his scent...and relaxed. For a happy moment, she kissed his jaw, his neck, because he never smelled like anyone else. So nice. "Ocean, today? And with a hint of citrus. Yesterday, it was cypress, I think."

"Hmm?" His puzzled expression made her laugh.

She rubbed her face against his shoulder. "I like the way you smell. Even though it changes a lot."

He snorted. "Got soap from Lillian for Christmas. She said Mako used smell to stay grounded."

"You pick different scents depending on how you feel?"

A nod and a smile.

Huh, so which one would mean sex?

When he snorted, she realized she'd asked that aloud. *Oh...drat.*

"Guess. I'll let you know when you're right."

Her eyes narrowed. "You're a guy. That means I'll always be right."

His laugh completed her day. "Yeah."

He bent his head to nibble on her neck, making her sigh. "I like how *you* smell."

Thank you, Frankie.

She ran her fingers through his hair, loving the feel of his body on top of hers, something she'd never thought she'd have again.

Braced on one elbow, he stroked the hair from her face and

smiled down at her. When the lines at the corners of his eyes crinkled, she stared up at him. He looked...happy.

She'd made him happy, and without thinking, she whispered the words that she'd barely thought. "I love you."

Shock bloomed in his eyes. "Kit."

An apology sprang to her lips, but she held it in. Welcome or not, it was how she felt. She wouldn't apologize for her own feelings.

He shook his head as if to say no—or that he didn't believe her. "That isn't—" He stopped at the sound of light footsteps downstairs.

Kit gasped. "It's Aric."

"Hell." Hawk rolled off the bed.

Snatching up her clothing, Kit ran into the bathroom to dress.

A minute later, she heard the door open, and Hawk called, "Kid, what you got there—cookies?"

"I did blue," Aric piped.

"I'll come down," Hawk said. The door closed, and his voice grew fainter. "I need a blue cookie."

By the time she got downstairs, Aric was coloring at the island. Frosting streaked his face, and his fingers were blue.

She'd heard the outside door close as she'd left the bedroom. A glance through the windows showed Hawk had just left and was striding across the courtyard to his own place.

An ache set up residence in her heart.

Hawk took his troubles out onto the lake.

"*I love you*," she'd said. Had to be the most beautiful melody in the world. One that drifted through his head over and over as the kayak skimmed over the water.

He paddled faster until cold drops of water sprayed over his face.

But he couldn't escape the words, the surge of joy that'd hit, or the fucking rock-bottom realization that saying the words back would fuck them up.

He sure wasn't the person she needed in her life. Not permanently.

He might be an okay husband; yeah, he'd do his damndest to make sure he was, but a father?

Love couldn't fix everything.

Lifting the paddle, he let the kayak drift and listened to the soft hiss of the bow cutting water.

Near the bank, the trumpeter swans, Han and Leia, with four half-pint gray cygnets watched warily. The thought of Aric looking at him that way was a knife in the gut.

Never.

It hadn't been that hard to take care of a quiet, timid boy. But as Aric got past the shit that'd happened with the PZs, he'd return to being a typical noisy, mouthy boy.

Kids pissed off their parents—that was just a fact of life.

Hawk traced the scar that ran down his cheek. Another fact was that children became their parents—and his father had been a monster. An abusive asshole.

That weakness was inside Hawk, just waiting for a chance to get out.

No, he wouldn't—couldn't—risk it.

CHAPTER TWENTY-SIX

T*he world breaks everyone, and afterward, some are strong at the broken places.* - Ernest Hemingway

"The Prophet is dead, Captain."

"No." Rage swept through Nabera, and he shouted into the phone. "No!"

In the house, the handful of loyal followers living there turned to stare at him.

It couldn't be true. It mustn't. He yanked in a breath and evened out his voice. "Tell me what happened."

Ezekiel worked in the Texas State Capitol building in Austin and got the news about their leader before anyone else. "A bunch of convicts started a fight, and somehow, Reverend Parrish got knocked over. The guards broke the fight up and found him on the floor. He'd been shanked. Bad. He died on the way to the hospital."

"Why would anyone hurt our prophet?" Nabera dropped onto a chair, grief a hard knot within him. He'd followed the Reverend since the day they met years ago.

"Captain." There was a pause, then Ezekiel cleared his throat. "The guards found no witnesses, but they think…"

"Spit it out, damn you," Nabera snapped.

"Two of the prisoners are brothers to a woman who was in our Texas compound. They might have, uh, had a grudge. Because of her. They were in the fight."

"They did it." Anger raged in Nabera.

"Nobody saw anything. But seems the reverend hadn't annoyed anyone—not enough for a murder. So, yeah, one of the brothers probably stabbed him."

"Because of a woman." Once again, it was a cunt at the heart of their problems. It started when Obadiah brought Kirsten into their midst. Like a serpent, she'd poisoned everything around her.

Now another traitorous bitch had spread her lies. "Women are to blame for our Prophet's death."

"Our Reverend is dead?" Shocked voices rose, and within minutes, there was not only grief, but fear enough to thicken the air.

Nabera pulled himself together. Parrish would expect him to be decisive. "Thank you for letting me know, Ezekiel. Will you and our Texas Zealots be all right?"

"Eh, when the Reverend was arrested and the cops descended on the compound, we went to ground. And now…"

"What?"

"I'm done, Captain. I felt I owed you the call, but I'm out."

How many of the faithful would feel the same?

Grief mingled with fury, and Nabera was glad he had the phone pressed tightly enough to his ear that no one in the room heard how the weakling was fleeing with the other rats. Jumping off a sinking ship.

He pocketed his phone, frustration growing. He couldn't let them leave yet. Parrish had been more than his prophet; he'd been a friend.

Cowards. If he didn't act, the patriots here would also abandon the cause.

And he'd let them...after they did one last thing for the Prophet.

His voice came out as hard and cold as the glaciers on the mountain peaks. "My people, one woman caused the disasters that have happened. One disloyal, unnatural slut. She's probably laughing at what she's accomplished. Laughing at *us*."

The angry expressions around him mirrored his own. "She must pay for what she's done."

Their faith called for vengeance. For action.

For blood and death.

On Wednesday, Hawk drove into town, still out of sorts. Nightmares had kept him awake, then he'd spent the morning and afternoon in his floatplane, and nothing had gone right. Landing on a lake, he'd almost run into a submerged log. He'd flown a guy and his injured dog out and to a veterinarian, and the poor lab's pained whining had twisted Hawk's gut. Then two climbers showed up an hour late, and he'd had to throttle his anger and remind himself that strangling customers might have consequences.

Pity, that.

Now, despite his plan to avoid Kit and Aric until he found the right words to tell her his decision, he'd been railroaded into this task. The Hermitage gang were grilling the salmon Audrey and Gabe had caught early this morning. Since Hawk wasn't cooking, JJ had asked him to pick up the kids at summer school.

He sighed, pulled over to the gravel shoulder, and parked his pickup in front of the pair of clapboard buildings. After a landslide destroyed the school last winter, Bull loaned out a couple of houses Mako had owned for the spring semester classes. One of the teachers was using a building for her informal "summer school" and an older-child day care.

Inside, Hawk headed for the dining room, which served as the daycare for preschool-aged children. A batch of short tables and chairs filled one end. Stick-figure-type artwork—like the pictures on his fridge—covered a corkboard wall.

At least half a dozen rugrats darted around the room like bats in a mosquito-rich environment.

"Hey, Hawk," Erica called from where she was putting shoes on a little boy. Her mother was the teacher responsible for this zoo. According to Knox, the young woman had recently dropped out of college to consider her career choices.

Hawk nodded to her.

"I heard you're picking up Aric today. He's in the reading circle." Erica motioned to a corner with a round, bright red rug and green beanbag chairs.

Yeah, there was Aric in a chair, immersed in a picture book.

Hawk started across the room and paused to admire the clay animals on a table. Some of the kids had done damn clever work.

A tinny-sounding "*mooo-mooo-mooo*" caught his attention. A little girl was pushing buttons on a white plastic gameboard that lay at Aric's feet. When she pressed a green button a loud "*meow*" sounded.

"Hey! That's mine!" Aric jumped up and grabbed the game, trying to pull it away.

"Mine!" The girl wrenched the plastic board free. Freeing one hand, she shoved Aric back. "Bad boy."

Moving that direction, Hawk snorted. *Fair enough.*

Face red with fury, Aric swept the closest books off the book-case, then started throwing the rest. Everywhere.

Shit.

A book hit the girl. She dropped the toy and screamed in pain.

The high, pain-filled sound hit Hawk like an IED, blinding him with memories. *His father's shouting, "You fucking stupid brat," and flinging the screwdriver at him. The pain as it ripped across his fore-head. Screaming, curling on the floor, holding his forehead. Father kicking him out of the way. "Dumb fuck." Blood everywhere.*

Hawk tasted blood. Pain told him he'd bitten the inside of his cheek. He shook his head hard and pulled in a breath, trying to escape the flashback.

Not. Now.

In the corner, Aric lifted a heavy book over his head to throw it...at the girl.

"Stop!" Hawk's voice came out an angry roar.

Aric froze.

Taking the boy by his arms, Hawk picked him up, strode to the other corner, and set him down. "You—"

His voice strangled and died. He not only sounded like his father but was looming over the kid. *Jesus, no.*

Aric crumpled into a scared ball on the floor.

Hawk's mouth went dry. The harsh sound of his own voice still rang in his ears, and his heart pounded faster than in a damned artillery barrage. What the hell was wrong with him?

He knew the answer. He was a monster.

Get a grip, asshole. Pulling in a breath, he went down on his haunches beside the boy that, face it, he loved with all his wretched heart. A child he shouldn't be allowed near. "Aric."

Aric kept crying.

"Hey..." Hawk reached out carefully.

The boy didn't move.

"Kid, I'm sorry I yelled." Hawk cringed inside. He was just as bad as his father, terrifying a child. There were no words to erase that fact.

He could only wait, silently, until the tears slowed.

Across the room, Erica held the little girl who was now calm. There was no blood. She'd be okay.

Aric sat up.

Slowly, carefully, Hawk pulled out his bandanna and used it to wipe away the snot and tears.

The boy didn't cower from him—such a brave kid.

Hawk pulled in another breath against the pain under his ribs. "Let's get you home."

The trip home had been silent. Hawk turned off the pickup, released Aric from the car seat in back, then lifted him and set him on his feet.

When he shut the pickup's door, the kid just stood there, staring up at Hawk with big eyes. Unhappy eyes that hurt something deep inside Hawk's chest.

"C'mon, kid."

Aric didn't move. Just held his arms up in a way he hadn't for weeks. And he had tears in his eyes.

Hawk wanted to sit down beside him and bawl too. Getting shot, getting knifed had been less painful. "Sure, buddy."

He lifted Aric carefully, an arm under his ass.

The kid's arm went around his neck, head on Hawk's shoulder. Why the fuck was the boy snuggling up to a monster?

Hawk pulled in a breath and carried his charge out to the courtyard. Time to man up, confess, and disappear for the good of all of them.

Everyone was already on the patio.

Wearing a baseball cap with her hair pulled through the back, Kit tossed a salad and chatted with JJ about some celebration for Audrey.

Frankie was learning to grill, something the city girl hadn't yet mastered. To one side, Bull offered suggestions.

At the end of the table, Audrey was unloading condiments from a tray.

Gabe and Caz were setting the table with Regan's help.

His family. So normal, so fucking amazing.

The sense of loss was like the bite of shrapnel, ripping his chest to shreds. As Hawk carried Aric to the patio, his boots felt as if they were weighted down with lead.

"Hey, honey bear." Kit hurried up, obviously having seen the tear-streaked face. "What's wrong?"

Hawk tried to hand over the kid, but Aric's arm tightened around his neck.

The boy had no sense of self-preservation.

Kit turned to Hawk, brown eyes filled with worry. And everyone on the patio went silent.

Time to gut himself, bleed out, and leave.

"I fucked up." Hawk pulled in a breath. "I shouldn't be around kids; it's not safe."

Rather than grabbing her son and backing away, Kit moved closer. "I don't understand."

Jesus.

"Hawk." Caz sat down on the picnic table within reach. "What happened, '*mano?*"

Brother. That wasn't a word he was worthy of.

Kit deserved an explanation; they all did. *Yeah, get it out, asshole.* "I yelled at Aric. Grabbed him too rough. Scared the shit out of him. I'll leave; don't worry, I'll—"

"No." Aric had both arms around Hawk's neck now. "No."

Kit's frown deepened. "I'm not sure I've ever heard you yell. What made you shout at Aric?"

"It's not his fault," Hawk said. "I was wrong to—"

"Rachel took my toy, and I t'rowed stuff. Books. At her." The tiny voice was so unhappy.

Hawk felt tears on his neck. "No, Aric, it's—"

"I yelled too," Aric said. "Am I bad?"

Oh, holy fuck. "Jesus, boy, no. No, you're just a kid, and hell, you shouldn't throw things. We talked about that, yeah?"

There was an up and down movement. Aric's face was still pressed against Hawk's neck.

"You're not bad. Kids can't be bad. Like it's a law or something."

There was a muffled snort.

Hawk glared at Caz.

Kit scrubbed her face with her hands. She was pale.

She should be. He was a monster.

And his brothers were assholes.

"Let me get this straight." She used the voice he thought of as her badass-mama one. "Aric and Rachel had a fight over a toy, and he lost his temper and threw books and yelled at her." Her eyes narrowed as she looked from Aric to Hawk, waiting for an answer.

Hawk didn't move. He wasn't about to incriminate the kid.

"Yes, Mama," Aric whispered.

"One down," Gabe muttered. He stood beside Caz, one foot on the bench. Bull was next to him.

Hawk's muscles tightened. Would he lose his brothers too?

"What did Hawk yell at you?" Kit asked, her attention on her son.

"Stop."

She sighed. "Because he wanted you to stop throwing things?"

Another nod.

"I'd've yelled too," JJ murmured. "A book could've caused a nasty injury."

"And he grabbed you. Maybe to move you away from Rachel?" Kit's guess got a nod.

"Did he hurt you, Aric?"

"Nuh-uh." Aric sniffled. "I got scared."

The sense of guilt almost buckled Hawk's knees, but he kept his balance; he was still holding the boy. At least he hadn't hurt him, thank fuck.

"Aric, why were you scared, *mijo*?" Caz asked gently.

"Cuz I—"

"Because I'm a monster," Hawk growled. "Don't pick on the kid; he should—"

"What?" Kit stared at him. "Why would you...? Hawk, no. Aric was afraid because Obadiah or the other PZ men would have beat him. Why would you think you're a monster?"

"Because his father was," Gabe said at the same time as Bull.

Hawk turned to stare at his brothers.

Caz nodded. "We heard you talking with Grayson."

His brothers knew; it wasn't the big secret that he'd figured. There wasn't the pity or disgust he'd feared. Just understanding.

And their knowing was more of a relief than he could have imagined.

Aric lifted his head and told Kit, "His mama and daddy were mean to him."

Hawk winced. That was exactly what Doc Grayson had said to Aric, that Hawk's parents could be mean. "*His dad hit him. So did his momma.*"

"I see." She took a step closer. Her hand was warm on his arm. "Tell me about your parents."

Fuck no. He needed to leave, dammit.

His brothers just waited. Audrey, Frankie, JJ, and Regan had gathered in a group next to them.

Aric still had both arms around Hawk's neck, holding on like a lifeline. How the fuck could the boy want to be around him?

"Hawk." Kit's gaze met his. "Fair's fair."

She'd told him about her aunt and uncle. And he'd scared her kid. Had led her on and got her to love him—to love someone way too screwed up to be a good man. He owed her an explanation.

Man up, asshole. "They were okay till my father lost his job. Had to move to another state to find even crappier work. Pissed him off. He took it out on me."

Hawk stopped, cold seeping into his blood.

"Not before?" Kit prompted.

"Not...much. Till he noticed I looked like him and wanted to toughen me up. Called me a pussy, a coward, stupid and clumsy." Hawk managed a laugh. "He scared me so much I really was."

Kit leaned her forehead against his arm. "You had your own Obadiah, didn't you? Where was your mother?"

Of course Kit would ask. She'd done everything she could to keep Aric out of the firing zone, even when she got hurt instead.

"Her family was around until we moved. Then she took his side...maybe to keep from getting slapped around herself."

Regan took up position beside Hawk, leaning against him, no less. "Wow, your mama was a stupidhead *pendeja*." She looked up, filled with righteous judgment.

He stared down at the girl. The first time they'd met, he'd terrified her and made her cry. What was she doing? And she'd called his mother the Spanish equivalent to asshole?

He glanced at Caz.

His brother's lips quirked. "What she said."

Regan grinned.

"You had that scar on your forehead even in the foster home. Your dad?" Bull handed him a beer.

Damn his brothers. He'd always managed to avoid this shit before. Now, though... He was fucked.

Stalling, Hawk downed half of the bottle before handing it back. *Get it out.* "He was fixing a doorknob. I startled him, and he dropped a screw. So, he threw the screwdriver at me."

Regan wrapped her arms around him, staring at the white line across his forehead. "I *hate* your dad."

Aric's eyes were filled with tears again—and so were Kit's as she pulled Hawk down to brush soft fingers over the long, ugly scar. Ugly because his parents hadn't taken him to get it stitched. Because a doctor might have asked him how it happened.

"No wonder you yelled at Aric. You have first-hand experience of what can happen when things are thrown," Kit murmured.

Hawk shook his head. "The memory got me. I lost it. Because I'm a—"

"Oh, please." Kit gave his arm a shake. "If every parent who yells at their child is a monster, then we're all in that category. I've yelled at Aric, haven't I, honey bear?"

Aric nodded. "An' you said sorry, like Hawk."

A snickering sound came from Regan. "Just like Papá. He yells and says sorry for yelling, but I shouldn't'a done whatever, and so I have to say sorry too."

"God knows Mako yelled at us," Bull said. "And grabbed us."

"How many times did we end up in a snowbank or the river shallows?" Gabe's expression was wry—because the stubborn bastard had landed there more times than the rest of them.

"Wasn't the sarge's fault." Hawk shot Gabe a glare. "He did his best."

"We all do our best. We all mess up, apologize, and try to make it right," Kit said softly. "No one is perfect."

Even as he was trying to work through that, she frowned. "Aric and I have sessions together. To help with parenting techniques since we both have our own triggers that kind of bounce off each other. You obviously have some triggers...so you'd better come to those sessions with us."

What the fuck. "I'm leaving."

Even as Aric yelled, "No," Kit said, "No, you're not."

He looked at Aric. Mouth set in a stubborn line, chin up and determined.

He looked at Kit, who wore an identical expression.

Every fucking person around him looked the same.

Christ, he was screwed.

But...now everyone knew. Knew what he had inside, what he feared. He looked at his brothers. More protective bastards couldn't be found. Their women were the same.

And so was Kit.

Hawk rubbed the back of his neck as he considered. He'd

stopped Aric when his behavior got out of control. Now, it appeared Hawk had a whole family to do the same for him if needed. He had backup. The knowledge was...freeing.

He tightened his arm around Aric and touched Kit's cheek. "Guess I'm staying put."

A few minutes later, Kit was sitting beside Hawk at the picnic table. Because her legs had gone wobbly.

Although Regan had dragged Aric away to help her put out the silverware, he checked Hawk's location every couple of minutes.

She knew exactly how her son felt. Her insides were still shaking.

Hawk would have walked away, from his home, his family, Aric —and her.

The man was so very tough—and had so much pain inside him. She leaned against his side. "We're a hot mess. All three of us."

Putting an arm around her, he kissed the top of her head in silent agreement.

She curled her fingers around his hand. "We'll figure things out. Maybe we'll have a rough patch here and there, but none of us is a quitter."

He didn't speak for a long moment. "Thought it'd be safer if I left. I'm sorry."

Even if it would hurt him, he'd do anything to keep them safe. Dear heavens, she'd seen his face when he told them he'd shouted at Aric. So devastated.

"You should be sorry." She rubbed her cheek against his shoulder. "Don't even think about leaving, or I'll sic Aric and Regan on you."

Because he was a total pushover when it came to the children.

"You got a mean side, woman." He brushed her hair out of her face with one hand and lifted her chin with the other.

Who knew gray-blue eyes could be so warm?

"I love you, too, you know." The words in his deep rasping voice filled her heart.

And then he kissed her.

CHAPTER TWENTY-SEVEN

The purpose of life is to be useful, to be honorable, to be compassionate, to have it make some difference that you have lived and lived well. - Ralph Waldo Emerson

"My God, Hawk has a really effective shout." Erica leaned on the receptionist desk in the municipal building. "He silenced them. We should hire him."

"Were the children upset?" Kit asked. There was no summer school today, and the young woman had come in to talk about Aric's fight yesterday. And about Hawk.

Erica snorted. "Aric was the only one who was really scared—and, honestly, a lot of things set him off. After he calmed down, your boy wrapped himself around Hawk like a monkey."

Kit smiled. Of course he had. Aric trusted Hawk right down to the ground. Like Kit did. "Aric is supposed to apologize to Rachel. If he forgets, can you remind him?"

"Sure. She gets to apologize for shoving." Erica rolled her eyes. "After Aric and Hawk left, I had a talk with the children about better ways to disagree and about saying you're sorry."

"You're an amazing caregiver. I'm glad Aric has you this summer."

"Oh, god, that's so cool to hear." Erica beamed. "I've decided that childcare is going to be my career. Who knew I'd want to follow in Mom's footsteps?"

Kit laughed. "I was hoping Aric would follow in mine, but I think Hawk enticed him into wanting to fly."

"Of course he did." Erica rolled her eyes. "Those Hermitage guys make anything look sexy."

Now there was a truth. "Oh, I wanted to tell you, we're having an all-female celebration on Saturday at the roadhouse. I hope you and your mom can come. Audrey's pregnant. "

"I heard! It's so awesome, and one more way to make sure our Chief and librarian stay here where they belong. I turned twenty-one last month, so yay, I can get into the bar." With a wave, Erica headed out, sidestepping two people coming in.

Time to work. Mentally donning her medical receptionist hat, Kit got the elderly woman and her husband squared away to see Caz in the health clinic.

Next up was a person reporting a fender-bender.

JJ came out to retrieve that one.

This job sure wasn't anything she'd ever imagined doing but was exactly what she needed for the summer. Between the police station, the medical clinic, the library, and the records office, the building was the heart of the town.

And she'd started to feel like she belonged in Rescue.

An hour later, Gabe strode across the lobby to her desk. His rough-hewn face held an unreadable expression rather than a smile. "Kit."

"Is something wrong?" She jumped to her feet, panic rising. "Aric?"

"No. Nothing like that. I have news about Parrish."

Fear tightened her stomach. "And."

"He's dead, Kit. He was shanked—knifed, essentially—during a prison fight."

Reverend Parrish, the Prophet, was dead. She shook her head in disbelief. "Are you sure?"

"Yes." A fleeting smile crossed his face. "I knew you'd worry, so I called the prison staff. There's no doubt."

"Oh." Worries she hadn't even imagined fell away. Was this what trees felt like when shedding their leaves? "It's horrible to feel so relieved someone is dead."

Gabe's expression went hard. "It's sad to be such a bastard that your passing causes more relief than regret. And, in this case, one of the women in the Texas compound had a brother who wanted to see Parrish pay."

"Chief." JJ stood in the doorway of the police station. "We have a pile-up out on Sterling, and the drivers are fighting. The troopers asked for help if we're available."

Gabe hesitated, gaze on Kit.

"I'm fine." She made a scooting motion with her fingers. "Off with you."

He tapped the top of her desk. "You're a good match for Hawk. I'm glad he found you."

Thank heavens he left, since it took a full minute before she picked her jaw up off the floor.

But then another two people came in needing directions to the library and records office.

During the hours at the desk, Kit processed her feelings about Parrish's death.

The Prophet had been a huge figure in the PZ compound, and her husband had blindly followed him.

Without Parrish, the Patriot Zealots had no leader. Captain Nabera had been second in command, but it was the Prophet who'd held them together.

Now, their fanatic cult would truly fall apart. And Nabera's world would be shattered. The thought was so very satisfying.

Kit took a breath and a deeper one, then smiled. The pissers would scurry into the woodwork like the cockroaches they were, and they wouldn't come back out.

She could stop looking over her shoulder in fear they'd come for her.

I am free.

And she was in love.

CHAPTER TWENTY-EIGHT

*F*ortune and love favor the brave. - Ovid

On Friday, the Hermitage courtyard was a busy place. Kit watched the children scurrying back and forth across the courtyard.

Regan's friends, Niko and Delany, were here to spend the night, and the kids were working to fill the woodshed.

Bull and Hawk had spent the day in the forest, cutting down dead trees. Now the four brothers and JJ were chain sawing the log sections, then splitting them into woodstove-sized pieces with a log-splitter and, so stereotypically wonderful—an axe.

The late afternoon sun was toasty, and the guys were shirtless.

Boy, oh boy.

Bull was simply huge, like one of those professional weightlifters. Caz was lean and ripped. Gabe and Hawk had muscles to spare and hard abs you could bounce a coin off.

Hawk, though, had those gorgeous tats. Not only on his arms.

Covering his upper back was a hawk with spread wings and raised talons.

Seriously, what woman wouldn't enjoy the sight of these men —she was alive, right? Honestly, she should take pictures and sell them on the internet.

Bad, Kit.

Back and biceps burning, JJ set the chainsaw down, then looked around for the next section to cut up. In her back pocket, her cell made a dinging sound.

After checking the text, she raised her voice. "Pizza incoming in forty minutes. You have just enough time to put everything away and wash up."

Caz laughed. "*Mamita*, the pizza place doesn't deliver here."

"No, but Audrey and Frankie do. They agreed to pick up the pizza after I called in the order."

Over by the woodshed, the group of children stared at her.

"Pizza?" Regan's happy grin took over her whole face.

As JJ's heart turned to mush, she totally understood how parents could spoil their children. "Pizza. After a hard day of working, we deserve a treat."

"Yay!" The girl ran over and grabbed JJ around the waist for a big hug. "You are the best mamá."

Stunned speechless, JJ didn't have a chance to respond before Regan went stiff. "I mean, um, thanks, JJ."

JJ turned, and Caz was watching, approval in his dark eyes. He tilted his head in a way that said he was leaving this in her hands. But she had no doubt what he wanted. Hoped for.

He'd given her himself...and now a daughter. *God, I love him. And Regan.*

Paperwork or not, they were a family.

Bending, she put a hand on each side of Regan's face, looking her straight in the eyes. Because that was what Caz had been teaching her and Regan—that a person didn't hide from their family.

"I love you so much, Regan." The thickness in her throat made it difficult to speak. "And, sweetie, I already think of you as my daughter."

Regan's chin trembled. "Really?"

As JJ stroked a hand down the soft brown hair, her eyes were burning. "I'd really, really like to be called *mamá*."

Regan burst into tears, burying her face against JJ's shoulder.

Pressing her cheek to the top of her head, JJ felt her own tears running down her cheeks. "My girl." *I have a daughter.*

As Caz wrapped his arms around them and enclosed them in warmth, JJ felt as if the entire world was filled with sunlight.

I have a family.

Inside the barn, Nabera stood on the hood of an ancient Ford and looked out over what was left of the Patriot Zealots in Alaska. Although the building stank of horse shit and hay, at least there were no government agents snooping around.

His fifty or so men stood in straight lines as he'd taught them and waited in silence.

Eagerness to begin rose inside Nabera as he shouted, "The Feds and state troopers have been searching for us and hindering any chance of finding work or even leaving the state. I have news that will change that."

He could feel his men's hope in their focused attention.

"Our Prophet is dead. But we aren't alone in believing in individual freedoms. Or insisting a woman keep to her proper place. We're not alone in thinking our nation's capital has become a disgusting abyss. Other militia groups hold those same beliefs."

The men were nodding.

"A group in Idaho has reached out to me. They want our help, and in return, they'll provide us with new IDs, help us move to Idaho, and let us join them."

The shouts of glee made him smile. The Idaho militia also wanted Nabera to head up an active resistance unit. One that would be on the forefront of the battle lines and actively working against the government. His troops would handle intimidation and reprisal.

The media, law enforcement, and government officials would learn that any action against the Idaho militia would cost them or their loved ones dearly.

"They asked us for one final task to pay our way into our new lives."

"What's that, Captain?" Luka asked. He and Conrad, the other lieutenant, were in the very front of the troops, standing straight and tall.

"Something I think we'll enjoy." Nabera smiled. He sure would. "We lived outside of Rescue for years. Thought we were part of the town. But they turned on us. Broke into our compound. Took our women."

The angry sounds coming from his troops filled his heart with joy.

He waited one moment. "I think it's only fair that we steal their women in return."

Eventually the shouts of agreement died down.

"This is the plan. We take the women and sell them to a boat waiting offshore. The money will start us off in our new lives. And Rescue will never see those women again."

The Idaho militia would use the PZ's revenge as an example for their own purposes. *See what happens if you get in our way? Can you guard your family against us?*

"Yeah, let's do it," Conrad shouted.

Nabera gave his lieutenant an approving smile. "We'll teach those bastards a lesson."

And Rescue would hear their women scream.

Hours later, Kit and Hawk climbed the stairs to her apartment. His hand was warm in hers, the skin calloused, the strength obvious. She smiled up at him. "What a perfect day."

"Yeah." Wrapping an arm around her, he bent to nibble on her neck. "Thanks for the cake."

Her heart softened with tenderness. Caz had mentioned that Hawk's favorite dessert was chocolate cake, so she'd made one. And, obviously, Hawk had known she made it for him.

After a long, sweet kiss, they continued up the stairs.

The evening had been wonderful, although pizza and cake for supper might get her banned from the good parenting list.

Everyone had been starving, especially the children, and the food disappeared like magic.

Clean-up afterward got jump-started when Caz started picking up plates and singing, "Heigh ho, Heigh ho".

The children laughed, and the table was cleared in no time.

In the kitchen, Gabe led off with Alabama's "Forty Hour Week", and Niko joined in. Apparently, the song was a favorite of his father, Chevy.

After that, Frankie had winked at Kit and belted out Dolly Parton's "9 to 5"—a totally female tune. Wasn't it fun that the guys had actually been at a loss? Of course, Frankie knew the lyrics... and hip-bumped Bull when singing about that her boss being out to get her.

Bull's big laugh had filled the kitchen, sending the children into uncontrollable giggles.

Yes, it had been a wonderful day.

At the top of the stairs, Hawk opened the door for Kit.

Crossing into the bedroom, she glanced at Aric's divided-off corner. "I feel as if I've abandoned my baby."

When Aric had begged to join the big kids for their overnight,

Regan and her friends thought it was a great idea. Niko insisted he needed another boy to make even numbers.

Hadn't Aric gotten puffed up with that?

"Relax, mama." Hawk ran his knuckles over her cheek. "JJ'll call if Aric needs a pick-up."

"I know." And the slumber party was just next door.

She should enjoy her time with Hawk—their own "overnight". Something they hadn't had since the helicopter trip.

In the bathroom, Kit brushed her teeth and stared in the mirror, trying to decide what to wear. And laughed at herself.

She'd just wear her usual and not make a big deal about it. Stripping down, she smiled and patted her breasts. "Ready, my pretties?"

"Did you say something?" Hawk asked.

Kit pulled on her nightgown on and walked out. "The counselor suggested I talk to my body—and compliment it." She bounced her breasts in her hands. "These are my pretties."

"Pretties?" Hawk was sitting on the bed, shirt off, still in jeans. His gaze lingered on her breasts, and his smile was slow and very masculine. "I'd agree with that."

She could see the heat in his eyes as he looked at her. It seemed he liked her nightgown. His gaze slid down. "Any other names?"

Darn it, did he have to ask that? Her face felt hot. "Peach. I hate the word pussy."

He grinned, the jerk. She'd heard someone in town say he didn't have a sense of humor. So wrong.

As she slid under the covers, he started to unzip his jeans. The zipper must have been old and made an almost grinding sound as if the gate, no—the *prison door*—was complaining about being opened?

Oh heavens, when she was nervous, her thoughts became bizarre.

But she knew what lay behind that prison door. She clapped her hands over her mouth to smother a snicker.

Halting, he studied her, obviously worried that she was nervous. "Stop?"

"No." She felt her shoulders start to shake. *Don't laugh.*

"Kit." The low growl held a warning. "Talk to me."

"Just thinking...your zipper sounded, um, creaky. Like a prison door."

He gave her an odd look as he finished unzipping. His shaft sprang out.

Sprang. Out.

"Oh, nooooo. The one-eyed dragon has escaped the dungeon. It's loose." Waving her hands in the air, she fell back on the bed.

Hawk stared. "Fuck me, I broke her."

She was giggling so hard she couldn't catch her breath.

Shaking his head—but he was grinning—he finished undressing and went into the living room. She heard him lock the door. He left the light on in there.

Back in the bedroom, he turned off the nightstand lamp.

By the time he finished she was sitting in the center of the bed, a lingering ache in her belly from laughing.

"You won't need this." He bent and pulled her nightgown off.

"Hey." She frowned at the light streaming in from the living room.

"I like to look at you." Hawk's mouth tipped up. "And the pretties."

Then he showed her how much he liked her pretties, using his mouth and fingers—and even his teeth. By the time he finished, her breasts were so swollen and her nipples so sensitive, even the slightest touch made her quiver.

Lying down beside her, he rolled onto his back. "Climb on."

Oh, she could do that. But when she straddled his hips, he put his hands under her bottom and pulled her up, past his stomach, past his chest, until her most intimate parts were right over his face.

"Yeah, there." His fingers tightened on her buttocks when she would have moved. "Happens I like peaches."

And he licked, lightly, up and over her pussy. Up and down. Around. When she started to whine, he relented and focused on her clit.

With a gasp, she grabbed the headboard.

He laughed and continued. Swirling and sucking, and pushing his tongue inside her. Driving her totally insane.

After she'd come so hard she'd seen stars, he rolled her onto her back, using his legs to spread her thighs. Pressing himself against her slick, throbbing entrance, he smiled. "Let me introduce you to my one-eyed dragon."

A long, satisfying time later, Kit lay beside Hawk with her head on his shoulder. His skin was warm and slightly damp, and smelled woodsy with a trace of pine.

He stroked down her arm, then up to play with her breast, teasing the nipple as if fascinated.

Capturing his hand, she kissed his fingers, then realized there was enough light to see his whole arm.

"What?"

"Your tattoos. I like how the colors are shades of brown and gold." She sat up beside him, holding his arm to see it better, then reached for his other arm.

Obligingly, he lay it across his stomach.

His right upper arm had a golden eagle—and, sheesh, she wouldn't want to be within reach of that viciously hooked beak. His left had a soaring bald eagle with trees as a backdrop.

He loved those predatory birds. Whenever he saw one, he'd stop and just watch. Aric was full of the tidbits of information Hawk had shared.

His left forearm showed military helicopters, and the dark tree branches wove the birds and choppers together.

She nodded. Combat had definitely influenced who Hawk was.

With her finger, she traced a ridged pink line past a helicopter into the trees. The knife wound was healing.

He saw where her finger was. "Least it didn't mess up the art."

That was his only concern? *Men.*

Looking closer, she saw smaller tats in the branches. A police badge. A serpent entwined rod—the symbol of medicine. The round sign from Bull's brewery. Then a bunch of military insignia. SEALs, Army Special Forces, the Night Stalker one. "Did all of you serve in the military?"

He nodded.

His right forearm was far more peaceful with a floatplane landing on a mountain lake in front of a log cabin.

But...what in the world? "Hawk, lakes don't have sharks, do they?" She traced the dark shape cutting through the water.

He chuckled. "Mako means shark in Māori. It was the sarge's military handle."

Oh. She touched the cabin and glanced at him.

"Yeah, that's where we grew up. I'll take you sometime."

It looked very primitive.

Whoa, there were knives embedded in the porch post. A hawk perched on the roof, and a big moose stood in the shadows of the forest. On the other side, guarding the shadows was an angel.

Hawk saw where her fingers had stopped. "For Gabriel. His mother named him after the archangel."

All of them, protecting the cabin where four boys and one battered sergeant had become a family.

CHAPTER TWENTY-NINE

N*ever draw fire; it irritates everyone around you.* - Murphy's
Laws of Combat Operations

Seated at one of the pushed-together tables, Audrey listened to
Tina, Lillian, and the postmistress vie for the raunchiest joke.

Honestly, she'd never blushed so much in her life. Well, aside
from the first few times she'd had sex with Gabe.

Effing-A, the jokes got dirtier with every round of drinks.

Hopefully, the Saturday night crowd at the roadhouse wouldn't
mind. It was late enough the room was only a quarter full now. So,
there weren't too many people to be offended.

Behind the bar, Raymond saw her looking around and raised
his eyebrows.

She shook her head; they didn't need anything.

The bartender was such a sweetie. When Frankie told Bull to
take the night off so she could get drunk and he wouldn't hear her
complain—or boast—about him, Raymond had volunteered to
work.

Poor guy.

After a dramatic pause, Tina yelled out the joke's punch line, and her audience burst into laughter. The postmistress pounded the table in approval.

Audrey tried not to pout. The party would sure be more fun if she could drink too.

"Hey, Audrey, have you and Gabe set a date, yet?" EmmaJean, the B&B owner, asked.

"We just did, actually." Audrey smiled. "It'll be at the beginning of November so I'll be past morning sickness."

"Ah." Frankie smirked. "You want to be able to enjoy your honeymoon."

Audrey felt her cheeks heat. Because…Gabe. "Um, yes?" She grinned. "A tropical beach has been mentioned."

Beverly, the midwife, sighed. "I love beaches."

She was echoed by Glenda, one of the owners of the arts and crafts store.

"Most excellent planning," Lillian said. "Tourist season will be over, and JJ can easily handle the police work."

"Speaking of our fine police officer, where is she?" Charlotte, the other store owner, asked.

Audrey flushed. JJ'd told Gabe he couldn't work tonight…so he and Audrey could have their own private celebration after the party.

She had the best friends.

"JJ doesn't get off duty until midnight," Frankie said. "If we're still here, she'll join us."

"That's only half an hour away." Kit snorted. "And it doesn't look as if we're quitting anytime soon."

"This is such a blast, having a women's night out. I hope we do it more often," Tina, Chevy's wife said. "Audrey's book clubs are amazing, but there isn't any alcohol. And men attend."

"At the moment, the romance book club is all women," Audrey said. Not that it was a rule, but that was how it'd turned out.

"You can thank me for that. Knox wanted to join the romance one to pick up sexy ideas." Erica giggled. "I told him no."

"Wise decision, my dear." Lillian pursed her lips. "Comparing book boyfriends to real-life ones can leave a man with a lifelong inferiority complex."

Regina barked a laugh. "No guy can compete with a book boyfriend."

Irene, the postmistress, snorted. "My sweet husband is the love of my life, but I'm afraid his big chest descended to his belly many years ago."

"My ex wasn't so sweet." Glenda wrinkled her nose. "He'd eat garlic cloves just so he could breathe on me."

"That's truly vile," Lillian stated. "You were wise to discard such a foul deformity of nature."

Audrey grinned. The mayor's Shakespearean insults were as fun as Frankie's Italian ones—and didn't require a translation dictionary.

"Oh, man, talk about vile? Last night, Chevy let out this huge fart. I almost pushed him out of bed and ran away to Cold Creek." Tina made a humming sound. "I could sure use me some hot panther shifters. *Mrow*."

Everyone at the table burst out laughing and shouted out names of their favorite heroes. *Calum. Ian. Adam.*

Sipping her alcohol-less drink, Audrey looked around the table. These women were present simply to celebrate her baby-to-come. In one year, she'd gained more friends—and family—than ever before. Her eyes burned.

Leaning in, Kit rubbed her shoulder. "Are you okay?"

That did it. Tears filled her eyes and overflowed. "I'm just so happy, and you are all here, and you mean so much to me."

Why in the world was she crying? Horrified, Audrey covered her face. "Sorry!"

"No, no." Laughing, Kit gave her a quick hug. "You're just getting the full effect of pregnancy hormones, my almost-sister."

Audrey wiped her eyes. "Seriously?" She obviously needed to research the heck out of pregnancy.

"Oh, yes. Mood swings are a thing." With a wry smile, Sarah raised her glass. "With each child, I had such a temper Uriah was sure I was incubating demons. Especially after I slammed the oven door so hard his bread fell."

Tina giggled. "When I was pregnant with Niko, I totally craved tortilla chips and salsa. Chevy even drove through a blizzard to get some. My whining was just that bad."

"No, child." Lillian gave a nod of approval. "Your whining was most effective. And good husbands are susceptible."

"Not Gabe. He'd never..." Audrey bit her lip. "No, actually, he probably *would* drive through a blizzard to get me something."

On her other side, Frankie nodded. "Of course he would. He adores you."

Oh great, more tears. Sniffling, Audrey wiped her face, then shot Frankie a glare. "You just had to say that."

The New Yorker smirked. "And I'm sooo going to tell him how you reacted."

"I'm rethinking my gratitude for you all," Audrey muttered—and grinned as they laughed.

At the Hermitage, Hawk glanced around the gazebo. Interesting evening. The kids were in bed, and the gazebo was filled with his brothers along with Dante, Knox, and Chevy whose women were at Audrey's celebration.

Leaning forward, Hawk warmed his chilled fingers at the fire pit. In his lap, Sirius gave him an affronted stare before settling back to sleep. Damn cat.

On the other side of the fire, Bull pulled his jacket closed. "Feels like winter will be early this year. But we're ready."

"The woodshed is almost full," Caz agreed.

They all liked being prepared, but Mako's survivalist preparations especially suited Hawk. His parents had often punished him by locking him up without food for a couple of days. He'd learned to keep a hidden stash of food.

Fingers now warm, Hawk sat back in his chair, jostling the cat again, and earning another stare. "Food storage is almost finished."

With everyone working, they had a good haul of salmon—smoked, canned, and in the freezers. Berries had been frozen or made into jam. Garden produce was getting put up. Bull and Frankie had made up spaghetti sauce and canned it for quick meals.

The apple trees Mako had planted years ago should yield a good harvest in September. Finally. As with most fruit trees, apples didn't particularly like Alaska.

They'd do some hunting to top things off.

"We're about ready too. A moose in the freezer would help." Chevy glanced at Gabe and added hastily, "once the season opens."

Gabe grinned. Poaching in the area decreased after he took over as police chief.

Smiling, Hawk picked up his mug of hot chocolate that, unfortunately, lacked rum. But he'd lost the rock, paper, scissors game and was designated driver to retrieve Kit, Audrey, and Frankie from the roadhouse later. JJ, too, if she joined them after her shift. His pickup would be filled with drunken women.

Or maybe not. Kit said she never had more than two, and Audrey wouldn't be drinking.

Drunk or sober, he and Kit would enjoy some adult fun. Hawk glanced over at Caz's where Aric was bunked down on the floor in Regan's room.

Following his gaze, Caz grinned. "I don't think either of them will wake before noon."

"We wore them out good," Bull said.

"They make a hell of a team." Gabe rested his feet on the edge of the firepit. "Damn, they were cute. Like mini-soldiers."

Hawk chuckled. Lillian had decided adorable clothing came under her grandmotherly purview and bought camo shirts and pants for Regan and Aric.

After the women left for their celebration, the kids stayed up past dark to play hide-'n'-seek games and see if their clothing worked. Aric had donned a black stocking cap to cover his blond hair. "The camo face paint topped it off."

"It worked." Knox tugged on his red beard. "They were purely invisible."

After the kids won the last game, Hawk snapped pictures before realizing the photos revealed it was after nightfall—far past Aric's bedtime.

Even worse, both kids had fallen asleep before baths. They were still face-painted and wearing combat clothing.

As if he was reading Hawk's mind, Caz frowned. "We should get up early and scrub the children down."

"Erase the evidence?" Chevy had a bullfrog's laugh. "That'd be smart."

Hawk rubbed the scar on his cheek and considered. It'd work if Kit slept late. Otherwise, she'd murder him for corrupting her son.

Then Gabe would arrest her. Which would be bad.

Hawk nodded. A few extra orgasms would ensure she slept late. Wouldn't be a problem.

No, he'd do his utmost for a noble cause.

As his dick stirred to life, he rose to his feet. "I'm going to head out and park at the roadhouse. Just in case."

"In case they decide to sing their way through downtown?" Bull nodded. "I could see Frankie egging Kit on to something crazy."

Appalled, Hawk stared at his brother. "Seriously?"

"My woman won't be drinking," Gabe said smugly. Then his

smile faded. "But Frankie and Kit together might be impossible for her to contain."

Caz shook his head. "JJ is unpredictable. She might vote for restraint—or not."

"Lillian can come up with some crazy notions." Dante nodded approval at Hawk. "Best to have a lookout, just in case."

Knox and Chevy exchanged worried looks before Chevy turned to Hawk. "They're supposed to text us for a ride, but if they leave the roadhouse?"

"God help Rescue," Knox muttered. "You call if that happens, Hawk."

Yeah, he'd do just that—after he retreated to a safe distance. And took some pictures. Many, many pictures.

"Will do."

Outside Bull's Moose Roadhouse, there were ample pools of darkness to help with staging the operation.

Captain Nabera's men had arrived in black SUVs along with a couple of black passenger vans. They drove into the lot without lights and parked in the shadows.

For transport of their prisoners, Nabera had rented two windowless cargo vans, unfortunately white—the only color available. For discretion, the driver parked them down on Sweetgale until needed.

At the back of the lot, Nabera stood next to one SUV and surveyed the area. The black vehicles were nearly invisible. His men were geared up and ready for action.

The Prophet would have been proud of Nabera's planning and his people's professionalism.

Inside the roadhouse, two newer recruits, who wouldn't be recognized, kept an eye on the targets.

A man walked past the roadhouse front window, light

gleaming off his shaved scalp. *Conrad.* As if without a care in the world, the lieutenant sauntered across the parking lot to Nabera.

"Report, lieutenant."

"Sir." Conrad came to attention. "The women are inside and drunk."

"Very good." Nabera eyed the roadhouse. "Kirsten is present?"

"Yes, sir." Conrad nodded sharply.

Nabera smiled slowly. "Now, the world will learn how the Patriot Zealots respond to traitorous women and to having our Prophet murdered."

And, before selling her, he would spend some quality time with the cunt who'd caused Obadiah's death and all their problems.

When her phone vibrated against her butt, Frankie pulled the cell from her back pocket and walked away from the noisy table of women. "Hey, JJ, everyone's asking where you are. Did something happen?"

"Police stuff," JJ grumbled. "Some bozos at the fishing camps started a brawl, and they called me to break it up. I should book the idiots simply for making me miss the party. Tell Audrey I'm sorry. Is everyone still there?"

"I'll tell her." Frankie eyed the tables. "We're down to just eight of us." The midwife had gotten a call, then the two sisters who owned the arts and crafts store left with Irene. A few minutes ago, the summer schoolteacher had bailed out, although her daughter, Erica, stayed.

JJ started laughing. "From the noise, your hardcore bunch includes Lillian."

Strutting alongside the table, Lillian was singing, "*Oh, you nasty boys,*" to the shouts and whistles of the other women.

Frankie snickered. "The Brit might have white hair, but *cavalo*, she has some moves."

"Well, I need to finish up here." JJ sighed. "Don't drink so much you can't have fun afterward with Bull."

"Right." Tucking her phone back in her pocket, Frankie made a face because she wasn't anywhere near drunk. Although her spirit was all-too-willing, her body wasn't in a drinking mood. Her stomach had been on the fritz for a few days now, probably because she and Bull were testing Asian dishes for the restaurant menu.

At just the thought of dim sum, nausea hit. The gin-and-tonic, which should've settled her stomach, threatened to resurface. She swallowed uneasily.

While Lillian conducted the enthusiastic singing of the next song, Frankie fled to the roadhouse's office.

Thank goodness she had a private bathroom in here.

If Kit caught her worshipping the porcelain god, Frankie would never live it down.

As Lillian waved her hand to direct the next verse in a raucous song, Kit glanced around the nearly empty bar. The noisy all-women celebration had driven most of the regular customers away.

Tucker and Guzman had fled an hour ago, as had Felix and Orion.

A couple of clean-shaven men with short hair sat at the bar—probably tourists. In the front corner, three older women were talking quietly.

The dark windows to the parking lot reminded her she'd wanted to step out back. Bull wanted her opinions on how to make the patio overlooking the lake more attractive. Although she'd studied the area before sunset, she needed to see how it looked after dark.

Slipping away from the table, she crossed the bar and went out the roadhouse's back door.

Whew, instant quiet. Her ears were still ringing. As she walked around the big patio area, a frosty night breeze rustled the lakeside rushes and cooled her overheated skin.

Lights traveling up the mountain caught her gaze. Whoever built the roadhouse had chosen an excellent location. Tourists drove by it on the way to the resort, and the townsfolk provided steady clientele.

Now, how to lure more of them in?

Well, the way the patio overlooked Lynx Lake was perfect for romantic evenings.

Kit bit her lip. Would Hawk like to come here sometime? Maybe—although he was more of a homebody. She really liked that about him.

She rolled her eyes. *Work, Kit.*

Now, what would evoke romance? Perhaps flowers to scent the evening air? She glanced up at the starry night sky and the quarter moon rising in the east. There were white flowers that would glow in the moonlight. Maybe some twinkle lights?

Slowly walking the perimeter, Kit made plans and enjoyed the faint singing from inside. From the off notes and slurred words, she could tell which ones had imbibed more than others.

Sarah had been careful. Her children were overnighting with a neighbor so she could enjoy sexy times with Uriah tonight.

The B&B owner, EmmaJean, was feeling no pain, and Tina? Oh, boy, that woman knew how to drink. It was good Chevy was picking her up.

Kit smiled a little. Hawk had mentioned he'd see if Aric wanted to sack out on the floor in Regan's room.

Who knew—maybe, she'd get sexy times too.

In the roadhouse parking lot, Hawk chose a space under a street-light, fairly close to the door. The women would see his vehicle when they left—and he could intercept them if they chose to storm the town.

He got out and leaned against the pickup. Since they hadn't texted for a ride, he'd stay outside and enjoy the night until they were ready. The air held the scent of an incoming storm. The forecast called for rain close to sunrise.

From inside the bar came the sound of women singing. *Jesus.* Having a pitch perfect ear, he was damned glad he wasn't any closer.

He caught a few words of their song and grinned. Raymond must be getting quite an education—and might invoice Bull for hazardous duty.

Turning to scope out the parking lot, Hawk heard his name called.

"Evening, boss. You're running late." The parking lot light gleamed off a shaved scalp as Milo, one of his handyman hires, walked out of the shadows with another man. "Meeting someone?"

Hawk tipped his head toward the roadhouse. "I'm the driver."

"From the sounds of it, they'll need a ride," Milo's friend said. "Nice ride, man. I like the new F-150s." He moved to Hawk's left to look in the pickup's side window.

"Hey, Hawk, did you see the crash just up there on Dall." Milo pointed to the road to the right.

Even as Hawk turned to look, he caught a motion out of the corner of his eye and brought his arm up.

Too late.

The crowbar struck his head with a grisly thud. Even as pain exploded in his head, blackness sucked him down.

Audrey was the only one abstaining from alcohol at the table. Poor pitiful me, she thought.

Then again, Frankie'd been sipping one drink most of the evening. Kit stopped with two, saying she'd puke otherwise.

Lillian had nursed her drinks, saying that as the years crept on, the buzz wasn't worth the ensuing hangover. And she didn't appear to require alcohol for boisterous revelry.

"We should sing about babies." Face flushed, EmmaJean gulped more of her drink. "Not a lullaby, but—"

The roadhouse door swung open so hard it banged against the wall.

Men flooded in. A handful headed straight toward the bar. The rest milled in the center of the room as if deciding where to sit.

"Boy, their evening is sure startin' late," Tina noted. "Oh *shit*."

"What?" Audrey followed her gaze.

At the door stood a tall, rail-thin guy with a black beard.

Nabera.

Everything inside Audrey went cold. She turned to tell Kit to run.

Kit wasn't there.

"Don't move!" The captain pointed a pistol straight at Audrey's table.

"You there. Put the gun down," Raymond called from the bar. He was tapping on the cell in his hand.

The men who'd been seated at the bar jumped over it and attacked him.

Cursing, Raymond fought as they grabbed his phone, then clubbed him to the ground.

Audrey pushed her chair back, looking for somewhere to run.

"What is the meaning of this?" Lillian snapped, rising. "Are you stark raving mad, Nabera?"

"You wish, don't you, Mayor Bitch? Lording it over the town." The man's gloating smile iced the blood in Audrey's veins. "That stops today...and so do you."

He motioned to a hatchet-faced man who shoved Lillian back down into her chair.

Audrey's hands closed into fists. As several men surrounded the table, their firearms in their hands, she reached around to her phone in her back pocket.

A man kicked her chair. "Don't move, bitch."

Eff-it-all. Her hands curved over her lower abdomen protectively. *Hang in there, baby.*

"Shut the outside lights and roadhouse sign off," Nabera called.

"Got it," a man yelled back.

The parking lot went dark.

Several men loomed over the three women seated in the corner. One man yelled, "Captain, we got some fucking politicians here."

As Nabera moved in that direction, Audrey managed to pull in a breath.

Across the table, Sarah was looking around, obviously evaluating what could be done. Erica looked terrified. Tina was—

"Well, well, we caught ourselves some state representative libtards along with our targets." Nabera sounded elated. "It wasn't as big a haul as I wanted, but they'll make up for it. Secure them all."

A man pulled out zip-ties, yanked Audrey's arms behind her back, and bound her wrists together. The other women were being restrained too.

When one grabbed EmmaJean, she screamed and fought back. A second man backhanded her, and she hit the floor hard and lay crying.

Lillian cursed until one of them shouted, "Shut the fuck up," and slapped her to make her stop.

Furious, Audrey yanked at the zip-ties until her skin ripped and blood trickled down her wrists.

Surely someone would come to the roadhouse and notice something, would call the police.

No help came.

A man with a shaved head was checking that each woman was bound. Audrey frowned. Wasn't that Milo, one of the carpenters remodeling the downtown buildings?

"Good job." Milo motioned to the women. "Stuff 'em in the transport."

"Yes, sir, Lieutenant," the man beside Lillian said.

Milo motioned toward the white van at the door. "You're driving that one, Luka."

"Got it, Conrad." The man behind Audrey hauled her up and across the room like a child. The back door of a windowless cargo van was open, and he shoved her inside. She twisted to keep from landing on her belly and hit her shoulder so painfully that tears filled her eyes.

But her baby was safe. For now.

Her friends' risqué singing had changed to...were those *screams*? On the back patio, Kit spun around as the hair on the back of her neck rose and goosebumps covered her arms.

She ran toward the back door and gripped the handle, then stopped. From inside came men's loud voices. Shouts. Women were sobbing and crying out in pain.

The months in the PZ compound had taught her the sounds of violence.

Her mouth went dry. The cold in her stomach wasn't from the night air but sheer terror. *Run!* She could crawl into the bushes or run down the gravel path into the darkness of the park. *I need to hide.*

No. Her friends were in there. Her bestie, Frankie. Audrey was *pregnant*.

I have to help, to do something. But she had no phone; she'd never bought one. She was so stupid!

She tried to turn the door handle, and it wouldn't move. Of course not. The patio wasn't open to customers, yet. It was just for an emergency exit; the door had locked behind her.

Dammit.

Heart thudding painfully hard, she looked around frantically, already knowing the left side of the building had the most bushes.

That way.

She crept around the corner and along the log wall toward the parking lot. In the dark, she peeked through the window into the bar.

Men—so many men—with guns. In the center stood a tall, thin black-bearded man...and Kit froze, unable to even breathe.

Nabera. Oh no, please no.

The PZ men were using zip ties and rope to tie up the women, then pushing them out the front door.

She couldn't let them take her friends.

The thought got her feet moving. In the shadows, she crept to the front of the building and peered around the corner.

A white cargo van was backed up to the covered front entry. A man dragged a struggling Erica out and tossed her into the cargo space. When white-haired Lillian was roughly shoved in, fury engulfed Kit.

Focus, Kit. She could almost hear Hawk's warning.

"That's the last," the man said to someone, then slammed the van door shut. "All yours, Luka."

"On it." One of the lieutenants, Luka had let his buzz-cut hair grow out to a couple of inches. Jumping in the driver's seat, he started the engine, then leaned out to yell, "Ready, Captain."

"Hold up while we do a final walk-through," Nabera yelled.

At the sound of Nabera's yell, Kit pressed her knuckles to her mouth to keep from whimpering. Her legs trembled so hard her knees started to buckle.

No. She couldn't—wouldn't—give in.

As fear sweat trickled down her back, she drew in a breath.

Situational awareness, sugar. Kit could almost hear Hawk's voice. Mouth tight, she forced herself to look around.

And blinked in surprise.

Luka didn't have any situational awareness. The lieutenant had his door open, his head tipped back. His fingers tapped on the steering wheel impatiently.

The van was running.

Everyone else was inside the building.

Oh, God, I can't do this.

She had to.

Find a weapon.

The gravel path around the side of the building was bordered by softball-sized rocks. Hawk whispered in her mind, "*Throw it. Or hit someone in the head with it.*"

She wouldn't let him down. Picking up a rock, she snuck to the side of the vehicle, any crunch of her steps on the gravel was masked by the women's crying and groaning inside the van.

"For fuck's sake." Luka moved suddenly, and Kit froze. He turned toward the screened divider between the cargo area and the cab. "Bitches. Shut. *Up.*"

As he started to turn forward again, Kit swung the rock with all her might and hit him in the side of the head. The impact jolted her fingers so badly the rock dropped.

No seatbelt held him in, and the unconscious man tipped sideways.

She grabbed his shoulders. Sweet heavens, he was bleeding so bad.

Focus.

"Out you go," she whispered. Gritting her teeth, she yanked

him out onto the gravel. Climbing into the driver's seat, she slammed the door.

Move, move, move.

She rammed the gearshift into drive, pushed the pedal for a trickle of gas, and rolled forward. Quietly.

The van was partway across the parking lot when a man came out of the roadhouse. "Luka, what the fuck!"

Kit stomped on the gas. The van rocketed forward, tires spitting gravel. The vehicle fishtailed at her hard turn onto Sweetgale, and screams came from the women in back.

Almost panting, Kit tried to think. The PZs would chase her. Where could she go?

No one would be at the police station if JJ wasn't back—and it was only her, anyway. One person couldn't defend against so many fanatics.

The town closed down at this hour. No one was around.

In despair, Kit tightened her hands on the steering wheel.

What about the Hermitage? They had guns.

Yes.

But she had to warn them. "Audrey, Frankie, Lillian —someone!"

"Kit?" It was Audrey's voice. "Oh, God, Kit. Wait—you're *driving?*"

Kit needed a second to get her voice to work again. "Yes, but they'll chase us. I'm taking us to the Hermitage." She gave a terrified glance at the side mirrors. Headlights appeared, coming out of the parking lot. "We need to warn the guys, and I don't have a phone."

"Who has a phone?" Sarah yelled.

"Me." Audrey answered.

Kit found a breath and used it. Took a bigger one.

"Ma'am, your hands are tied in front," Audrey was telling someone in back. "Can you get my phone from my back pocket?"

"I guess there's a benefit of being so big my wrists won't meet in back." The woman's voice was old and gruff. "Turn around." A second later, she said, "Got it."

"Hurry, hurry," Kit whispered under her breath.

"Punch in 3-2-8-3 to unlock it," Audrey instructed quickly. "Then hit the badge icon."

A second later, Gabe's voice sounded. "Goldilocks, how's the party? Hawk should—"

Audrey's voice rose. "Gabe, Nabera attacked the roadhouse. Kit's driving a van to the Hermitage, and the PZs are—" Audrey's hasty speech broke off at the sound of cars approaching from the rear. "Oh, *God*."

"*Nabera. Fuck.*" Gabe low voice rose to a shout. "Men. Our women are coming in hot with PZ bastards chasing them. Bull, batten us down. Caz, get weapons out. Prepare for incoming."

Kit glanced in the rearview mirror as the headlights in back came closer. There was a spatter of gunfire before she screeched left onto Swan Ave. Women in the back yelped in pain.

Seconds later, she turned left again onto the tiny dirt road leading to the Hermitage. She was very familiar with the road now.

First came the *this-isn't-the-road-you're-looking-for* corner. Almost, almost...

She slammed on the brakes, skidded, and slowed just enough to curve left around the virtual U-turn.

The SUV behind her couldn't slow fast enough. Brakes squealed, as the vehicle spun out on the corner and slid into a tree with a horrendous bang.

Maybe it'd block the others.

Speeding up, Kit peeled down the gravel road. Past the forest, past Hawk's landing strip.

"Tell Kit to pull into Mako's garage." That was Gabe's voice on Audrey's phone, loud enough for Kit to hear. He sounded impossibly calm.

"Got it," Kit yelled back, heading for the last house.

Don't drive into a ditch; keep it on the road.

Ugh. Wasn't that fun? In the office bathroom, Frankie ran water to wash her face and then rinsed out her mouth. *Double-ugh.*

No wonder Kit never drank much. In fact, Frankie might never be able to drink gin and tonic again.

So, was it the Asian food that'd made her sick, or did she have a stomach flu?

Out in the office she shared with Bull, she grabbed a breath mint off her desk to eradicate the lingering taste of sickness. With luck, the group hadn't noticed her disappearance, although *face it, woman*, she'd been gone longer than a song or two.

Oh well. Humiliation was good for the soul, right?

Odd noises trickled into the office, and she frowned. Was there someone shouting in the bar? And swearing? A bunch of drunks must have come in late.

Cazzo, the night had been so fun too.

The office door was flung open, and a bearded man stood in the doorway. "Found one," he yelled.

"What—" As she stared at him, he pulled a *pistol*—and her breathing simply stopped.

When another bearded man pushed past him and headed for her, Frankie retreated a step. Hands closing into fists, she dropped into a defensive stance. "I'll kick you into next week."

The clicking of a trigger being pulled back was loud in the room. "Try it, bitch," came from the man holding the pistol. The muzzle of the weapon pointed directly at her.

She froze, unable to take her eyes off the gun.

The other man grabbed her arm, yanked her around, and bound her wrists behind her with a long strand of rope.

What is going on? She pulled in a breath. "Can you tell me—"

He slapped her. "Shut up."

Pain seared her cheek. Her eyes watered and turned the room into a blur.

The man pushed her out into the bar, and she bit back a cry of protest at the empty tables. Where were her friends?

Outside, a white cargo van pulled up to the front of the roadhouse and parked. The driver opened the back door.

The man beside her ordered, "Tie her legs."

When the driver grabbed a bunch of loose ropes and knelt, she tried to kick him. "*Vaffanculo!*"

An arm came around her throat, cutting off her air. The PZ behind her snapped, "Don't. Move."

Once her ankles were tied, the two men threw her in the van. Landing on her side, she skidded painfully across the ridged metal flooring.

Blinking away more tears, she struggled to sit up. The cargo portion had no windows. No seats. Just an empty space.

No, it wasn't completely empty. In the dim light, she could see a lump farther forward.

A man. Also bound. Unconscious.

Cavalo, it was Hawk.

"Well, well." A man in the van's open door gripped her feet and jerked her toward him.

Tall and emaciated. Black beard. Cold, cruel eyes. "I remember you, girlie. The lying bitch of a waitress. You're Kirsten's friend, Frankie."

Ice crawled up her spine and into her bloodstream. Her lips felt numb as she whispered, "Nabera."

"Our Prophet is dead, cunt." His weird fanatic's eyes filled with hatred as he grabbed her hair and yanked her head back painfully. "You and Kirsten are to blame."

"Want me to cut her throat?" someone asked from behind Nabera. "And my so-called asshole boss?"

"Don't tempt me, lieutenant." Still holding her hair, Nabera ran his hand over her breasts. "Nice and ripe."

Her stomach almost revolted again.

"She'll sell for a lot," the man called the lieutenant said.

Nabera's mouth twisted. "We'll need the money, especially if we can't recover the others."

Did that mean her friends had gotten away?

But...sell her?

When he squeezed her breast, she kicked out at him.

He stepped sideways, the *bastardo*.

Cazzo, she'd really hoped to damage him, no matter what it would have meant for her survival. He was going to *sell* her?

"Cunt." He jerked her hair so hard a painful sound escaped her. "Before I sell you, I'm going to enjoy hearing you scream."

The van door shut, leaving her in darkness and terror.

Inside Mako's garage, Kit stomped on the brake pedal, bringing the van to a skidding halt just before it hit the far wall.

As the garage door banged shut, she shut off the engine.

One of the PZ vehicles roared up outside, halting with a grating crunch of gravel. Doors slammed. Men shouted.

And then gunfire sprayed the house.

Kit jumped, wanting to cringe at the horrible noise.

As lights flickered on in the garage, Dante walked up to the side of the van. "Stay put, people."

Outside, more vehicles roared up. So many more. Dread filled her.

She'd led the fanatics right to the Hermitage.

To her son.

The shaking inside her grew. She tried to move—and couldn't. One hand was clamped so tightly onto the steering wheel her fingers ached.

The back of the van opened. "Ladies, I'll get y'all released in a jiffy. I have scissors here." Dante's gruff Oklahoma twang was distinctive. The vehicle bounced as he climbed in. "If you're hurt, tell me. If you're sober enough, we need some help to shoot those bastards."

"You tickle-brained fustilarian, let me up." Lillian sounded spitting mad. "I'll shoot the boils off those mammering, beetle-headed maggot-pies. If they—"

A gasp and squeak interrupted the diatribe. Kit heard someone getting kissed.

Dante had his woman back.

Snipping noises sounded. The van rocked as the women climbed out. At least one was crying.

"Dante, can't help just yet," Tina said as the freed women grouped together at the side of the van. "Way too much to drink. I'm still seeing double."

"And me," EmmaJean admitted. "Give us time though. We'll help."

"Come along. We'll get y'all sorted." As if he heard gunfire every day, Dante led most of the women out of the garage.

Move, Kit told herself. *I need to move.*

Her body wasn't listening.

"Hey." Audrey opened the driver's door. "Are you all right?"

"I can't stop shaking." Kit pulled in a breath and pried her fingers from the steering wheel. After she managed to slide out, Audrey hugged her hard.

"You saved us, my valorous girl." Lillian took Audrey's place for a quick hug.

Audrey winced as the hammering noise of bullets increased. "Dante says Regan and Aric are safe down in the tunnels."

"Which means it's our job to ensure the ill-bred hedge-pigs don't get in." Lillian pointed at the door. "Weapons, my girls. We will *destroy* those fusty carbuncles."

Audrey nodded. "We will."

Kit's mouth tightened. I hate guns. But it didn't matter. No matter what, she'd do what she must to protect her son and everyone else here. She straightened her spine and told her knees to stop shaking. "Let's go find us some of those guns."

———

"JJ." Caz's voice came across the police car's internal speakers. "Do not come back to the Hermitage."

"What? Why?" JJ had just pulled into town, planning to switch cars and head home. "Am I needed out at the roadhouse?"

"No! Don't go there, either."

What were those noises in the background? She stiffened. That was *gunfire*. "Caz, what is going on?"

"Nabera and his men tried to capture the women at the road-house. The women got away—and are here."

JJ stared at the speakers.

"The PZs are attacking the Hermitage—in force. Maybe fifty or so. Get the troopers here. The Feds. We need help." Caz pulled in a breath. "Stay away from here, *mamita*. The *cabrones* are all over the road outside. There is no cover out there except for their cars."

"But—"

"I must go. Be safe, *mi corazón*"

His heart—he'd called her his heart.

Somehow, she'd parked in front of the municipal building. Her need to head for the Hermitage with lights and sirens blazing couldn't be allowed. She forced herself to turn off the engine.

Duty first.

She summoned help from the state troopers and the FBI, then the DEA, warning them that the good guys, women, and children were in the Hermitage buildings. And she added another caution that there might be good guys attempting to attack the PZs from the rear.

Because she knew Mako's sons. They wouldn't sit quietly when attacked.

When an FBI special agent told her to wait for them to arrive, she hung up on the idiot. As if she'd sit on her hands when her man and her daughter and her friends were in danger?

Never.

But some help would be nice.

She slid out of the police car.

A light showed in the coffee shop across the street. Sarah was at Audrey's party, and Uriah was probably waiting for her to come home. He might not know what had happened.

As JJ ran across the street, her worries tangled with hope. Last fall, no one in town had trusted her. Since then, they'd taken her in and made her one of them.

Would they follow her now...into war?

CHAPTER THIRTY

I *f the cost is the loss of a life, then let it be my loss and not that of my brother... -* Unknown

With relief, Bull spotted Aric and Regan obediently sitting on the tunnel steps and waiting for him. Both were wide-eyed and frightened, something no child should be.

Fucking PZs.

"Let's go, kids." He picked Aric up, took Regan's hand, and headed downstairs into cooler air that smelled of moist dirt. "Follow me, Dante. Ladies."

Going up, Caz passed them, his arms filled with a load of weaponry to equip the women who'd volunteered to help. Gabe had already set Knox and Chevy up in Hawk's sniper nest to keep the attackers busy.

Bull could see that Caz had left the armory door closed and concealed.

"Sirius and Gryff are in a storage room." Caz smiled at Regan. "They hate noise, so they're safer there, *mija*."

"Okay, Papá."

Caz exchanged glances with Bull, both of them hurt by the girl's scared little whisper. "Go with Bull now, *chiquita*."

"Time to get you tucked away." Moving quickly, Bull led Regan, Dante, and the non-combatant women past the armory and then past the heavy door to Mako's amply-weaponed disaster shelter—totally unsuitable for civilians.

Instead, he stopped at a storage room, more than adequate to keep them out of the line of fire.

The women filed past him. As he'd figured, Frankie wasn't in this bunch. She wasn't the type to sit out a fight.

"People, do not leave this room." Bull gave them a hard stare. "Am I clear? Out here are nervous people with weapons, and anyone leaving this room is liable to get shot by someone with an itchy trigger finger—or might catch a bullet from the assholes outside."

The women nodded. He knew them all except for three middle-aged women who...damn, they were state legislators.

Politicians. "Ladies, that goes for you three also. Stay here."

"We will," the oldest one said.

Setting Aric on the ground, Bull crouched down. The boy was trembling. *Dammit.* "Aric, your mom's upstairs, helping with the guns, but she needs you to stay here. Regan, you too. Keep an eye on Aric, please."

"I will, Uncle Bull." Her chin trembled, but her answer was steady.

He gave her an approving nod. Toughest kid ever.

Damn the bastards for putting these two through this shit.

"Bull," Caz shouted from above. "Get moving. We need more firepower. And '*mano*, no one saw Hawk at the roadhouse."

Fuck. Bull stiffened as his worst worries were confirmed. Hawk wouldn't have let the women be taken if he was operational. Trouble was, no one had expected an attack on the roadhouse.

It only took one bullet.

"Hawk?" Aric was stricken. So was Regan.

Caz, you idiot. Bull pulled in a breath. He wouldn't lie but wouldn't deny them hope either. *Dammit, bro, be okay.* "Hawk's sneaky, so we'll just have to wait and see."

Aric's mouth trembled, but he nodded.

Regan put her arm around him.

"Stay strong." Bull ran his hand over Aric's hair, then squeezed Regan's shoulder. "I'm proud of you both."

Farther in the room, Dante was pointing the women toward blankets on the hard dirt floor. The only light came from a camp lantern in one corner. The accommodations weren't comfortable, but better than bullets.

Dante glanced over. "Go on, boy. I'll be up in a minute."

At the stairs, Bull stopped to let Caz and Audrey go past on the way down.

Caz paused to say, "I'm sending Audrey up to Gabe, then guarding the ground floors. You escort Dante and Lillian to my place, *sí?*"

"Got it." Bull ran up the stairs, his need to see Frankie growing by the moment.

At the kitchen island, Lillian was loading a Glock.

His spirit hurt at the thought of the older woman joining the battle. "Lillian, maybe you should—"

"My dear boy, you will not deny me my place on this stage." Her smile was cheerful, her eyes grim. " '*Hark! the shrill trumpet sounds, to horse, away. My soul's in arms and eager for the fray.*' "

Guess that was his answer. If he argued, he'd probably get served up the St. Crispin's Day speech.

"Hey, dude." By the dining room table, Erica waved at him. "I'm assigned to you."

"You?" Spotting movement, Bull turned.

Kit and Sarah were upstairs on the landing outside Mako's rooms, both carrying weapons.

He scanned the living area, and dread lodged in his gut. "Kit, where's Frankie?"

Kit looked over the railing. "Isn't she with the women in the tunnels?"

"No." Fear increasing, he turned to Lillian.

Surprise, then concern filled her face. "I didn't see her."

Upstairs, Sarah leaned over the railing. "Dear God, I don't think she was in the van. Erica, did you see her?"

"I...no, she wasn't." Erica's eyes were wide. "How could we not notice?"

Bull bit back his snarl. The women had been terrorized and tied-up in a dark van, and as driver, Kit wouldn't have known who was in the cargo area.

His hands closed into fists as he fought the need to charge into the PZs until he found her.

Don't be a fool.

Either she'd escaped in the commotion at the roadhouse, or was shot and left behind, or she hadn't escaped. None of which he could do anything about right now. His jaw was so tight his teeth ground together.

The quickest way to her was to eliminate the bastards outside.

Exhaling, he saw that Kit had a hand over her mouth and was shaking. Yeah, there was guilt to spare and no time for it.

"We'll find her." He hardened his voice. "For now, move out, Kit."

Her mouth firmed, and then she and Sarah hurried toward the stairs to the attic.

The dining room table held a pile of weaponry, obviously for Bull. He strapped the Colt 45 around his waist, slung the bag with ammo over his shoulder, and picked up the HK semi-automatic rifle.

"We're ready." Loaded up, Dante stood beside Lillian.

Bull nodded to Erica. "Let's go."

With the three behind him, Bull hunched slightly as he strode through the fucking-low tunnel. A side tunnel held the steps to Caz's house. "Erica, wait here."

With Dante and Lillian behind him, he went up the stairs to the door, punched in the code, and ushered them through. "You know how to get into the attic?"

They both nodded.

Back in the tunnel, he led Erica past Hawk's and turned into his side-tunnel and up the stairs. He put in his code, opened the door, waved her in, then kicked it shut.

Two more flights upstairs got them into the small attic area.

Each house had a sniper's roost. The walls were reinforced with metal and sandbags. Camouflaged slits in the roof and walls allowed the shooter to move and target different areas.

The room was dark with the only light from outside. Not that there was anything in here to trip over. Just bare floor.

"Stand there a moment, Erica." Down on one knee inside the door, he felt for the display controls and flipped it on. The light-muted screen was close to the floor to avoid stray bullets. The display split into several windows with the feeds from their outside cameras.

Fuck. In the dark night, he couldn't tell how many black SUVs lined the road, but it looked like a lot.

Erica made a scared sound.

Keeping her busy would help.

"Let's get you set up." He donned one of the wireless intercom headsets. After handing another one to the young woman, he showed her the loopholes on the right side of the room. "Pick out the targets closest to you and fire away. After a few shots, move and shoot from a different slit."

"Got it." Her voice was shaky, but she knelt at a narrow opening that overlooked the dirt road.

The inter-house intercom dinged in his earpiece.

"People." Gabe's voice came through loud enough to be heard over the gunfire. "Fence is amped up to max."

Bull snorted. Electric fencing spanned the gaps between each house and from the end houses to the lake. Normally, the zap was only strong enough to deter bear and moose, but the charge *could* be increased.

No one would survive climbing the fence today.

"Sound off, people," Gabe ordered and started, "Ready at Gabe's—Gabe and Audrey."

Bull spoke, "Bull's place is ready—Bull and Erica."

"Ready at Hawk's. Lillian and Dante," Dante said.

"We got Caz's. Knox and Chevy."

"Here at Mako's," Kit said. "Kit and Sarah."

Bull nodded. The Hermitage was as prepared as they could be.

Over at the front, Erica continued to fire, making small sounds as she did. Good woman.

A long screech of pain came from down below. Yeah, someone had tried to climb the electrified fence. The bastard would have some burns to show for it.

Another yell came from farther away. Probably Mako's fence.

"Caz will watch for ground floor or lakeside incursions." Gabe said. "In thirty seconds, I'll flip on the flood lights. It's a target-rich environment, team. Have yourselves some fun."

Off to one side, Erica gave a choked laugh.

Spirits lifting slightly, Bull shook his head. Leave it to the old man to make a full-fledged attack sound like a light-hearted evening's entertainment.

There was a reason Gabe was their leader.

Bull took up position at a horizontal slit on the room's left side. "When the area's lit up, shoot as fast as you can. They'll be blinded."

"Got it." Erica moved to a new spot.

The bright floodlights came on, illuminating the road that ran past the outside of the semicircle of houses. A few bodies lay stretched in the gravel to show the effectiveness of the Hermitage's defenders.

But, Jesus. Two oversized passenger vans and another four

SUVs lined the road—and there was a white cargo van a lot farther away.

A shitload of PZs were using the vehicles for cover. Four dozen or so of the assholes must be out there.

Even as he started firing, Bull's teeth gritted together. So much for getting his ass outside and searching for Frankie. *Dammit. Dammit all.*

He'd give his own life to save her, but he couldn't risk the children or leave his brothers a man down. *God, Frankie, be alive. Be safe.*

From here, he'd do what he needed to do.

Searching for her would be a fuck of a lot easier if every PZ bastard was dead.

Where the hell were they shooting from?

Standing on one side of the white cargo van, Nabera squinted against the lights blazing down on his men who were much closer to the five two-story houses.

The amount of gunfire from the defenders was impressive.

He could see narrow windows on the first floors—smaller than man-sized—with metal grills, no less. The second-floor windows were slightly bigger, but dark. He couldn't spot any movement.

There were no windows in the attic spaces, but before the lights had blinded him, he'd seen muzzle flashes from high up.

People were shooting from the houses. For fuck's sake, they were more than adequately armed—and prepared. Even hosing them down with machine guns hadn't stopped them.

Hoping to breach the houses from the lakeside, he'd ordered two men to climb the eight-foot fences between the houses. Only they'd discovered the fencing was not only electric, but high voltage. Two more men disabled.

Fucking Hermitage bastards. He'd kill them all once he got through their defenses.

Swearing under his breath, Conrad joined Nabera. "We can't keep this up for long, Captain. They'll have sent for the state troopers, and our roadblocks won't hold them off forever."

At least the plan to isolate the town had proven effective.

Since Sterling was the only road to Rescue, they'd set off explosives, creating landslides to block the highway on each side of the town. Once they had the women, the Zealots would drive up Dall Road to McNally's Resort and leave their SUVs in the crowded parking lot. His men would scatter into the forest and make their way to a small lake and the floatplanes there. For Nabera and the captives, a rented helicopter waited on the helipad to fly them to the rendezvous point outside of Seward.

But Conrad was right. By now, they'd have heavy equipment working to clear away the landslides, and the troopers and the Feds would be on them the minute the road was clear.

What a fucked-up operation. They needed to get out of here.

Nabera glared at the five buildings. The bastards had destroyed the compound. The Prophet. The movement.

His *life*.

Humiliation was an ugly taste in his mouth. He and his men wouldn't run from the assholes like whipped curs.

He'd rather die.

As the floodlights went out, leaving the area in darkness, Nabera scowled. Were the off and on lights a deliberate plan or a problem with the electric lines?

No matter.

How could he turn this fiasco around? The group in Idaho paying their way had expected him to net several women. Kidnapping and selling the Mayor Lillian as well as the wives and girl-friends of the men who'd attacked the Zealots' compound would have been an effective demonstration. Selling two people—one of them a man—wouldn't bring much money. Even worse, Idaho would be less than impressed with the night's work. Would they renege on their agreement? Dammit. He and his men needed new IDs and a way out of Alaska.

Nabera eyed the Hermitage buildings. They had a stand-off—and the Zealots had a time limit.

The men in there wouldn't hand over the escaped women—their women—in exchange for Nabera's hostages. However…it was doubtful they cared about the three politicians. Would they agree to that exchange?

The Idaho militia would be more than satisfied if Nabera made the libtard state representative women disappear.

"Conrad, that bitch in the van." He had to raise his voice over the snapping of gunfire and the occasional cry of pain from his men. "Does she have a man in those houses?"

"Yeah. That'd be Bull. He owns the roadhouse. And my boss who's tied up with her?" Conrad smirked. "That's Hawk—Bull's brother."

Brother and girlfriend. Yeah, the Hermitage might go for an exchange.

"Tell the men to stop shooting."

Conrad pulled out his phone.

As the gunfire decreased to sporadic firing from the houses, Nabera yanked open the back of the van.

For fuck's sake. The prisoners were back-to-back, trying to untie each other.

Grabbing the woman's leg, Nabera dragged her away from the man. "Bull!" he shouted loud enough to be heard inside the distant buildings. "Bull, let's talk!"

The defenders stopped firing a few seconds later. They obviously had some way of communicating in there.

"Talk," came a deep bellow.

"I got your pretty girlfriend. Frankie, right?" He drew his K-bar knife. The light from the quarter moon barely penetrated the back of the van, but he could see how the bitch glared at him.

Not going to cooperate? There were ways.

Nabera pulled Hawk sideways, ensuring he couldn't kick, then ripped his shirt open.

"Watch this, bitch." He cut a deep groove across the man's gut —and the tough bastard didn't make a sound.

In the dim light, the pooling blood looked black against his skin, and Frankie let out a choking scream. "No!"

Nabera held the blade up. "You need to yell '*Bull*' real loud, or I'll poke so many holes in this bastard's gut that no surgeon will be able to repair him."

Horror filled her expression. She sucked in a breath and let loose. "*Bull!*"

"Yep. That should do it." Seeing the blood dripping off his knife, Nabera had to fight the craving to finish the job.

Not yet.

He shouted to the buildings, "Bull. I have Hawk too. I'll trade them for the three bitches—the state representatives. Do it, or I'll cut these two to pieces. You'll hear them screaming. Before they die."

"*Nooo.*" Even though Regan's voice had only come out a thin whisper, she clapped her hands over her mouth. That...that horrible man would kill Frankie and Uncle Hawk?

Beside her in Hawk's bedroom, Aric whimpered.

She put her arm around him. He was only a little kid. He shouldn't be hearing this.

But it wasn't *her* fault he was here. He'd snuck out, and the women hadn't seen him...or seen Regan following him. In the tunnel, he'd run really fast, and when she caught him, he wouldn't go back.

He'd wanted into Hawk's house—and, okay, like she really wanted to see what was going on, too, and she knew the code to open the door. When Papá taught her the emergency drills, she'd learned the passwords.

Aric shivered as he peeked out the window. "That was Captain Nabera," he whispered. "Is Hawk in the white car?"

"The big van?" Regan bit her lip. Frankie's scream had come from that way. "I guess."

"The captain's gonna kill him." Aric was shaking harder. "Will somebody go get him 'n' Frankie away? Your dad?"

Regan studied the van. No trees around it, no buildings. Just really short bushes and tall grass. Even Papá couldn't sneak there. Maybe if he crawled on his belly, but that'd take forever.

They didn't have forever.

She and Aric were a lot littler than Papá. "We could get there." *Maybe.* Now she was shaking too. "We're good at sneaking."

"We can't get past the fence." Camo paint still streaking his face, Aric stared down at the bare road.

"Can." Papá was going to kill her for leaving. She'd be doing pushups, like, forever. "One end of the tunnel comes out on the other side of the fence."

"'Kay," Aric whispered.

She peeked in Hawk's nightstand. If he was like Papá... He was. A sheathed knife lay in the top drawer. "Here. Just in case."

Aric shoved it into a pocket of his camo pants.

She already had the folding knife Papá had given her. Because she was smart and careful and responsible.

He'd probably take her knife away now.

"My Hawk. No, no, no." Kit's hands on the rifle trembled, and she pulled in a breath. The small attic room was filled with the acrid, smoky stench of gunpowder. "I'll kill Nabera."

As if she could. Her shooting wasn't exactly accurate.

"Too far away," came Sarah's whisper.

Kit gritted her teeth. Sarah was right.

The white van was past Gabe's house at the other end of the semicircle on the road coming in. It was almost to the forest, but not quite. The captain must have been the last to arrive.

He was too far away to shoot. Probably too far for anyone except Hawk, who supposedly could hit anything he could see in a scope. The captain hadn't come close to the houses—he wouldn't take the same risks as his troops.

Nabera had Hawk. And Frankie. The knowledge was so painful she set the rifle down.

Four of the PZs ran from the SUVs toward the white van. She closed her eyes in despair. With the location of Frankie and Hawk known, Nabera would set guards there.

Damn him.

In her headset, she heard Gabe, Caz, and Bull talking.

"I'll tell Nabera I want to meet him outside to discuss the exchange," Bull said. "I can agree, then stall by working out precautions for the exchange."

Gabe said, "Tell him to work out a way that no one knows we turned the women over. He'd understand your reasoning."

"If you keep his attention, I can try to get Hawk and Frankie loose. But there isn't much cover." Caz sounded worried. "And not enough time to go slow. I'll have to take out those four guards too."

Gabe said, "Even if they don't see the guards drop, Hawk and Frankie will be seen when you try to leave. If they can even move."

Kit stiffened. How badly might Hawk and Frankie have been hurt?

The captain—of course, he'd hurt them.

We have to get Hawk and Frankie away from him.

"Nabera will expect us to try something; he'll be watching," Bull agreed. "I'll try to keep his attention, but—"

"I'll set up somewhere in the brush where I can take out

Nabera or the guards on the van, if needed." Gabe made a growling sound. "This is a forlorn hope, guys."

A forlorn hope. Hawk's westerns had told her the term meant a suicidal assault. A bunch of men sent right into the kill zone.

Kit scrubbed her damp palms over her face.

Even though Caz was completely silent in the forest, he couldn't hide when there wasn't any cover. Especially if Nabera was suspicious. And if their captain was watching, the guards would be especially attentive too.

What would pull Nabera's attention away from the van? Could Bull do something— Her thoughts stuttered to a halt.

There was a guaranteed way to keep Nabera's focus. Her whole body shook in protest of the idea.

All she'd ever wanted was to stay as far from Nabera as possible.

She had to swallow twice before her voice would work. "Guys, I have an idea."

Nabera watched as two people came out of the closest log house and strolled toward him as if the guns of his men weren't targeting them. As if they had all the time in the world.

They were stalling, the bastards.

In a blinding wave of light, the floodlights came on. It made it easy to see the two walking down the road. Halfway to him, in the long stretch between the cargo van and the line of SUVs, they stopped and waited.

The location was logical, forcing him to join them, so anyone with a firearm would be able to shoot negotiators.

Here at the cargo van, he was safe.

He didn't like putting himself at risk.

Damn them. Time was running out. The landslides across the roads wouldn't keep the state troopers away too long.

With Rescue's Chief of Police inside the Hermitage, there was undoubtedly something planned. Not that he could do anything. There was a Zealot stationed on each side of the van.

At the open back door, Conrad was saying to Hawk, "You fucking bastard. Even if we trade you, I'll hamstring you before we let you go. You won't walk so high and mighty then, *boss*."

Mood lightened, Nabera laughed. "Come, Conrad. Join the men and take charge of them while I negotiate."

When his lieutenant's face fell, Nabera added, "I'll make sure you get a moment with Hawk before handing him over."

Grinning, Conrad joined him.

Nabera turned to one of the van's guards. "They were trying to untie each other. Leave the door open so you can check on them as you patrol."

"Yes, sir." The man scowled at the prisoners. "If they try it again, I'll cut their fingers off."

"Good man." A minute later, Nabera and Conrad passed the two guards stationed between the houses and the van. They'd watch for anyone leaving the houses.

Nabera nodded to them. "Stay vigilant, men."

They both straightened. "Yes, sir."

A grim satisfaction filled Nabera. No one would get past his men.

As Conrad continued forward to take command of the Zealots at the SUVs, Nabera veered toward the two waiting people.

Built like a tank, Bull was the owner of the roadhouse.

The person beside him was much smaller. Had they really brought a woman to negotiate? Unbelievable. Was it one of the state representative bitches?

No, this woman was younger. Golden-brown hair, average height, obviously terrified.

A second later, he recognized her...and grinned.

She *should* be terrified. Anticipation filled him to overflowing, and his dick shot to attention.

The woman was Obadiah's wife. *Kirsten.* No matter what they negotiated, she wouldn't be returning to the Hermitage. Not alive.

Caz silently opened the tunnel door and exited into an area of thick underbrush. Only a week or so ago, he and Regan had been out here, cleaning up the area, after he'd shown her how to use the tunnel system and locks.

Crouching in the darkness and bushes, he looked around. Behind him was Gabe's house and past it, one of the SUVs on the road. Farther to the west, toward the forest was the white van. *Ya valió madres.*

Sí, no doubt about it, their plan was fucked. There was a good chance he wouldn't return from this. Wouldn't see his little girl or JJ again.

At least his women would live. JJ loved Regan and would raise her.

From shadow to shadow, from cover to cover, he eased away from the buildings toward the white van. The area around the lake held a fair amount of reeds and bushes, but closer to the road? Just short shrubs and grasses. Too short.

In the quiet night, Bull's deep voice boomed, even louder than normal.

Kit's higher tones were clear and understandable even where he was. "You are the stupidest person. How did you ever get to be captain?"

Caz saw her gesturing emphatically, making herself the center of attention. Risking herself for Frankie...and for Hawk.

You found a fine woman, mi hermano. Now, let's get you free to have a lifetime to love her.

As the guards turned to watch Bull and Kit confront their captain, Caz gained another few feet.

Reaching the last decent-sized clump of bushes, he went down on one knee and paused.

There was no cover, and the quarter moon was high in the sky. Even with Kit and Bull drawing attention, the guards would eventually remember to scan the area.

However, the floodlights didn't reach this far and watching the brightly lit negotiations would destroy the PZs' night vision. Quickly, he mapped out a possible route that'd require him to belly-crawl for part of the way.

A stealthy movement in the stubby brush close to the van caught his attention. Was that a raccoon?

No, *no*. It was a small boy crawling through the thicker clumps of grass in the drainage ditch beside the dirt road. On the same route was a girl.

His girl.

As terror swept through him, his jaw clenched to prevent his curses from spilling out like a furious fountain.

Following the plan, Regan finally reached the road and crept beneath the white van. She was trying to breathe without making any noise, and her hands were scraped and burned like fire. Her camo jeans were all ripped up.

And she was so scared. *I want Papá.* Tears stung her eyes, but she couldn't cry.

The little shadow that was Aric moved closer to the back of the van. He was in place.

Mouth tight, she got out her knife and opened it. Her job was to be the distraction. And even attack if she had to.

Down by the houses, Kit was yelling again, and Bull's shout

was even louder. The noise they made didn't quite hide the tiny creak from the van as Aric slipped inside.

Footsteps crunched on the gravel as a guard walked around the van.

Oh no. Regan wiggled closer to the back, just in case the man looked inside and saw Aric.

He kept walking.

Her knife hand was shaking. *She* was shaking. Friggers, she wanted to run home.

Why was she *here?*

For Hawk. Right. And for Frankie.

And even for Aric.

She tightened her grip on the knife and silently repeated what Uncle Bull said anytime she whined about something being too hard. *"Pain is acceptable. Quitting is not. Blood is acceptable. Quitting is not. Falling is acceptable. Quitting is not."*

Her lips pressed together. *I won't quit.*

Nabera started yelling nasty words. Then Bull shouted something.

Hurry, Aric.

How they'd get Frankie and Uncle Hawk out of here...she didn't know that.

Maybe she was a stupidhead, cuz she'd believed Aric when he said Hawk would fix it.

She really, really hoped the kid was right.

What the fuck was going on out there? Hawk turned his head, wincing as the movement sent his headache into high gear. He could sure hear Kit's voice way too clearly. Although she was shouting, he could hear her fear.

Why in hell was she outside instead of safe in the Hermitage? His jaw tightened as Nabera bellowed in anger.

He pulled at the ropes around his wrists. No give. He'd never felt so fucking helpless.

Feeling a slight dip of the van, Hawk eyed the open door. No one blocked the light from outside. Frankie hadn't moved.

There was a whisper of sound, a slight movement of the air. Something small had crawled into the cargo area. A cat, maybe? There were too many shadows to see clearly.

A cold little hand touched his cheek, and he heard the tiniest of whispers in his ear. "Hawk."

Son of a fucking bitch.

Terror shot shards of ice right into his heart. Aric. *God, no.* He'd rather die than have the boy hurt.

Before he could figure out what to do, Aric crawled behind him and started sawing at the ropes around Hawk's wrists.

Damned if the kid didn't have a knife.

This might take a while. The fucking PZs had used lots of rope in tying him up—and the child had only a four-year-old's strength.

But he was so silent that even Frankie hadn't realized he was in here.

There was no light for Aric to see, and Hawk gritted his teeth as the sharp blade cut him several times in the process. But the strands were loosening, falling away, one by one.

With all his strength, he yanked at the ropes. The last ones broke, and he was free—even as the knife sliced down his wrist.

Aric squeaked in dismay.

Frankie gasped.

"Shhh." Hawk took the knife and cut the ropes binding his ankles. Good blade. Actually, it felt damn familiar in his hand.

Outside, gravel crunched.

Fuck. The guards must have heard Aric's squeak and were heading around the van toward the back.

Hawk pulled the boy against his side and breathed, "Stay down."

Regan had heard a sound like a mouse from inside the van. *Friggers, Aric.*

The guards had heard too. Under the van, she saw feet moving toward the back of the van. Tucked behind the rear wheel, she waited.

Closer, closer.

She picked her spot—the place above the man's boot. Braced on one hand, she stabbed her knife really, really hard into his leg.

"*Shit!*" His leg jerked away, pulling the knife right out of her hand.

Oh no. She scrabbled backward as fast as she could.

There was a thump, like he hit the van, and then he dropped to his knees. She tensed, knowing he'd look under the van. Would shoot her.

Only...he fell over sideways and just lay there, not moving or anything.

She wiggled even farther back under the vehicle.

Stabbing a leg couldn't kill someone...could it?

Why was Kit yelling at Nabera? What was her bestie *thinking?*

Get away from him, Kit. Frankie couldn't stop trembling, terrified for herself, for Hawk, and now for Kit.

A few seconds ago, Hawk whispered, *Shhh,* only she hadn't made any noise. Then something thumped against the side of the van.

She felt movement behind her. Hawk? Had he gotten free?

"Shhh," he whispered again, only a breath of a sound.

The ropes around her wrists pulled tighter, then fell off completely. As blood surged back into her hands, she smothered a moan. *Cazzo,* that hurt.

He closed her half-numb fingers around a knife handle and whispered, "Cut your legs loose."

Hearing a guard's footsteps approaching, she sawed frantically on the ropes binding her ankles.

The PZ appeared in the van's doorway.

Half-standing, Hawk grabbed the man's shoulders and yanked. The PZ's head hit the top of the doorway with a gut-wrenching crunch, and he dropped bonelessly to the ground.

Frankie's ankles were free. As her circulation returned, her feet returned to life in waves of searing pain. *Ow, ow, ow.*

Jumping out of the van, Hawk bent to pick up the PZ's rifle.

As Frankie followed him out, she felt something behind her and spun.

And then her arms were full of a little boy.

Madonna, it was Aric, trembling like a leaf.

She hugged him hard even as fear for him tore holes in her heart.

Silently, Hawk crept around the van to where the other guard should be. The one who'd thumped on the van.

A body lay on the ground, unmoving...with a matte black knife in his back.

Caz was here.

Hawk glanced around, seeing an area of taller brush. Probably there.

With a grim smile, Hawk turned his head and winced as his headache increased. Farther down the road, two guards stood between the van and the Hermitage.

Near Gabe's house, Nabera was still shouting at Bull and Kit.

Dammit, Kit. His gut clenched.

First things first. Those two guards were far enough away that Aric and Frankie should be able to reach Caz without being seen.

His eyes narrowed. Just how the hell had Aric gotten out of the Hermitage anyway? Caz sure wouldn't have brought him.

Someone else might, though.

Frowning, Hawk spotted a jack-knife sticking out of the dead guard's leg. Someone else, indeed.

Bending, Hawk spoke softly. "C'mon out, Regan."

After a second, she appeared, taking his hand to stand up. Flinging her arms around him, she buried her face against his side.

Yeah, Caz had an incredibly lovable, incredibly brave kid.

Holding the AR-15 off to one side, Hawk bent and whispered in her hair. "You did great, Regan. But time to leave. Take Aric and Frankie to your dad. I got this now. Yeah?"

Her head moved up and down.

Caz would intercept them and guide them back. Protect them on the way.

Arm around Regan, Hawk moved to the back of the van. With a happy gasp, Regan grabbed Frankie.

Setting the rifle in the van, Hawk picked Aric up for a hug and a quick whisper. "Thanks for the rescue, buddy." Fuck, he loved these kids.

Man up, Calhoun. After putting the boy down, Hawk whispered to them, "Stay crouched and go there." He pointed where he estimated Caz was and a route where the van would mostly block them from the sight of the PZs

Aric signaled okay, and the three moved off.

Hawk stayed on guard until they disappeared into the taller foliage.

Still talking to Kit and Bull, Nabera sounded increasingly frustrated. Yeah, the bastard was going to snap. And when he did, he'd pull his fucking pistol and start shooting.

Hawk checked the AR-15's magazine, pleased it had a full load. Bringing it up into firing position, he winced. His arms were less than optimal after being wrenched behind his back for so long. His aim would be crap.

Where was a tripod when he needed one?

His eyes narrowed as he studied the van. Yeah, the roof would provide adequate arm support.

At the back door, he went up onto the van's bumper step pad and leaned forward, propping his elbows on the roof. Good thing he was tall.

He found a stable position. Resting his cheek against the stock, he zeroed-in on Nabera.

Target acquired.

"You are stupid—a real dumbass," Kit shouted, even as she edged even closer to Bull. She couldn't help herself. It was taking all her courage to keep yelling at Captain Nabera.

His face had darkened, his expression furious.

More fear welled up inside her. Her whole body kept trying to sink into the dirt. The heavy body armor Gabe had insisted they wear didn't help.

Her throat was so dry, her voice cracked.

Hearing it, Bull took over. "We can't let anyone know we handed you the politicians, so..."

Tuning out the discussion, she darted a glance at the white van. Was their scheme working?

The two PZs in the road between them and the van were staring at her and Bull... probably waiting for Nabera to hit her. No woman ever raised her voice around him, let alone called him names.

If Bull hadn't been with her, and if Nabera hadn't agreed on safe conduct, she'd be dead.

With a hard breath, she made herself taller. "No." She flipped her hand in the air at Nabera. "That's not acceptable, you moron."

"Woman, we're talking," Bull said loudly and gave her shoulder a shake before telling Nabera, "We'll bring out the politicians if—"

"Stay on guard, people," someone shouted from behind the lined-up SUVs.

As if reminded of his hostages, the captain turned toward the white cargo van.

No!

"The big bad Nabera doesn't know what to do with real women," Kit snapped out and almost laughed as his attention whipped back to her. "The PZs are terrified of women. There's no other reason they'd try to make sure we don't talk."

As angry retorts came from the PZs behind the SUVs, fear blasted through her, and her bones felt as if they'd turning to water. Had she and Bull stalled long enough?

Get free, Hawk.

"Or maybe the PZs just have tiny dicks, and that's why you joined." She made herself smirk. "I *know* that's true for nubby Nabera."

"I changed my mind, you fucking cunt." Nabera yanked his gun free of the holster. "You'll be my prize and—"

Before he could raise it, a shot rang out from the SUVs even as something slammed into Kit, knocking her backward.

And then there was pain.

One of the bastards shot Kit.

No, fuck, no! He couldn't live without her. And Aric. Blackness clamped down on Hawk's mind.

She was still staggering—falling—when Bull plowed into her, taking them both into the far too shallow ditch next to the road. Hawk gritted his teeth against a scream of rage.

Training and long experience had kept him immobile despite his shock. The rifle sights were still centered on his target.

He softly pulled the trigger.

Nabera dropped like a rock.

One.

Hawk aimed at his second target—the leftmost PZ guard in the road. Pulled.

Two down.

Before Hawk could move to the other guard, someone took the bastard out.

Fine, then.

Hawk went for his fourth choice, the PZ near the center of the SUVs. With the floodlights on, Milo's shiny scalp was easy to see. Damn him, he was shooting at Bull and Kit.

A wave of fury seared along Hawk's nerves. Was Milo the bastard who'd shot her?

Die.

Hawk breathed out. Pulled.

Milo, aka Lieutenant Conrad, wouldn't be doing any more carpentry.

Hawk's next shot took out Luka.

And then the entire area erupted with gunfire.

Grief bitter in his mouth, Hawk glanced at Bull. Still flattened in the dubious cover of the ditch with Kit beneath him.

But...wait.

Had she moved? Was she...squirming?

She was *alive*.

Dear heavens, she couldn't breathe! Gasping for air, Kit tried to move but was totally pinned down. Was she buried? Was she dead?

"Stay put, Kit."

Bull's deep voice came from just over her head. She could barely hear him what with the shooting.

Oh. He was on top of her, pressing her into the dirt.

No wonder she could barely pull in a breath, and her shoulder hurt like heck. But she was alive to complain.

She blinked. "Where's Nabera?"

"Dead," Bull muttered. "I'm guessing Hawk got loose."

As hope rose inside her, so did her fears.

Because all around them, it sounded like World War III had begun.

———

Lying in the brush to one side of the road, Gabe grinned at the sweet effectiveness of one of the finest snipers he'd ever known.

The hawk was flying free. In fact, he'd beat Gabe to killing Nabera by a fraction of a second, then taken out one of the two guards without missing a beat. Gabe got the other.

Despite heavy fire from the Hermitage, Kit and Bull were still in a lot of danger. The PZs were after revenge for Nabera's death.

Gabe turned his rifle toward the SUVs. He'd get as many shots off as possible before his muzzle flash would pinpoint his location and end his effectiveness.

Suddenly, headlights of multiple vehicles barreled down their private road, drawing up behind the white cargo van. Doors were slamming and a hailstorm of shooting began—all aimed at the PZs.

The cavalry had arrived.

———

JJ pulled in a breath and tried to get a sense of the battle.

With their cars fanned out on the dirt road, her volunteers were picking off the well-lit PZs like they were in a shooting gallery. From this angle, the pissers had no cover.

Even though JJ almost shook with the need to check on Caz,

she knew he was probably safe inside the Hermitage. Regan would be even safer down in the tunnel system.

When JJ reached the white cargo van, she recognized Hawk. He was standing on the van's back step-pad and shooting over the roof. The thin moonlight also showed the blood that soaked his sleeves and matted his sand-colored hair.

"You look like shit, Hawk," she yelled over the noise of gunfire. "You okay?"

"Yep. Am now." He fired again, then stepped down beside her, avoiding the body that lay in the dirt.

Behind a pickup on the left, Uriah fired twice and made a satisfied sound.

On the right, Tucker shot and grunted. "Three."

"Loser," Guzman retorted from beside him. "I got four."

Hawk eyed the vehicles and the men. "No state troopers?"

"They're delayed," JJ said. "It seems Sterling is blocked with landslides on each side of town. These are volunteers from Rescue."

He grinned. "Probably better shots than the Feds, anyway."

"I know, right?" Their town had a lot of hunters. She grinned. "I told them it's open season on the pissers with no permits required."

Hawk snorted.

The firing from the SUV area was diminishing. A rifle was flung out into the dirt. Then another.

Someone shouted, "I surrender!"

"Stop, please, stop!" another PZ yelled.

That did it. The PZs—the ones left alive—threw down their weapons.

Gunfire still came from the Hermitage and her troop. Her voice came out loud and piercing over the noise. "Ceasefire."

The last shots stuttered to a halt.

Hawk nodded at her. "Looks like they're all yours, Officer."

"Damn." So much for checking on Caz. She scowled at him. "No good deed goes unpunished."

He huffed a laugh.

She sighed. Her troops, her command.

"Patriot Zealots, stand up with your hands on your head." She glanced at Hawk and asked the question burning in her heart. "Is Caz okay?"

"Yeah. He took Frankie and the kids back to the Hermitage."

"Oh good." Her sigh of relief clogged in her throat. "Wait, what? The *kids*?"

Kit heard the shooting stop after someone—had that been JJ?— yelled for a ceasefire. Didn't matter. Right now, she wanted to curl into a ball and shake. Maybe she also wanted some covers to pull over her head.

Only she needed to find Hawk.

Her hands clenched at another influx of worry. How badly was he hurt?

Thank heavens Aric was safe down in the tunnel.

Bull's weight moved off her. "Stay down, Kit." He stood with a low groan.

She'd felt him flinch right after they hit the ground. "Are you hurt?"

"Caught one in my back armor. Like you got in the front." He scanned the area as he spoke. "We'll both be sore tomorrow."

The armor. Heavens, no wonder her shoulder hurt so bad. She'd been *shot*.

She lifted her head to watch the people following JJ down the road toward the SUVs. Huh, that was Tucker, wasn't it? And Sarah's husband?

"JJ." Gabe came out of the bushes to meet his officer and slapped her shoulder in obvious approval. "Nice timing."

"I think we're good. Up you come." Bull helped her up to her feet.

"Kit." The gravelly growl made her heart bound. "Jesus, woman." Hawk grabbed her and lifted her off her feet in a rib-crushing, breath-stealing embrace.

"Hawk." Arms around his neck, she clung with all her might. "You're alive. I was so worried."

And she was shaking far harder now than she had been when shouting at Nabera.

"You're wearing armor, thank Christ. I thought you were dead." Hawk scowled at Bull accusingly. "Why the *fuck* were you in the kill zone?"

"Bro, she insisted—and she was right. The minute she appeared, Nabera forgot you even existed." Anxiety filling his face, Bull gripped Hawk's shoulder. "Is Frankie—"

"Fine. I sent her to Caz before nailing Nabera."

Kit breathed out a sigh of relief. Her bestie was safe.

"Sugar." Slowly, tenderly, Hawk kissed Kit, then rubbed his cheek against hers. And just held her.

It was what she needed. Everything she needed. She pressed even closer. He was alive.

His arms tightened as she clung to him. Eventually, she lifted her head. "Are you all right?"

"Bruises and cuts, nothing major." With an unhappy sigh, he straightened and let her loose.

"I know. We have stuff to do," she muttered.

"Yeah." He eyed her. "I got good news and bad news." He wore the same expression as Aric after he'd knocked over a newly seeded planter.

"What did you do?"

"Me? Nothing." His eyes crinkled with mischief. "Your son, though..."

CHAPTER THIRTY-ONE

The only redemptive feature of war is the brotherhood which it forges. - Max Hastings

Finally released by the Fed who'd interviewed him, Hawk headed toward his house.

The entire area outside the Hermitage still crawled with state troopers, FBI agents, and first responders. Damned if cleanup wasn't taking longer than the battle. Would the talking ever end?

Jesus, he hurt. His head pounded like it'd been flattened under a Bradley tank. His ribs throbbed enough he would guess that the bastard Milo had kicked him a few times. His shoulders ached. And his gut and wrists? He glanced at his blood-soaked sleeves and flannel shirt. At least the bleeding had stopped.

And he was alive and moving...unlike a lot of the PZs. Ambulances were still hauling away the wounded assholes. The state troopers had taken charge of the rest.

Hawk felt like he'd been out here for days, but past the floodlights, it was still night. The moon had been blotted out by black clouds. Carried on the rising breeze, the air stank of gunpowder, sweat—and death, and all he wanted to do was escape.

"Yeah, that PZ guy's in really bad shape." A medic was telling a state trooper as Hawk walked past. "My partner's watching him till an ambulance returns."

Hawk sighed, then turned. "Got a plane. I can fly—"

"*No mames, güey.* No, you cannot." Caz's voice came from behind.

Hawk turned, feeling relief. The Fed had said that none of the Hermitage group was seriously wounded, but hearing wasn't seeing.

Lines of exhaustion showed in Caz's brush-scratched face. But none of the blood on his clothing appeared to be his.

Hawk glanced at the medic, then Caz. "Bro. The floatplane's—"

"*No.*" Caz threw his hands up in open exasperation. "Can you say *concussion?* You were unconscious. You fly nowhere until I say otherwise."

Next to the state trooper, the Soldotna first responder tilted his head at Caz and told Hawk, "What he said. A crash landing doesn't improve anyone's health."

"Fine." To be honest, he was exhausted. "In that case, got anything for a headache?"

Caz's grin flashed. "Come, 'mano. I was looking for you anyway."

They went through the garage into Caz's house and out onto his deck. Audrey was there, sitting next to a table with an assortment of medical shit.

"Hawk!" Over on Bull's deck next door, Aric scrambled off Frankie's lap.

Worry stabbed at Hawk, sharp as a stiletto. Kit should be with her son. "Where's Kit?" Had she been hurt worse than he thought?

"She's fine." Frankie smiled. "She's still being questioned by some Feds."

Hawk nodded his thanks for the info, then bent to catch the incoming rocket of a kid. His head throbbed in pain, his ribs stabbed, and damn, it still felt like he'd had a belt of pure happiness. "Hey, Aric."

Caz sat down and pointed to the wider deck chair. The one he called a loveseat. "Sit."

With the kid curled up next to him like a puppy, Hawk glanced at Audrey. "Anyone get hurt at your roadhouse party, blondie?"

"Raymond. But I talked to him. He has bruises and a headache—probably like yours—but nothing major." Audrey shook her head. "The rest of the women, well, we've got bruises from banging around in the van. Everyone who was shooting got cuts and splinters, but nothing worse."

Mako had carefully designed the sniper roosts. The narrow rifle openings and steep angle from the ground decreased the chance of catching a bullet. "Splinters?"

"When they couldn't tell exactly where the shooters were, the PZs turned loose with machine guns." Caz checked Hawk's midsection and scowled. "I'll need you to lie down for that one. Let me get your arms first."

Moving one blood-drenched sleeve out of the way, the doc started cleaning the slices on Hawk's wrist

"Machine guns are scary. Enough bullets got through that we got showered with wood splinters and pieces of shingles," Audrey said lightly. She had wood chips in her long hair and scratches on her face and arms.

Gabe said she'd kept shooting in the roost by herself after he'd left to provide backup for Bull and Kit.

Hell of a woman.

"That's when Knox's rifle barrel got hit. Chevy said Knox

bitched about his bruised fingers, grabbed another rifle, and went back to shooting."

Hawk could only smile. They grew them tough in Alaska.

Still, everyone—except the PZs—had been fucking lucky.

"Aric, how are you doing, sweetie?" Scooting closer, Audrey leaned forward to kiss Aric's cheek.

He didn't release his hold on Hawk's shirt but gave her one of his crooked smiles.

Finished cleaning Hawk's arms, Caz glanced up. "I'll glue and tape, but only if you try not to mess up my work."

"Sure."

Holding out a butterfly strip for Caz, Audrey frowned at Hawk's wrists. "Did Nabera do all that? Or was it that Milo guy?"

Oh, hell.

Aric stiffened, and his big eyes filled with tears. "I'm sorry."

"I'm not." Hawk gave the kid a comforting squeeze. "Gonna catch a few cuts if you use a knife in the dark."

Catching on, Caz confirmed with a nod. "*Sí.*"

Audrey's expression held dismay. She hadn't realized what she was asking.

"You got me free; that's what counts." Hawk kissed the top of Aric's head. "Might get new scars to remind me of the bravest kid I know. I'd like that."

Aric stared up as if trying to see if Hawk was being honest. Then he relaxed and went limp against Hawk's side.

It was way fucking past the kid's bedtime.

But—Hawk tightened his arm about the boy—they were both happier being together.

Hours later, in Mako's place, Kit was snuggled up against Hawk's side. Aric lay, sound asleep, across their laps. She was exhausted, one shoulder throbbing from the impact of the bullet, the other one from shooting a rifle. Her fingers ached. Scratches burned.

Yet the oddest contentment filled her.

Her loved ones were alive and safe.

Tilting her head, she rubbed her cheek against Hawk's arm. "I didn't think those law enforcement people would ever leave."

Outside, dark clouds had covered any hint of dawn, and rain pounded from the sky, washing away the remnants of the battle. It might have helped send the Feds and troopers on their way.

"I know, right?" Audrey agreed.

Sitting beside her, Gabe gave her curls a tug as he smiled. "We actually got off lightly, Goldilocks."

"Lightly?" Frankie sniffed. "Sooo many questions. They even managed to wear Lillian out."

First, JJ's "troop" and the six friends who'd been inside the Hermitage houses had finally had been allowed to leave. None had appeared too upset. Some, if anything, the opposite.

Knox and Erica, Chevy and Tina, Dante and Lillian—they'd competed for the most outrageous whopper of a story. Their interviewer—an FBI agent—had looked at them as if they were crazy. The state troopers had just laughed.

"Having three state representatives almost kidnapped short-ened our questioning," Bull said. Beside him on the sectional, Frankie was curled up with her head on his thigh, and Gryff lay across his feet. "Since the PZs attacked the Hermitage to capture them, there wasn't any doubt about who the good guys are."

"Especially when the Chief of Police and his officer live here," Frankie murmured in agreement.

Gabe grinned at Caz, who had JJ and Regan tucked against him. "Thanks for getting the unused weapons into the armory before the Feds saw them."

Kit rolled her eyes. The armory was not only in the tunnel, but the door was locked and camouflaged. Talk about paranoid. Yet their sarge's survivalist preparations had saved them all.

Smirking, Caz tugged on JJ's hair. "It is best to avoid giving the law enforcement types anything extra to worry about. *Sí*, officer?"

"Ooooh, you'll pay for that one." JJ twisted far enough to pinch his ribs, then pinched Regan too.

"Hey! I didn't do anything," Regan's protest was handicapped by giggles.

"Actually... You did." Smile fading, JJ moved to sit beside the girl. "You snuck away from where you were safe and left the Hermitage. With Aric."

Regan stiffened, then her gaze dropped, and she nodded.

JJ lifted the girl's chin. "I am so very proud of your courage. And I was terrified at how badly my girl could have been hurt."

As Regan's eyes filled with tears, she burrowed into JJ's side... and Caz gathered them both in.

Kit had to wipe away her own tears before cuddling closer to Hawk. Her heart felt overly tender, aching as much as her shoulders did.

"I'm not sure I'm ready for kids," Gabe said under his breath as he rested his hand ever so gently on Audrey's abdomen.

Sympathizing with his worries, Kit whispered, "They're terrifying," and heard Hawk's almost silent, "Yeah."

After kissing the top of Audrey's head, Gabe raised his voice. "I don't know about the rest of you, but I need a shower."

"You really do, although, at least you're not covered in blood. Which you should be." Sitting up, Audrey scowled. "I saw you in the bushes, shooting as if you had a brick wall for cover instead of a few measly leaves."

"Ah..." Gabe eyed Audrey, obviously searching for a response, then shrugged. "I got nothin'."

"My crazy hero." Audrey shook her head and stood. "Let's go. I'll scrub your back."

"Forget showers, I want a long, long bath." Frankie sighed before glowering at the rope burns on her wrists.

Knowing the hot water would make the abrasions sting, Kit flinched. It was her fault that Frankie and everyone else had been injured. If she hadn't met and married Obadiah, then—

No, she couldn't think like that. She'd made the best decisions she could at the time. And many wonderful things had happened. Like Hawk. And Frankie finding Bull.

As if hearing her, Frankie looked over. "*Amica mia*, thank you. Caz said if you hadn't kept Nabera and the guards' attention on you, no one could have freed Hawk and me. I have an idea how hard it must have been to face Nabera."

"Yeah," Hawk said in his deep rasp. "That took guts."

Kit pulled in a shaky breath. It had been so very close, but they were all here and alive. And she had her son on her lap and Hawk beside her.

Life was good.

So was balance. She looked at her bestie. "After getting me out of the compound, you said it was *my* turn to save *you*—and I owed Hawk a rescue too. Nabera gave me a chance to pay you both off at once."

Kit grinned at Frankie, then Hawk. "You're welcome."

CHAPTER THIRTY-TWO

*L*ove *is something sent from heaven to worry the hell out of you. -* Dolly Parton

Behind Kit in the back of his canoe, Hawk stroked the paddle through the aqua-blue water. Fog drifted over the lake in a silent contrast to the battle last weekend.

For two days, they'd dealt with law enforcement groups and repaired the damage to the Hermitage. The garage doors would sure never look the same. They'd have to buy new ones so the women and kids wouldn't constantly see the ugly reminders of violence.

Backstroking lightly, he angled the canoe closer to the bank. Now that the town's floatplane dock was in good repair, more planes landed on the lake. The roadhouse was benefiting from the visitors.

In the bow, Kit paddled smoothly and quietly. Next time, he'd teach her to steer.

Next time.

They had a future together. The knowledge was simply,

fucking wonderful, although, yeah, it might take a while to truly accept it.

On the bank, a flock of snow geese were snacking on the grasses and sedges in preparation for their fall migration.

Winter was coming—but the long, dark nights wouldn't be the same. Not when Kit and Aric would be with him.

"Wow, look." Kit pointed to a moose rubbing the velvet off its antlers on a tree trunk.

"It's almost rutting season, so remember that the males can be irritable."

For a change, he wasn't one of the irritable males. He'd never been more content.

An hour later, he lay on a heavy horse blanket with Kit straddling his hips.

The canoe rested on the bank, and they'd found a grassy area well hidden by bushes and overhanging trees.

She was so beautiful when naked. The sunlight made gold and red glints in her brown hair—soft hair that whispered over his chest as she bent over him, thoroughly impaled on his dick.

As she planted little kisses on his face, he breathed in the scent of vanilla and lavender.

She'd already come twice from his fingers and tongue, and her eyes were half-closed, her mouth swollen.

Her breasts were heavy in his hands, and when he tugged a reddened nipple, her cunt tightened around him in response.

"Hawk." Her beautiful voice held an appealing sultriness now. "Don't you want to get off?"

He'd be happy like this forever, with her smiling at him, with her ass settled on his groin, her breasts right there for him to play with.

But with her question, his cock set up urgent demands. He wouldn't last much longer.

"If you insist." Watching her carefully to ensure he didn't set off a panic attack, he rolled them over to put her beneath him.

Rather than panicking, she giggled. "You really do like being on top."

On top, standing, beneath, behind. He enjoyed any position when it came to making love with her. "Today, my dick wants to play hammer."

And because it'd been a patient cock, it deserved a reward.

Her laugh turned to a moan as he demonstrated.

Oh, sweet heavens, she was going to come *again*. The heavy pounding had re-awakened every nerve in her body.

Hawk was watching her closely, the way he did whenever he got rougher with her. Now, his eyes crinkled slightly as he bent her right leg and pushed it outward so his pelvis rubbed against her clit with each thrust.

Oh, oh, oh. As her muscles went stiff, everything inside her tightened, and the relentless beat tossed her right over the edge into a lake of pleasure. A bottomless lake it seemed as each forceful thrust set off more and more sensations.

With a guttural sound, he sheathed himself deep. Heat filled her as he buried his face in her hair and let himself come.

Minutes later, her insides continued zinging with aftershocks of pleasure, and her heart had barely slowed. Smiling, she tangled her fingers in his thick blond hair and held his head against her. He was still thick inside her, and the heavy weight of his body was ever-so-satisfying.

Could there be anything more intimate than this?

When he propped himself up to look down at her, she traced a finger over the slight smile on his lips.

He nipped her finger and grinned at her false yelp of pain.

And then he kissed her, soft and deep, so gently for such a deadly man.

When the kiss was done, it took her a second, then she glowered at him. "You bit my finger. A kiss won't let you escape—"

By the time he finished the second kiss, she'd forgotten she had fingers at all.

Slipping out of her, he propped himself up next to her side. A chill lake breeze wafted over her overheated body, making her nipples contract.

Of course he noticed.

"So pretty." Smiling, he drew a finger around one breast, and she shivered under his touch.

"I see why parents enjoy the months their children are in school," he murmured.

She laughed. Yesterday had been the first day of school, and Aric had brought home a drawing for the refrigerator and so many tales. Chocolate milk for snack, and how his newest friend made a big burp. His teacher wore a shirt with penguins on it. On the swing, he went really high—higher than Rachel. "He's probably having as much fun in school as we are here."

"Doubt it." Hawk kissed her again, so tenderly, her eyes dampened.

"I love you, you know." His blue-gray eyes were serious. "Both of you."

"I know. We love you too."

His hand cupped her cheek, his thumb stroking her lips. His gaze went distant, focusing on the trees, the mountains. A crease appeared between his eyebrows, and his jaw went tight.

"Hawk? What's the matter?"

"I'd like you to move in." His voice deepened to a rough growl. "With me."

Taken by surprise, she blinked.

As if he needed to clarify, he added, "To share my house instead of living in Mako's cabin."

This...she wasn't expecting this. Well, okay, yes, maybe she was. *Eventually*. But to ask her and Aric into his very masculine, very private space was a huge leap for him.

For a long moment, all she could do was stare at him as her heart simply brimmed over.

"Hell, too fast." Releasing her, he rubbed the scar that ran down his cheek. "Do you want to be together?"

She kicked her vocal cords into gear. "Yes. Yes, I do."

The tension in his jaw relaxed. "Do you want to stay in Rescue?"

When she didn't answer immediately, the muscles in his face tightened again. "I'd like to stay close for my brothers." His lips twisted as he admitted, "And for me. It's healthier for Aric to be around family too. But if you'd rather move to Anchorage to work, we can do that. Or I can support you."

Oh heavens, he really did love her. Enough to offer to move to Anchorage—somewhere she knew he wouldn't like.

Yet he'd set boundaries. He wouldn't do something truly unhealthy for him or Aric—and she loved his honesty.

His beard was soft beneath her fingers as she caressed his cheek. "I think that's more than I've ever heard you say at once."

He shrugged.

Aaaand there he was again, her word-stingy warrior.

"You took me by surprise." She didn't even need to ask her son what he wanted. He'd loved the deadly ex-merc from the very beginning. "Of course, we'll move in."

Tugging her man down, this time, she took her own kiss and took a moment to savor the joy spilling like warm rain from the air and welling up from the ground.

"Because we love you, Hawk. Both of us."

CHAPTER THIRTY-THREE

G ood job. You men got the makings of a fine team. - First Sergeant
Michael "Mako" Tyne

For fuck's sake. The school's parking lot was so full, Gabe had to park well down the street. Cars lined the shoulder of the gravel road. Had the entire population of Rescue shown up for this event? "There are a lot more people here than we expected."

"Poor Chief. You sound so grouchy." Laughing, Audrey slid out of his Jeep before he could walk around and help her.

He was looking forward to the days when she'd be so big, she'd need an assist. Being a wise man, he kept that thought to himself.

Instead, he took her hand and laced their fingers together. "Actually, I think it's great the town is so invested in our children."

As they walked down the side of the road, he smiled down at her. The afternoon sun brought out the golden colors of her hair and lightened her gray eyes to silver. Her blue hoodie displayed the graphic, *Come to the nerd side. We have Pi.*

His highly-educated, research-loving librarian was fucking adorable. No wonder the town loved her.

They walked through the gate of the newly installed fence onto the school grounds. There were children everywhere and adults carrying food, blankets for picnicking, and drinks. The light breeze carried the scent of charcoal and grilled meat.

Off to one side, the Roadhouse servers were clustered around Bull. Spotting Gabe, his brother broke off and strode over. "The place looks good, doesn't it?"

"It does." Sarge's Investment Group—aka SIG—the corporation they'd set up to manage Mako's investments and properties, had donated the one-story house and the land it sat on. At the edge of town, the property had plenty of acreage for the school to grow.

Last fall, the news coverage about the school-destroying earthquake and landslide had brought in a flood of money. It'd taken until now to remodel the house into the school administration building and add the four new portable classrooms around it. The construction of the playground and athletic field was nearly finished.

In celebration of the beginning of classes last week, the school was having a Sunday afternoon open house and celebration.

Perfect timing, really. This morning, termination dust had sprinkled the tops of the mountains with white. It was September, and summer was officially over.

Bending, he kissed Audrey's soft hair, breathing in her light citrus scent. By next summer, there would be three of them.

"Uncle Gabe, Uncle Bull, Audrey!" Regan ran across the grassy grounds followed by her small pack of children and Gryff. His niece was a natural leader, and Gabe couldn't be prouder. "Come and see our classroom first."

Herded by the kids, they started with the third-through-fifth-grades' classroom. Ms. Wilner, the same teacher Regan had last year, was standing beside her desk, talking with visitors.

With a warm smile, she hugged Audrey, then looked her over carefully. "Thank goodness, you're all right. I'm sorry I didn't stay longer at the party. I could have helped; I'm a good shot."

Gabe stared at the curly-headed instructor who was very clearly sincere. She would have willingly put her life at risk to defend others.

Back in L.A., he'd quit the force when it seemed as if the entire civilian population was against him. Here, his problem would be keeping the civilians from getting killed when trying to help.

Damn, he loved this town.

Standing to one side of the grounds, Kit was darned glad that Knox and Chevy had caged off her new landscaping plants last weekend. She'd been thinking only of keeping moose from nibbling, but boy, the mob today would have trampled her knee-high baby shrubs and slender trees.

But the crowd provided an excellent chance to observe the flow of people on the property and make plans.

That curve there should definitely be turned into a pathway.

The area just below the rise cried out for a shade tree and a comfy bench for a student or teacher who wanted a little quiet time.

"Ms. Sandersen?" a man called.

Tensing at an unfamiliar voice, Kit turned.

A businessman with white hair and a receding hairline stood at a polite distance.

She was apparently still a bit nervy after last weekend, wasn't she? *Get it together, Kit.* She was not only in a crowd, but...she had backup, as Hawk would call it.

JJ, who was patrolling the crowd, was veering closer.

Chatting with Principal Jones, Bull had his gaze on Kit.

On the playground, Hawk was pushing Aric on a swing...and watching. He glanced at the white-haired man, then grinned.

Okay then. Kit smiled. "Yes, I'm Ms. Sandersen. Can I help you?"

"I'm hoping you can." He held his hand out. "I'm John Biese, and I handle the facilities and grounds management at McNally's Resort."

She shook his hand, pleased that his handshake was all business. "It's nice to meet you."

"I have to admit to poor behavior. The COO and I were eating lunch—and eavesdropping—when you were telling Hawk what you would change about the resort's landscaping." He gave her a rueful smile.

She winced. How badly had she criticized the grounds? "I'm sorry?"

"No, your ideas were spot on. I asked around about your job history and think you might be a good match for us. As it happens, our grounds manager's wife hates Alaska."

Hate Alaska? Kit's gaze took in the rolling forests and the gorgeous mountains christened with the first snow. Around her were the townsfolk, everyone here to support their school. Who could hate this paradise?

Kit tried for a polite response. "I've heard that not everyone likes this state."

But what did this man mean by her being a good match for McNally's?

"Unfortunately, that means they're moving back to Kansas." Biese spread his hands. "If you're interested, I'd like to set up a time to discuss the position of grounds manager for the resort."

Just like that, her breathing went away for the winter.

Breathe, fool. She inhaled and kept her voice even. "I'd definitely be interested."

"Excellent." He pulled out a card and handed it to her. "If you could call and schedule an appointment with my admin, we can go over what we're hoping to accomplish. I told him I hoped to hear from you, so he'll be expecting a call."

She nodded. "I'll do that."

With a pleased smile, the man bowed slightly. "I can't wait to see the changes you'll make."

As he strolled away, she stared at the card.

"Everything good?" Hawk's rasping voice settled her. When he put a steadying arm around her, she leaned against his side.

"I might have a job at McNally's as their grounds manager," she said faintly.

With a finger, he tipped the card to read it. "Biese is a good guy."

She tilted her gaze up. "You knew this was coming?"

"Nope. Back in June, he asked about you." Hawk hesitated. "I passed him to Frankie. Figured she'd know how much to tell him."

In June? Hawk had barely known her at all. But he'd still been looking out for her. She leaned her head against his chest. "I love you."

Bending, he planted a kiss on her lips, then lingered and—

"Mama." Aric's high voice interrupted them.

In jeans, bright red sneakers, and a new dinosaur shirt, he charged across the lawn, and she almost cheered. Her exuberant boy was back.

"What's up, honey bear?" She bent for a happy hug.

"Come 'n' see my room." He took her hand and announced importantly, "*My* art is there."

"Oh, well, we better check it out, then." She grinned and saw Hawk doing the same.

Since the summer daycare program had given Aric friends and a familiarity with classroom-type activities, he'd taken to preschool like a champ.

With her boy pulling on her left hand, Hawk's arm around her, and a new job on the horizon, Kit felt as if she was glowing with happiness.

. . .

At a table near the playground, Caz watched Regan climbing the equipment with her buddies, Delaney and Niko. Gryff lay nearby, having decided the girl needed his furry protection more than Bull or Frankie.

People were stopping to talk with Caz and checking how the Hermitage people were doing after the battle last weekend.

He'd noticed JJ and her volunteer soldiers getting congratulatory pats on the back. Caz approved. Heroes should be celebrated. And the way the town had embraced JJ as their own meant more to her than they'd ever know.

On a small stage near the soccer field, Principal Eugene Jones had extended his welcome to the townsfolk and was finishing with the time-honored naming of anyone who'd done anything for the new school or the celebration.

"Again, thank you for your help and for coming today." Jones raised his voice slightly. "Now, I know we'd all like to have some music while we're eating and socializing. As it happens, we have our police chief and his brothers here with their families, and that means some incredible music, if we can get them to sing."

Caz eyed the stage and realized two violins, several guitars, and his own drum set were there, almost hidden in the back.

"*A la verga,*" he said under his breath.

"Get on up there, boy," Dante called from the next table over. Beside him, Lillian wore a smug smile.

Definitely what the fuck. Dante must have raided Mako's cabin for their musical instruments while the tricky Brit kept Kit and Aric busy in the garden.

"What do you say, folks?" Principal Jones asked. "Give a yell if you want them to play."

A hearty cheer meant Caz and the others wouldn't escape playing a set. Not that he minded. Playing for an enthusiastic crowd was like being plugged into a battery.

"C'mon, Papá." Regan ran over and pulled him to his feet. On the way, she snagged JJ too.

"I'm on duty," JJ objected.

Coming up beside her, Gabe set his hand on her shoulder and gave a small push toward the stage. "Officer, if I have to sing, so do you."

Audrey sniggered. "What he said. Get moving, Officer."

Smiling, Caz gave JJ a quick kiss. "*Princesa*, it wouldn't be the same without you. You would not want to disappoint us or your town, would you?"

Although her eyes narrowed at his manipulation, she let Regan lead her forward. Because his woman had the biggest heart in the world.

As Caz stepped onto the stage, he smiled when he saw Hawk carrying Aric with Kit beside him. The hawk loved music—and didn't care if anyone was listening or not.

With Frankie beside him, Bull joined them. Gryff jumped up and lay down at Frankie's feet.

After tuning up, everyone turned to Gabe for directions.

"I wasn't expecting this, but at least we know the perfect song." Gabe grinned. " 'Be True to Your School'."

They laughed—because for the last couple of weeks, they'd played the Beach Boys' song to get the kids in the mood for classes.

Caz tucked Aric between his knees to help drum—the boy had skills—and led off with a quick drumroll. A nod told his family when to jump in.

It wasn't long before the crowd was singing along in rowdy enthusiasm.

Caz smiled in contentment, feeling as if he was nestled in the heart of his family and his town.

They'd finished their set onstage with "Turn! Turn! Turn!" a cover by The Byrds Hawk had always loved.

"To everything there is a season."

In the past, the tune had left him in a melancholy mood, but not today. Not with Aric dragging him and Kit off to greet people and then to check out the food.

The kid was always hungry.

And seasons could change for the better.

"A time of war, a time of peace."

On Wednesday, they'd shopped and set up Aric's new room. The next day, Kit and Aric had moved into Hawk's house—their house, now. Although they didn't own much, everyone at the Hermitage had helped, Bull had fired up the grill, and the rest of the evening became a celebration.

He'd worried about Aric's reaction needlessly. The boy seemed to have expected them to live together, and he loved getting his own "*just like Regan's!*" room.

The first night, he'd snuck into the master bedroom as if to check that Hawk and Kit were where they belonged, then had slept peacefully in his room since.

Hawk frowned. It did seem a mite unfair that he had Kit in his bed, and Aric was alone downstairs.

Will she kill me if I buy the boy a dog?

"See?" Aric called, giving Hawk's hand another tug. "There's stuff to eat." He pointed to the tables filled with potluck foods. Around the grounds, people were sitting at picnic tables or on blankets on the ground.

"Yo, Hawk." Over at a grill, Guzman waved a spatula. He and Tucker'd taken charge of grilling salmon. With a few others, Knox, Chevy, and Erica were staffing the hamburger and hot dog grills.

After getting plates of food, Hawk led his small crew over to where the family had pushed together a couple of picnic tables.

"Over here, Aric." Regan patted the empty spot beside her and pointed to two more spaces for Kit and Hawk.

As Aric climbed onto the bench, Kit grinned at Hawk. "I guess we're sitting here."

"Not going to argue with her." He set Aric's plate in front of him, his own plate next to it. "The two of them could take us."

Kit laughed.

"Hermitage people, may we join you?"

The smooth resonant baritone was one that lived in Hawk's memories, and he turned.

Doc Grayson stood at the end of the table, with a little girl, maybe a bit over a year old, on his hip. Beside him, a short, curvy blonde held the hand of a girl about Aric's age.

With a whoop of pleasure, Bull stood and held his hand out. "Zachary Grayson. Damn, it's good to see you, and you, too, Jessica."

The psychologist had been Mako's friend, and one of the rare people to visit their remote, off-the-grid cabin. Every year or so, he'd show up to check on the paranoid survivalist and the four messed-up street kids.

"Grayson." Hawk took his turn shaking hands with the man who'd kept them from being totally fucked up.

Grayson smiled and studied him with keen gray eyes. "You're looking well, Hawk."

Hawk nodded his agreement, pleased to see the doc hadn't changed much. As usual, he was in black jeans and a black shirt. Still lean and fit, although the black hair had more silver creeping into the temples.

The pretty blonde had to be the wife Bull mentioned they'd met at Mako's funeral. She hugged Bull, Caz, and Gabe, then patted Gabe's cheek. "You look so very much healthier. I'm glad."

Then she smiled at Hawk. "You must be Hawk. I'm Jessica."

Hawk took her hand gently, then shot a glance at Zachary. "Good job."

"I think so."

Audrey joined Gabe. "Welcome back to Rescue, Doc. Hi,

Jessica. I'm Audrey." She smiled at the preschooler, then at the toddler in Grayson's arms. "Hi, you two."

The one-year-old bounced. "Hi. Hi." She held her arms out.

Audrey looked at Jessica. "May I hold her?"

"Yes." Jessica grinned as Grayson handed over the child. "She's Aubrielle, and I don't think she has a shy bone in her body."

Audrey smiled at the baby. "You are adorable."

Yeah, Hawk had to agree. The kid was fucking cute.

Turning, Audrey beamed at Gabe. "We should have a girl."

Gabe opened his mouth. Closed it.

As Audrey walked over to show the baby off to JJ and Frankie, Gabe just looked perplexed.

Caz shook his head sadly. "*Viejo*, has no one explained these things?"

"Yeah, bro." Bull grinned. "Your boy juice already picked out a gender, and she'll blame you for not giving her what she wants."

"Fuck," Gabe said under his breath. "I'm screwed."

Hawk felt a hand take his.

"Who's that?" Aric stared at the little blonde girl who was his age. He looked up at Grayson. "Is she your girl?"

"Yes, she is." Zachary went down on one knee and held out his hand. "It's good to see you again, Aric."

With no reluctance whatsoever, Aric took his hand. "Hi, Doc."

Hawk almost laughed. Doc Grayson had a way about him.

Holding his hand, Grayson smiled. "I'm getting hungry. Have you found anything good to eat?"

Aric had no problem advising about food, and the questions continued as Grayson learned about school, about favorite games, about Kit. As Hawk knew from his own talks with the doc, Grayson possessed a boundless store of patience.

Quietly, Kit joined Hawk and whispered, "Is this the psychologist?"

Hawk nodded, putting his arm around her.

"And what about Hawk," Grayson was asking. "Is he your friend too?"

"No," Aric said, his chin going stubborn, and the answer was a blow to Hawk's heart.

"Indeed. But I can tell you love him very much."

"Uh-huh." Aric leaned forward, put his other hand on Grayson's sleeve, and whispered loudly, "He's my papá."

Hawk froze.

"Ah, I see. How did that happen?" Zachary flicked a glance at Hawk and Kit. Laughter had lightened his gray eyes.

"Grammy says I'm Hawk's boy. She *said*." Aric waited a second as if to let Grayson try to dispute the infinite power of Lillian. When the doc nodded acceptance, Aric laid out his reasoning. "So that means Hawk is my papá. Like Regan's papá."

"Very logical." Grayson leaned forward and whispered too. "Have you called him that to see what happens?"

Aric shook his head, then intently watched his shoe make a hole in the dirt.

"This is a very good time," Grayson said firmly. "I know you're brave enough to give it a shot."

Aric's head came up. "'Kay."

He turned. Stubborn chin, bottom lip trembling. So much like his mother. Eyes filled with worry and hope met Hawk's. "Papá."

A muffled sob came from Kit. "Yes." That there was no hesitation in her whispered agreement meant the world to Hawk.

"Yeah, Aric." Hawk's heart almost burst with love as he picked up...his son. His voice came out rougher than gravel. "Yeah, you're mine—and I'm your papá."

Aric wrapped his arms around Hawk's neck, and the strangling hug was one of the finest Hawk had ever received.

Fuck, he was a father.

Picking up Kit's hand, he kissed her fingers. He'd be a husband damn soon if he had anything to say about it.

Rising, Grayson smiled up at Hawk. "Very good work."

The compliment—and verification—was incredibly gratifying.

Hawk nodded to Kit. "His mother gets most of the credit. He's never doubted her love."

Grayson studied Kit for a long moment, then smiled. "There's nothing more important."

After kissing the top of Aric's head, Hawk put him down.

"Aric." Grayson put his hand on his little daughter's shoulder. "This is Sophia. Sophia, this is Aric who can probably find you some potato chips."

"Yes!" With no hesitation, Sophia walked right up to Aric. "I need a hot dog too. An' ketchup."

"'Kay." Aric took her hand and pulled her toward the food. "There's cookies. We'll get a lot."

Chuckling, Grayson held out his hand to Kit. "I'm Zachary Grayson. I met your son when you were still in the hospital."

To Hawk's surprise, Kit's eyes filled with tears as she took his hand. "You're the one who paid for my hospital and the therapy visits. Thank you."

Grayson didn't even try to sidestep. Just smiled and squeezed her fingers. "You're very welcome."

Jessica laughed and slung an arm around Kit. "Hey, I now have a serious craving for those cookies your son was promoting. Let's go get some."

Hawk watched Jessica hand Kit a tissue as she pulled her away. "Your woman has a big heart."

"She does," Zachary agreed. "So does yours, Hawk. I very much approve."

Hawk felt the words deep in his chest, almost as if Mako himself had been there to give his blessing. "Thanks."

Bull smiled as Zachary and his family joined their table, fitting in seamlessly.

Regan, Sophia, and Aric sat together, sampling foods from the potluck. The faces they made when a taste didn't meet their approval kept everyone laughing.

Audrey had squished in beside Jessica and Kit—and was asking pregnancy questions. After a moment, Frankie joined them, giving stories of being Kit's birthing coach and asking Jessica about her labor.

Whoa. Bull retreated. Women were sure not the weaker sex. And damn, now he needed a drink.

Opening the cooler, he set several bottles of beer in the center of the table. "People, I have the brewery's new seasonal beers. Let me know what you think."

He'd also brought a bottle of wine for Frankie. Opening it, he nabbed a few clean glasses and walked over. "Ladies, would anyone like wine?"

Jessica took a glass. Kit already had a beer Hawk had brought her.

Bull started to pour some wine for Frankie.

She shook her head. "Thank you, but no."

"No?" Bull frowned. "It's your favorite."

"I..." Her color rose, surprising him. She didn't blush easily.

Worried, he ran his hand down her hair. She couldn't seem to shake that stomach bug. "Sweetheart, if you're not feeling good, I can take you home. Or maybe Caz should check you over?"

"I'm fine!" To his surprise, she glared at him. "*Che cavolo,* I don't know how to say it plainer."

What the fuck. She had a temper, but there was always a reason for it. This wasn't like her. "How about we..." How could he politely suggest they needed to talk?

"No. I am fine." She crossed her arms below her breasts, her gorgeous eyes shooting sparks. "And I already saw Caz, so there."

A glance down the table showed no help forthcoming from the others. Grayson's eyes were filled with amusement. Caz was grinning.

Even his damn dog seemed to be laughing at him.

Well, okay, at least she wasn't deathly ill.

Bull sighed. He'd found himself a temperamental New York Italian. A laid-back Polynesian was outclassed.

Crouching beside her, he took her hand and kissed it. "I'm sorry. I'm just worried."

He'd leave it at that because she had a tender heart to go with her temper.

And there it was. The anger disappeared. She ran her hand over his shaved scalp and down his cheek. "My *orsacchiotto.*"

He'd never tell her how much he loved being called her teddy bear.

Then sparks hit her eyes again. "You are so *stubborn.* I wanted to tell you tonight. In private." She threw her hands up in the air in exasperation.

"Jesus, tell me what?" Was he wrong? Was she ill?

"We're having a baby."

"Baby?" *What. The. Fuck?*

"What happened?" he asked, not in accusation, but in shock.

Down the table, he heard Grayson murmur to Caz, "Mako assured me he'd told you boys about the birds and the bees."

Frankie leaned her head against Bull and confided, "I, um, messed up taking my birth control pills a while back. I needed a refill, but then I got hurt at the compound, and Kit was in the hospital, and everything was going on, and my family showed up and...oops?"

Oops.

A baby.

A sense of wonder was rapidly overtaking the surprise. A baby. *Their* baby.

Maybe even a little girl who might have her eyes.

Frankie put her hand on her midsection. "When I was growing up, I always wanted a big brother. So we should start our family with a boy." Her mouth set in a stubborn line. "So that's what has to happen."

Across the table, Gabe started to laugh. "Hate to tell you, bro, but *'your boy juice already picked out a gender, and she'll blame you for not giving her what she wants'.*"

Bull burst out laughing, plucked Frankie up from the table, and spun her around.

His shout of "We're going to have a baby!" silenced everyone on the entire school grounds before cheering filled the air.

Much later, the festival began to wind down.

Gabe saw Zachary Grayson rise, obviously to start gathering his family. "Hey, Doc. A question. Something I've been wondering for a while."

Zachary inclined his head. "Of course."

"You're maybe around fifteen years older than us, so how the hell did you have a doctorate when you visited us when we were young?"

"I didn't."

Gabe barely kept his mouth from dropping open. Bull, Caz, and Hawk looked equally shocked.

"When Mako and I talked, just before he stole you from the foster home"—Zachary put his foot up on the bench and rested his forearms on his thigh—"he ordered me to get my ass out of combat and into psychology."

"Ignoring the sarge's orders was never wise," Bull said.

"And I didn't. When I visited your cabin, he learned I was pursuing a doctorate and started calling me 'doc' then and there. I objected." Zachary gave them a wry smile. "He ignored me."

Caz's snort of sympathy made them all laugh.

"So you were still studying for your degree when you dragged us out to the woods to *chat*?" Bull asked.

"Now, Bull, we went out to the woods to work. Or walk,"

Zachary said mildly. "If a few words happened to get spoken, that was entirely at your discretion."

Even Hawk grinned. Because it was that same ever-so-reasonable tone that had gotten each one of them to wander out to help the doc with whatever he needed assistance with—and had them spilling their guts. Maybe because they knew he'd listen with an open heart and mind.

"You were damn good at it," Hawk said.

"I'd had some experience. My father was a psychologist. We discussed various therapies around the dinner table, and I'd read all of his books long before I enlisted." Zachary smiled slightly. "My mother volunteered in pediatric units in the hospital, which meant her only child did too."

No wonder four messed-up foster kids hadn't been able to outmaneuver him. And Gabe had to admit that he'd tried more than once.

Bull spoke for everyone. "However you came by the experience and wisdom, you did good, Grayson. Thanks."

"It was my very great pleasure to lend a hand now and then." Grayson looked at them all, his gaze direct and honest. "You've grown into men the first sergeant would be proud of."

Blinking hard at the burn in his eyes, Gabe glanced at his brothers. Yeah, he wasn't the only one.

"Jessica, it's time we were headed to the B&B," Grayson said.

"No!" Aric scowled at him. "Sophia stays here."

When Hawk cleared his throat with the same intonation the sarge had used as a warning, Gabe almost laughed.

Aric's lower lip poked out in a pout, but then he politely asked Grayson, "Can Sophia stay, *please?*"

Grayson's eyes were alight with laugher, but none showed in his voice. "Sophia needs a bath and bed. May she come and visit you tomorrow?"

Aric considered. "'Kay."

As Grayson and his family took off, the rest of them began to pack up.

Gabe took Audrey's hand. His beautiful, pregnant woman had held up until now, but she was obviously flagging. "Might I send you home with JJ and Regan? I need to make sure the last stragglers leave without any fights."

"Oh, please." Audrey snickered. "You'd love it if there was a brawl."

She knew him well. "Busted. Last year's fight was a lot of fun."

Laughing, Bull slapped a hand on his shoulder. "Hawk, Caz, and I'll stay too. Just in case."

"All right. I'll see you in a while." Audrey went up on tiptoes to kiss him.

"Wait up, Audrey." JJ tried to give Caz a G-rated peck on the cheek and ended up lured into a full, *sex-in-the-near-future* kiss instead.

Gabe grinned, and when Regan started giggling, he exchanged fist-bumps with her.

Off to one side, Kit had pulled Hawk down for a hug and kiss, and damn, but it was good to see his brother happy. To see him with a woman who would protect that soft heart of his. And a family he could guard with all the protectiveness in his soul.

Bull pulled Frankie to one side, asking her to go home with Kit and Aric—and though her belly was still flat, he gave it a gentle rub. "Our baby."

"It's going to be a while before you see him, but then, it'll be all diapers and lack of sleep." Her delighted smile showed the idea didn't bother her in the least. "Hmm."

She turned and raised her voice, "Hey, Hawk, I expect you to babysit our boy like you did Aric before he was yours."

Still holding Kit, Hawk lifted his head. "*What?*"

"Wait, we're already reserving babysitters?" Audrey spun. "Hawk, same here!" She bumped Frankie with her hip. "I know *our* baby will be a sweetheart. Yours, though..."

As the women headed away, mock-bickering and teasing each other about temperamental offspring, the shocked expression on Hawk's face was priceless...because they trusted him with their babies.

Gabe shook his head. His brother had never seen himself clearly. The rest of them knew that, of them all, their hawk had the softest heart.

Within a few minutes, there were just the four brothers at the picnic table with Gryff snoozing at Bull's feet.

Gabe gazed around at the new school buildings and the bright banners flapping in the light wind. Townsfolk were packing up cheerfully with everyone mingling together. The store owners, Charlotte and Glenda, chatted cheerfully with off-the-gridders, Tucker and Guzman. Lillian was instructing Orion and Felix about ways to heat the greenhouse at the house they'd just moved into.

Throat tight, Gabe looked at his brothers. "When the sarge died, he ordered us to save this town. To bring it back to life."

Bull's gaze dropped. Caz pulled in a breath. Hawk's eyes gleamed with tears for a moment.

"It wasn't just to save the town; it was to save us. To remind us of what's important—that we'd given enough time to death, that it was time to remember how to live."

Gabe picked up his beer, waited as his brothers lifted theirs, then grinned at Hawk. "Use your words."

Hawk said in a deep rasp, "To Mako."

Gabe, Caz, and Bull echoed, "To Mako," their voices rough. Bottles met with soft clinks.

Gabe knew they were thinking of the townsfolk who'd come together as a community, of the love he and his brothers had found, of the children they had now and the ones to come.

With the words that were in their hearts, Gabe spoke to the man who'd raised four lost boys against all odds. "Rest well, Sarge. Mission accomplished."

AUTHOR'S NOTE - PART ONE

My dears:

I know it's tough to leave Alaska and the people in Rescue; however, the series is at an end and this is truly goodbye. I don't know about y'all, but sometimes I'm in the mood for a shorter series rather than one that keeps going. So when you're in that mood, come and revisit the Sons of the Survivalist.

Love you all!

Cherise

AUTHOR'S NOTE - PART TWO

To my readers:

About abuse: Recovery after abuse is something that has to be taken at your own pace. No one gets to say, "You should be healed by now." No one gets to say, "You should be having sex with me." And in the same vein, no one gets to say, "You shouldn't be having sex yet."

Nope.

Healing can be slow or fast. Everyone copes in different ways. As with jumping in cold water, some of us plunge right in, some start with one toe and go inch by inch. Others might retreat a couple of times before forging ahead.

And each of us might need different methods to heal.

Gardeners know that the soil, rainfall, sunlight, and temperature where a fern will thrive will not make a geranium happy. Humans have the same variety. So, my dears, find the place that will give you what you need to bloom.

With all my love,

Cherise

TIMELINE

Since there is some crossover between the Masters of the Shadowlands series and the Sons of the Survivalist series (Master Z just can't keep from getting involved, right?), I thought y'all might like a chronological order of events.

The thirteenth book in the Masters of the Shadowlands series was: *Beneath the Scars* (Master Holt & Josie's story).

Several months later in the fall comes *Defiance* with Master Z & Jessica, which takes us to Alaska to meet the sons of the survivalist.

The Effing List occurs the following spring.

The first book in the Sons of the Survivalist, *Not a Hero,* overlaps the ending of *The Effing List*.

ALSO BY CHERISE SINCLAIR

Masters of the Shadowlands Series

Club Shadowlands
Dark Citadel
Breaking Free
Lean on Me
Make Me, Sir
To Command and Collar
This Is Who I Am
If Only
Show Me, Baby
Servicing the Target
Protecting His Own
Mischief and the Masters
Beneath the Scars
Defiance
The Effing List

Mountain Masters & Dark Haven Series

Master of the Mountain
Simon Says: Mine

ABOUT THE AUTHOR

Cherise Sinclair is a *New York Times* and *USA Today* bestselling author of emotional, suspenseful romance. She loves to match up devastatingly powerful males with heroines who can hold their own against the subtle—and not-so-subtle—alpha male pressure.

Fledglings having flown the nest, Cherise, her beloved husband, an eighty-pound lap-puppy, and one fussy feline live in the Pacific Northwest where nothing is cozier than a rainy day spent writing.

Printed in Great Britain
by Amazon